Snowmageddon

Neta Jackson
Dave Jackson

CASTLE
ROCK
CREATIVE

Evanston, Illinois 60202

Published in Evanston, Illinois. Castle Rock Creative.

Scripture quotations are taken from the following:

> The Holy Bible, New International Version®. NIV®. Copyright © 1973, 1978, 1984, 2011 by International Bible Society. Used by permission of Zondervan Publishing House. All rights reserved.

> The Holy Bible, New Living Translation, copyright ©1996, 2004, 2007 by Tyndale House Foundation. Used by permission of Tyndale House Publishers, Inc., Carol Stream, Illinois 60188. All rights reserved.

> The New King James Version®. Copyright © 1982 by Thomas Nelson, Inc. Used by permission. All rights reserved.

"O Come, O Come, Emmanuel" translated by John M. Meale, 1851 (Public Domain).

ISBN: 978-1-939445-00-1

Cover Design: Dave Jackson

Cover "cake-topper" image: Julian Jackson

Printed in the United States of America

Windy City Stories

by Dave and Neta Jackson

The Yada Yada Prayer Group Series (Thomas Nelson)

The Yada Yada Prayer Group, Neta Jackson (2003)
The Yada Yada Prayer Group Gets Down, Neta Jackson (2004)
The Yada Yada Prayer Group Gets Real, Neta Jackson (2005)
The Yada Yada Prayer Group Gets Tough, Neta Jackson (2005)
The Yada Yada Prayer Group Gets Caught, Neta Jackson (2006)
The Yada Yada Prayer Group Gets Rolling, Neta Jackson (2007)
The Yada Yada Prayer Group Gets Decked Out, Neta Jackson (2007)

Yada Yada House of Hope Series (Thomas Nelson)

Where Do I Go? Neta Jackson (2008)
Who Do I Talk To? Neta Jackson (2009)
Who Do I Lean On? Neta Jackson (2010)
Who Is My Shelter? Neta Jackson (2011)

Lucy Come Home, Dave and Neta Jackson (Castle Rock Creative, 2012)

Yada Yada Brothers Series (Castle Rock Creative)

Harry Bentley's Second Chance, Dave Jackson (2008)
Harry Bentley's Second Sight, Dave Jackson (2010)

Souled Out Sisters Series (Thomas Nelson)

Stand by Me, Neta Jackson (2012)
Come to the Table, Neta Jackson (2012)

Windy City Neighbors (Castle Rock Creative)

Grounded, Neta Jackson, Dave Jackson (2013)
Derailed, Neta Jackson, Dave Jackson (2013)
Pennywise, Neta Jackson, Dave Jackson (2014)
Pound Foolish, Neta Jackson, Dave Jackson (2014)
Snowmageddon, Neta Jackson, Dave Jackson (2015)

For a complete listing of
books by Dave and Neta Jackson visit
www.daveneta.com
www.riskinggrace.com
www.trailblazerbooks.com

Prologue

IMA! IMA!"

Rebecca wiped applesauce from baby Benjy's face and tipped her ear in the direction of her four-year-old's yell from the front porch. Not a hurt cry . . . not danger . . .

"Jacob! Don't yell!" she yelled back. "If you want to speak to me, come to the kitchen!" Quickly rinsing out the facecloth from the kitchen tap, she tackled Benjy's face again. Applesauce in his ears, in his hair, on his shirt . . . what a mess! She should've spoon-fed him instead of letting him try to feed himself, even if he was almost one.

"Ima!" Four-year-old Jacob appeared at her elbow, dark eyes bright. "Can I play outside with Nathan? He's in front of his house with the babysitter—you know, the big girl from up the street. They're playing hopscotch. Nathan yelled at me to come over. Can I go, please?"

"No, no, not now, Jacob. You are all cleaned up for Rosh Hashanah service, and your papa will be home any time now. Another time." *Perhaps.* Isaac wasn't too happy with the children playing with *goyim*, but Jacob and Ruthie liked the two children across the street, and there weren't any other Jewish children on their block.

Which was a big problem. Even though they technically lived within the parameters allowed by their synagogue, they had not been able to find a house in the blocks populated by Jewish families just a few streets away and had gotten special permission from the rabbi to purchase this house on the south corner of Beecham Street. "Temporarily," the rabbi had warned. Isaac agreed. Her husband was quite eager to be enfolded within the Jewish community rather than on its fringe. Which would be nice for the children, Rebecca

1

thought. Sure, they had lots of friends at the Hebrew school and play dates back and forth between other Temple Beth Zion families. But it was times like this—neighborhood kids playing outside, Jacob and Ruthie wanting to join in—that it would be nice for the kids to just pop outside to play. And to be honest, she could use a few minutes of peace and quiet to finish preparing the family meal and get herself ready for service this evening—

"Ima! Please! Just till Abba comes home, okay?"

Rebecca sighed. "All right, just till your papa comes home. And don't get your clothes dirty!"

Jacob was already thundering down the hall and out the front door.

"Ruthie!" Rebecca slid the high chair tray out a few inches, then plucked Benjy out of the chair and swung him onto her hip. "Ruthie, I need you!"

Her five-year-old daughter appeared in the doorway. "I'm making a card for Dodah Mary. See?" The little girl waved the folded piece of paper she'd been working on.

"I know, sweetie. Your *dodah* will love it. But I need you to play with Benjy for a few minutes while I finish setting the table. Papa will be home soon, and we need to be all ready to eat so we can walk to service." *And I need to finish getting dressed.* She put the baby down on the floor.

"Okay." Ruthie took Benjy's hand and pulled him up onto his feet. "Come walk with your sister, Benjy. Can you walk? . . . Ima, look, he's walking!"

Rebecca smiled at the unsteady efforts of Benjy trying to coordinate his feet while clinging to his big sister. "Just don't let go of his hand."

As the little girl coaxed her baby brother into the front room, Rebecca peeked into the dining room and surveyed the table. Plates, candles, silverware—all set. Fluted glass dishes with dates and pomegranates were already on the table. The baked apples sweetened with honey were ready to come out of the oven, and the round Challah loaf could be sliced at the table. But she still had to dish up the black-eyed peas and fritters. All *pareve* foods tonight— no meat, no dairy. Made it simpler to keep kosher . . .

Rebecca busied herself in the kitchen, serving up the last few dishes for their New Year's dinner, cleaning up Benjy's high chair and the floor beneath, wiping down the counters . . . and jumped when she heard the deep masculine voice say, "*Shanah Tovah*, Rebecca."

Rebecca turned. Her husband stood in the doorway, still wearing his black hat and black coat, the fringes of his *tallit katan* showing from beneath the hem. "I didn't hear you come in! *Shanah Tovah*, Isaac." She moved quickly to his side, rose on her tiptoes, and kissed his bearded face.

He kissed her back on the cheek and removed his hat, but a frown creased his forehead. "What is Jacob doing across the street?"

"Oh! Did he see you? He promised to come in right away when you got home. He just went out a few minutes ago to play with the Singer boy. I'll get him." Rebecca sidled past her husband in the doorway and hurried to the front door. Sure enough, Jacob was hopping on one foot on the hopscotch diagram drawn in sidewalk chalk in front of the second house from the corner. "Jacob!" she called. "Papa's home! You need to come now." She waved at the teenage girl, the Singers' frequent babysitter from the black family up the street, who was cheering on the little boys. "Thank you, Tabby! But send Jacob over now."

"I'm coming, Ima! Just let me finish this throw!" As Jacob turned at the top of the hopscotch grid and started back, Rebecca's eyes strayed to the brick two-flat next door to the Singers, third house from the corner. A large sign was stuck in the ground in front. She squinted . . .

FOR SALE.

For sale? How long had *that* been there? Must be new. At least she hadn't noticed it before. A Latino family lived there, using both floors it seemed. She'd noticed at least five or six adults coming and going, and they all seemed to be related. They mostly spoke Spanish, which she didn't understand, so she usually just smiled and nodded if they happened to cross paths, which didn't happen often since they lived on opposite sides of the street. She'd never learned their names—and now they must be moving.

At least it wasn't the Bentleys, the older African American couple who'd moved into the only other two-flat on this block

3

last spring. Friendly folks. They'd actually come knocking at the door with fresh-baked cinnamon rolls, even though Rebecca had to throw them out because they weren't kosher. Or the Jaspers, Tabby's family, at the other end of the block near the dead end. Tabby's mother, Michelle, was one of the few people she did know on the block, at least a little bit. They'd talked a few times in the grocery store. The woman was pregnant—surprise, surprise, at forty-something. Rebecca smiled to herself. As a trained midwife, she'd guessed right away. Nice neighbors. She'd been tempted to ask Tabby to babysit a few times but was pretty sure Isaac wouldn't be open to the idea. "Jews take care of our own," he always said. Still, she was glad the Jaspers weren't moving.

"Jacob!" she called again. "Come now!" To her relief, Jacob obeyed and ran across the quiet street. "Wash your hands," she chided as he darted past her into the front room where her husband was playing "horsey" with Benjy on his knees, grinning at the baby's happy giggles. "Isaac, give me a few minutes to finish getting ready, and then we can eat. The meal is basically ready."

Rebecca hurried into their bedroom at the back of the one-story bungalow, taking off her apron as she went. Her long-sleeved white blouse and long dark skirt were fine. Sliding her *snood* off her head, she shook out her thick dark hair until it fell past her shoulders, then grabbed a brush and gave her hair a quick brushing. Now for her *tichel*, her head wrap. She reached for the long silvery-blue patterned scarf with the silver threads that ran through it . . .

A last look in the mirror. Creamy skin. Brown eyes delicately fringed by dark lashes and brows. A touch of color on her lips and cheeks. Isaac would be pleased. Even though he rarely said so, she knew he liked the way she did her makeup and the pretty way she wrapped her *tichel*, hiding the thick hair that was for his eyes alone.

A few minutes later the Horowitz family had gathered around their table. Just as she usually did for Shabbat, Rebecca solemnly lit the two tall candles, their glow flickering in the eyes of Ruthie and Jacob as she held her hands over the candles, then drew her hands inward three times in a circular motion. In a singsong voice she began: *"Baruch ata Adonai Eloheinu melech haolam . . ."*

✦ ✦ ✦ ✦

Rebecca stuck another clip onto Jacob's *yarmulke*. That should hold it. "Ready." Isaac locked the door, then helped her bump Benjy's stroller down the front steps.

"Should've asked that foreigner to replace the bushes," Isaac muttered as they started down their front walk.

"What?"

"The bushes. Last winter when that Iraqi or Irani or wherever he's from drove his big pickup down the sidewalk."

"It was an emergency, Isaac. You know that. The street was blocked and the ambulance couldn't get through for the old lady up the street."

"I know, I know," her husband muttered. "But that big plow of his damaged two of our bushes. See? They never did recover over the summer."

Rebecca let it drop.

"Will they blow the shofar tonight, Abba?" Jacob's feet danced with excitement. Dusk was settling and the day's mild temperature was sinking into the fifties—a perfect early September evening.

"Yah. Or maybe tomorrow morning," his father said . . . and then he stopped. "What's that?"

Rebecca followed his eyes across the street to the third building from the corner. The sign in front of the two-flat. "It says For Sale, I think."

Isaac stared, tugging absently on his beard.

"Abba! Come on!" Ruthie pulled on her father's coat sleeve. "We'll miss the blowing of the shofar!"

"Hush, child. One moment." Isaac turned to Rebecca, his eyes bright behind his studious glasses. "A two-flat for sale. Maybe another Jewish family can buy it—or even two—and we will no longer be alone on this block." The father suddenly began walking to the corner as Jacob's and Ruthie's short legs trotted to keep up. "Quickly, Rebecca. We missed our chance last spring when the *goyim* bought the other two-flat." His pace picked up. "We must tell Rabbi Mendel. This will be good news for the New Year!"

5

Chapter 1

*B*zzzzzzzz!

Estelle Bentley's head jerked up. Wha . . . what? She must've dozed off. Was someone at the door? Land sakes, what time was it? She glanced at her watch. Three fifteen . . . too early for DaShawn to be home from school. Besides, the boy had his own house key. Who could it be? Maybe the mail carrier. Whoever. Huh. Guess she better go see.

Hefting herself out of the overstuffed chair in the living room, Estelle padded in her house slippers down the stairs of the two-flat she and Harry owned, past their tenant Mattie Krakowski's door on the right, and pulled open the outside door.

The front stoop was empty.

She peered into the mailbox marked Bentley. Nothing there either.

Hmph. Whoever it was didn't even give a body time to get to the door.

Annoyed at having to climb the stairs for no good reason, Estelle muttered all the way into the kitchen at the back of their second floor apartment. DaShawn would be home soon anyway, might as well fix him a snack. He'd be wanting something sweet, especially if he smelled the—

Estelle's eyes flew wide open! Her cake! In the oven! That buzzer hadn't been the front door. It was the oven timer, set to go off at . . . Oh, good Lord! Don't let Michelle Jasper's birthday cake be burned!

Grabbing two potholders, Estelle pulled open the oven door and hauled out the Bundt pan holding the lemon pudding cake she'd put in an hour ago. She eyed it critically. Golden brown on top . . .

6

slightly pulled away from the sides . . . hmm. So far, so good. A few more minutes in the oven hadn't seemed to hurt it after all.

The round Bundt cake had cooled and was sitting regally in the center of the kitchen table, a lemon-sugar sauce dripping prettily down its sides, when she heard her step-grandson pounding up the front stairs. "Hey, Grams!" Thirteen-year-old DaShawn Bentley came breezing into the kitchen, tossed his backpack into a kitchen chair, and pulled open the refrigerator door. "We got any milk?" The slender black teenager pulled out the plastic jug, got himself a glass from the cupboard, filled it, and chugged down the milk in one long draft. "Ah, that's good."

Estelle, meanwhile, stood with one hand on her hip and one hand leaning on the back of a kitchen chair, giving him the eye. "Well, hello to you, too, young man. Where's my sugar?"

DaShawn grinned as he wiped his milk moustache off with the back of his hand. "Oh, sorry, Grams. I was so thirsty." He gave his step-grandma an awkward hug and plopped into a kitchen chair—and then spied the cake. "Oh, man. Lemon cake! Can I have a piece?" He reached out a finger as if to take a taste but pulled it back when Estelle slapped his hand.

"You let that cake be, DaShawn Bentley, if you want *any* food to eat in this house before the sun comes up tomorrow." Estelle snatched the cake plate off the table and whisked it into a far corner of the kitchen counter. "It's Sister Michelle's birthday today— Miz Jasper to you, don't you forget—an' I'm takin' this cake over to help 'em celebrate."

"Can I come? When you gonna go over? Tavis and Tabby told me it was they mama's birthday. I know they'd want me to come too."

Estelle hid a smile. She'd planned for all of them to go across the street to the Jaspers' with the cake—Harry and DaShawn and herself. Had even told Michelle's husband she wanted to make a cake since he was working all day out at the airport, and he'd said, "Only if you and Harry and DaShawn come along to help us eat it."

But all she said now was, "Hmph. We'll see 'bout that if you eat your supper."

DaShawn settled for an apple from the fridge, then headed for the back door with his basketball.

"Where you goin'?" Hmm. That boy's "short Afro" was definitely in need of a trim. Hadn't they agreed on two inches, no longer?

"Just gonna shoot some hoops. Tavis said he's comin' over."

Estelle frowned. "Wait just a minute. His mama told *me* the doctor said Tavis isn't supposed to play sports this fall, and school just started three days ago. Don't you go helpin' that child break doctor's orders. Lord, Lord, that boy's still not a hundred percent after gettin' himself shot this summer."

DaShawn rolled his eyes. "Oh, Grams. Shootin' some hoops in the alley ain't gonna hurt Tavis. He's pretty much healed up. The doc just didn't want him gettin' elbowed in the stomach or knocked down—that kinda thing."

Estelle folded her arms across her ample chest and tapped her foot. "Well . . . you hold off long enough for me to check with his mama. If she says okay, then okay."

DaShawn rolled his eyes again, but he plopped down in a chair while Estelle used the kitchen phone to call Michelle Jasper's work number at Bridges Family Services. It was tempting to say, "Happy birthday!" when her neighbor answered, but since the cake was a surprise, she kept her query to whether Tavis was allowed to shoot baskets behind the Bentley garage.

"All right." Estelle hung up the phone. "His mama says he can play for about twenty minutes. Just shootin' though. No runnin' around, you hear me?"

DaShawn grabbed his ball. "Thanks, Grams." And he was out the back door and down the outside stairs. A few minutes later she could hear the *thump thump thump* of the ball on the alley pavement and the indistinct voices of the two boys.

"Thank You, Jesus, that boy gonna be okay," she breathed. It'd been nothing short of heart-stopping when the two Jasper boys—Destin and Tavis—got shot back in July by some gangbangers who mistook them for drug dealers, when all they were doing was trying to make some money selling an energy drink.

Well, Harry and Corky would be home soon. She better get supper on so they could eat right away and have time to skedaddle over to the Jaspers with dessert, 'specially if Harry wanted to take

Corky out to do her doggy thing before they went over. Couldn't blame the dog. Working security at the Amtrak station downtown wasn't the best place to let a dog specially trained to sniff out drugs do some free sniffing and running around.

Estelle pulled out a frying pan and then eyed her lemon creation on the counter. Might be a good thing to hide that cake from Harry or she'd be slapping his hands too.

✧   ✧   ✧   ✧

"You lookin' mighty fine in that blue caftan, Estelle." Harry Bentley held his wife's arm as they stepped off the curb between two parked cars and started across the residential street. "You sure we don't want to send DaShawn over to this birthday party while you an' me—"

"Nice try, Harry." Estelle giggled. They'd been married only four years, but Harry—all six feet of him, shaved head and graying Van Dyke beard to boot—still knew how to sweet-talk her. "DaShawn!" Estelle's voice rose. "Don't you go runnin' ahead now. We're gonna ring that doorbell together."

"Anyone else comin'?" Her husband craned his neck, looking up and down the street.

"Don't think so, but it don't matter if they do. There'll be plenty of cake to go around." She eyed him curiously. "What you lookin' at?"

Harry pulled his eyes back and assisted her up the opposite curb. "Did you see that For Sale sign across the street in front of the other two-flat?"

Estelle stopped on the sidewalk in front of the Jaspers' brick bungalow. "What sign?" She peered into the waning dusk.

"There's a For Sale sign in front of the two-flat next to the Singers' place. Haven't seen it before. Know anything about it?"

Estelle shook her head. That'd be the Alvarezes . . . She didn't really know much about the family who lived there. A Spanish-speaking couple plus some other adults, all seeming to be related. Friendly when she'd stopped by with cinnamon rolls, back when she and Harry moved into the neighborhood several months ago.

But they hadn't actually gotten to know them yet. And now . . . looked like they were moving.

"I'll stop by this weekend, see what's up. Hope they're okay." She felt badly that she and Harry hadn't made more of an effort to get to know the Alvarezes. They'd gotten to know several families on the block pretty well—the Jaspers, Grace Meredith, the Singers, the Jalilies. Even the elderly Molanders next door and the "two dads" next to the oversized house at the end of the block. Only so much one could do in a few months with thirteen families on their little dead-end block. But still.

"Saw the Horowitz family, too, when I was comin' home, all decked out in their . . . you know." Harry fluttered his fingers down around his waist. "Those fringes he wears. Looked like they were off to the synagogue. Saw several other Jewish families out walking too. But it's only Thursday."

"It's Rosh Hashanah, Harry," Estelle said patiently as they continued up the Jaspers' walk. "For two days. The Jewish New Year, you know." Harry probably didn't know, but it didn't hurt to give her clueless husband the benefit of the doubt. Though, Lord knows, they were surrounded by enough observant Jews in this part of Chicago, they ought to learn a little more about them and their religious holidays.

Once on the Jaspers' front porch, she nodded at their antsy grandson. "You can ring the doorbell now, DaShawn."

Michelle Jasper answered the door. "Estelle! Harry! What are you—?"

Estelle held up the Bundt cake with its ring of birthday candles. "Happy birthday, Michelle! We brought your birthday cake."

"Oh, Estelle. You didn't have to do that." The attractive forty-something, her smooth caramel complexion glowing in the porch light, seemed flustered. "I hope my husband didn't ask you to—"

"Girl, are you going to invite us in, or are we going to eat this cake out here on the porch?"

Michelle laughed. "I'm sorry! Come in! Hi, DaShawn. The twins and Destin will be happy to see *you*." She led the way through the living room and turned into the dining nook just off the kitchen, which also faced the street. Some of the "Chicago bungalows" on

Beecham Street had living rooms and kitchens on opposite sides at the front of the house with bedrooms in the back, like the Jaspers. Others had kitchens at the back.

Estelle leaned in close to Michelle's ear. "That baby bump lookin' mighty cute on you, young lady."

"Uhh. Not so young." Michelle laughed self-consciously as she took the cake from Estelle. "But I'm four months now. And no 'maternity smocks' these days like my mother wore to hide a pregnancy. You wouldn't believe what the stores have in the maternity section. All stretchy and clingy, designed to show off everything."

"Don't I know it. I—"

"Yaay, cake! Let's cut it!" The two Jasper boys and DaShawn were clamoring to get on with it, but Tabby Jasper glared at them. "Mama's gotta make a wish an' blow out candles first, and then we gotta sing." The girl used a kitchen match to carefully light the candles—more like fourteen than forty, but Estelle figured no way could she fit forty-plus candles on that cake. "C'mon, Daddy, you start."

Jared Jasper, still in his open-collared dress shirt and slacks from his work day at O'Hare Airport, winked at his daughter from behind his wire rims and started in somewhere between baritone and tenor: "Happy birthday to you, happy birthday to you . . ." Everyone else joined in, mangling where the birthday person's name should be inserted with everything from "dear Michelle" to "Sweetheart" to "Mo-om" to "Miz Jasper" to "Sister Michelle," which caused everyone to giggle as Michelle paused to make a wish, and then blew out the candles.

"Bet I know what you wished for," Tabby grinned, then smirked at her dad, who shook his head secretively. Michelle pretended not to notice.

"*Now* cut the cake!" Tavis shouted.

"Did you hear the doorbell?" Harry asked. "I think someone's at the door."

"I'll get it!" Tabby darted into the living room.

Michelle handed Estelle a knife and asked her to do the honors. Estelle was serving up slices of lemon cake when Tabby returned. "It's Miss Grace."

Grace Meredith, the Jaspers' next-door neighbor, just-turned-thirty, came in, her pale face flushed and long brunette hair carelessly caught up in a clip at the back of her head. "Oh! There you are, Estelle. I was actually looking for you and Harry, but you didn't answer your doorbell, so I—" She suddenly noticed the birthday cake. "Oh, dear! I'm interrupting a birthday party. I'm so sorry."

Michelle gave the younger woman a hug. "No, no, you're not interrupting. The Bentleys brought over a cake and there's plenty. Guess my 'no-fuss birthday' is turning into a party after all. Stay and have some cake!"

Grace shook her head. "Thanks, but I really can't stay. My assistant is picking me up fairly early tomorrow morning—we're driving this time, down to St. Louis. We'll meet the band there and . . . Anyway, sorry, I've got a bit of an urgent problem. Uh, Harry and Estelle, could I talk to you privately for a minute?"

Estelle looked at Harry, who shrugged and followed Grace into the living room. Lord have mercy! She'd completely forgotten that Grace was scheduled for a concert tour this month. Handing the cake knife back to Michelle, she followed her husband and Grace into the next room.

Grace lowered her voice. "Don't want Michelle's kids to hear but . . . we saw Max."

"Max?" Harry was immediately on alert. "What do you mean, 'we'? Where?"

"Ramona and I. On the 'L.'"

"Honey, sit down." Estelle steered the young woman to the Jaspers' couch. Ramona was Grace's teenage houseguest—or whatever you call someone you're hiding for her protection. Hiding from that no-good, smooth-talking Max What's-his-name who was out on bail until Ramona could testify at his trial on charges of transporting drugs and taking a minor across state lines. "Now, dear, start at the beginning."

Chapter 2

G RACE TOOK A DEEP BREATH. "Okay. Ramona and I went down-town this afternoon. I wanted to do something special with her since I was going to be gone for the next ten days. We went to the Loop, took the 'L' because I didn't want to have to park . . ."

Estelle's mind jumped to the jumbled events of last spring when Grace was returning by train from a West Coast concert tour and met this young girl, still a teenager, traveling with a man named Max at least ten years her senior. Something fishy about the whole thing . . . though only much later did Grace find out she'd been a mark for unknowingly transporting drugs in her luggage from LA to Chicago. Good thing Harry, traveling under-cover as a blind man with a seeing-eye dog, had been on the tail of this drug dealer. The pair had been caught in Chicago—but charges were dropped against Ramona if she'd testify against Max, and tenderhearted Grace had taken the girl in until Max's trial came up.

". . . so we did some shopping, then caught the Redline home," Grace was saying. "Except Ramona saw Max on the Belmont plat-form get on a car ahead of us, so we quickly got off and caught a different train. Pretty sure he didn't see us, but Ramona is kind of a wreck. She was going to stay home by herself while I'm gone, but under the circumstances, I don't think that's a good idea."

"Honey, don't you worry. We can put her up till you get back." Estelle gave Harry a look. *Right, Harry?*

"Yeah, yeah, sure." He gave her a look right back.

"Oh, thank you." Grace, her worry lines disappearing, gave them both a hug. "I knew you'd understand—especially you, Harry, being the one who arrested Max and worked out the deal for Ramona."

"Yeah," Harry grumbled. "Just didn't count on him making bail."

"Well, then, it's all settled," Estelle soothed. "Tell Ramona to bring her things over tomorrow when I get home from work . . . say, around three o'clock." Wasn't sure where they'd put her in their two-bedroom apartment, but they'd make do somehow.

Michelle Jasper poked her head into the living room. "We've still got cake left. At least take a couple pieces home with you, Grace, for you and Ramona."

"Well, okay." They trooped back into the dining room, where Michelle quickly wrapped up a couple of pieces of the lemon cake, then Grace said she really did need to go, still had to pack.

Estelle held up her hand. "Everybody? I don't think it's a coincidence that Grace popped in here tonight just before she leaves on tour. Why don't we all pray for her before she goes? You know she'll be needin' it—all that travel and singing and talking to young people. And for Ramona's protection while she's gone."

"Good idea," Harry said, and the Jaspers, Bentleys, and Grace all made a circle standing around the table joining hands. Estelle started in, followed by Harry, then Jared, then Michelle . . . and then the prayers turned to Michelle and the baby she was expecting . . . and the new year at school as the twins and DaShawn started eighth grade and Destin began his senior year.

"And bless our neighbors, the Alvarezes, who look like they're selling their two-flat down the way," Estelle added. "We don't know why they're movin', but Lord, we ask You to bless them as they make this transition. And bless whoever moves into that two-flat, that they will be blessed by this neighborhood and bring us a blessing."

"Amen," several voices murmured together, along with a "Huh? Who's moving?" from one of the kids.

Estelle opened her eyes and caught Harry looking at her quizzically. She shrugged and gave him a little smile. Her prayer did get a little out of hand, adding the Alvarezes on top of everybody else. Not sure what made her pray that way, just a little tug in her spirit that God was up to something.

14

Estelle stood aside as Harry unlocked the front door of their gray-stone. "I didn't know Grace was leavin' on tour again," he growled as DaShawn disappeared up the stairs ahead of them. "Thought she was still taking some time off for her voice to recover after that last one. Don't think it's wise leavin' Ramona alone, not until Max is put away in prison for good."

"You've got homework to finish!" Estelle called after DaShawn. Then she turned to her husband. "I agree, Harry. Grace told me about the tour a couple weeks ago, and I was going to ask you if Ramona could stay with us—then I promptly filed it in my brain under F for Forgetter. But at least she asked us tonight, even though it's last minute. We can do that, can't we?"

Harry snorted as they climbed the stairs. "Do we have a choice? Problem is, we only got the two bedrooms. An' I ain't kickin' DaShawn outta his. That boy has had too much disruption in his life as it is."

"Oh, Harry. I don't think the boy minds. Easier for him to sleep on the couch than Ramona." Easier on her and Harry, too, since at least she could boss DaShawn to vacate the living room and most days he had to leave early for school. Not so with Ramona, who was just treading time until she could testify at her ex-boyfriend's trial, still weeks—maybe months—away. It wouldn't exactly be convenient having the girl underfoot for a whole week, but still. Like Harry said, what choice did they have?

Harry just grunted as they topped the stairs and came into the living room, where DaShawn was flipping through channels on the TV. "Hey! Didn't your grandma just say you still have home-work to finish? Besides, the news is on." He held out his hand for the remote, and once in possession sank onto the couch. He tried to find the news channel, but Harry's black Lab had trotted in from the other room and kept bumping his arm, nosing Harry for atten-tion. "Hey, cut it out, Corky. Yeah, yeah, I'm glad to see you too. C'mon, settle down. It's a work day for you tomorrow, too, don't forget."

Estelle chuckled. That dog. The way those two interacted, you'd think Corky was a pet, not a service dog. But she was just as glad Harry had been assigned to the canine unit when he'd gotten the job with Amtrak Security's drug interdiction team. Made her feel a bit safer when he was on the trail of drug traffickers who were using the rails to move their payloads. No one would mess with Harry as long as Corky was around.

The news was all about the anniversary of 9/11 coming up that weekend. Estelle shook her head. She didn't want to live that all over again. Leaving Harry and Corky to watch the news, she made sure DaShawn was actually on task at the dining room table and put the teakettle on for a cup of chamomile tea. Tuning out the somber TV voices coming from the living room, her mind focused on how to work a Hispanic teenager into their upcoming week. She was hoping to go visit Leroy this weekend—had been a couple of weeks since she and Harry had been able to visit her son. Probably not a good idea to take Ramona along—the Lighthouse for mentally challenged adults could be stressful for the uninitiated. And Leroy's burns were still healing . . . No, she didn't feel like explaining *that* whole mess to Ramona. The girl had enough on her plate as it was.

But church on Sunday would be good. She'd introduce Ramona to Edesa Baxter—Edesa could speak Spanish with the girl, while neither the Bentleys nor Grace spoke more than a few phrases. Yes, yes, introducing her to Edesa at SouledOut Community Church was a good idea . . . And next week she'd just take Ramona to work with her at the Manna House shelter, where she made lunch for the residents five days a week. Ramona could also help her with the cooking and sewing classes she taught, just like any other volunteer.

The teakettle whistled. Estelle poured hot water over her teabag and let it steep. Already she was beginning to relax about having Ramona stay with them. But going to see Leroy . . . that was a different story. Estelle stuck a second teabag in her mug of hot water. Maybe two would calm her nerves.

✧   ✧   ✧   ✧

Ramona was waiting on the front stoop with her duffle bag when Estelle got home from cooking lunch at the shelter the next day. "I gotta go back over to feed Oreo every day," she informed Estelle as she lugged her duffle bag up the stairs. "I told Miss Grace *el gato* would be more comfortable staying at his own house instead of that fancy cat hotel she used to take him to. She left me the key."

"Of course, honey." She herded the lithe teenager—was she seventeen? eighteen?—up the stairs, wondering how Ramona got into those skinny jeans. But later Estelle thought one of them should probably go over with her when she fed Grace's cat. What if that Max fellow somehow figured out where Ramona was staying and that Grace was out of town? Wouldn't put it past that sleazy character to break into the house and wait for the girl, figuring he'd catch her there alone. Max had good reason not to want Ramona to testify against him at his trial—

No, no. She wasn't going to go there. She had to trust God for something.

Estelle had finally talked Harry into letting Ramona stay in DaShawn's room and putting the boy on the couch . . . which worked out Friday evening since it wasn't a school night and the boy didn't have to get to bed early. DaShawn and Ramona ended up playing video games, hogging the TV in the living room. Harry had rolled his eyes at Estelle and disappeared into their bedroom with the newspaper. Estelle busied herself in the kitchen making cookies to take to Leroy.

Estelle was up early Saturday morning, but neither Ramona nor DaShawn had shown any signs of life by the time she and Harry got ready to leave for the Lighthouse. "You leave any of those cookies for us?" Harry asked, eyeing the cookie tin Estelle was carrying as they climbed into the black-and-silver RAV4. Harry's little SUV had become the "family car" once he'd been assigned the Dodge Durango equipped to cart Corky back and forth to work.

"Of course, silly. But I hid them—otherwise between those two teenagers up in there, they'd all be gone before we got back."

"Yeah, well, they better not," Harry growled. "Those ginger cookies you make are my favorite—oh, see what I mean about that house going up for sale?" He pointed across the street as he nosed the car out of its parking spot and headed for the end of the block.

Sure enough. A big red-and-white For Sale sign stood out in front of the two-flat. It was the only other two-flat besides their own on this modest block of mostly brick bungalows—most of which were only one story, or one-and-a-half if the attic space had been remodeled into bedrooms. The blinds on the two-flat were all pulled down, making the building look rather forlorn, as if the residents had already emotionally moved away.

Estelle frowned. "Doesn't seem right, people moving away from our own block without any kind of good-bye. I mean, I know we haven't gotten to know them beyond deliverin' those cinnamon rolls and gettin' their names, but . . ."

Harry cast a sideways glance her way and chuckled. "Uh-huh. I feel an Estelle Happenin' comin' on." But his tone turned serious. "Look here, hon, you can't feel responsible for everybody's comin' and goin' on this block. Some people like their privacy."

"Mmm." She knew Harry was right, but still . . . wouldn't hurt to drop by and express regret at the Alvarezes leaving the neighborhood, see if they needed anything. "Oh! There are the Horowitzes!" She rolled down the window as they came up to the stop sign at the end of the next block, where a family in conservative Jewish dress was waiting to cross the street. "Happy Rosh Hashanah!" she called. "Happy New Year!"

The father in his long black coat and flat-brimmed hat didn't seem to hear, but the two children—a girl and a boy—giggled and waved, and the mother, who was pushing a hooded stroller, gave a pleasant nod.

"Honestly, Estelle." Harry shook his head. "The Horowitzes strike me as people who basically want to be left alone. These religious Jews mostly keep to their own, you know. Are you sure about this Rosh Hashanah business? Kind of embarrassing if you got the wrong holiday or something."

"A lot you know," she sniffed. Ruth Garfield, one of the sisters in her Yada Yada Prayer Group, kept them well informed about Jewish holidays. "Just drive, will you? I promised Leroy we'd take him out to lunch and I don't want to be late."

Chapter 3

L EROY WAS WAITING FOR THEM in the day room of the Lighthouse—a compact three-story building that had been converted from a small hotel on Chicago's South Side into a residential facility for up to thirty mentally challenged adults. Estelle signed the visitor register at the front desk and then walked toward her son, who stood up to meet them. "Hey, Ma," he said, shoulders hunched, hands in his pockets. "It's 9/11 today. Not a happy day. A lot of people died back then."

Estelle felt like smacking her head. The anniversary had been in the news all week, but she'd totally forgotten that morning. "Yes, a sad day to remember," she agreed. "All the more reason to be grateful we woke up this morning"—she almost added, *"in our right mind,"* like people often said in church, except sometimes Leroy wasn't in his right mind—"and can be with people we love." She gave her son a hug.

The day room was nicely furnished with seating clusters of lightweight sofas and chairs so they could be rearranged easily, depending on the event taking place in the multipurpose room. Card tables with games on them—checkers, chess, Monopoly—were positioned here and there. A bookshelf only half-filled with paperbacks and magazines stood in one corner. Even though the lighting was adequate, Estelle wished there were more big windows to let in more daylight . . . but what could one expect from a renovated old hotel in the heart of the city? Even if the day room did have big windows, they'd look out on buildings crowded close on either side.

"How you doin', son?" Estelle gave Leroy a kiss on his right cheek, not knowing how sensitive the burn scars were on the left side of his face and neck—the only scars visible testifying to the much larger burn scars down the whole left side of his body. She gave an involuntary shudder, remembering that day . . . "You feelin' all right?"

"I'm okay. We, uh, goin' someplace to eat? Somewhere outta this neighborhood?"

"Sure, son." Harry joined in. "Where would you like to go?"

"How 'bout Bubba Gump's?" A crooked grin spread across Leroy's face, crinkling the hazelnut-colored skin around his dark eyes. "We saw *Forest Gump* last night. That's a really funny movie." His shoulders shook in a silent chuckle.

Estelle cast a look at her husband. Bubba Gump's, situated on Chicago's famous Navy Pier, would be a fun place for sure. Fun and pricey.

Harry caught the look and shrugged. "Bubba Gump's it is."

Estelle flashed him a grateful smile, took Leroy's right arm, and let him escort her outside to where they'd parked the RAV4.

Turned out to be an expensive lunch, as parking in Navy Pier's parking garage wasn't cheap. But the temperature was mild, even though the day was cloudy and promised a drizzle or two, so they sat outside on Bubba Gump's patio under the blue and red umbrellas. Leroy studied the menu for half a minute, then tossed it aside. "I want the Shrimp Shack Mac & Cheese."

"Mac 'n' cheese!" Harry looked askance. "We're at Bubba Gump's, for Pete's sake, son! You can have mac 'n' cheese any ol' time. Get yourself some shrimp."

Leroy pouted. "It's got shrimp in it. I like mac 'n' cheese."

Estelle kicked Harry under the table and gave him a look that said, *The mac 'n' cheese is only ten bucks! If that's what he wants, don't complain!* Then she said sweetly, "Harry, why don't we split the scampi and pasta . . . See there?" The scampi was pricey, but not so bad if they split it.

As they waited for their food, Leroy seemed to sink into himself. After several long minutes of silence, Estelle tried to make conversation. "How's it goin' at the Lighthouse, baby? You doin' okay?"

Leroy shrugged. "I guess. It's kinda big. Not like home."

"You making any new friends? How about that girl we met . . . Brenda. Was that her name?" He'd introduced them to Brenda the last time, a rather plump white girl with wavy brown hair, not bad looking except for a facial tic. She'd seemed normal enough, kind of like Leroy when he wasn't in one of his schizophrenic episodes.

Leroy nodded. "Yeah. Brenda was cool. She could talk about all kinds of stuff. But . . ." He shrugged. "I think she bit one of the staff. They put her back in the hospital."

A waiter brought their food. Leroy started to dig in, then looked sheepishly at his mother. "Oh, yeah. You wanna say grace. Gotta be thankful."

Estelle hid a little smile as she took Harry's and Leroy's hands and bowed her head. *Train up a child in the way he should go . . .*

She kept the blessing short, then busied herself dividing the large bowl of scampi onto an extra plate the waiter had bought. "So, how's the mac 'n' cheese, Leroy?"

"It's okay." He stirred the creamy pasta with his fork. "Kinda different with shrimp in it. I like yours better." His voice suddenly got husky. "I miss your cookin', Ma."

Harry cleared his throat.

Estelle blinked rapidly. No way did she want to cry. "I know you do, son." Not that he'd been eating her cooking for a few years even before he'd ended up at the Lighthouse. Those few years after it'd gotten too dangerous for her during some of his episodes, when she'd moved out and let him stay in the house rather than kick him out . . . only to have the local druggies take advantage of him and turn her house—*her* house!—into a drug house. And then there was the fire . . .

It was nearly three o'clock by the time they got home. Estelle stared out the window most of the way up Lake Shore Drive. At one point she felt Harry's hand on her thigh. "Babe," he said, "I know what you're thinkin'. You still want to take care of your boy. But you know he can't move in with us. Just can't. Even if DaShawn wasn't living with us. Leroy needs the care he can get at the Lighthouse. It's a good place."

"I know."

Rain droplets started to sprinkle on the windshield. The lake on their right blended gray and mist-like into the horizon, while fog hid the tops of the high-rises on their left. "But maybe we could bring him to our house for a visit. I could cook somethin' he likes."

"Estelle." Harry's voice was patient. "Sure, invite him for Thanksgiving. But on most weekends, just drivin' to the South Side and back again for a regular visit takes a big hunk out of a day. If we had to pick him up, bring him up here, then take him back, turn around an' come home—that's a whole day just drivin'!"

"I know."

They rounded the S-curve and left Lake Michigan behind as they headed for the Rogers Park neighborhood. More silence. Then . . . "But if he lived closer, we could visit more often. And it'd be easier to have him visit us."

Harry patted her knee. "I know, babe. But you know it wasn't easy finding a decent residential program that fits his needs. Long waiting lists. We were fortunate there was room at the Lighthouse when he got out of the hospital. It comes highly recommended."

She sighed. Thanksgiving seemed like such a long way off. All Leroy wanted was some home cooking. Least she could do as his mama. Might help the guilt she still struggled with about having a happy home with her new husband and his young grandson, while her own damaged son lived in an institution.

Well, the holiday season would be upon them soon enough.

Estelle absently eyed the bungalow on the corner as Harry turned into their block. If they were Jewish like the Horowitzes, their holidays would've already started . . . *wait.* She'd been so smug hollering "Happy New Year" to the Horowitzes earlier that day. But if Rosh Hashanah was only two days, that meant it was over at sundown last evening, and the sober Days of Reflection had begun, or whatever it was Ruth Garfield called it.

Well, she wasn't going to mention her boo-boo to Harry.

✦ ✦ ✦ ✦

Harry stomped back into their bedroom the next morning, rumpled plaid robe unbelted over his pajamas, his face glowering. "How long is that girl gonna be in the bathroom? We'll never get to church on time at this rate!"

Estelle straightened up from making the bed. "I'll go chase her out." Stuffing her feet into her worn slippers, she schlepped to the bathroom and knocked on the door. "Ramona! There's a line out here. Others need to get in!" No answer. Just the noisy drone of the hair dryer from the other side of the door. She knocked again. Louder. "Ramona!"

The loud droning stopped. The door opened and Ramona's tousled head appeared, her long dark hair falling over her face. "Oh. *Lo siento,* Miss Estelle! I borrowed your hair dryer. Is okay?"

"That's fine, Ramona. But take it into the bedroom and dry your hair there. Mr. Harry needs to get in here." Not to mention DaShawn, who was still in bed, and herself. So much for having only one bathroom per unit in these older two-flats.

An hour later all four of them were dressed, somewhat fed, and in the RAV4 on the way to SouledOut Community Church. "Are we going to Mass?" Ramona asked timidly from the second seat.

"Mass!" DaShawn scoffed. "What's that?"

"Mass . . . you know, going to the church." Ramona sounded hurt. "*Mi familia* goes to Mass back in Los Angeles."

"Don't be rude, DaShawn." Estelle twisted in her seat and gave the boy a frown. "The Catholic Church celebrates Mass—kind of like our Communion—as part of their worship service. Were you raised Catholic, Ramona?"

"*Si.* But . . . I wasn't going so much in high school. I went with Miss Grace to her church a couple times though. Never went to a Protestant church before. It's different."

Estelle stifled a snort. *Honey, you have no idea how different Protestant churches can be from each other.* "Well, we hope you like Souled-Out. There's somebody I want you to meet, a friend of mine who speaks Spanish fluently."

It wasn't even a ten-minute drive to the Howard Street Shopping Center where SouledOut was located, but Harry hadn't said a word. Estelle tugged on his arm to hold him back as DaShawn escorted Ramona through the double-glass doors of the church. "Sorry about the inconvenience of having Ramona here, Harry," she murmured. "It's only for a week."

"Aw, don't mind me. Just not used to having a teenage female in the house. All Willa Mae an' me had was Rodney, and now DaShawn—just boys, you know. Not used to all the girly stuff. But . . ." Harry shrugged. "Can't see her stayin' alone for a whole week across the street. Wouldn't be safe."

"I know. Thanks, honey. It'll be easier once the work week starts."

"Speakin' of which, Gilson has me scheduled for a run to Texas this week—probably be gone two nights, goin' an' comin'. I'll let you know for sure when I get to the office tomorrow."

"Oh." Estelle tried to hide her disappointment. She didn't like the long runs, especially when they took him away from home for two or three days in a row. But it was all part of Harry's job when Amtrak got intel of a drug shipment coming to Chicago via the rails. Bad timing with Ramona staying the week . . . but couldn't be helped.

Electronic band music suddenly spilled into the parking lot from the double-glass doors. "Uh-oh, they've started worship already!" And she'd wanted to introduce Ramona to Edesa Baxter before the service. Well, there would be time later.

✧　✧　✧　✧

The two-hour worship service seemed to fly by, as far as Estelle was concerned. She really liked Pastor Cobbs's sermon he called "God's Word in My Mouth." She needed the reminder about praying the Scriptures. But once the African American pastor with the salt-and-pepper hair gave the benediction, there was a general stirring and scraping of chairs as the mixed congregation of blacks and whites and various shades of tan stood up and began to mingle.

Ramona leaned in close to Estelle. "Who's the cute guy who read the Bible earlier and gave the announcements and stuff?" The flirtatious hint in the girl's voice was hard to miss.

"That young man," Estelle sniffed, "is *Pastor* Nick Taylor. He's the associate pastor to Pastor Cobbs, and you can just tuck your eyes back in their sockets, young lady, because he's married. That's his wife, Kat, over there." Estelle jerked her head toward a young white woman with a head full of brown curly hair having an animated conversation with another woman, attractive, coffee-skinned, holding a toddler on her hip.

"Oh. Too bad." Ramona sighed dramatically. "He's *bonito.*"

Estelle ignored that comment. "The woman Kat Taylor is talking to is Edesa Baxter—she's the person I wanted you to meet . . . Oh, Edesa!" she called. "You got a minute?"

The young woman with the toddler flashed a smile in their direction. "*Si! Un momento.*" She turned back to her companion and exchanged a few more words.

Ramona looked puzzled. "But . . . I thought your friend was Hispanic! You didn't tell me she's black. She's got all that, you know, twisty hair." Ramona made tiny corkscrews with her finger up by her head.

Estelle chuckled. "Edesa's from Honduras, Ramona. Central America has black people, too, you know."

The woman in question, the toddler still on her hip, was making her way toward them. "*Hola,* Estelle. And who is this charming young lady?" Edesa beamed at Ramona.

"This is Ramona Sanchez, a, um, friend of ours. And Ramona, this is Edesa Reyes Baxter. That's *her* husband, Josh Baxter, back there." Estelle pointed toward the soundboard at the back of the room, where a sandy-haired young man was winding up electrical cords. "And *this*"—Estelle tickled the cheek of the toddler on Edesa's hip—"is Julian. Hey, Julian sweetie, you got some sugar for Auntie Estelle?"

The little boy tucked his head into his mother's shoulder.

Ramona giggled. "Let me try . . . Julian?" She pronounced it *Hul-yan* in a singsong voice. "*Hul-yan.* Peek-a-boo, I see you . . ."

The little boy peeked shyly and grinned at the singsong voice.

"*Tsk, tsk, mi amiga,*" Edesa chided gently, grinning at Estelle. "You should know by now how to pronounce Julian's name in Spanish." Then she dimpled at Ramona. "*Usted se aloja en la casa de los Bentleys?*"

Estelle figured she must be asking if the girl was staying at their house.

Ramona rattled off a reply in Spanish, but Estelle got lost after "*Mi familia vive en Los Angeles,*" so she left them to it and wandered off to find Harry, who was talking to Pastor Cobbs at the snack table in the back, both of them chowing down on large, sugary doughnuts along with their coffee. She was just about to scold Harry for adding to his waistline, but decided not to—not with Pastor Cobbs as his partner in crime.

But just then Pastor Cobbs's wife sailed into view. First Lady Rose had no such compunction. "Joseph Cobbs! You put that doughnut down right this minute. You know what the doctor said about sweets!" She turned on Harry. "Shame on you, Brother Bentley, leading your pastor on like this. You should be a better example." And the petite grandmother dragged her husband off.

It was all Estelle could do to stifle a belly laugh. Couldn't have done it better herself.

Harry wiped telltale sugary crumbs from his mouth with a napkin. "I see Ramona and Edesa over there joined at the hip. Mission accomplished?"

Estelle poured herself a cup of coffee from the large urn, adding three packets of lo-cal sweetener. "Mm-hm. Like turning on a spigot. Must be a relief talking to someone in your own language." She shook her head. "Sure wish I'd taken more than one year of Spanish—and that was in high school." One of the reasons, she guessed, she hadn't made more of an effort to get to know the Alvarezes in the neighborhood, as they didn't seem to speak much English and she'd be lost after *"Buenos días"* and *"Cómo estás?"* But she really didn't want them to move away without connecting somehow . . .

Hmm. She eyed Ramona and Edesa across the room, still talking and laughing together in Spanish. Maybe there was a solution to that after all.

Chapter 4

A BIG POT OF JAMAICAN RICE AND BEANS AND OXTAILS had been simmering in the slow cooker all morning, making for a ready-
to-eat lunch when they got home. "You and Miss Edesa seemed to
get on," Harry said, spooning a huge helping onto Ramona's plate.

"Oh, sí. Gracias! She's very nice. I liked talking to her. And that
bebé is so cute. His big sister too."

Estelle chuckled. That would be five-year-old Gracie, the homeless baby Edesa and Josh had adopted before they even got married. Or maybe it was they got married sooner than planned so
they could adopt Gracie . . . it was hard to remember the exact
sequence of things. Gracie's creamy tan skin, inherited from her
Latina birthmother, made most people assume she was the natural
offspring of Edesa and Josh's mixed marriage.

Ramona's dark eyes danced. "She asked if I would like to babysit sometime. That would be so cool. I like little kids."

"Hey, Ramona," DaShawn sputtered between mouthfuls of
rice and beans. "You wanna shoot some hoops out back with us?
The twins and Destin are comin' over once they get home from
church."

"DaShawn! Don't talk with your mouth full. Besides, I might
be needing Ramona this afternoon. I, uh . . ." Estelle didn't look at
Harry. "I'm thinking of going over to the Alvarezes this afternoon,
the ones with the For Sale sign out front, just to see if they need
anything while getting ready to move. But they don't speak much
English, so I'm wondering if you'd go with me, Ramona, to, uh,
help translate."

Ramona shrugged and nodded. "Sí. I am glad to help."

". . . Especially," she laughed a short while later as she and Estelle made their way across the street, "since it got me out of doing

27

the dishes with DaShawn. Do you think *Señor* Harry minds very much?"

"Hmph. Does him good to get his hands in the dishwater now an' then." Estelle mounted the steps of the two-flat and paused in front of the two doors side by side. The doorbell on the left said 1st Floor. After a few rings, a somewhat square-faced woman with dark hair pulled back into a long ponytail at the nape of her neck opened the door and looked questioningly back and forth from Estelle to Ramona.

"*Buenas tardes, Señora* Alvarez." Estelle beamed. "I am your neighbor, Estelle Bentley. My husband and I live across the street in the other two-flat." She turned and pointed.

The woman just looked at her. Estelle poked Ramona, who rattled off a sentence or two that included Estelle's and Harry's names. The woman nodded. Her manner wasn't unfriendly, Estelle decided, probably just wondering why they were there.

"We saw your sign"—again Estelle turned and pointed—"and came to see if you need any help with your move. And we brought you some supper. You must be busy." She held out the casserole. Again Ramona translated.

A little smile appeared on the woman's face as she took the dish. "*Eres amable.*"

"She said, 'You are kind,'" Ramona murmured.

In bits and pieces, Estelle tried to say they were sorry to see them move out of the neighborhood and asked if they were moving far. That seemed to loosen Mrs. Alvarez's tongue because she began waving her hand around and rattling a stream of Spanish, worry lines puckering her forehead. Ramona tried to keep up but it was a little hard because the woman barely took a breath for several minutes.

"Something about her husband's parents in Guatemala . . . sick . . . they need to go back and take care of them . . . take over the family business—didn't catch what it is," Ramona said.

Estelle nodded sympathetically. *Guatemala.* She'd just assumed they were from Mexico. Showed how much she knew.

The woman was pointing at the For Sale sign, shaking her head and shrugging as she continued to speak. Even before Ramona translated, Estelle figured she was saying they didn't have a buyer yet, which was a big worry.

Ramona summarized. "She's saying they can't move until they sell the house, but they need to move soon."

"Oh! Well, tell her we are going to pray for the right buyer, and we'll pray for their family in Guatemala too." Estelle laid a hand on the woman's shoulder, lifting up her other hand in prayerful petition, just as she did in church.

"You mean . . . right now?" Ramona hissed. "Like, right here?"

"Of course. The sooner the better." Ignoring Ramona's obvious discomfort—Mrs. Alvarez seemed a little startled also—Estelle pleaded with Almighty God to bring the right buyer for the two-flat, asked God to comfort the Alvarez family who were so far away from family who were sick, and prayed for healing and comfort and blessing . . .

She was well into her prayer before she realized Ramona wasn't translating. The girl was just staring at her. "Ramona," she whispered. "Translate, please."

"Oh." Ramona squirmed. "Well, all right . . ." The girl cast a nervous glance at the woman in the doorway. But Mrs. Alvarez had her eyes tightly closed and was moving her lips as if she, too, were praying.

Ramona cleared her throat. "Uh, *Señor Dios* . . ." she began.

✧   ✧   ✧   ✧

DaShawn off to school, Harry and Corky off to work . . . Estelle took a deep breath. Time for another cup of coffee, then she better get moving herself. Staff meeting at Manna House every Monday at ten.

A half hour later she pulled on her fall coat, grabbed the car keys to the RAV4, and called out, "You ready, Ramona? Time to go."

The girl appeared in the dining room, chewing her lip, no coat.

Estelle frowned. "We need to leave, honey. You're coming with me to Manna House this morning, like we talked about."

"I know, but . . ." The girl fidgeted. "I'm a little, you know, nervous to go back there. I mean, what if Max shows up, like he did that time when I was staying at the shelter?"

29

Estelle pursed her lips. She hadn't thought of that. Fact is, she'd almost forgotten that Ramona had stayed at Manna House Women's Shelter for a few weeks after Max got arrested, and after Harry had arranged to get the charges dropped against Ramona in exchange for testifying against him. But when Max got out on bail, he'd somehow tracked her to the shelter, scaring the bejeebers out of half the residents. Which was why Grace Meredith had taken her in.

But she didn't want to leave the girl here all week either. "Don't think there's any way he'd still be checking the shelter for you, Ramona. But I'll see if Sarge or one of the guys can put in some extra time on security this week. Really, I think we'll be fine. Can't live in fear, you know."

Reluctantly, Ramona got her tan suede jacket and followed Estelle down the stairs and out to the car.

But once at Manna House with ten minutes to spare, Estelle wondered what she should do with Ramona during staff meeting. It'd be one thing to keep an eye out for her while they prepared lunch together or worked with the sewing class afterward. But—

"*Hola!* Sister Estelle!" Edesa Baxter came clomping down the stairs to the lower level, baby on one hip and Gracie by the hand, where Estelle was preparing a tray with a coffee carafe and all the "fixin's" for the staff meeting. "Have you seen Sabrina McGill? She promised to come over with Lil' Turkey to watch Gracie and Julian during staff meeting, but she's not here yet."

"That you, Edesa?" A voice floated out of a small office off the dining room, which took up most of the lower level beneath the main floor of the shelter. A mop of curly red hair poked out of the doorway. "Precious called an hour ago, said both Sabrina and Lil' Turkey came down with a bad cold and couldn't make it this morning . . . Oh, hi, Ramona! Didn't know you were here."

Gabby Fairbanks, the program director at Manna House, came out of her broom-closet office and gave Ramona a hug. "It's nice to see you again—say, didn't I see you at SouledOut on Sunday? Thought that was you, but didn't get a chance to say hi." She looked questioningly at Estelle. "Is Ramona—?"

"Ramona is staying with us this week while Grace Meredith is on tour," Estelle said hastily. "Thought she could volunteer today, help me with lunch and classes and stuff. But I forgot about staff meeting, not sure what she—"

"I can take care of Gracie and Julian," Ramona piped up. "May I, *Señora* Edesa?"

Edesa beamed. "That would be great, Ramona. *Gracias.* There's a small playroom upstairs on the main floor—staff meeting's right next door in the schoolroom. Come on, I'll show you."

Ramona took Gracie by the hand and followed Edesa and Julian up the stairs.

Gabby Fairbanks gave Estelle a sly glance as they disappeared. "Got your hands full, I see. Everything okay at the Bentley household? DaShawn? Harry? You?"

"Hmph. We're fine. Takes more than an old man who thinks he's 007, a pubescent thirteen-year-old, and a teenage runaway with a drug trafficker stalking her to ruffle the waters at *my* house." Estelle grabbed her coffee tray. "See you upstairs, Firecracker."

Gabby's laughter followed her all the way up to the main floor.

✧   ✧   ✧   ✧

Staff meeting was pretty much the usual with Mabel Turner, the shelter's director, presiding. Problems with the furnace. Updates on new residents. Ideas for a Christmas fund-raiser. Then Edesa reported on the House of Hope—the Manna House affiliate for homeless moms with kids, where Edesa's husband, Josh, worked as property manager. Last but not least, Gabby Fairbanks offered a calendar of special events for the fall, including a Fun Night in October.

Estelle chuckled at that. It had been one of Gabby's hair-brained Fun Nights here at Manna House where she'd first met Harry and they'd danced the Macarena. *Goodness!* What a fool she'd made of herself—at her age! Except Harry always said he knew from that night on she was the woman for him.

How long had it taken her? She chuckled again. Not too long . . .

Once the staff meeting was dismissed, Estelle grabbed Ramona and hurried down to the kitchen. "Only got an hour to get lunch on, so we gotta hustle, girl." She started pulling ground beef, lettuce, cheese, and other food items from the refrigerator for the do-it-yourself taco salad she'd planned. "Here, chop this lettuce . . . Gabby!" she hollered in the direction of the Firecracker's office. "Who's on the chore chart helpin' with lunch this week?"

The two shelter residents in question, Piper and Sybil, moseyed in fifteen minutes late, but having Ramona as an extra volunteer helped and the makings for taco salad—Mexican-seasoned hamburger meat, shredded lettuce, chopped tomatoes, canned pinto beans, grated cheese, sliced black olives, salsa, sour cream—along with lemonade and pitchers of water were laid out on the counter between kitchen and dining room by the time the lunch bell rang. The shelter residents lined up—twenty-five or thirty by Estelle's guesstimation—and were semi-quiet while Mabel said grace. Then the hubbub began as they helped themselves buffet-style. Ramona sat at a table with Edesa and her kids, giving Estelle time to pull up a tall stool in the kitchen to eat her lunch by herself. She needed a breather.

She'd just started teaching a new sewing class right after Labor Day, so her project today would be fairly simple: making a newspaper pattern for an apron, cutting it out from the colorful remnants she'd bought at the fabric store, and teaching basic steps to using the two sewing machines donated to the shelter. But—like all the classes she taught at the shelter—it wasn't easy to maintain consistency since some residents came to the shelter for just a few days, others stayed a few weeks, some for a few months. So she usually chose projects that could be completed in a couple of hours since there might not be a "next time" for some. But still, it was rewarding. Those who signed up for the class seemed to enjoy learning to do something with their hands with a finished product to show for it. And now and then a resident turned up who knew a whole lot more about sewing than she did.

Once they'd finished cleanup after lunch, her sewing class students started to gather in the dining room. Ramona admitted she'd never sewed a stitch in her life, but the class wasn't large, so Estelle let her choose a remnant of sturdy purple cloth and showed her how to cut out her own newspaper pattern.

By the time Estelle climbed wearily into the RAV4 for the drive home a couple of hours later, Ramona had a half-finished apron rolled up in her backpack. "Will you help me finish it tonight?" the girl asked, her dark eyes dancing with anticipation as they drove through early rush-hour traffic.

"Mmm." Right now, getting home, cooking enough supper for DaShawn's hollow leg, and overseeing the boy's homework felt like plenty for one evening. So much for her boast to Gabby that adding Ramona to the household mix was easy peasy. And it wouldn't get any easier—not with Harry being gone two nights this week on a security run.

Turning onto Beecham Street and heading for the cul-de-sac at the end of the block in order to turn around, Estelle saw Michelle Jasper sitting on her porch in what must be a new porch swing. She didn't remember seeing it the night they'd gone over with the birthday cake. "You're home early!" she called across the street as she and Ramona climbed out of the car in front of their graystone. Usually her neighbor got home around six or even later. "Is that a new swing?"

"Yes!" Michelle hollered back. "Birthday present from Jared and the kids! Come over and sit a minute!" She patted the seat of the swing beside her.

Estelle waffled. What she really wanted to do was get upstairs, kick off her shoes, and sprawl on the couch for the next thirty minutes. She'd been on her feet for hours. But after a brief hesitation she gave Ramona the house key and told her to go on in, she'd just be a few minutes.

Crossing the street and climbing the few steps to the Jaspers' front porch, Estelle lowered herself gingerly onto the porch swing beside her neighbor. The chains creaked. "You sure this thing is strong enough to hold two?"

Michelle grinned, her warm nutmeg skin seeming to glow in the late afternoon sun. "Positive. The other night it held all three of my kids, who were acting like it was a ride at Six Flags." She sent the swing into a gentle sway with the push of her toes. "But nobody's home from school yet. Really, I should come home at this time every afternoon. It's so peaceful."

Estelle chuckled. "Know what you're sayin'. The lull before the storm." She gave Michelle a sideways glance. "But you're not usually home this early. You doin' okay? Baby Bump not givin' you any trouble?"

"I'm fine. Had a staff meeting at Bridges that ran longer than usual, so I decided to bring my reports home and do the paperwork here." Her mouth twisted in a guilty grimace. "But . . . the swing calleth."

The two women swung back and forth gently for several long moments. This was nice, Estelle decided. Technically it wasn't fall yet, but the summer humidity had backed off and the late afternoon sun had a warm, lazy feel. Too nice to be inside.

"How long you plannin' on working, with the pregnancy an' all? I mean, you don't exactly have a desk job, not with all the clients you have to check up on." Frankly, Estelle didn't know how anyone survived a job as a caseworker, pregnant or not.

"Oh, baby's not due till the first week of February. I'll probably work until Christmas. We need the money you know, 'cause I'm going to stay home with the baby for a while. Oh, here's something interesting announced in staff meeting today. Bridges finally got the funding to add a group home to its family services. There's such a need."

"Group home? For foster kids? That's who you mainly supervise, don't you?"

"Yes . . . I mean, no. Yes, that's a lot of what I do, follow up on foster kids we've placed. But no, this will be a group home for adults with mental health challenges. All of us at Bridges are convinced most adults with mental health issues do better in smaller home-like settings."

Estelle snorted. "Yeah, that's what I think too. But . . ." Her words caught on a lump in her throat. "It doesn't always work for them to live at home once they're grown."

"Exactly. Even people with mental health issues need independence from Mom and Dad."

"Mm-hm." Had she ever told Michelle about Leroy? What if—? Her heart beat a little faster. "When you thinkin' about starting this group home? And where's it goin' to be?"

Michelle shook her head. "Don't know. We haven't even started looking for a suitable place. Had to get the funding first. Could be anywhere in the city. And we need to hire the house parents. Could be a single person or a couple, just depends."

Estelle nodded absently, her mind elsewhere. Might be a place for Leroy down the road, depending on where it would be located. She wondered if the group home residents had to be clients of Bridges Family Services. If so, that might disqualify him. Still . . .

"Well, that's an interesting prospect." Estelle hefted herself up out of the swing. "I better get on home. DaShawn will be home soon. But keep me posted how it works out."

Michelle got up, too, and followed her to the top step. "Sure, depending on how things move along. But I might be on maternity leave before anything happens. These things can move like molasses on a cold day." She gave Estelle a hug. "Thanks for coming over to share my swing. I'm trying to not be so busy-busy, and the swing helps. Come on over anytime you need to relax!"

Estelle waved good-bye as she trundled down the Jaspers' walk and crossed the street. A porch swing was relaxing . . . but the front stoop of their two-flat was barely big enough for the plastic lawn chair where Miss Mattie sometimes sat. Maybe she would take Michelle up on her invitation.

At her own walk she caught movement out of the corner of her eye and saw Mrs. Alvarez down the block shaking a throw rug over the side of the iron railing of her front stoop. Should she cross back over and say hi? No . . . she was too tired. Another day. There'd be time. They didn't even have a buyer yet for the place.

Wearily Estelle mounted the steps . . . and then her own thoughts rebounded like a slap upside her head. *They didn't even have a buyer yet for the place.*

But they needed one.

The sooner, the better.

Like now. It'd be a quick sale for sure.

Energy seemed to flow through her bones like a recharged battery. She whirled like a top and hustled back down her steps. "Michelle!" she hollered. "Michelle, wait!"

Chapter 5

Estelle couldn't wait to tell Harry her idea. But he seemed distracted at supper, chowing down on the chili and cornbread she'd made, had to be asked twice to pass things, and answered questions about his day with a dismissive, "Okay, I guess." As soon as he was done, he excused himself from the table, saying he wanted to take Corky for her nightly walk and get to bed. Had to be at work early.

She followed him and the dog to the back door. "You okay, hon? I made a peach cobbler for dessert."

"Yeah, I'm okay." Her husband glanced back into the dining room, where DaShawn and Ramona were arguing over who got the last piece of cornbread. "Just . . . I got a call from Rodney today. Says he wants to talk about DaShawn."

Little alarm bells went off inside Estelle's head. "About what?"

"Didn't say. It was a voicemail. Haven't called him back yet."

"You don't think . . ." Estelle didn't want to put her next thought into words. Harry's son *was* trying to get his life straightened out after doing time for drugs. He'd gotten a job driving for Lincoln Limo and had moved into his grandmother's apartment after she died a few months ago. He'd also mentioned that if things worked out between him and DaShawn's mother, he'd like to talk about DaShawn coming to live with them.

DaShawn's mother, however, was a piece of work. Hooker, drug addict, foul-mouthed vixen . . . what Rodney ever saw in Donita was a good question, though that had been in his druggie days. Estelle knew that as far as Harry was concerned, the only good thing that ever came out of that relationship was his grandson—a grandson he didn't even know he had until DCFS called to ask him to take the boy when Rodney was arrested on drug charges.

Donita had shown up at their house a few months ago, demanding her rights to see her son, but Harry had said if she ever showed up again, he'd call the cops. Harry was *not* happy Rodney was seeing her again, but he and Estelle both figured it wouldn't last. No sense worrying about losing DaShawn over the remote chance Rodney and Donita would actually make it trying to be a family.

Harry didn't respond to Estelle's unfinished question, just headed down the outside back stairs with the black Lab scrambling behind him on the leash. Estelle stood at the open back door listening until they disappeared into the alley. Well, the man had a lot on his mind. She'd wait before telling him her idea for a buyer for the Alvarezes' two-flat. At least until he found out what Rodney wanted to talk about.

Harry and Corky seemed to be gone a long time, longer than usual. Estelle guessed he was walking off his worries about DaShawn going to live with his dad. Might as well help Ramona finish her apron after all, as it'd be easy to machine-hem it all the way around. She scooted DaShawn and his homework down to one end of the dining room table and set up her sewing machine on the other.

They were just finishing up the apron ties when Harry returned and poked his head into the dining room. "Sorry we took so long," he wheezed, a bit winded from the climb up the back stairs. "Ran into Molander next door. He was grousing as usual about the neighborhood changing again—all hot and bothered by the For Sale sign across the street."

Estelle followed him into the kitchen as he refilled Corky's water bowl, which the dog lapped in loud wet slurps. "Don't think he's sorry to see them go, though," Harry snorted. "The 'Mexies,' he called them—"

"Guatemalan."

"What?"

"They're from Guatemala, not Mexico." Estelle frowned and glanced toward the dining room, where Ramona and DaShawn were still at the table. She didn't want the kids picking up that kind of talk.

"Huh." Harry chewed on that for a moment and then sighed. "Don't think that would've made a difference for Molander. He's hoping some 'decent folks' buy the two-flat—actually, what he said was 'decent American folks.'" He snorted. "Coming from Molander, he probably means '*white* folks.'"

"Oh, don't let him get under your skin, Harry." Estelle reached for the peach cobbler and peeled off the aluminum foil covering it. "Old people have a hard time changing, and they've been in this neighborhood longer than anybody, except maybe Miss Mattie downstairs. But, uh, speakin' of the Alvarezes' two-flat . . ." She turned back to Harry to spiel her great idea—but he'd already disappeared.

She found him in the bedroom packing his overnight bag. "So you've got an overnight run tomorrow?"

"Yeah." Harry motioned for her to close the door and lowered his voice. "Two nights actually. Be back Thursday. At least I hope so. Got intel about a new cartel moving drugs from Mexico to Chicago this week through Dallas. Gilson assigned Corky and me to the Texas Eagle. Got a few other undercover cops on the other runs, just in case."

Estelle watched him pull out his wraparound sunglasses and plaid flat hat from his top drawer and stuff them in his case with the nondescript tan corduroy sport coat and equally nondescript open-neck shirt—his usual "undercover" outfit. Harry downplayed the danger, but she knew he had to focus in order to successfully pull off his role as an ordinary blind guy traveling with his seeing-eye dog.

Yeah, Harry had too much on his mind right now. He'd just have to wait to hear her brilliant idea for solving three problems with one smooth move.

✧　✧　✧　✧

Tuesday was a shorter day at Manna House because Estelle's only responsibility was preparing lunch for the residents and staff. Ramona still seemed a bit jumpy every time somebody clattered down the stairs, which happened quite often since the lower level of the shelter housed not only the kitchen and dining room, but a rec room with a Ping-Pong table, a laundry room, and Gabby

Fairbanks's tiny office as well. Estelle kept the girl busy chopping vegetables for a cauldron of hamburger-vegetable soup, but she could tell Ramona was visibly relieved when they were back in the car on the way home.

"Still worried about Max showing up, honey?" Silly question.

Ramona shrugged but gave a brief nod.

"How did you ever get hooked up with him anyway?" Nosy question.

Ramona didn't answer, just stared out the passenger side window. Estelle decided not to press and was just going to change the subject when the girl said, "*Mi familia*, always fighting, always yelling. Nothing I do is right . . . so I ran away, stayed with *mi amigas*, one here, one there. Ended up nowhere to go. Then I met Max at this big dance in LA. Lied about my age to get in—supposed to be over eighteen. He treated me nice, said not to worry, he would take care of me . . ." Her voice quivered.

"Oh, Ramona." Estelle's surge of sympathy for Ramona was quickly swallowed up by anger that a man ten years older than this child would take advantage of her, making her dependent on him, sucking her into his illegal drug trafficking, posing as a couple, and taking her two thousand miles away from home! Estelle smacked the steering wheel with one hand, which made Ramona jump. "Hope the judge puts that sleazeball away for a long, long time," she muttered. The rat should be charged with kidnapping too.

Once home and in her house slippers, Estelle tried to call Harry, but she wasn't surprised when her call went to voicemail. He and Corky must be on the Texas Eagle already. While working undercover, he usually put his phone on silent and checked his calls later in private. Hmph. So much for getting in touch with him if she had an emergency. She wasn't sure when the train got in to Dallas—Harry was vague on the details, though she supposed she could look it up online. Hopefully he'd call tonight.

She was just starting supper when Ramona showed up at her elbow. "Miss Estelle?" The girl seemed antsy. "DaShawn isn't home yet, but I need to go over and feed Oreo. You said you want him to go with me, but he has soccer practice or something after school today. I don't want to go when it's dark. Should I, you know, just run over now?"

Estelle was tempted to say yes. Kind of silly to insist that someone go with Ramona to Grace's empty house. It was just across the street, next to the Jaspers. But . . . what would Harry say if Max showed up, heaven forbid, and they hadn't taken precautions? "Oh, all right. I'll go with you." No way was she going to put her shoes on again though.

Grace Meredith's black-and-white cat meowed pitifully when Ramona let them in the front door. The girl disappeared into the kitchen to feed the cat as Estelle casually looked around. The concert singer had left her house as neat as a *Good Housekeeping* photo except for a jumble of sheet music scattered on the spinet piano in the living room. Estelle fingered a few notes on the keys . . . if only she'd learned to play. But no one she knew back in the day had a piano growing up on the South Side.

Ramona reappeared a short while later carrying the loudly purring cat. "You still going to have your prayer meeting here tonight? Miss Grace probably wouldn't mind."

Tonight . . . *right*. It was Tuesday. She had started praying weekly with Grace Meredith last spring when Grace's doctor grounded her for several months after her voice gave out on a long winter tour. Then they'd added Michelle Jasper. Even Nicole Singer at the other end of the block had come a few times—though that was a bit awkward at first, since it was Nicole's husband who had hired Michelle's son, Destin, to sell his energy drink and pushed him to expand his territory . . . a fiasco that landed both Jasper boys in the hospital. But as far as Estelle knew, there'd been some reconciliation between the two families, thank God.

The prayer thing had become pretty regular on Tuesday nights. They met at Grace's house because everyone else had kids, though they hadn't met last week because Tuesday was the first day of school after Labor Day. And this week Grace wasn't back yet from her tour . . .

"Mmm. Don't feel comfortable meeting here with Grace gone," she told Ramona. But why stop praying just because one person was gone? Harry was gone . . . They could meet at her house tonight. And maybe she could send DaShawn over to the Jaspers' to do his homework if they'd have him.

Ramona wandered off to play with Oreo, so Estelle called Michelle at work to tell her about the switch.

"DaShawn?" Michelle said. "Sure, send him over. He might as well eat supper with the twins too. I already made a pot of chicken and rice in the slow cooker. There's plenty. Then Jared can supervise homework time." She laughed in Estelle's ear. "Let him be the meanie for a change."

Estelle couldn't resist asking. "Uh . . . did you get a chance to tell your boss about the two-flat that's for sale on our block?"

"Not yet. Sorry. She's been out sick the last two days. But I promise I'll let her know as soon as she comes in."

Huh. That was disappointing. Estelle had been hoping for a quick answer. But . . . all in God's time. She dialed Nicole Singer next. Nicole homeschooled her kids and hadn't been as regular, but maybe she'd like a chance to get out of the house.

"Prayer at your house tonight?" the young mom answered. "Uh, yeah, sure. The kids just got home from school, so I'll need to spend some time with them, but I'll ask Greg if he'll watch the kids tonight. You said seven, right?"

Just got home from school? That was new. Estelle was sure Nathan and Becky had been homeschooled last year. Well, she'd ask Nicole about it tonight.

Supper for just her and Ramona was a snap—tuna salad on toast—so Estelle was ready when the doorbell rang and Michelle came up the stairs, followed shortly by Nicole. Estelle set out a tray with a teapot and cups on the coffee table, and the women made small talk as they settled down in the Bentleys' comfortable living room. A smile tipped the corners of Estelle's mouth as she watched Ramona pour tea for their guests, her long dark hair falling over her light honey skin, such a contrast to Nicole's blonde waves and peachy pink cheeks. Hopefully Nicole didn't feel uncomfortable being the only white person in the room, what with Grace out of town.

Estelle glanced at Michelle. It was almost funny that she and Michelle were both considered "black," even though the two of them practically fell off opposite ends of the "brown skin" color chart. But the mix felt comforting, a little bit like her Yada Yada Prayer Group. Estelle missed meeting with that motley crew of "sistahs" now that Yada Yada was meeting only once a month on the last Sunday of the month . . . ever since they'd decided to start other mini prayer groups in their own neighborhoods or at work.

Well, this was Estelle's "mini group." There were other women on the block she should probably invite. Farid's wife, Lily? Or Mrs. Molander? Hmm. That would be a challenge. But she and Harry had moved into the neighborhood just this year, so it seemed best to go slow, let God open the doors.

"—so quiet. What'd you do with Harry and your grandson?" Nicole was looking at her expectantly.

Estelle realized she hadn't been paying attention. "Oh, uh . . . Harry's out of town on, uh, business, and DaShawn's at Michelle's house. Doing homework, I hope."

Michelle made a face. "Supposedly. I'm just grateful DaShawn's around to keep the boys company. It's been hard on them since, you know, the shooting, especially since neither of them can play sports this fall. Hard on Destin especially, since it's his senior year. He was really hoping for a basketball scholarship."

Nicole squirmed. "Michelle, I am so sorry—"

Michelle reached over and squeezed Nicole's hand. "Please, Nicole. We're not blaming you—not blaming your husband either. We're past that. But I would like prayer for the boys. Destin's off his crutches, but they're both still healing."

"Sounds like a good place to start our prayer time." Estelle grabbed the hands on either side of her. It felt good to pray for Michelle's boys. Even Nicole, the shyest one among them, offered a prayer . . . Maybe it was important for her to do that.

When they finished, Estelle asked, "So what's this about Nathan and Becky coming home from school? You're not homeschooling this year?"

Nicole flushed. "Yeah. Big decision. We, um, got in a lot of debt while Greg was out of work, so even though he's got a new job, I'm working part time as a temp. I'd like to get back into paralegal work, but I don't want to work full time right now. We'll see how it goes." She smiled wanly at Michelle. "So glad Tabby is able to babysit the kids on the days I can't get home by three."

They prayed for Nicole and Greg as they adjusted to new family schedules and thanked God for the new jobs. Ramona didn't say much, but Estelle prayed for her anyway, keeping things vague, unsure how much about the girl's situation had been shared with others.

"What about you, Estelle?" Nicole looked at her watch. "I should probably get home soon, but I can stay a few more minutes."

Estelle could hardly keep the excitement out of her voice. "I do have something I'd like us to pray about. I've already mentioned this to Michelle, but . . . you know the two-flat next to you, Nicole?"

"The one that's for sale? What about it?"

"Well . . ." Estelle took a deep breath. "The Alvarezes have a family emergency back home in Guatemala, so they're eager to sell quickly. And Bridges Family Services where Michelle works"— Estelle nodded in her direction—"just happens to be looking for a building where they can start a group home for mentally challenged adults. Seems like it might be a match made in heaven!" She beamed. "I thought it'd be good if we could pray about it— you know, as neighbors who care about our neighborhood."

But the look on Nicole Singer's face stopped her.

"What? You're not serious! A group home on *our* block?" Nicole looked from Estelle to Michelle and back again, eyes wide. "I . . . I'm sorry, but I think it's a terrible idea! I don't want people with . . . with all sorts of mental problems living next door to us." Her voice rose. "I mean, think about our kids!"

Chapter 6

*T*HINK *ABOUT OUR KIDS INDEED.*

Estelle banged pots around the kitchen the next morning as she threw vegetables and beans and a ham bone into the slow cooker. Huh. That's exactly what she'd been doing when this idea jumped into her head. A group home on Beecham Street? A possibility that Leroy might qualify to move in? Her son living close by but not in the same house? It would be an answer to a mother's prayer.

"Bye, Grams!" DaShawn's yell from the front of the house was followed a nanosecond later by heavy feet thudding down the stairs.

"Wait! DaShawn! You forgot your—" The slam of the front door left Estelle holding the paper bag she'd grabbed off the kitchen table with the Dagwood sandwich she'd made not fifteen minutes earlier. Hmph. No way was she going to run after him. She tossed the bag into the refrigerator. "That boy can make his own lunch from now on," she muttered. "Maybe he'll remember to take it then."

Covering the slow cooker and turning it on low, Estelle untied her apron and hustled into the bedroom to put on her shoes. "Ramona?" she called. "We gotta leave in a few minutes. Busy morning at the shelter today." The community nurse came in on Wednesday mornings, and Estelle conducted her knitting class for those waiting to see the nurse. Not to mention helping to keep order and calm the anxious residents who just *had* to see the nurse *right now.*

No answer from Ramona. Sighing, Estelle finished stuffing her feet into her most comfortable shoes and knocked on DaShawn's closed bedroom door. "Ramona? We gotta go." No answer. She opened the door and poked her head in. The girl was busy sending a text on her phone. "Ramona!"

The girl looked up, startled. "Oh. Sorry, *señora*. I got a text from Miss Grace asking how I'm doing, so I was telling her what we've been doing at Manna House."

"Oh, well, that's nice . . . but we have to go. Can you do that in the car?"

"Gotta do it now. She's doing a concert thing at a high school in Louisville this morning, then they're heading for Indian-some-thing—"

"Indianapolis."

"Yeah, guess so. Okay, I'll just finish this sentence. Be there in one minute."

Estelle left the bedroom door open and went for her sweater. So Grace was in Louisville, heading for Indy . . . Where else was she going? She should've asked for the tour schedule. Heavens! She wasn't even sure what day Grace was coming home.

Which was exactly what Harry wanted to know when he called that night from the Texas Eagle on his return trip from Dallas. "Grace home from her tour yet? How long is Ramona gonna be there?"

"I don't really know, hon. She's in Indianapolis tonight, I think. But I'm sure she'll be home this weekend sometime."

"This weekend like what . . . Friday? Saturday?"

"Said I don't know! What's up with you, Harry? What time are *you* gettin' home?"

She heard a dramatic sigh on the other end. "Supposed to get in about two o'clock tomorrow—if the train's on time. Right now we're runnin' about an hour behind." His voice turned sultry. "Just missin' you, babe. Couldn't we send DaShawn and Ramona somewhere tomorrow night? Out to a movie or somethin'? I want my own bed and my big, beautiful wife in my arms—"

"Who you callin' your *big*, beautiful wife, mister?"

"Aw, Estelle, you know I love every curve of you. Glad you're not one o' them skinny model types. Not for me, babe. I like my woman with some meat on her."

"Listen to yourself, Harry Bentley. Honestly. You're one track from gettin' yourself sidelined somewhere in Oklahoma." But she couldn't help chuckling. She wasn't looking forward to another night sleeping alone either. But they better talk about something else. Both sets of big ears were still up and rummaging around in the kitchen for bedtime snacks. She knew better than to ask him about the assignment he was on while he was still en route. Maybe she'd tell him now about her great idea for the Alvarez's two-flat—

"Uh, is DaShawn around?" Harry said. "Let me say hey to my man."

Okay. Later for that too. Estelle padded into the kitchen and handed the phone to DaShawn, who was hunched over a big bowl of Cheerios. "It's your grandpa."

As soon as those two were off the phone, she was going to text Grace Meredith and ask when she was getting home. Sure would be nice to have the house back to themselves when Harry got home tomorrow. Well, except for DaShawn. But that boy usually went to sleep with his earphones on.

✦ ✦ ✦ ✦

Estelle thought she'd hear from Harry the next morning, letting her know when he'd be home. When she hadn't heard by the time she and Ramona left for Manna House, she sent him a text—*What's your ETA?*—but didn't get a reply.

Not that she had much time to worry about Harry. Thursday was her cooking class at the shelter, which was supposed to meet after lunch cleanup from two till three, but she still hadn't settled on what to make. Lunch was going to be corn chowder and biscuits, so soup was out of the question. Last week they'd done Southern-fried chicken—a big hit—and the week before it was cheese omelets. Whatever they made today, she'd probably have to make a trip to the grocery store for ingredients.

Estelle glanced sideways at Ramona as they navigated the narrow residential streets just north of Wrigley Field leading to the shelter. Hmm, maybe her answer was sitting right here in the car. "Ramona, what's one of your favorite traditional foods, like your mom makes at home?"

Ramona snickered. "That's easy. *Enchiladas verdes* with chicken. The ones *Mama* makes are so good."

"Think you could show the cooking class today how to make them?"

The girl looked at her, mouth dropping. "*Sí*, I have helped *mi madre* many times! But . . . we would need some special ingredients—tomatillos and serrano peppers and this special cheese, *queso fresco*, and—"

Estelle chuckled as she backed into a parking spot. "You make a list and we'll sneak out during lunch cleanup to do a bit of shopping. You game?"

A text pinged on her cell phone while they were at the big Dominick's grocery store on Sheridan Road after lunch. *Ah, Harry.* She dug in her purse for her phone. If the train had made up the time, he should be getting in pretty soon. But it wasn't Harry. The text was from Grace Meredith:

Sorry I didn't give you my schedule before I left. Much needed day of rest today in Indy. Four concerts so far, two to go Friday nite & Sun A.M. Voice a bit weak today—pls pray. Everything OK with Ramona? Thanks SO much for keeping her while I'm gone. See you Sunday evening.

Estelle grimaced. Sunday evening . . . Harry wasn't going to be happy about *that.*

Ramona dumped a hunk of *queso fresco* into the grocery cart and surveyed the other items. "Boneless chicken breast . . . tomatillos . . . serranos . . . corn tortillas . . . cilantro . . ." she murmured. She ticked off a few more things, then grinned. "That's it."

The cooking class had grown from three to five while they were gone and Estelle worried there wouldn't be enough for everyone to do. But to her surprise, Ramona started putting everyone to work. "Kathy, you chop that onion and the garlic cloves . . . Piper, start cooking chicken breasts in the chicken broth . . . Sybil, these tomatillos need husking—here, I'll show you . . ."

While Ramona helped her crew put together the fresh green salsa and shred the cooked chicken, Estelle supervised the two newcomers—Cha'relle and Roz—frying the tortillas in a little hot oil and draining them between paper towels . . . but she had to play nurse with vinegar and cool water when the oil got too hot and spattered Cha'relle's arm.

In spite of that minor mishap, soon everyone had at least two enchiladas on her plate, and Estelle winked at Ramona as the five guinea pigs *mmm'd* and sighed, "Oh man, this is good."

Ramona practically bounced into the RAV4 as they left the shelter an hour later. "That was fun! Can we do that again? Teach Mexican dishes to your cooking class, I mean."

Estelle chuckled. "Maybe so. You did a good job today. Though I usually try to teach a variety of dishes." *And you're only coming to the shelter with me this week because your hostess is out of town, young lady.* One more day at the shelter and then the weekend . . . then Grace would be home to take over Ramona's care until Max's trial.

Speaking of which, she still hadn't heard from Harry and it was already past four. Was the train just late, or did he have some kind of security incident? She checked her phone when she got home. Still no text. Should she call? No . . . no, he'd call when he could. She had to trust God for Harry in this job. And trust Harry too.

✧ ✧ ✧ ✧

The call came just as Estelle was trying to decide whether to drag out leftovers for DaShawn and Ramona's supper or cook up something new for Harry when he got home.

She snatched up her cell phone. "Harry Bentley! Where in the—"

"Is Ramona with you?"

"What? Yes. She's here. She's fine. What's the—"

"Good. Don't go out tonight. Keep both kids inside. It's . . . Don't worry. Everything's fine. Just keep everyone home tonight. I can't talk now. Gotta go. Will talk to you later."

The call went dead.

Estelle sank down into a kitchen chair and stared at the phone. What in the world?

She looked at her watch. DaShawn would be home shortly. Ramona was waiting for him to get home from soccer practice so she could go across the street to feed *el gato*.

Well, Grace's cat would just have to go hungry tonight.

Chapter 7

A WAKENED OUT OF A FITFUL SLEEP, Estelle felt the bed creak and covers move. "Mmm, that you, Harry?"

"Hmph. Better be me. C'mere, babe." She felt Harry's familiar arms go around her and pull her close, spoon-like. "Sorry I woke you."

Estelle peered blearily at the digital clock on her nightstand. *12:03.* "How come so late?"

"The job. Uh, tell you 'bout it in the morning, okay?" His breathing slowed and she felt his body relax against her back. Well, at least he was home safe and sound. Whatever it was could keep.

But Harry was still asleep when Estelle crawled out of bed at six thirty. Hopefully he could go in late today. She had to get DaShawn off to school and herself and Ramona down to Manna House. Edesa Baxter usually taught a Bible study on Friday mornings for the shelter residents, might be a real nice thing for Ramona . . .

She looked at her husband's inert form under the comforter. *If* Harry thought it was all right for Ramona to go with her this morning, that is. What was that business last night all about?

DaShawn complained about having to make his own lunch, but at least he stuffed it in his backpack before running down the stairs to meet up with the Jasper twins.

Estelle hated to do it, but she shook her husband awake shortly after DaShawn left. "Harry? Sorry, but Corky's whining, wants to go out."

Harry's muffled voice was hard to catch. "Just let her out . . . backyard . . . make sure gate's closed."

Oh, great. No way did she want to go all the way down the back stairs to the yard. She'd send DaShawn, but he was already gone.

She shook Harry again. "Hon, I gotta leave in half an hour. You okay with Ramona goin' to the shelter with me this morning? I mean, after what you said last night . . ."

With a groan, Harry threw off the covers and swung his legs over the side. "Uhhh. Guess I better get up. I'll tell you after I check with Gilson." He reached for his phone.

The dog was still whining at the bedroom door. "Oh, all right," she muttered. "C'mon, Corky." She took the dog to the back door and went out on the landing. She could see the back gate by the garage . . . closed. The side gate was probably all right.

She stayed on the back landing long enough to see the dog make it down the back stairs and head for her usual corner by the garage, then she went back inside. Harry was off the phone and pulling his pants on. "Captain wants me in by ten. We got some moppin' up to do from the bust last night."

"What about Ramona?"

"Oh." Harry frowned. "Yeah, sure, take her with you. Probably better than leavin' her here. Just tell people there not to let *anyone* in who isn't staff or resident."

"Harry. Tell me. What's going on?"

He eyed the door. "Is she . . .?"

Estelle quickly closed the door. "She's dryin' her hair, can't hear a thing."

Harry sighed. "Don't want to upset her. And it's kind of a long story, don't really have time right—"

"Harry!"

"Okay, okay!"

Still getting himself ready for work, Harry said nothing went down in Dallas as they'd suspected. He thought he might have to phone Captain Gilson that either he'd missed their man, or the intel on the drug shipment had been flawed. Until midnight on his way home, that is, when a man matching the description and photo of the supposed "mule" boarded the train in Little Rock, Arkansas—with no baggage, only a backpack. "I walked Corky by the backpack as the guy was getting settled in coach and she didn't react. No drugs there. If this was our man, I figured he'd checked them in his luggage. Which meant

I had to wait till we got to Chicago when he'd try to recover the stuff."

"But what does that have to do with Ramona? The mule wasn't Max, was it?"

Harry snorted. "No. He'd have to be pretty stupid to pull a stunt like that while he's out on bond. But while I was keepin' an eye on our guy at Union Station after we pulled in—late, like I said—I overheard him on his cell phone sayin', 'Yeah, yeah, I know. Track down the girl while I'm in town. I got it'—something like that."

"Oh no. Ramona?"

"Can't be sure, but it's possible Max got some of his crew in the network lookin' for her. See why I wanted you to be extra careful last night? But we got the guy before he left the station with his dirty bag—thanks to Corky." Harry frowned. "By the way, where is Corky?"

"Oh. Uh, I'll get her." Estelle had totally forgotten she'd left the dog outside. Scurrying to the back door, she expected Corky to be on the landing, whining for her breakfast. But no dog. Estelle went to the railing and scanned the tiny yard below. "Corky? Corky! Here, girl!"

No sign of the dog. But now the back gate stood halfway open.

Estelle swallowed. The gate must not have been latched securely. Harry was not going to be happy. Not one bit.

✧   ✧   ✧   ✧

By the time they found the dog—even Ramona went along to help look—they were all late for work. At first Harry was alarmed that someone had taken her—a smart, beautiful Lab like Corky would be worth something on the black market. But no, the dog had only wandered up the alley and through the gate at Beecham Street's dead-end leading into St. Mark's Memorial Cemetery, where Harry often walked the dog. But even after they found her happily chasing a squirrel around a tree, Harry was so upset he didn't even say good-bye when he put Corky into the back of the Dodge Durango—his work vehicle, specially outfitted for the Amtrak canine unit—and backed too fast out of the garage.

Estelle shook her head as she heard the Durango squeal down the alley. Looked like she and Harry would have their own mopping up to do that night.

✧ ✧ ✧ ✧

Edesa Baxter had already started her Bible study in the main room of the shelter when Estelle bustled in, trailed by Ramona, who was feeling disgruntled because Estelle had refused to add feeding Grace's cat to the already botched morning schedule. Good grief. Oreo had dry food set out as well as the canned. He'd survive till this evening. Huh. When she was a girl, all the dogs and cats lived outside and mostly took care of themselves. Of course that was down South, but still.

". . . anybody know why the disciples were so shocked when they came back from food shopping and found Jesus talking to this Samaritan woman?"

At least four hands flew up from the group of ten or so women gathered in a half circle of mismatched chairs and sofas. "'Cause she was a ho!" . . . "Nah, she married all them men—'cept the last one. They was jus' livin' together." . . . "'Cause Jews wasn't s'posed to talk to Samaritans." . . . "Or women. Especially *that* one. Maybe people would get the wrong idea, her bein', ya know, kinda a woman of the night, know what I'm sayin'?"

At the front of the circle, Edesa grinned. "Sounds like some of you have heard this story. *Bueno.* Just think about it. Jesus was not only a teacher, a rabbi, but the long-awaited Messiah. Yet He talked to this woman respectfully, in spite of the bad choices she'd made, in spite of her reputation. He really cared about her as a person . . ."

Estelle felt a tug on her sleeve. "Okay if I stay to listen?" Ramona whispered. "Promise I'll work extra hard to help with lunch."

"Sure, sure. No problem." Estelle headed downstairs with her bags, chuckling. Exactly what she'd hoped would happen. And maybe after getting things squared away in the kitchen, she could take in a little of Edesa's Bible study herself. That young woman sure was born to teach—though she'd gotten her master's degree in public health.

Estelle stashed the supplies she'd brought from home, double-checked that the hamburger meat she'd taken out of the freezer yesterday was thawing in the fridge, set out the large cans of beans and tomatoes she'd need for the batch of noontime chili, and was just getting ready to head back upstairs when her cell phone rang.

"Estelle?" Michelle Jasper sounded breathless. "Hope I'm not bothering you at work. I can't really talk now—on my way to a meeting. But I wanted to let you know I told Charlotte—that's my boss, Charlotte Bergman—about the two-flat that's for sale, and she asked if we could get her some info—sale price, condition of the building, you know, all the facts a realtor usually provides. Not sure I'll have the time—I still volunteer at Lifeline Care Center on Saturday mornings, which takes a big bite out of my day. Can you—?"

"Don't you worry. I'm on it. Oh, praise Jesus!" Estelle ended the call before realizing she hadn't even said good-bye. Well, Michelle would understand. *Oh, Lord, oh, Lord, thank You Jesus!* She just knew God was going to move some mountains to get that group home up and running on Beecham Street.

✧　✧　✧　✧

Ramona was pretty quiet on the way home. That was fine with Estelle. Her mind was racing sixty miles an hour about the best way to get the information Michelle's boss wanted. Did the Alvarezes have a realtor? Or were they doing the sale themselves? All the sign said out front was For Sale. Well, she'd pop over there this afternoon and just ask.

Mattie Krakowski, their first floor tenant, was sitting in the plastic lawn chair on the front stoop when they pulled up in front of their graystone. "Hello, Miss Mattie," Estelle said as she mounted the few steps to the front door. "Have you met this young lady? This is Ramona. She lives across the street with Grace Meredith but is staying with us a few days. Ramona, this is Mattie Krakowski.

She lives on the first floor." Estelle decided not to mention that Mattie used to own this two-flat . . . too long a story.

"*Buenos tardes*, Miss Mattie." Ramona extended her hand.

Mattie Krakowski squinted up at her, ignoring the outstretched hand. "Hmph. Another foreigner. Where you puttin' all these young'uns? Second floor apartment ain't that big. And a dog too. They're upstairs now."

They . . .? "Who's upstairs, Miss Mattie?"

"That man o' yours an' his big dog. Home early, if you ask me."

"Uh, thank you, Miss Mattie. Enjoy this nice fall weather." Estelle quickly ushered Ramona inside and murmured, "I'm sorry she was rude to you, Ramona. She's not usually like that."

Ramona muttered something in Spanish and hustled up the stairs. Estelle followed. Sure hoped she wouldn't get so cranky when she got to be Mattie's age.

Harry was asleep, sprawled across the bed in their room. Well, that was good. He probably needed to catch up after all that business with the drug bust last night. She was glad he'd been successful, but right now she was more concerned with knowing whether Max What's-his-face was trying to silence Ramona before she could testify about *that* drug delivery.

Estelle shook her head as she put on the teakettle. Lord have mercy. Hard to believe Ramona had gotten sucked into that mess, hooking up with a drug dealer, being all friendly with Grace Meredith on that train trip from LA back to Chicago, then helping Max hide drugs in Grace's luggage . . . Who would've thought Ramona would end up agreeing to testify against her no-good boyfriend and staying with Grace?

Harry, that's who. He's the one who went to bat for Ramona after the bust.

The teakettle whistled just as Ramona poked her head into the kitchen. "Miss Estelle—?"

"Shush now." Estelle jerked her head in the direction of the bedroom. "Mr. Harry's sleepin'."

"Oh. Sorry." Ramona lowered her voice. "Do you think we could go over a little early to feed Oreo? I haven't been there since Wednesday night and it's Friday afternoon already."

"I'm sure Oreo will be just fine for another hour or so until DaShawn gets—" Estelle stopped herself. If she was going to go over to the Alvarezes, she'd need Ramona to translate. "On second thought, fine. I'll go with you. Then you can go with me to the Alvarezes. A prospective buyer asked me to get more information about the two-flat."

The cat, as Estelle had predicted, was perfectly fine, with enough dry food and water to last at least another day. Though Oreo protested mightily when they came in and followed Ramona everywhere she went. Impatient, Estelle decided to walk a bit outside till those two finished their mutual admiration society.

The weather had been exceptionally fine all week—sunny, moderate temperature, no rain. A nice prelude to fall. And she really did need to do more walking outside before Chicago's winter set in. Wouldn't hurt to lose a few pounds either.

Grace's house, which was next door to the Jaspers, was just two doors away from the cul-de-sac that topped the dead end of Beecham Street. Estelle walked around the cul-de-sac, then down the opposite sidewalk, past their own graystone, heading for the far corner where she'd cross to the other side. Surely Ramona and Oreo would've finished their love fest by the time she got back to Grace's cute bungalow.

As she came to the house on the corner, she saw the two older Horowitz children sitting on the front steps of their house, balancing paper plates on their knees. "Hello!" she called. "Are you having an early supper?" Those two munchkins sure were cute.

The girl ducked her head shyly, but the little boy burbled, "Yep! Ima says we gotta eat 'fore the sun goes down."

"And why is that?" Estelle tried to hide her smile.

"'Cause Mama doesn't do any cookin' on Yom Kippur," his sister piped up.

"I see." Estelle had to wrack her brain to remember what Ruth Garfield had told the Yada Yada Prayer Group about Yom Kippur. Came after Rosh Hashanah . . . called the Day of Atonement . . . the most important Jewish holiday of the year . . .

"Ima lets *us* eat, though. Just the big people hafta fast," the boy added.

"Well, your mama knows what's best for her children." Estelle flashed the kids a big smile and started to cross the street.

"Do *you* have any children?" the little boy called after her.

Estelle turned back. "I do," she beamed. "I have a son, his name is Leroy. But he's grown—you know, he's a man now. And I'll tell you a secret. He *might* move into that house across the street that's for sale."

The two Horowitz children looked at each other, then back at her, their eyes wide. "But our papa wants a Jewish family to move in there. Maybe even two," the girl protested. "He even talked to the rabbi about it!"

Chapter 8

ESTELLE'S HUSBAND WAS HUNCHED blearily over a cup of black coffee at the kitchen table when she and Ramona got back to the house. "Now it's the Horowitzes!" she fussed. "First Nicole Singer has a conniption when I mentioned the group home idea, now Mr. Horowitz is already talking to his rabbi about a Jewish family moving in."

Harry stared at her. "*What* in the world are you talking about?"

"The Alvarezes' two-flat, of course."

He still gaped. "And . . . ?"

"And the group home Bridges Family Services wants to start. It's a marriage made in heaven."

Harry's eyes narrowed. "What kinda scheme are you plotting now, Estelle Bentley?"

Estelle clamped her lips. Snatching the coffeepot, she poured the rest of the coffee into a mug—a mere half cup at best. "Thanks for leaving some for me," she snapped, marching out of the kitchen and into the dining room. She'd get sugar from the tray on the buffet.

Two heaping teaspoons later, Estelle sat at the dining room table, her emotions tumbling. She not only felt frustrated by what the Horowitz girl had said, but no one answered the doorbell when she and Ramona stopped at the Alvarezes. How was she supposed to get more information about the property for Michelle's boss? As for Harry, couldn't she count on support from her own husband? *What's goin' on, Lord? Didn't You put that idea into my head about Bridges buyin' that two-flat for their group home? Why all this opposition all of a sudden? Even Harry's not—*

Her half-baked prayer skidded to a stop. Come to think of it, she never did tell Harry about her idea. So he really *didn't* know

57

what she was talking about. Also, he'd left upset that morning about Corky getting out, which *was* her fault because she didn't actually go check the gates. So coming home and dumping her frustration about what the Horowitz girl said wasn't exactly good timing—especially when she and Harry hadn't done any "mopping up" from that morning.

Estelle sighed. If only she had another cup of coffee to jumpstart her courage. But she didn't, so . . .

"Harry, I—"

Harry was at the kitchen counter making a fresh pot of coffee. "What?" he growled, not turning around.

She couldn't help the smile. "You read my mind. I was hoping for a fresh cup of coffee."

"Didn't read your mind. I wanted another cup too."

"Oh. Well, thanks anyway. Besides, that's not why I came in here. I . . . well, first of all I want to say I'm sorry about not double-checking the gates this morning. That was lazy of me and cost all of us a lot of time and worry. I'm really sorry."

His silence probably lasted only five seconds, but it felt like five minutes.

"Okay. Thanks." Harry sighed. "But Corky's care isn't your responsibility. I was tryin' to catch another forty winks an' put it on you to let her out. So bottom line, it's actually my fault."

"Oh, honey." She hurried across the room and massaged the tight muscles in his neck. "You deserve to get another forty winks now an' then. I don't mind helping with Corky. But I promise next time I'll be more careful. None of us wants that dog to go missin', even if she's not exactly the family pet."

He sighed and turned. "Thanks. Corky's not really 'my' dog, either. Belongs to the canine unit. But she doggone sure has worked her way under my skin." He wrapped his arms around Estelle and pulled her close. "I forgive you, babe. And I'm sorry for stayin' upset all day. Forgive me?"

"You know I do." A load slid off Estelle's back. Even her discombobulation over the Horowitz kids' innocent slip. After all, the For Sale sign was there for the whole neighborhood to see. It was only natural to pass on the word to people who might be interested—like she and Michelle had done. But it did mean she needed to get a move on.

The coffee gurgled its finish. Pouring each of them a fresh cup, Estelle said, "And second thing. I realized I haven't told you about my idea to help out the Alvarezes. I mean, you'd just gotten that phone call from Rodney, an' then you had to leave for a couple days, so it didn't seem a good time to bring it up . . . No wonder you didn't have a clue what I was talkin' about."

Harry snickered. "To help out the Alvarezes, eh? Didn't you say something about a group home movin' in there? You wouldn't be thinkin' about Leroy, would you?"

"Oh you." But they sat. And talked. Estelle started with Monday when Michelle told her about Bridges Family Services getting the go-ahead to start a group home . . . and finished with her encounter with the kids down the street. "But Harry, if it all worked out, wouldn't that be wonderful? If Bridges located their group home to the two-flat, maybe Leroy could transfer there. He'd get the supervision he needs but in a home-like setting, and he'd be close to us, but not underfoot. Seems like it'd be so good for everyone, all the way around."

Harry patted her hand thoughtfully. "Yeah, yeah, it would. But babe, don't get your hopes up too high. Would Leroy even qualify? I mean, he's not a client of Bridges Family Services."

"I know, I know. But even leaving Leroy out of it, it'd be great for the Alvarezes, who need a buyer quickly, and Bridges *is* looking for a residential home."

Harry scratched his chin. "True. Just not sure how quickly a sale like that could happen, babe. A group home that's part of a social service agency would need to get a special variance from the zoning board—and who knows how long that would take."

Estelle stared at him. Needing a zoning variance had never crossed her mind.

✧　✧　✧　✧

At least Harry had the weekend off. Captain Gilson was pretty good about tweaking the schedule when one of his agents had forty-eight-hour duty—which in Harry's case had turned out to be more like sixty. "Gotta take the Durango in for a tune-up before winter, rotate the tires, stuff like that. Might as well do it now rather than wait," he said at breakfast, which they were eating alone since both Ramona and DaShawn were still asleep. "But you and I are going *out* tonight, babe. Okay with you?"

"Never thought you'd ask," she teased. Estelle slid a fresh stack of pancakes onto his plate. "Have you called Rodney back yet?"

"Uhh . . ."

She lifted an eyebrow.

"Well, kinda. Left him a voicemail three or four days ago that I had to go out of town and would call when I got back."

"Uh-huh. Now you're back."

"Yeah, yeah, I know. I'll call him sometime today."

Once Harry was off to the garage, Estelle stripped their bed, put on clean sheets, and puttered around waiting for Ramona to wake up so they could go over and speak to the Alvarezes again. DaShawn was still a lump on the living room couch . . . It really would be good when Ramona could go back to Grace Meredith's house and DaShawn could get his room back. Ten days—including two weekends—was really a long time.

It was almost noon by the time Ramona got herself up and moving, but she was willing to go with Estelle to speak to Mrs. Alvarez. Estelle glanced toward the Horowitz house at the end of the street as they headed over. No one about. Probably at Yom Kippur services. At least Mr. Horowitz wouldn't be pursuing the two-flat today.

As they approached the two-flat, Estelle noticed the For Sale sign out front was different. It now said Trujillo Realty and a phone number. She'd never heard of that company before. But there was a website on the sign. Well, that might be a good way to get information about the property. If nothing else, she could pass on the contact info of the real estate company and let Michelle's boss follow up . . . if she would.

Hmm, it might be better to do a little lobbying at Bridges. Maybe Mrs. Alvarez would let her take a look around and she could give an eyewitness pep talk to this Charlotte Bergman person.

The woman of the house answered the door and pushed open the screen. *"Hola."* With Ramona translating, Estelle said she knew someone who might be interested in looking at the house. Did they have any information about the property she could give to them?

The woman's face lit up. *"Sí, sí. Casa en exhibición. El próximo Domingo."*

"She said there's an Open House next Sunday."

"Tomorrow? Or next week?"

Ramona questioned Mrs. Alvarez. "Next week."

Estelle frowned. If only they could get a jump on this before an Open House brought a slew of potential buyers. Bridges' chances might've been better if the Alvarezes hadn't signed with a real estate company.

"Ask her if the person who's interested could come during the week." After all, Bridges was closed on the weekend. Charlotte Bergman might not be able to come on a Sunday.

Mrs. Alvarez frowned. "No, no . . ." and rattled off something in Spanish.

"She says they're not supposed to show the house unless the realtor is present. She said to come to the Open House."

Estelle   sucked in her breath. If only she'd been a better neighbor and gotten to know Mrs. Alvarez personally. Couldn't really blame her for not letting total strangers into the house. "All right," she said. "I will tell the person who's interested to come next week." She dug around in her purse and pulled out a notepad as Ramona translated. "But if you want to know more about this buyer, you can call me." Estelle scribbled her phone number and tore out a page. "My phone number." She pointed to herself.

Mrs. Alvarez took the note and nodded. *"Sí, sí. Gracias."*

As they left, Estelle turned and gave the two-flat a once-over. Seemed in good condition. Tuck-pointing neat. Lawn was cut, bushes trimmed. The brief glimpse into the entryway had been uncluttered with nice wooden wainscoting. Hopefully the inside would be the same.

✧   ✧   ✧   ✧

The night out with Harry was just what Estelle needed after being apart a good chunk of the week. Ramona and DaShawn had been invited to the Jaspers' for a marathon of the *Star Wars* movies starting at five—giving Estelle and Harry a perfect escape to enjoy a leisurely catfish dinner at Leona's Restaurant over on Sheridan Road. By mutual consent they agreed not to talk about Harry's work or the Manna House shelter or their kids . . . which worked for a while. But while waiting for Leona's specialty cheesecake to arrive after their dinner plates had been cleared, Harry seemed to zone out, his eyebrows knit in a frown.

"Harry? What are you thinking?"

"Huh? . . . Oh, sorry, babe. I was just thinkin' about Rodney's phone call."

"Hmm. So much for not talking about the kids."

"Yeah, yeah, I know. Sorry. It's just on my mind . . . He wants to invite DaShawn to spend Columbus Day weekend with him and Donita—you know, three-day weekend."

"At your mom's place."

Harry rolled his eyes. Even though it had seemed like a good thing for Rodney to take over his grandmother's apartment when she passed, Estelle knew Harry had a hard time with Donita living there too.

"Yeah, that's the plan. He said they'd do something DaShawn might like to do—go to a Bears game or bowling or somethin'." Harry sighed. "He didn't say so, but I'm guessin' this is a trial run before askin' DaShawn to come back and live with them."

Estelle hardly knew what to say. She reached out and took Harry's hand. "I know that's hard for you to think about, hon."

"You're right about that."

"DaShawn's no fool, either," she said. "Maybe a weekend with the two of them will open his eyes to how good he's got it with us."

Harry snorted. "Yeah. Maybe so." He blew out a big breath. "No use mopin' about it. Gotta leave it in the Lord's hands, I guess."

A noisy party of some sort was heating up in one corner of the restaurant. Harry leaned close to Estelle. "What time did Jaspers say they'd be sending the kids home?"

"Around eleven I think. They've got church tomorrow too."

Harry tapped his watch, a sly grin easing the lines in his forehead. "It's only eight thirty, babe. What do you say we sneak back home, light a few candles, put on some music, and, you know . . ."

✦   ✦   ✦   ✦

Sunday dawned breezy and sunny, with the promise of the high sixties. Today was the day! Grace Meredith would come home, Ramona would go back to stay with her, and DaShawn could sleep in his own room.

But, Estelle admitted to herself as she bustled around the kitchen putting out a get-it-yourself breakfast of cold cereal and toast, she'd actually enjoyed Ramona's company every day at Manna House. The girl had pitched in with the lunch chores Estelle had given her to do, and her *enchiladas verdes* had been a big hit with the cooking class. Maybe she'd talk to Grace about Ramona volunteering at Manna House a couple of times a week— if she wanted to, that is. Surely the girl needed something to do while she waited to testify.

"I like your church," Ramona said as they drove home from the two-hour worship service at SouledOut. "I like all the different people—you know, Anglos, blacks, Hispanics. At Grace's church . . ." She shrugged. "Not so much."

Estelle smiled to herself as Harry turned onto Beecham Street. She didn't know much about the church Grace attended, just that it was in the suburbs and Grace went there because her brother's family attended.

"I like Miss Edesa too," Ramona said wistfully. "She asked me again if I'd like to babysit her *niños*. I would, but . . ."

"Oh, honey, I'm sure you can stay in touch with Miss Edesa. In fact, we'd be glad to take you to SouledOut with us on Sundays if Miss Grace doesn't mind."

"Really? That's great. I'll—"

The RAV4 suddenly swerved as Harry pulled over to the curb. "Harry! What—?"

"Ramona, get down!" Harry ordered gruffly, unbuckling his seatbelt. "Estelle, DaShawn—you stay put. Don't anybody get out of the car."

Out of the corner of her eye, Estelle saw Ramona unbuckle her seatbelt and slide down to the floor behind the driver's seat. "What's the matter?" the girl whimpered.

"Gramps?" DaShawn scrunched down too.

"Just wait here." Harry reached under the driver's seat, pulled out the heavy-duty flashlight he kept there, and got out. Estelle gaped. What in the world was he doing? She watched as he casually walked up the street. Harry had pulled over to the left curb before getting to their house, but now he walked past their graystone, gradually angling across the street. What was going on?

And then Estelle saw it. A strange car—black, looked new—sat in front of Grace Meredith's house. She could see a man in the driver's seat, arm resting on the open window, as Harry slowly approached from the rear of the car, gripping the flashlight slightly behind his right leg.

"Lord have mercy," Estelle breathed softly. "Harry, please be careful."

Chapter 9

HARRY SLOWLY CAME ALONGSIDE THE BLACK CAR. Through her open window, Estelle heard him say, "Sir, get out of the car. Keep your hands where I can see them."

The man turned his face and looked up at Harry. White guy. Thirties.

"Sir, I said, get out of the car."

Harry stepped back as the door opened and the man got out—tall, dark-haired, wearing a sport jacket and open-necked shirt. Estelle squinted. Something familiar about him . . .

The man kept his hands spread and spoke. Estelle strained to hear. Did he just say, *"Mr. Bentley"*?

Suddenly Harry slapped his head and burst out laughing. *What in the world?* Estelle saw him shake the man's hand, then put his hand on his shoulder and beckon him back toward the RAV4. "Estelle! Kids! It's okay. Friend of Grace's."

Ramona and DaShawn sat up in the back seat. Estelle got out of the car. Now she recognized that face—Grace's agent. And, well, more than a "friend," according to Grace.

The young man was grinning in a boyish way. He held out his hand to her. "Mrs. Bentley? Jeff Newman. We met before—at your wonderful welcome home party for Mrs., uh . . . you know, Mattie, um . . ."

"Mattie Krakowski." Estelle chuckled as she shook his hand. "Well, this is certainly embarrassing. Harry thought you might be . . ." She trailed off. Maybe it was Harry's place to say what he thought. "Yes, I remember you. And Grace has certainly told us about you."

Ramona had bounced out of the car. *"You're* Mr. Jeff? Ohmigosh, Miss Grace *lives* to get your phone calls! You're even cuter than your picture."

"Ramona!"

But Ramona rattled on. "She's not here, you know. She's on tour. Not getting home until tonight."

"I know." Jeff Newman smiled. "Actually I knew she was getting back today, just wasn't sure what time. Tonight, you say? Hmm." He rubbed his five o'clock shadow thoughtfully. "I didn't tell her I was in town. Flew in from Denver a couple hours ago and rented the car. I, uh, wanted to surprise her."

"Well, you're a few hours early." Estelle started walking toward their house. "You're welcome to come in and wait till she gets back. Ramona"—she indicated the young woman—"has been staying with us. She's also waiting for Grace to get home."

"I see. Of course."

Harry, meanwhile, had gotten back into the RAV4 and drove it up the street and around the cul-de-sac to park in front of the graystone facing the right way.

"Think I'll move my car too," Jeff said. "Like I said, I want to surprise her."

Five minutes later Harry was entertaining Jeff Newman in the Bentleys' second floor living room, while Estelle enlisted Ramona and DaShawn to help set out the makings for tuna sandwiches, chips and salsa, and some boxed mac 'n' cheese, which cooked in about fifteen minutes. Estelle hated the boxed stuff—nothing like the sumptuous mac 'n' cheese she made from scratch—but it was useful in a pinch and helped fill up the teenagers.

As they ate the impromptu lunch, Ramona and DaShawn peppered Grace's agent with questions about the music industry. The agency he worked for, Bongo Booking, worked exclusively with singers and musicians. Even though he politely answered their questions, Estelle noticed the young man seemed a bit nervous and kept looking at his watch.

"Here, I'll help you clear," he said, jumping up when she started to gather up the empty plates.

Estelle chuckled. Grace better hold onto this one. He was a keeper.

"Uh, Mrs. Bentley, I appreciate your hospitality very much, but I'd like to go over to Grace's house and wait for her there. I already, um, talked with your husband and he thought it'd be okay. But he said you, or maybe Ramona, had the key?"

Wait for her there? Was that appropriate? Estelle frowned. Did they have permission to give this man the key to Grace's house? She glanced into the dining room and caught Harry's eye. He nodded his head and gave an *it's okay* sign. Well, if Harry thought it was all right . . .

She lifted the key from the key hooks that hung near the back door and handed it to Jeff.

He beamed. "Thank you so much. I will tell Grace to give you a call when it's all right for Ramona to come over. Sound okay?"

Mm-hm. Estelle couldn't help the smile tickling the edges of her mouth as Jeff said his thank-yous and good-byes, and disappeared down the stairs. Sounded like Jeff Newman wanted a little time alone with Grace when she got back. Well, well . . .

✧   ✧   ✧   ✧

Estelle's phone rang around four thirty. Was Grace home already? But a woman's voice speaking Spanish filled her ear. "One moment, one moment," she said and handed the phone to Ramona, who was packing her stuff in DaShawn's bedroom. "Psst. Can you translate for me?"

Ramona listened, then put the phone on Mute. "It's Mrs. Alvarez. Her husband says it is okay for your buyer to come see the house today. Don't need the realtor."

Estelle's eyes widened. Today? Without the realtor? She had no idea how to get hold of Michelle's boss on short notice. She didn't even know if this Charlotte Bergman was interested yet. She thought quickly. "Tell her the person who's interested isn't available today. But I could come and take a look at the house and give this person a report." If the realtor had trouble with that, she was just a neighbor who dropped in and then told an interested party about the house.

Ramona spoke into the phone, then handed it back to Estelle. "She said okay. Maybe thirty minutes."

Thirty minutes . . . That gave her enough time to pull up information about the building on the real estate website. Moving quickly, Estelle turned on their home computer, found Trujillo Realty, and looked up the listing on Beecham Street. There it was . . . Wow, almost $500,000. They hadn't paid that much for this two-flat—but then again, the first floor had needed extensive rehab. And it *was* two units, making it $250,000 for each.

Did Bridges Family Services have that kind of funding?

Most of the rest of the information seemed standard: Brick exterior, two bedrooms on first floor, three on the second. Full bath on each floor. Half bath in semi-rehabbed basement. Two-car detached garage in back. Gas heat . . .

Estelle interrupted the football game Harry and DaShawn were watching on TV to say she was going out for a few minutes, then hustled across the street. No sign of life at Grace Meredith's house yet—although Grace's assistant usually just dropped her off in a rental car after a concert or tour, so no telling. Well, Grace would call when she was ready for Ramona to come over.

Mrs. Alvarez answered the door and politely showed Estelle around the first floor. Good smells wafted from the kitchen. The house was sparsely furnished, but everything was neat and tidy. The wood furniture was simple and plain, but colorful woven rugs and throws brightened all the rooms. Would they sell the house furnished? Estelle couldn't imagine moving tables, chairs, and beds back to Guatemala.

She should have brought Ramona so she could ask questions!

Estelle pointed toward the ceiling. Could she see the upstairs too? Mrs. Alvarez seemed a little reluctant but led the way up the stairs from the entryway. Here, three men Estelle had seen from time to time were watching the same ball game as Harry, surrounded by packing boxes. *"Mi espouso, mi hermano, y el primo,"* Mrs. Alvarez said.

Her husband stood and shook hands with Estelle. "My wife, she told you we must move? Family emergency back home."

Estelle felt relieved. He spoke English. "Yes. I am sorry to hear that you must go. Thank you for letting me see the house. For . . . a friend."

The other men nodded and showed teeth as they smiled at her, then turned back to the TV. Again, Estelle noted that furnishings were sparse, but bright rugs and throws gave a pleasant air. The three upstairs bedrooms were not as neat—the single men lived up here, Estelle surmised—but overall the painted walls and wood floors seemed in good condition.

"*Gracias,*" Estelle said as she and Mrs. Alvarez went downstairs. Well, that was that. Had she learned anything the fact sheet she'd printed out couldn't have told Michelle's boss? Not really. Estelle felt a little guilty. Was she just being nosy? Yes, she admitted to herself. Just wanting to imagine what it'd be like for Leroy if he lived there. Wherever he lived, she'd want it to be a good place, pleasant, in good condition.

The Alvarezes' two-flat would be a good place.

O Lord, please make it all come together —

"Estelle!"

Estelle's head jerked up. Grace Meredith and Jeff Newman were just emerging from her front door, Grace's arm tucked in his. The young woman waved. "We were just heading over to your house to pick up Ramona!"

The pair met her on the sidewalk, grinning, a hint of happy laughter in their faces. "You can be the first to know." Grace giggled and held up her left hand.

A beautiful marquis solitaire on a white-gold band sparkled in the late afternoon sunlight.

Estelle beamed. "Girl, let me see that rock!" The ring was at once stunning and simple. Kind of like Grace herself. "I am so happy for you! C'mere, girl, let me give you some sugar. You, too, young man." She hugged Grace and then burst out laughing as she hugged Jeff. "You told her, didn't you, that you almost got yourself arrested by my Harry this afternoon?"

Chapter 10

Estelle thought her story about Harry confronting Jeff with his heavy-duty flashlight would make Grace laugh, but the concert singer immediately grew alarmed. "Do you think Max has found out where Ramona is staying? Have you seen strangers prowling about my house?"

"No, no . . . I'm so sorry, Grace. I didn't mean to upset you. Harry was just being extra vigilant after you and Ramona saw Max on the 'L' platform that day. But like you said, Max didn't see you, and we have no reason to think he knows where Ramona is. He—" Estelle caught herself. She'd almost mentioned what Harry overheard at the train station just before making that last drug bust. But it would only worry her more. "Well! Come on over to the house. I'm sure Ramona will be excited to see you. She packed up her stuff hours ago and is ready to go home."

As they all trooped over to the graystone, Estelle winced inside. *Home . . . Where is home for Ramona really?*

As predicted, Ramona went bonkers when Grace showed off the engagement ring. "Just now?" she squealed. "Mr. Jeff gave you a ring just now?"

Grace cast a grin in Jeff's direction. "Well, my first surprise was finding him in my kitchen with a towel around his waist serving up Pad Thai. He—"

"You cooked dinner for her?" Estelle was impressed.

Jeff grinned sheepishly. "Not exactly. Takeout. Had it in the car. Warmed it up."

"Oh, *now* he confesses." Grace gave Jeff a poke. "After breaking and entering my house without permission."

"Well, Mr. Bentley said—" Jeff started.

"Hey!" Harry threw up his hands in self-defense. "This young man asked me if it'd be all right, told me he wanted to surprise you so he could propose. What could I do? Had to give him my blessing—I mean, the key."

Everybody laughed. Except Ramona. "So you're gonna get married now?"

"You bet. That's the idea." Jeff gave Grace a squeeze.

"When?"

"Oh my goodness. We haven't talked about *when*." Grace laughed lightly. "He just popped the question half an hour ago—right after the coconut ice cream."

Estelle could tell Harry's mouth was watering. They might have to order some takeout from Siam Pasta this evening too.

"But . . . if you get married," Ramona said slowly, "what's gonna happen to me? What will I do?"

✧   ✧   ✧   ✧

Couldn't blame the girl, Estelle thought as she bustled through her chores the next morning. Everything in her life must feel up for grabs—though Grace had tried to reassure her that a wedding wouldn't be till after the New Year, which was still several months away, and surely the trial would take place before then.

Hmph. Not so sure about *that*. These court cases sometimes took a long time to get on the docket. Harry had shaken his head slightly, an unspoken word not to say anything right then. Might, might not.

She was just about to head down the stairs to leave for work when the phone rang. "Miss Estelle? Oh, I'm glad I caught you." It was Ramona. "Can I go with you to Manna House this morning? I talked to Miss Grace about, you know, volunteering at the shelter, like I did last week when I stayed with you."

"Well, I . . ." Estelle wasn't sure what to say. She'd had the same thought herself, but she wasn't sure she wanted to be responsible for Ramona five days a week.

"Not every day," Ramona hastened to add. "Just a couple days, like maybe today and cooking day. 'Cause today, you know, I could babysit for Miss Edesa during your staff meeting like I did last week. And help with your sewing class after lunch."

Help wasn't exactly the word for Ramona's contribution to the sewing class last week, but Estelle was sure Edesa Baxter would be glad for childcare she could count on each Monday. And Ramona *had* been a big help with the Thursday cooking class . . .

"Well. Sounds like a good idea. Meet me at the car in two minutes?"

Grace came outside with Ramona. "Sorry this is so last minute. Are you sure it's all right for her to go with you? I mean, you hosted her all last week . . ."

"It's fine. Glad to have her." Estelle glanced up and down the street but didn't see the black rental car. "Jeff gone already?"

Grace's cheeks got pink. "Actually he stayed at the airport hotel last night. Had an early flight to Nashville this morning. Chicago was just a stopover."

Estelle chuckled as she climbed into the car and rolled down the window. "Well, next time he's comin' through town, you let me know. I think we oughta have an engagement party!"

"Oh, *sí!*" Ramona grinned. "A big *fiesta!*"

"Grace, are you up for hosting our prayer time at your house tomorrow night? We met at my house while you were away."

"Oh yes! I'm going to need it!" Grace waved good-bye as Estelle pulled away.

Ramona prattled all the way to the shelter about helping to plan a party for Miss Grace and Mr. Jeff. *Music . . . dancing . . . fireworks . . . a piñata!* Well, why not? Harry would probably roll his eyes at another one of her big ideas, but an engagement party was the least they could do to encourage this young couple. Not just a party, but also a time to bless them, pray for them, and even "roast" them a little . . . Well, maybe they should wait until the wedding reception for that.

Edesa Baxter was delighted that Ramona was offering to come babysit during the Monday staff meetings at Manna House for the next several weeks. Estelle shooed them off to get the kids settled and glanced at the kitchen clock. She still had ten minutes before staff meeting. She pulled out her cell phone and dialed. "Michelle?

Hope I'm not bothering you at work. . . . Okay. Just wanted to know if you got the information I stuck in your mailbox last night . . . Good, good. . . . Yes, that's what I pulled off the realtor's website, but I also walked through the house yesterday . . . Uh-huh. Seems in decent condition. There's an Open House next Sunday. Do you think your boss could come? There'll probably be other potential buyers, but if she's interested, maybe she could talk to the realtor during the week—I mean, the Alvarezes are eager to sell. The sooner, the better . . ."

❖ ❖ ❖ ❖

With the apron project finished, Estelle gave the women in the sewing class a choice: a decorative pillow or a simple tote bag. The tote bag won hands down. "When you're homeless, you need somethin' to carry around your personals, ya know?" one woman said. Setting out a stack of newspapers and colorful fabric remnants, Estelle said the first step was to make a pattern the size they wanted their tote bag to be, using her sample as a guide. "Be sure to allow an inch on both sides to allow for a seam," she cautioned—but several patterns had to be thrown away anyway and started over.

By the time each woman had a newspaper pattern pinned to her fabric piece and cut out, the time was up. "Next week we'll sew these together, and then you can decorate them with felt flowers or whatever you'd like to pretty them up," Estelle promised. But she noticed that Ramona rolled hers up to take home with her.

"If I get mine done at home, I can help you more next week," the girl reasoned.

Did Grace sew? Estelle hoped so. She didn't think Harry would appreciate more young people underfoot this week.

After dropping off Ramona and parking the car, Estelle saw her next-door neighbor to the north standing on her front stoop, getting her mail. "Hello, Lily!" she called, even though the young mother was very shy and rarely seen outside the house.

The woman looked up. Lily Jalili wore her usual black headscarf, a remnant of her Iranian culture, even though her husband had told Harry they were not Muslim. The woman offered a tentative wave, but then went back to looking through the mail. Just as well, Estelle thought. Lily's English was spotty, and Estelle wasn't even sure what language they spoke, which she sometimes heard when the family was in their backyard or calling to their two kids. Arabic? She should look it up.

Estelle had no sooner set down her own bags and taken off her jacket when the doorbell rang. Oof. Another trip down the stairs. To her surprise, Lily stood on the stoop. "Can you read to me?" The young mother thrust an envelope at Estelle. "I don't understand."

Puzzled, Estelle took the envelope. On the outside, scrawled in ballpoint pen, it said: "Occupant, 7332 Beecham." Inside was a single sheet of paper, also handwritten. Estelle's eyes widened as she skimmed over it silently.

Attention: Occupant, 7332 Beecham
From: Isaac Horowitz, 7310 Beecham

The two Red Twig Dogwood bushes you damaged in front of our house with your snowplow in February are dying and must be replaced. I want full-sized bushes to match the rest of the hedge, which I estimate will cost a total of $150 for two mature bushes plus shipping and handling. Make check out ASAP to:

Isaac Horowitz, 7310 Beecham.

"Um, I think this is for your husband." Oh, brother, that was lame. But she'd heard it was Farid Jalili who'd plowed the sidewalk during the big snowstorm last winter so that an ambulance could get through when Mattie Krakowski fell and broke her hip. His work truck was a familiar sight in the neighborhood: *Farid's Lawn Service.*

"But who is—?" Lily pointed to the word *Occupant.* "Not us."

"It, um, just means the person who wrote this does not know your name. 'Occupant' means, uh, the person who lives at this address."

Lily frowned. "Please. Read to me."

74

Reluctantly, Estelle read the note aloud.

Consternation flared on Lily's face. "Money?" She shook her head vigorously, words foreign to Estelle flowing from her mouth. Then, realizing Estelle did not understand, Lily pointed to herself and said emphatically, "No money! No, no!"

She took back the sheet of paper and flounced down the steps, but on reaching the sidewalk turned back and put her hands together. "Thank you. Thank you. I am sorry."

Estelle told Harry about it when he and Corky got home that evening. "It seems such a petty thing for Mr. Horowitz to do," she fussed. "After all, wasn't it an emergency? I heard Farid saved Mattie's life by driving the plow on his truck down the sidewalk." She wagged her head. They hadn't moved into the neighborhood until spring, but the Jaspers had told them about the unplowed, clogged street full of stuck cars, making it impossible for emergency vehicles to get through.

Harry nodded thoughtfully. "True. But I did notice a couple of the Horowitzes' fancy front bushes are pretty much dead when I was out walking Corky. Still, I'm sure Farid doesn't have extra money just lying around. He told me business is really tight. Lots of competition with other yard services."

Estelle heaved a sigh. She'd been trying to get to know all their neighbors since they'd moved in last spring, hoping to create a sense of community here in this little neighborhood. They'd made a few friends already, like the Jaspers, and Grace Meredith, and even Greg and Nicole Singer. And their neighbors on either side— the old Swedish couple, the Molanders, and the Jalilis—a little bit. But guess it was going to take more than homemade cinnamon rolls, which she'd delivered to each neighbor on the block when they'd moved in, to get beyond the social walls around each family.

Hmph. *Occupant* indeed!

Chapter 11

ESTELLE LEFT VOICE MESSAGES for Michelle Jasper and Nicole Singer that their weekly "sister prayer" on Tuesday night would be back at Grace Meredith's house. *I'll be there!* Michelle texted back. No reply from Nicole. Should she try again? No, Estelle didn't want to bug the woman—especially after the tense way their last prayer time had ended. At least Nicole would know from her voicemail that she wasn't holding their difference about the group home against her.

Both Estelle and Michelle arrived promptly at seven Tuesday evening. "You're engaged!" Michelle shrieked when Grace waggled her ring finger. While waiting for Nicole to arrive—Ramona was nursing a headache, they were told—they bombarded Grace for details of Jeff's proposal and cracked up at some of Grace's backstage stories from her recent concert tour. But when Nicole still hadn't arrived by seven thirty, Estelle couldn't help wondering if Nicole was deliberately avoiding her.

"Guess we better go ahead with our prayer time," she said. "Nicole's probably just busy with the kids, now that she's working and they're going to public school. I'll check in with her tomorrow." Well, before next Tuesday anyway.

Michelle's prayer requests were personal: college plans for Destin if he didn't get a basketball scholarship—which looked slim now with his injury and long recovery—and wisdom for how to make ends meet on Jared's salary when she stopped work to have the baby next February. As for Grace, she admitted she was nervous about trying to juggle marriage with a career that involved concert tours. "I know I'm marrying my agent—is that weird or what? But where will we live? Here in Chicago, or in Denver where Bongo Booking is located?"

When it was Estelle's turn, she brought up the group home possibility again—at least Nicole wasn't there to object this time—and Grace, who was hearing it for the first time, thought it was a wonderful idea. "By the way," Michelle jumped in, "Charlotte checked out the information from the real estate agent and said she'll try to come to the Open House on Sunday. Charlotte Bergman is my boss at Bridges," she added for Grace's benefit.

"That's great!" Estelle's spirit lifted. Maybe it was time to open her heart about her hopes and dreams for Leroy. She'd never shared about her son and his schizophrenia with these new friends, but she felt safe with these women. "And there's something else . . ."

Michelle and Grace listened empathetically to Estelle's story and her longing to have Leroy live closer to them, though Michelle cautioned that there was already a list of clients Bridges Family Services had vetted as possible residents for the new group home. "But I can really understand why you'd want your son to be closer, Estelle. Guess we'll just have to put Leroy into the prayer hopper, too, and let God work it out."

"Seems to me like Estelle's boy oughta get priority," Ramona piped up. Estelle jumped. She hadn't noticed that Ramona had slipped into the room and curled up in a chair off to the side. "I mean, with the Bentleys living right here on the block."

"It's a bit more complicated than that," Michelle said gently. "And it's still a big question whether Bridges will even buy this two-flat for their group home. One step at a time."

For some reason, Estelle felt rattled by Ramona inserting herself into the conversation, even though what she'd said was supportive. She needed to tell the girl that the things they shared in this prayer circle were confidential. Not sure she was ready to tell the whole neighborhood about Leroy.

✧　✧　✧　✧

It felt good to get back into the semblance of a normal routine that week at the Bentley household. Ramona came again on Thursday to volunteer at Manna House, and Estelle took advantage of her presence to teach another Mexican-themed favorite to the cooking class—taco soup. "We don't make such a soup at home," Ramona whispered to Estelle.

"Probably been Americanized," Estelle admitted. "But the ladies will love it, you'll see." And they did, in spite of the warm fall day that had spiked into the eighties.

And so did Harry and DaShawn when she served them the leftovers for supper that night. DaShawn piled on the toppings—sour cream, grated cheese, and crushed tortilla chips—and consumed two big bowls.

"I'm gonna need to walk that off," Harry said, pushing back from the table. "C'mon, Corky." He got the dog's leash and headed out the back door. But a moment later he poked his head back in. "Hey, Estelle. You wanna come walk with us? It's a beautiful night. Even a full harvest moon."

Who could resist a romantic invitation like that? Estelle hung her apron over DaShawn's neck and told him he had dish duty, then made her way down the outside stairs to their little backyard where Harry and Corky were waiting. "Whew, it's still warm," she said, mopping her face. "You'd think this was midsummer."

"Ha. Enjoy it while you can. Winter will be here sooner than you can say 'Windy City.'"

They sauntered down the alley, pausing to let Corky do her sniffing and poking about the trash cans. "Wouldn't the cemetery be a nicer place to walk?" Estelle hinted. Beecham Street was surrounded on the east and north by St. Mark's Memorial Cemetery, causing the dead end.

"Yeah, sure. Just easier to clean up after Corky where there are trash cans. She'll be done by the time we get around to Lincoln Paddock's place, then we can go through the little gate."

As they neared the south end of their alley, Estelle heard pounding in the backyard of the last house. Curious, she peered over the gate beside the garage and glimpsed Isaac Horowitz building some sort of wooden structure. "We can see better from the sidewalk," she whispered to Harry, hurrying around the side of the garage. The Horowitzes' house sat on the corner where Beecham Street intersected with Chase Avenue.

The whole family was in the backyard. The father was testing the square wooden frame that stood a few inches taller than he was, which had wooden lattice nailed to it on three sides and across the top. His wife was decorating the structure with panels of colorful cloth around the sides and large greenery over the top, while the baby fussed in his stroller nearby.

"Hello!" Estelle called over the four-foot hedge. "Are you building a booth for the Feast of Booths?"

On hearing her voice, the two older children popped out of the inside of the structure. "We're camping out tonight! We get to sleep in our booth for Sukkot!"

"Hush," the father said. "No need to tell the whole world."

"Well, glad it's a warm night for your campout."

Rebecca Horowitz picked up the fussing baby and came over to the hedge. "You know about the Feast of Booths?"

"Only a little. It remembers the temporary dwellings when the Israelites were in the wilderness, I think."

Rebecca Horowitz smiled. "Very good. But we are praying it does not rain till Sukkot is over."

"How long is that?" Estelle tried to ignore the looks from Harry.

"A full week . . . till next Wednesday."

"Oh my. I've heard about the booths that Jewish families build for this festival, but I've never seen one. It's beautiful." Now Harry was tugging at her sleeve. "Well, God bless you!"

When they were out of earshot, Harry growled, "So how do you know so much about these Jewish festivals or whatever they are?" They walked on, crossed the street, and continued up the alley on the other side of Beecham.

Estelle chuckled. "Don't forget Ruth Garfield is in my Yada Yada Prayer Group. She made sure we all got educated about such things. 'You *goyim!*' she'd say. 'Even Jesus celebrated the Jewish festivals. You think God's people started with you? Don't forget—grafted in you are!'"

Now even Harry was chuckling. "She has a point. Not sure the Horowitzes think we're grafted in, though—at least not the mister."

"Oh! Speaking of Yada Yada," Estelle said, "we're supposed to meet this Sunday evening. We skipped August since so many sisters were out of town, so I really want to go. especially now since we meet only once a month."

"Uh-huh." Harry was clearly distracted by Corky, who had found something interesting behind a row of trash bins.

As they passed behind the Singers' brick bungalow, Estelle heard Nicole's children playing in the backyard. Hmm. She hadn't called Nicole yet to find out why she hadn't come to the prayer time at Grace's house on Tuesday night. Okay, she'd call for sure this weekend.

And thinking about the weekend . . . "Harry? I'd like to go see Leroy on Saturday. That okay with you?"

"Sure, except I've got to work on Saturday. It was either that or Sunday and Gilson let me pick. You okay going by yourself?"

"I guess. Sure." No reason why she couldn't. But the ride to and from the South Side was a lot more pleasant when she had company. Maybe they could go Sunday afternoon instead—

No, the Alvarezes' Open House was Sunday. She definitely wanted to be here for that. Especially if that Charlotte Bergman from Bridges Family Services was coming to check it out for a group home. And Yada Yada after that . . . Nope, had to be Saturday.

✦ ✦ ✦ ✦

Estelle wasn't quite sure how she did it, but somehow she sweet-talked DaShawn into going with her to visit Leroy on Saturday. He was playing soccer this year as an eighth grader, but Stone Academy's games were all on weekdays after school. High school next year would be another thing, but until then, weekends were still fair game. She wasn't sure he'd say yes— after all, DaShawn had only met Leroy a few times, at holidays or a birthday dinner. And DaShawn was Harry's grandson, had been living with his grandpa a few months before she and Harry started dating. Those two were thick as thieves, so it wasn't like she'd spent much time alone with DaShawn, just the two of them.

Maybe it was offering to go to Lou Malnati's for pizza for lunch. She was pretty sure there was one not that far from the Lighthouse. And it turned out to be just the thing. Leroy loved pizza, and seemed to enjoy DaShawn's kidding around. In fact, he was more "with it" than he'd been the last time she and Harry visited.

Maybe she should bring DaShawn to visit Leroy more often. If those two got along, that'd be another good reason to move Leroy closer to the family.

"That pizza place was slammin'!" DaShawn said on the way home. "Hey, Grams, I been thinkin'. I'd really like to have a party for my birthday. But it'd be so cool to go someplace like Lou Malnati's or Gino's East instead of just ordering pizza or whatever. I mean, I'm gonna be fourteen. Whaddaya think?"

Estelle glanced at the boy beside her. Fourteen already? He certainly had been getting taller. He was already eye-to-eye with her, not counting the Afro he kept trying to grow. "Your birthday's October . . . what day?"

"My birthday's the tenth, but that's the weekend I'm gonna be with my dad, and I'd like to have a party with my friends. Never done that before, but all the kids at school invite friends to their birthday parties."

"So . . ." Estelle turned off Lake Shore Drive and headed up Ridge Avenue toward their neighborhood.

"So, I was thinkin' maybe next weekend?"

Estelle's head started spinning. A party. Next weekend. With friends. At a restaurant. "Uh, just how many friends are you thinking of inviting?"

"I dunno. Not too many—maybe five or six. There are some kids at school who are pretty good friends. This guy named Jaivon invited me to *his* birthday party last year, remember? And the Jaspers for sure—they're like my best friends."

For which she and Harry would be eternally grateful. A Christian family. Right in the neighborhood. Nice kids. But she needed to buy some time. "Well, I've gotta talk to your grandpa first before you go inviting Tavis and Destin or any of those other boys."

DaShawn shot her a look. "*Destin?* I don't mean *Destin*. He's like, too old. Good grief, he's goin' to college next year. I meant the twins, Tavis and *Tabitha*." He twisted his head away, trying to hide the sudden grin that widened his face. "She's pretty cool, you know, for a girl."

Estelle had a hard time keeping a straight face. Hmm. She hadn't seen *that* coming.

Chapter 12

Estelle ran DaShawn's request by Harry as they were getting ready for bed that evening.

"A birthday party at a restaurant? Five or six boys besides us?" Harry ran a hand over his shaved head. "I dunno, Estelle. Sounds rather expensive."

"Uh, not just boys. He wants to invite the Jasper twins—Tavis *and* Tabitha—too." She winked at her husband. "In fact, I caught a hint DaShawn's kinda sweet on Tabitha."

"What? He's just a kid."

"Uh-huh. A *fourteen*-year-old kid. Bet when you were that age, all you did was think about girls."

Harry rolled his eyes and Estelle laughed. "Anyway, he wants to have his party next Saturday, since he'll be at his dad's on his actual birthday—"

"What?" Now Harry's face clouded. "He's gonna be gone on his birthday? How did we miss that? Rodney will just have to choose another weekend."

Estelle lifted an eyebrow. "Harry, that's probably why Rodney asked for that weekend. He wants to be there for his son's birthday for once. He wants a second chance to be a father. You of all people should understand that."

Harry sank down onto their bed, rubbing a hand over his shaved head. Then he sighed. "Okay, okay, I get it. It's just . . . I'd feel better about it if that Donita woman wasn't in the picture."

"His mother."

Harry rolled his eyes again. "Yeah. His *mother*. But you've seen what she's like, Estelle. I don't get it. Just don't see why Rodney puts up with the likes of her."

Estelle laid a hand on her husband's shoulder. "I know. We can't do anything about that right now. But we can celebrate DaShawn's birthday, even if it's not on the actual day. I think it's kinda nice that DaShawn wants to have his birthday party while he's with us."

"Hmph." Harry ambled off to the bathroom, but was back a few minutes later, still holding his toothbrush. "Tell ya what. Maybe we can talk DaShawn into having a birthday party with his friends here at the house—but if he wants to go out somewhere special for dinner, I'd like to take him out, just him and me. Fourteen's a good time for some man-to-man talk."

✧ ✧ ✧ ✧

Ramona called the next morning and asked if she could go to SouledOut Community Church with them again. "Of course," Estelle said, cradling the kitchen phone between ear and shoulder as she stirred the scrambled eggs. "Tell Grace she's welcome to come, too, if she'd like."

"Nah, she's gonna have Sunday dinner out in the 'burbs with her brother's family—hasn't told them she's engaged yet. Wants to do it in person I guess."

Estelle couldn't blame Ramona for wanting to attend church where there was a mix of Spanish-speaking folks with whites and blacks and other nationalities. She hadn't ever been to the church where Grace and her brother attended, but Estelle's impression was that it was basically white and middle-class. Grace had enjoyed a visit or two to SouledOut, but connecting with family had been important to her in the past year when a lot of things had fallen apart for her and she'd basically been grounded from her career for several months.

Family connection *was* important, even when times were good. If Leroy lived close by, maybe he'd even be willing to come to SouledOut with them.

The only downside to bringing Ramona with them that morning was that Edesa and Josh Baxter wanted to talk to her after the service about maybe helping out with the middle school youth group that fall. So they were later than usual getting home after the service, and Estelle could tell the Open House was already going on by the time they dropped Ramona off.

"Harry," she said as he parked in front of their graystone, "I think I'll go ahead and pop into the Alvarezes' open house now if you don't mind. There're plenty of leftovers from last night you and DaShawn can eat for lunch."

"Why the rush? Isn't the open house all afternoon?"

"Yes . . . but Michelle said her boss from Bridges was going to stop by and look at the house, you know, as a possibility for the group home they want to set up. I'd like to meet her."

Harry looked at her a long moment as they stood on the sidewalk. Then, "I know you'd like to see this happen, Estelle. And it's not a bad idea. Just . . . take it easy how hard you push. This is primarily about the Alvarezes being able to sell their house as quickly as possible so they can get back to Guatemala."

His words stung. He might as well have said, *"It's not about Bridges wanting to set up a group home, and it's not about you."*

"Thanks," she said dryly. "I'll remember that." Turning on her heel, she flounced across the street to the Alvarezes' two-flat. A car pulled up, parked, and a white couple got out and walked up the walk to the open door. Estelle paused on the sidewalk and took a deep breath. *Okay, Lord, I don't want to run ahead of You. But it would really be nice if Harry and I could be on the same page about this. I need his support.* Another deep breath and she climbed the few steps to the front door. After all, didn't it seem like a God-thing that this house needed a quick sale, and Bridges just got funding to buy a building, and her son needed something like this—all in her own neighborhood?

A good-looking Hispanic man in suit and tie, maybe forty-something, who Estelle presumed was the realtor, met her just inside. "Welcome," he said, his English accented. "Please, come in and look around. We have coffee and cookies in the dining room, as well as printed information about the house. If you have any questions, please feel free to ask. My name is Mario Valdez." He smiled and handed her his card.

"*Gracias*," she said, then immediately wanted to slap her head. The man spoke perfectly good English. Was she trying to show off? But he had already turned to greet someone who came in behind her.

Mr. and Mrs. Alvarez were nowhere to be seen. Guess it was standard for homeowners to not be present at an open house, but she was disappointed. She would've liked to introduce them to Charlotte Bergman as the person she'd mentioned who might be interested. Except . . . she had a problem. A few people were wandering around the first floor, but she had no idea what Michelle's boss looked like.

This was dumb. She might have to call Michelle and ask her to come over to the open house and help them connect. But maybe she'd take a look upstairs first.

As she topped the stairs, she heard animated voices from one of the back rooms—but not speaking English. Sounded Yiddish . . . or Hebrew, she wasn't sure. Her heart-speed picked up a little— one of the voices sounded like Isaac Horowitz. She hesitated in the upstairs living room, unsure whether to continue and risk running into him or to go back downstairs . . . when a woman's voice spoke behind her. "Excuse me. Are you Estelle Bentley by any chance?"

Startled, Estelle turned. She hadn't noticed anyone else on the second floor. The woman was on the stocky side, had short graying hair, fiftyish. "That's right."

The woman grinned and thrust out her hand. "Charlotte Bergman. Michelle Jasper told me you might be here. Thanks for giving us the heads-up about this property."

Estelle shook her hand. Firm grip, no nonsense. "How did you—?"

The woman chuckled. "You fit her description exactly."

Hmph. No doubt. So far she was the only African American she'd seen at the open house.

"It was the caftan you're wearing that gave you away. Michelle says you make a lot of your own African-inspired clothes."

"Ah. Well, yes. These caftans are comfortable." Not to mention they hid a lot of body flaws. After all, she wasn't twenty anymore.

Charlotte Bergman looked around and headed slowly toward the dining room. "I like the idea of a two-flat for a group home. Gives both the host couple and the residents some privacy—yet they can share common space, meals, things like that. And the second floor kitchen would give residents the opportunity to do some cooking themselves—depending on the residents, of course."

"Zayt moykhl. Did you say group home?" a pleasant voice interrupted—this time male. Estelle had been so distracted by meeting up with Charlotte Bergman, she hadn't noticed Isaac Horowitz and his companion had come out of the kitchen into the dining room. It was the other man who spoke—very distinguished-looking with a salt-and-pepper beard, black hat, and plain black coat even though the day was still warm. He was average height, but looked shorter next to Isaac's beanpole frame. His hands were clasped behind his back, peering at them through round wire rims.

"A gut ovnt." Michelle's boss nodded. "I am Charlotte Bergman from Bridges Family Services. And you are . . .?"

"Rabbi Jacob Mendel. Temple Beth Zion. *Redt ir Yidish?"*

"Yo, a bisele."

Okay, so she'd forgotten that Michelle's boss was Jewish—a non-practicing Jew, Michelle had said. Estelle was starting to feel left out. She leaned in. "Ms. Bergman is looking at this two-flat as a possible group home for adults. It would be ideal." Might as well make dibs on the place, Chicago style.

"This is a residential neighborhood," Isaac Horowitz said stiffly. "You would need a zoning variance to put a group home here."

The rabbi nodded. "Yes, yes, I would think so. Would take a very long time. And I understand the owners are eager to sell quickly." He touched his hat with a fingertip. *"Biz shpeter,* Ms. Bergman."

The two men made a detour around them and headed down the stairs.

Charlotte Bergman looked after them, her expression slightly amused. "Hmm. I wonder what the rabbi and his friend are wanting with a two-flat."

Estelle sighed. "His friend lives on the corner—the Horowitzes. Neighbors. According to his kids, they are eager for more Jewish families to move into this block."

Michelle's boss nodded. "I see. Yes, that would make sense, given the tight Jewish community if you're Conservative or Orthodox." She wandered through the second floor, peeking into various rooms, examining the kitchen. "Mm, seems in good shape. Would need an inspection of course to see how sound it is structurally."

"But is it true? You would need to get a zoning variance?" Harry had said something about that, which she'd basically ignored at the time. But now Estelle was worried. In a city like Chicago, appeals to the zoning board could drag on for months.

Charlotte headed for the stairs. "Not really." She tossed an impish grin over her shoulder. "The FHAA includes substantial fair housing laws for persons with disabilities."

"FHAA?"

"Fair Housing Amendments Act. Shouldn't have any trouble on that account. But—"

"But what?"

"This is the first property we've looked at. I'm sure the board will want to look at several properties to compare accessibility to transportation, neighborhood openness to a group home, property taxes—things like that."

Uh-huh, things like that.

On the first floor, Charlotte Bergman reiterated her appreciation for the heads-up about the availability of this property, but would Estelle excuse her? She wanted to talk to the realtor before she left.

Isaac Horowitz and the rabbi were nowhere to be seen. A few more people had arrived; some of the earlier ones had already left. Had anyone made an offer? No way to know at this point.

Estelle trudged home slowly. Of course Bridges Family Services would want to look at several properties before deciding. Like Harry said, the whole thing was a long shot—she needed to remember that. Out of her hands. Up to the Lord to bring it all together.

But there was one thing Charlotte said that especially bothered her: neighborhood openness to a group home. Was that a make-it-or-break-it issue? The Horowitzes definitely had other priorities for this block. Nicole Singer didn't like it, but would she fight it? Mattie Krakowski and the Molanders would probably give a thumbs-down if asked—neither of the old-timers liked change, and a group home would probably be too much. So far that was four probable naysayers to three who were open to the idea: Bentleys, Jaspers, and Grace Meredith.

But that was only half the neighborhood.

Her footsteps picked up speed. Maybe it was time to get a petition going.

Chapter 13

Estelle stared at the computer screen. Is this what she wanted to say?

> As neighbors of the 7300 block of Beecham Street, we support a proposed group home for mentally challenged adults in the two-flat at 7323-25 Beecham, sponsored by Bridges Family Services. Given Bridges's excellent reputation in the Chicago area, we are confident that the home will be well supervised by the staff couple who will live on the premises, as well as the staff at Bridges itself, and that the residents chosen to live in the group home will have been vetted as to their suitability for a residential dwelling, which they are entitled to under the Fair Housing Amendments Act (FHAA).

She stared at what she'd written a while longer, then deleted "a proposed" and substituted "the idea of a" since the group home hadn't actually been proposed yet. But maybe knowing the neighborhood generally supported "the idea of" a group home might influence Bridges's decision.

"Hey, babe!" Harry hollered from the living room where he and DaShawn were watching a football game on TV. "Thought you wanted to go to your Yada Yada group tonight. It's almost five o'clock."

Estelle jumped. Oh no! Where had the time gone? It'd been two months since they last met and now she was going to be late. She saved the document, then scurried around getting her shoes on and grabbing an apple from the fridge. She was still wearing the caftan she'd worn to church, so she was good there. Kissing the top of Harry's shaved head as she passed through the living room, she said, "Sorry, hon. I didn't make any supper for you and DaShawn. Will you be all right?"

"After all that leftover chicken and greens we ate for lunch? We'll be fine . . . what?!" Harry suddenly leaped up, stabbing a finger at the TV. "I don't believe it! Did you see that, DaShawn? What a stupid play. What's the matter with that coach?"

Estelle slipped out and made her way downstairs. Huh. She knew what "We'll be fine" meant—popcorn, chips, ice cream, pop, cookies.

It was only a ten-minute drive over to Avis Douglass's apartment. Pretty sure that was where they were meeting this time. Back in the day when they met weekly, they met at a different house each week—which was kinda nice, everyone getting a chance to be hostess, not a burden on any one of the sisters. Would everyone be there tonight? Well, not "everyone," since Nony Sisulu-Smith and her family had finally moved to South Africa, and Hoshi Takahashi was still doing postgraduate work on the East Coast. But most of the rest of the Yada Yadas had hung in there with the prayer group.

Had it really been six . . . no, seven years since she'd joined the group? Taken her in was more like it. After that fire at Manna House when she'd been staying at the shelter because Leroy . . . Estelle shuddered. No sense dragging up that whole scene again. But, bless her, Leslie "Stu" Stuart, one of the Yada Yadas and a social worker, had offered her a place to stay, which turned into something more permanent—housemates. Ha! What a pair they'd made! Total opposites: Stu was tall, skinny, white, super-organized, and quick with the "right" way to do things. Estelle was not-so-skinny, black, more laid back, organized enough, relaxed, had her own way of doing things. She chuckled. Yeah, "housemates" until Harry came along and swept her off her feet four years ago.

When the Manna House shelter got rebuilt, she'd gone back all right, but this time as a volunteer, and then as part-time staff. And continued with the Yada Yadas.

Estelle turned onto Avis's block and started looking for a parking spot. Everybody must be home on a Sunday evening . . . *Oh, there. Somebody just pulled out.*

Five minutes later she was huffing up the stairs to the Douglass's third floor apartment. She could hear the chattering a whole flight before she topped the stairs and pushed open the door, which had been left cracked a few inches.

"Hey, Estelle! Thought you weren't comin'!" Yo-Yo Spencer sauntered over in baggy crop pants and tank top and gave her a fist bump—Yo-Yo's version of a hug. The young woman still wore her blonde hair spiky even though she was in her early thirties. The purple streaks were new though. "How's the ol' man?"

Estelle chuckled. "He's fine—but don't let Harry hear you call him an old man."

Most of the women were standing around sipping iced tea. Several greeted her warmly and somebody handed her a frosty glass, but once Avis Douglass caught her eye, their hostess called out, "Estelle's here, sisters. We can start now."

Estelle sank into the closest chair and glanced around the room as the others found seats in the well-appointed living room. She'd already seen several of these women that morning at SouledOut—Edesa Baxter and her mother-in-law, Jodi Baxter . . . Stu, her former housemate, all leggy in tight jeans and boots . . . and Avis, of course, one of the worship leaders at SouledOut, her wrinkle-free, coffee-no-cream skin belying her age. She'd seen Florida Hickman that morning too—still with a touch of "street" in her, even though she'd been clean for a decade at least—but Estelle didn't see her now. Hadn't Florida said she'd be here tonight?

But Ruth Garfield was there—she and her husband, Ben, attended a Messianic congregation. Hmm. Had Ruth and Ben built a booth in their yard for Sukkot like the Horowitzes? She couldn't imagine those two middle-aged "Jews for Jesus" sleeping in the yard, in spite of their young twins. It was good to see Delores Enriques—she must've come straight from work, as she was still wearing her nursing scrubs. And Estelle couldn't help noticing Adele Skuggs's nails decorated with flourishes and tiny rhinestones—probably advertising that Adele's Hair and Nails had hired a *"nail artiste."* Hmph. All that bling wasn't Estelle's thing.

Didn't see Becky Wallace though. In fact, "Bandana Woman" hadn't been at their last meeting in July either. *Lord, Lord, hope that girl isn't back on drugs —*

". . . so we praise You, Mighty God, for bringing us together tonight, knit together as one in love and spirit." Avis was already opening in prayer. "We pray especially for our sisters who are far away and those who can't be with us tonight. We come just as we are into Your presence, with all the challenges we face, our hopes and fears, casting all our cares on You."

Murmurs of "Yes, yes" spread around the room. Estelle sucked in a breath and blew it out, reining in her wandering thoughts. *That's right, Lord. I do need to bring all my hopes and fears, all my cares, to You.* This was why she needed her Yada Yada sisters—to encourage her and keep her focused on Jesus when life seemed to be spinning out in all directions.

The room seemed to rustle expectantly after Avis's "Amen," as everyone opened their eyes and looked around with mischievous grins. But Estelle barely had time to wonder if she'd missed something when Avis called out, "You're on, Florida!"

Florida Hickman came marching out of the Douglass kitchen bearing a flaming sheet cake, which she set down on the coffee table in front of Jodi Baxter. "Blow, girl, 'fore them fifty-one candles burn down the house!" Florida snickered, as the rest of the room broke into a slightly off-key version of "Happy Birthday."

Estelle groaned inwardly. She'd totally forgotten that Jodi had a September birthday. Somebody should've sent around a reminder—which was something Jodi always did for other people's birthdays.

Jodi's face had turned pink. "Aw, c'mon you guys. I thought we didn't celebrate birthdays after you hit the big 5-0."

"What d'you mean?" Adele Skuggs tossed her head. "I've earned ever' one of my birthdays, and don't y'all forget I'm turning fifty-two in November."

But her last words were drowned out as everyone else screeched, "Jodi, *blow!*"

It took several blows to put out the fifty-one candles, and only then did the orange writing on the white-frosted cake become visible:

Happy Birthday, Jodi ~ "God Is Gracious"

Jodi teared up and she fished for a tissue. "Thanks for the reminder, everyone. I'm still learning to live in the meaning of my name."

Got that right, Estelle thought. She'd never been curious about the meaning of her own name until she started coming to the Yada Yada Prayer Group. But Jodi had looked it up. "Estelle—Star" . . . and she'd been taken aback at all the different ways her prayer group sisters had found to apply that word to her in meaningful ways. "Star—You are God's own twinkle in His eye" . . . "Estelle, you are like the morning star, brightening our lives with your love and energy even after the other stars have faded" . . . and more.

As Florida busied herself cutting the cake and passing pieces around, Avis suggested they go around the circle and each give a blessing to Jodi. Edesa flashed her wide, beautiful smile. "Me first! Mama Jodi, thank you for raising such a wonderful son, and for blessing our marriage. *And* for being a wonderful *abuela* to our babies!" Everybody clapped and hooted.

When it was Estelle's turn she got up and went to Jodi, brushed aside the brown straight bangs, and planted a kiss on her forehead. "Jodi Baxter, gotta say, you're the first white girl I've ever known who was willing to eat humble pie and admit you don't know everything"—behind her Yo-Yo started to snicker—"as well as being willing to step outside of your 'good Christian girl' comfort zone to hang with this motley crew of colorful sisters. So come on up in here and let me give you a hug. You're my sister for real." Estelle pulled Jodi to her feet and enveloped the woman in a big hug.

More clapping and hooting. More blessings. Jodi's mascara was soon a mess.

Finally Avis moved them on. "We want to have time to hear any prayer requests tonight, especially since we're only meeting once a month now. And we'd love to hear updates on any prayer groups that you've begun in your own neighborhood or workplace. But we'll have to be brief since most of us still have to go to work tomorrow."

Some of the prayer requests were predictable. Ruth Garfield asked prayer for energy to parent her six-and-a-half-year-old twins. "Complaining I'm not. But Ben and I aren't as young as we used to be." Which got a laugh, because both Ben and Ruth had already been in their fifties when the twins were born. But, she reported, they had started to meet with another Jewish couple who were curious that the Garfields had become Christians. "If Ben doesn't scare the bejeebers out of them. You know him, likes to play devil's advocate, he does."

Jodi said she'd started to pray with another teacher at Bethune Elementary, and Avis—the principal who'd hired Jodi—joined them from time to time. "Has to be unofficial, of course, since it's a public school. But we're hoping a few more teachers will join us."

Yo-Yo needed a job with more pay, as she was still trying to get her two brothers through community college. And no, she hadn't started a new prayer group and wasn't likely to either. "Good grief. I haven't even read more'n four books in the Bible. Just the Jesus ones, like you all told me to when I got baptized. Startin' a prayer group is way beyond my pay grade. Read my lips, ladies: 'Baby Christian on Board.'"

More smiles and assurances it was okay.

"Has anyone heard from Becky Wallace?" Avis asked. No, seemed like she'd dropped off the radar. Stu offered to check up on her and let everyone know.

Estelle checked her watch. Would she have time to bring her prayer group sisters up to speed on what was happening in her neighborhood? Her mind was so focused on what she might say, she almost missed Avis's gentle tease. "Okay, let's hear from our newlywed." Avis smiled in Estelle's direction.

"Who, us? Newlyweds? Hmph. Been almost four years now—and at our age, feels like eight." She tried to keep a serious face, but the group dissolved in laughter, and Estelle couldn't help grinning. "Besides, you should talk, Avis Douglass. You an' Peter weren't exactly spring chickens when you jumped the broom a few years ago."

"Yeah, but at least they jumped the broom," Yo-Yo snickered. "Don't remember you an' Mr. Harry *jumpin'* anything, 'cept maybe into—*mmph*."

Florida had clapped her hand over Yo-Yo's mouth. "I think we done with that," Florida said, her words dripping sugar even as she released Yo-Yo with a warning eye. "Sister Estelle, how them two boys doin' who got shot last summer?"

The silliness aborted, Estelle waved a hand. "Oh, they're doin' fine. Goin' to school, though neither one can play any sports yet. Which is 'specially hard on the older one, 'cause he was hopin' for an athletic scholarship when he graduates next spring. I'm sure the family would appreciate us keepin' them in prayer. But . . ."

Estelle tried to collect her thoughts. She didn't want to be talking about the Jasper boys. She'd already shared a couple of times about the Tuesday night prayer group she'd started in the Beecham Street neighborhood, first with just Grace Meredith and then as Michelle Jasper and Nicole Singer got added. But she didn't really want to share about all the little dramas going on with her neighbors. She wanted the Yadas to start praying about the group home possibility. At least these sisters already knew about Leroy, thank God . . .

So she plunged in, telling about the amazing coincidence of one of their neighbors needing to sell their two-flat, then finding out the social service agency where Michelle Jasper worked was looking for a place to start a group home for mentally challenged adults, at the very time she'd been feeling a strong need to find a place for Leroy closer to her and Harry.

"Don't believe in coincidences." Adele said. "Sounds like God doin' His thing." Several others murmured in agreement.

"*Sí, sí,* that would be wonderful, *mi amiga.*" Edesa leaned over and gave Estelle a hug. "I can see how a group home nearby would be a real answer to prayer for you."

"Oh Jesus!" Estelle closed her eyes and waved a hand heavenward. "Yes, yes. Please pray with me, sisters, that God will close the mouths of the lions and finish what He has started, right there on Beecham Street!"

There was a brief silence, and Estelle waited for one of the sisters—Avis probably—to start praying. But instead Stu spoke. "So which lions are you talking about?"

Estelle opened her eyes. "What?"

"What do your neighbors think about a group home moving into the neighborhood? Has the idea been getting some flak? Wouldn't be surprised—as a social worker, I've seen that happen quite a bit."

Estelle felt flustered. "Oh . . . you know. There are always naysayers. But there's a lot of support too. And if God is for us, who can be against us?"

Stu dropped it. And the group did pray for God's will to be done regarding the group home and Estelle's desire to have Leroy close by, before praying for the other prayer requests that had been shared.

But Estelle felt disappointed as she drove home. Why did Stu have to focus on the negative possibilities? It had sort of taken the wind out of the sails of how the group had prayed. *Let God's will be done?* That felt a lot wimpier than the kind of prayer she'd hoped for, more like, *Thank You, God, for what You're going to do! Move every mountain! Shut the mouths of the lions and naysayers! And we'll give You all the glory when that lease is signed!*

Yeah. That kind of prayer!

Chapter 14

Estelle almost forgot that Ramona wanted to come to work with her on Mondays until she came out of the house the next morning and found the young woman leaning against the RAV4.

"Did you hear that Miss Edesa and Mr. Josh asked me to help with the middle school kids at church?" the girl said, practically bouncing into the front seat. "Oh, right, I told you yesterday on the way home from church. But Mr. Josh called me last night to talk more about it. He said they're going to have a Harvest Party at the church on Halloween, and he wants me to talk about *el Día de los Muertos.*"

"The what?"

"*El Día de los Muertos,* the Day of the Dead. Something we celebrate in Mexico."

Estelle grimaced. *Day of the Dead?* Sounded even worse than Halloween, which wasn't her favorite holiday—although she'd had fun dressing up as a princess or a black cat back in Mississippi when she was a little girl and collecting all that candy. "So why do people in Mexico celebrate the, uh, Day of the Dead?" she asked carefully.

Ramona shrugged. "Not sure. All I know is that *mi madre* used to make a little altar with the pictures of her parents and light candles and say prayers for them. But mostly we celebrated All Saints' Day at the Catholic Church the first day of November." She grinned. "Mr. Josh encouraged me to do some research. Miss Grace said she'd help me."

Estelle tried not to roll her eyes. She hoped Edesa and Josh knew what they were doing. Most of the black churches she knew frowned on doing *anything* on Halloween. But then, SouledOut was a big mix of cultures.

At Manna House, Edesa Baxter was grateful that Ramona showed up again to babysit Gracie and Julian during the weekly staff meeting. "She's really sweet," Edesa whispered to Estelle as the staff and volunteers gathered in the small schoolroom on the main floor. "What's going to happen to her?"

Estelle shook her head. "Don't know. After she testifies in that drug trial, hopefully she can go home to LA, where she's got family." She hesitated. Should she say anything about Harry's concern about keeping Ramona safe until the trial? Actually, yes. The more people looking out for her, the better. "Until then, we—"

But just then Mabel Turner opened the meeting with a prayer, then launched into that morning's agenda. Estelle *did* roll her eyes when Gabby Fairbanks, the program director, outlined her plan for a costume party at the shelter the last Saturday of October— since the thirty-first actually fell on a Sunday this year.

"It'd be great if all the staff participated," Gabby enthused. "We can set the tone—no ghoulish costumes, no witches or ghosts or vampires. In fact, we could maybe have a theme, like fairy-tale characters or great American heroes. The residents would love it. Most of them have all too little fun in their lives—the right kind of fun, that is."

Estelle wagged her head. Could she get out of this one? What she'd really like to do that weekend is stay home, turn out all the lights to keep the trick-or-treaters away, and watch *Driving Miss Daisy* or some other sweet movie on their DVD player. She couldn't imagine Harry being willing to dress up. Except . . . he had a soft spot for Miss Gabby. After all, he'd turned up at the Manna House Fun Night at Gabby's invitation four years ago and danced the Macarena, which was how she and Harry had met . . . and the rest, as they say, was history.

And of course there was DaShawn, who still liked to dress up as some movie character and go trick-or-treating with his buddies. Hmph. Wasn't he getting a little old for that?

The agenda moved on: updates on new arrivals, how to use a new group of volunteers from one of the suburban churches, a possible fund-raiser for the aging furnace. But Estelle's mind got stuck on DaShawn. His birthday was coming up—and so was the party he wanted this coming weekend. Help! She needed her own staff meeting with Harry tonight!

✦　✦　✦　✦

Harry cleared his throat at the supper table that night. "So, DaShawn. Let's talk about this birthday party you're wanting to have this weekend."

"Yeah!" DaShawn had his mouth full of fried chicken, but that didn't stop him. "Did Grams tell you about my idea to go to Lou Malnati's? The pizza is so good!"

"I got that. But let's talk options . . ." Harry had his speech ready. "It would be expensive to take a group of hollow-leg teenagers like yourself to Lou—"

"Aw, Gramps! I've never had a real birthday party."

Harry and Estelle looked at each other. He cleared his throat again. "I know that. And we want to celebrate your birthday, but—"

"What if I just invited the twins? That'd be just two more, plus the three of us—only five altogether."

"Now hold on, son. Hear me out. We *want* you to have a party. And we want you to have a good time with your friends. But think about it—what's there to do besides eat if we go out to a restaurant? And you'd have to all be quiet and orderly—does that sound like a party?"

"But—" DaShawn frowned.

"C'mon now. Hear me out. What if you invited some of your friends for a party *here* Saturday evening—you could play basketball out in the alley, play some games, maybe watch a movie, and eat your grandma's good cookin', topped off by birthday cake an' ice cream."

Estelle shot him a look. This was sounding like a lot of work.

" . . . and *then,*" Harry continued, "if you've really got your heart set on having a birthday dinner at Lou Malnati's, how about you and me go there next Sunday, just the two of us?"

A slow smile spread on DaShawn's face. "Really? Just you an' me? That'd be cool. An' I guess we could have a party here . . . Can I invite some of the kids from school? How many?"

"Three," Estelle said quickly. "With you and the twins, that makes six. Even-Steven for games. And I will send an actual invitation with our home address and phone number so the parents can check us out. Which is what we do when you get invited to somebody's party we don't know."

"Okay, okay." DaShawn threw up his hands in surrender. Then he jumped up and gave both Harry and Estelle a hug. "Thanks, Gramps. Thanks, Grams. Sounds good. Uh, can I go call Tavis and Tabitha now? Maybe they can help me think of some fun stuff to do." Without waiting for an answer, he grabbed the kitchen cordless and darted from the room.

Estelle opened her mouth to call him back to clear his dishes, but Harry said, "Oh, let him go. I need to talk to you anyway." He jerked a thumb in the direction of the black Lab, who was curled up in her bed by the back door. "Corky and I have to do another undercover run this week—to Denver this time. Probably be gone two nights again."

Estelle stared at him. "What? This week? Please tell me you won't be gone during DaShawn's birthday party on Saturday."

"No, no. Have to leave tomorrow—be back on Thursday. But, uh, I think some of my clothes could use a run through the wash tonight."

Estelle's cell phone rang. Ha. Saved by the bell. "Feel free to throw in a load. I need to get this—it's Grace . . . Hello, Grace?" She wandered into the living room to give Harry plenty of room to gather his laundry on his own. The man wasn't helpless.

"Hi, Estelle. Sorry to call your cell, but your home phone was busy and I needed to ask something before tomorrow."

"No problem. Everything okay?"

"Yes, yes, everything's fine, but . . . I was wondering how you'd feel about Ramona coming with you to Manna House every day, like she did when she stayed with you that week." Grace sounded breathless. "It's just . . . I'm working on some new music for a fall tour, and it was really helpful to have Ramona gone this morning. And I know she really enjoys going to the shelter. It gives her something positive to do, and less time to get depressed about having to wait around for Max's trial to be scheduled. If she's not a bother . . ."

"No, no, she's not a bother." Though Estelle did feel the extra responsibility of looking out for her and keeping her busy. She thought fast. "Tell you what. Let me talk to the director tomorrow about having Ramona come as a regular volunteer, see what she says. Ramona is younger than most of our volunteers, but . . . anyway. Tuesday is my short day, I only have lunch to do, no classes or meetings. So if you can manage keeping her home tomorrow, promise I'll get back to you when I get off work."

"Thanks, Estelle. See you tomorrow night for prayer? If I haven't told you before, it makes a big difference in my week to stop and take that time to pray with my sisters."

"Thanks for that encouragement, Grace. Yes, I'll be there."

As she clicked the Off button, Estelle chewed her lip. Prayer with her neighborhood sisters tomorrow. And she still hadn't checked in with Nicole Singer to see why she didn't come last week.

Couldn't keep putting it off. What was she afraid of? She dialed the Singers' number.

"Estelle!" Harry's voice sailed from the bedroom. "Have you seen my gray pants?"

"Sorry! On the phone!" A man's voice answered the rings. "Oh, hello, Greg. Uh, is Nicole available? It's Estelle Bentley."

"Hi Estelle." She could picture Nicole's husband—five-eight, dark hair, hazel eyes, tanned from his job as a salesman for powerboats and outdoor equipment, nice looking if you liked the type. "Nicole's busy right now reading to the kids. Can I have her call you back?"

"Yes, please. Tonight, if possible."

"Sure. Tell Harry hello for me."

That was nice. Greg Singer seemed a lot friendlier ever since Harry had befriended the man while he was going through a job crisis last summer. She wondered what *he* thought about a group home moving in next door.

Estelle had just finished loading the dishwasher when Harry came in the back door from his hike to the basement with his laundry. "Gotta take Corky out for a good run," he said, getting the dog's leash. "She won't get much exercise the next few days traveling by train." He sounded a bit harried.

Relenting, Estelle said, "Don't worry about the laundry. I'll move it into the dryer. Take your time with Corky." If Harry was going away for a couple of days, the least she could do was give him a good send-off.

By the time Harry got back and they finished packing, helped DaShawn with some homework, and watched the tail end of the news, they were both tired and ready to fall into bed. It was only when she'd turned out the light and snuggled up against Harry's broad back that Estelle realized Nicole Singer had never called her back.

Chapter 15

ESTELLE FELT A PANG AS HARRY KISSED HER GOOD-BYE the next morning. They didn't talk about it much, but deep down she knew these special assignments could turn deadly. She wouldn't really relax until he was safely back home again on Thursday.

He must've seen the look on her face because he said, "Now, don't worry, babe. Nobody's gonna bother a blind man with his seeing-eye dog. If Corky and I ID our perp, I call in the troops."

She covered her worry with a mock eye roll. "Pooh. What I'm worried about is you an' Corky havin' so much fun playin' cops and robbers that you don't get back here in time to help me pull off this party for DaShawn."

"Now, babe, I promise I'll take the day off Saturday and do whatever needs to be done for the party. But gotta go." He kissed her again, hollered, "Bye, DaShawn!" and waited for, "Bye, Gramps!" from the other end of the house. Then he was out the door.

DaShawn sauntered into the kitchen moments later, backpack slung over one shoulder, and grabbed his lunch out of the refrigerator. "Hey, Grams, any chance you made those invitations yet? You said I could invite three, right?"

"Uh, right. But no, haven't had any time yet to make them. I'll have time today though, so you can take them tomorrow."

The boy shrugged. "Okay. See ya. Gotta go." He started to leave, then turned back. "Oh, the twins and I came up with a great idea for the party—a scavenger hunt in the neighborhood. Tabitha said their middle school youth group did one last year and it was a blast. Could you help us think of some things to go on the list?"

Estelle blinked. "Uh, well, okay." What did she know about doing a scavenger hunt?

Only later when she was in the car heading for Manna House did she realize how sneaky DaShawn had been. Instead of asking *whether* he could do a scavenger hunt at his party, he asked her to *help* . . .

Lord, Lord, You gotta help me stay two steps ahead of this teenager! . . . *And Harry.* Somehow between the two of them an easy peasy birthday dinner at a restaurant had turned into a party that meant cookin' a lot of food for teenagers and planning enough activities to keep them busy for a whole evening. She couldn't just order pizza, either, since Harry was taking DaShawn out for pizza at Lou Malnati's the next day.

She sighed. Well. As for that scavenger hunt, maybe Gabby Fairbanks could give her some ideas. Planning activities for the residents at Manna House was her job. And she had two teenagers herself.

"Mabel in?" she asked the receptionist in the glass-enclosed cubby when she swept into the foyer at Manna House. She didn't recognize the girl at the desk who nodded without looking up, chewing gum as she applied a coat of bright red polish to her fingernails. Shaking her head, Estelle knocked at the door across from the receptionist. Even if this was just a homeless shelter and not a fancy office downtown, the staff needed to be more professional than *that*.

"Estelle!" The woman behind the desk looked up and smiled. Mabel Turner was an attractive black woman with rich nutmeg skin who wore her hair straightened and cut in a short bob. She'd recently turned fifty—big shindig at the shelter—but was still raising a teenage nephew. "Everything okay?"

Estelle plopped herself down in a wooden chair. "Oh, you know. Life with Harry Bentley is never dull. Plus raising a grandson. But I'm too blessed to be stressed."

Mabel chuckled at the cliché.

"That's not what I'm here for . . ." Estelle rehearsed Ramona's story briefly and ended with the request from her current hostess, asking if the girl could come daily as a regular volunteer. "Might be a couple months—until she has to testify at that man's drug trial. After that, we're hoping she can go home."

The shelter director nodded thoughtfully. "Yes, I remember when Harry brought her here last summer. I also seem to remember a bit of drama when the man she's supposed to testify against showed up here looking for her." Mabel raised an eyebrow at Estelle. "Is this the safest place for her to be on a regular basis? What if he comes back?"

Estelle frowned. She hadn't thought about that. Except, here there were lots of people around during the day. Maybe it was safer than just her and Grace alone in the house back on Beecham Street.

"I think it should be all right," Estelle said slowly. "After all, the front doors are kept locked and anyone who comes here has to be buzzed in. Besides, we could alert the receptionist—" She stopped and tipped her head in the direction of the foyer. "Who's the girl at the desk? Don't recognize her."

"Lacee. One of our new residents. Don't you remember? I mentioned in staff meeting yesterday that Angela Kwon is on vacation this week. Different staff and residents are filling in."

"Oh. Right." Her mind must've been elsewhere. "Anyway, just had a thought. Ramona could help me with lunch and some of my classes, like she did two weeks ago, all of which happens on the lower level. If Max did show up, she wouldn't be here on the main level and we'd have time to be alerted. What do you think?"

Mabel shrugged. "Makes sense. Come to think of it. We could use more help doing shelter laundry—bedding after someone leaves, kitchen laundry, and donated clothes, things like that. If she'd be willing to do that when she's not directly helping you . . . Sure, we can always use another volunteer."

"Great. Thanks." Taking her leave, Estelle passed Miss Gum-Chewer and headed for the stairs to the lower level. She'd call Grace with the good news, and then . . . her next stop—Gabby Fairbanks's office.

Estelle was home by two thirty. She had a text message from Harry. *California Zephyr left on time, 2 pm. Should arrive Denver tomorrow*

morning 7:15. If all goes well, should be on the 7:10 tomorrow night, get in around 3 P.M. on Thurs. Love you, babe.

Thank God for cell phones. She didn't even *have* a cell phone five years ago. Sure made things easier for Harry to keep in touch with her while he was on these undercover assignments.

DaShawn had soccer after school. Which meant she had plenty of time to make him some sort of an invitation. With a cup of fresh coffee, she sat down at the computer and decided on a simple one-page flyer using a casual font.

DaShawn Bentley is 14!
And we're having a party at the home of
Harry & Estelle Bentley
7328 Beecham Street, Chicago
(just south of St. Mark's Cemetery)
5:00 P.M. till 10:00 P.M.
Please feel free to call with any concerns or questions.

. . . and she added their phone number. There. That ought to do it. She'd print out three copies and let DaShawn give them to his friends at school. Oh—maybe she should print out another one for the twins.

Estelle handed the invites to DaShawn when he got home. "So, tell me the names of the boys at school you want to invite?"

"Uh, well, there's Jaivon—already told you about him. I went to his party last year. And Simon—he's my science lab partner. And, uh, Kristy."

"*Kristy?* A girl?"

DaShawn shrugged. "Yeah. She's pretty cool. Sits at my lunch table. Tabby knows her. I mean, I don't want Tabby to be the only girl—she might feel funny."

Estelle felt flustered. A boy-girl party? Hadn't seemed like a big deal—in fact, it seemed kind of cute—when DaShawn said he wanted to invite the Jasper girl. But a girl she didn't know? Still, he had a point about inviting a second girl if Tabby was going to come. "Do you know any of their parents?" Now she felt like she was grasping at straws.

DaShawn gave her a funny look. "I guess I met Jaivon's parents at his party last year, but . . . how would I know their parents?"

"Well." Estelle felt like she had to regain some control over this party-to-be. "When you give your school friends this invitation, tell them to have their parents call me to confirm. Got it?"

"Okay, okay." But DaShawn didn't look too happy about it.

Supper was quick—she had to get over to Grace Meredith's house by seven. But what about Nicole? She hadn't called back . . .

Sucking in her breath and feeling slightly self-righteous for making the effort, Estelle called the Singers. This time Nicole answered.

"Oh . . . hi, Estelle. Yes, Greg gave me the message but, uh, the evening got away from me."

"Well, just wanted to tell you we missed you last week and to let you know we'll be meeting tonight at Grace's house. Can you come?"

A pause. Then . . . "Probably not tonight. Still trying to juggle getting everything done at home now that I'm working, you know. But thanks for calling. Maybe another Tuesday night."

Estelle felt a little sad as she hung up. Maybe the problem was juggling her new schedule, like Nicole said . . . or maybe not. She sighed. *Lord, even if we disagree about the group home, I don't want to let that come between us.*

She couldn't help feeling a little relieved when she hustled over to the prayer meeting and it was just Grace and Michelle. No sign of Ramona, either, who sometimes joined them and sometimes didn't. Now she could ask Michelle about her boss's reaction to the Open House on Sunday without stepping on Nicole's toes.

Michelle gave a so-so nod and a shrug. "She said it was a possibility. Would need an inspection, of course. She did say there were some real advantages to a two-flat. But I know she also plans to look at a couple of other properties this weekend, so don't get your hopes up too high, Estelle."

Estelle nodded, but inside she felt like crying. She *was* getting her hopes up, because it seemed like God was knitting together a real possibility for her Leroy to move into a more home-like setting close to them. *Oh, God, isn't that what You want for him too?*

She felt a hand on her knee and looked up. Grace had knelt down beside her. "Estelle, we know how much you want Leroy to move close to you and Harry. You've told me several times to 'do what you can do' and leave the rest to God . . . right?"

Estelle gave a wry smile. Easier to say than do.

"So let's put what's best for Leroy into God's hands . . ."

Estelle felt a little better after the three of them prayed, and they moved on to other sharings and requests. But what Grace said about "do what you can do" also stuck in her mind. As she was getting ready to leave their prayer time, she said, "If I pass around a petition for neighbors to sign who are open to the idea of a group home in our neighborhood, would both of you sign it?"

"Of course," Michelle said. Grace added, "Sure, if that would help."

Estelle walked back across the street, now dark at eight o'clock. A half-moon peeked through the scattered clouds. With DaShawn's party hanging over her head, she didn't think she could take a petition around the neighborhood until Sunday afternoon at the earliest. But, yes, she'd definitely get to it early next week.

As she mounted the steps to their graystone, she heard voices in the foyer. Mattie Krakowski and . . . a man's voice. Pushing open the outer door, she saw Mattie standing in her open doorway on the left, talking to Karl Molander from next door, of all people. Karl and his wife, Eva—a Swedish couple in their late seventies with a host of health issues—pretty much stayed inside most of the time. But tonight the older man had a clipboard and was holding it steady as Mattie, squinting closely, scrawled something on the paper attached to it.

"Hello," Estelle said cautiously. "Don't mean to interrupt. Uh, everything okay, Miss Mattie?"

The old woman cupped a hand to her ear. "Eh?"

Estelle raised her voice. "Is everything okay?"

"Oh, sure, sure. Just signing this here petition for Mr. Molander."

Estelle's neck prickled. "A petition?"

Karl Molander turned his gaze on her. "That's right. Mr. Horowitz down the street asked for my help. Sounds like some do-gooder agency wants to buy that two-flat across the street and dump some mental cases in it, who probably should be locked up in a psych ward. We're letting the agency know how the neighbors feel about it . . . Oh, thanks, Mrs. Krakowski." The man retrieved the clipboard from Mattie and held it out toward Estelle with a slightly roguish smile. "Would *you* like to sign, Mrs. Bentley?"

Chapter 16

ESTELLE HAD TO CLENCH HER JAW to keep from spitting out, *"Are you kidding?"* Instead, she held out her hand. "May I see the petition?"—though her voice croaked. Molander handed her the clipboard.

We the undersigned, it said, *are opposed to a social service agency purchasing the two-flat at 7323–25 Beecham Street for the purpose of housing mentally ill patients. We are a residential neighborhood of families, not zoned for social services.* Just four names were on the petition so far: Isaac Horowitz, Karl Molander, Eva Molander, and Mattie Krakowski. So . . . he hadn't gotten around the whole block.

She handed back the clipboard, wishing she had a cup of coffee or something to spill on it. "No, I won't sign this." She had a hard time keeping her voice from shaking. "It's alarmist. I have a son with mental-health issues, and he certainly doesn't belong in a psych ward. A residential group home would be just the thing. Besides, this petition is premature. As far as I know, the social service agency hasn't made an offer on the Alvarezes' two-flat. You're getting the neighborhood riled up about nothing. Now, if you'll excuse me . . ."

Estelle hustled up the stairs as fast as she could, mentally kicking herself the whole way. Why in the world did she say anything about Leroy to those two! But seeing that petition had rattled her.

Argh! She felt like throwing something. She'd hoped to pass around *her* petition stating a positive perspective of locating a group home in this neighborhood. But now . . . if Karl Molander kept his petition going, most of the neighbors would get a negative slant from the get-go.

Tea. She needed a cup of tea to calm her nerves. Glancing into DaShawn's bedroom on the way to the kitchen, she saw the boy sprawled on his bed, headphones on, supposedly doing homework. Estelle paced around the kitchen, distracted, but somehow managed to heat water and make some herbal tea. Cupping her hands around the mug, she sank down at the kitchen table. *O Lord, what to do?*

Her thoughts knocked into each other like rocks in a tumbler. Would Molander tell other people she had a "mentally ill" son? Would the neighbors be prejudiced against him if Leroy *did* move into the neighborhood? And that petition . . . She'd told Molander, "It's premature." Huh. As much as she hated to admit it, *her* petition would've been premature too.

What should she do? If only Harry were here. He'd been more laid back about this issue, even though he was certainly open to a group home on the block. Maybe she should call him . . . No, a call might interrupt something going down on the train. She was supposed to wait for him to call her.

Which he did as she was getting ready for bed awhile later. Harry was chuckling. "You should've seen it. Corky nosed out a kid's backpack in the observation car—probably had some weed in it—but it freaked him out that she just sat in front of the bag and wouldn't budge. Told me to call off my dog—ha. I pretended I didn't know what he was talkin' about, and he made like a ghost, haven't seen him since." Harry said the perp they were really after would probably board the train in Denver—according to their intel—heading for Chicago with a significant amount of heroin, so for now, he was pretty much just enjoying the ride heading west.

Estelle told him about Karl Molander showing up at Miss Mattie's door with Mr. Horowitz's petition against the group home. "Really?" Harry seemed to think that was funny too. "Didn't think Molander had an activist bone in him."

"Harry, be serious. Help me know what to do. He and Isaac Horowitz want to derail this before it even sees the light of day!"

"Okay, babe. Sorry." Her husband was quiet for several moments. "Look, let's both sleep on it. Can't do anything about it tonight anyway. Better than that, let's pray about it, leave it in God's hands, and ask for some wisdom about how to respond."

Estelle sighed. He was right of course. "Okay, hon. I—"

But Harry had already started praying. "We give it all to You, Jesus, 'cause bottom line, nobody can make this happen *or* stop it without Your say-so. We're askin' for some wisdom about the best way to respond. An' I'm throwin' in a personal request, Jesus, that Estelle will be able to leave this in Your hands tonight and get some sleep. Give her that peace that passes understanding, just like You promised in Your Word. So, guess that's it, Lord. Amen."

Estelle couldn't help smiling. "Thanks, honey. You get some sleep too."

"Ha. Don't worry about that. It's tomorrow night I might have to be a watchdog if we don't ID the perp before he gets on the train in Denver. 'Night. Love you, babe."

Estelle woke with a start. *That's it!* She'd slept like a log—thank You, Jesus!—and woke a few minutes before her alarm went off with an idea God must've dropped into her subconscious.

Create a petition where neighbors could check *either* yay or nay.

That would be fair. Something like . . . *Do you approve or disapprove of Bridges Family Services purchasing the two-flat in our neighborhood for a possible group home for mentally challenged adults?* She could add a link or a phone number—something—for more information. Then neighbors could check yes or no.

Would the naysayers go for such an idea?

Did she have time to talk to Isaac Horowitz and Karl Molander before they kept taking their petition around?

She threw off the covers and swung her feet over the side. She'd just have to make time. But it could wait till this evening. Isaac worked during the day, and even though Karl Molander was retired, most of the neighbors worked during the day, so he probably wouldn't be running their petition around till this evening anyway.

Ramona was waiting by the car when she came out. "Hi, Miss Estelle! Miss Grace told me you got the okay for me to come every day. Thanks. I get tired of staying in the house all the time. But"—she climbed into the passenger seat—"did the boss lady really say I had to do the laundry?"

Estelle chuckled. "Don't worry. It's not that bad. The laundry room has two washers and two dryers. Done in a snap."

"Oh. Okay . . . Hey, did Miss Grace tell you that her *novio* is coming to town in a couple weeks? Don't exactly remember when, but didn't you say somethin' about wanting to have an engagement party next time he came around? Guess what, now's your chance."

Estelle's mind scrambled. Grace did say something last night about Jeff coming, but it was an offhand comment, not like a big announcement. And she'd totally forgotten about offering to throw an engagement party.

Good Lord. When would she learn not to open her mouth and offer to do stuff without really thinking about it?

Wednesday was the day the community nurse came to Manna House from nine till noon, and she used the dining room for her mobile clinic. When Estelle and Ramona arrived at the shelter, the lower level was already a madhouse. Which was why Estelle had started a knitting class for those waiting. The current project was simple knitted slippers. Ramona didn't know how to knit, so Estelle gave her the job of managing the clinic sign-up list and calling people's names when the nurse was ready.

But between ripping out mistakes on too many pairs of slippers and having to step in a time or two to calm a belligerent resident who thought *she* needed to see the nurse *right now* even though it wasn't her turn, Estelle felt as if she spent more time doing damage control than actually accomplishing anything.

At least lunch was a done deal: make it, serve it, eat it, clean up. And as she and Ramona got ready to leave, Gabby Fairbanks came out of her broom-closet office waving a sheet of paper. "Some ideas to put on your scavenger hunt list. Don't worry. The kids will have fun. But don't forget prizes."

After dropping Ramona off at Grace Meredith's house, Estelle made a pot of fresh coffee, exchanged shoes for slippers, and settled down at the computer. She felt torn. Should she create an alternative petition about the group home for the neighborhood? Or work on plans for DaShawn's party? Even with Gabby's helpful suggestions, she still needed to finalize how to do the scavenger hunt, come up with a menu, and go shopping for food. And prizes. And what if it rained on Saturday? She needed a backup plan.

But she went with the petition. She'd hoped to wait until after DaShawn's party to take up the cause for the group home, but Isaac Horowitz and Karl Molander had played their hand. No time to wait. And besides, she reasoned, she should get DaShawn's input on the menu and party activities. What did she know about eighth graders these days?

By the time DaShawn got home, she'd printed out a new petition and was ready to try to sweet-talk Karl Molander and Isaac Horowitz into taking this one around instead. She'd added another wide column to check: *Would you like more information about the feasibility of group homes in residential neighborhoods? Add your email address here.*

She went next door to the Molanders' first. If Karl was doing the "dirty work" for Isaac Horowitz, she had to catch him before he continued his rounds this evening. Eva Molander answered the door after she rang the bell. "Oh! Mrs. Bentley." The white-haired woman smiled pleasantly but didn't invite her inside.

"Is your husband home? I'd like to speak with him for just a moment."

"Oh, oh." The woman shook her head. "Karl's not doing so vell today. His heart you know. Resting right now. Can I, uh, give him a message?"

"Well, yes." Should she leave her alternative petition? She decided no. Not without some conversation. "Could you have him call me about the petition he was taking around the neighborhood yesterday? I have an idea I'd like to discuss with him."

"Oh, yah, yah. I vill do that." The older woman shook her head. "Such a shame. So many changes in the neighborhood." The door closed.

Well. One down, one to go. Sucking up her courage, Estelle marched down the street and up the steps to the Horowitzes' brick bungalow. Rebecca Horowitz answered the doorbell, her toddler on her hip. "Yes? . . . Oh, Mrs. Bentley." She stepped outside and shut the door behind her. The young mother had a colorful print head wrap covering her hair in a becoming way. Estelle hadn't realized those head wraps could look so pretty—more like the ones she wore with her African caftans. Some of the head coverings she saw Jewish women wearing at the grocery store were downright dowdy.

"Uh, yes. Is your husband home? I wanted to speak to him about the petition he and Mr. Molander were taking around the neighborhood." She kept her voice pleasant, neutral.

Rebecca's eyes took on a wary look as she jiggled the little one. "The petition. Yes, I know what you're talking about. Isaac's idea."

Suddenly Estelle remembered—Rebecca's name was not on the petition. She'd assumed Isaac's wife just hadn't signed it yet. But did she have a difference of opinion from her husband's?

"Isaac isn't home from work yet. But I will tell him you stopped by." The little boy fussed and his mother whispered, "Shh, shh. It's all right, *boychick*." She turned back to Estelle. "Do you want him to call you?"

"Well, yes. But maybe you can show him this." Estelle handed the new petition to Rebecca. "I wondered if he'd consider using this petition instead, which gives neighbors a chance to check yes or no. It seems like it would be a better sense of the neighborhood, as everyone can express their opinion—not just sign or not sign." Which, Estelle saw now, would've been the same problem with her first draft petition.

Rebecca glanced over the sheet of paper, nodding. "This is good. I will show it to Isaac when he gets home." She hesitated and glanced about, as if to make sure no one else was listening. "Just to let you know, Mrs. Bentley, Isaac and our rabbi are interested in the two-flat across the street, hoping some Jewish families might move in. It would be . . . *zaier gut*. Very good." She turned to go back in. "Thank you for coming by. I will show it to Isaac."

Estelle stood on the doorstep a few moments after the door shut behind the mother and toddler. There was something wistful about Rebecca's comments. Was it lonely being the only Jewish family on the block? Maybe she should invite her to the Tuesday night prayer . . . No, that wouldn't work. She was Jewish, not Christian. Still . . .

✧   ✧   ✧   ✧

DaShawn wanted *real* food for his birthday party—mac 'n' cheese, fried chicken, ham, sweet potatoes, greens and ham hocks, maybe mashed potatoes and gravy . . . and chocolate cake with lots of white frosting.

"What? This isn't Thanksgiving, young man. Mac 'n' cheese, fine. Chicken, fine. A pot of greens, fine. But I'm not spending the whole day cookin' in the kitchen."

"And chocolate cake?"

"Fine. Chocolate cake." Hm, could she get away with picking up the chicken at Popeyes or someplace? Order the cake at the Jewel? But she'd make the mac 'n' cheese and greens herself. No way could her two specialties be duplicated by any store or restaurant.

Her cell phone rang. Her heart rate picked up. Was Isaac Horowitz calling? No . . . it was Harry.

"Hey, babe! The Zephyr was a couple hours late, but I'm on board. Getting ready to pull out. Not sure if the train will make up the time or not. I'll keep you posted about my arrival time." His voice sounded jovial.

"Is everything all right, Harry?"

"Better than all right, babe. We got our man unloading his stash from a locker at the Denver train station. Train being late helped, messed up his timing. He tried to run, but Corky held him until we got backup. He's their problem now. So I'm technically off duty— 'cept I still have to keep up my undercover role until I get back. Which is a pain. Oh . . . just heard the last call for supper in the dining car. Gotta go, babe. Talk to you in the morning, okay?"

Well. She hadn't got in a single word edgewise. Still. He was safe and sound and coming home. That's what mattered.

Estelle stopped by DaShawn's bedroom. "So, did you give out your invitations today?"

"Yeah." He didn't look up from what he was doing.

"What's the matter? You don't sound too happy about it."

"It's fine. Just . . . felt kinda dumb telling them their parents are supposed to call you."

"Sorry. That's just the way it is."

"Whatever."

Estelle shook her head and closed the door. Hmph. That boy better be grateful he was even getting a party.

Chapter 17

SOMETHIN' SURE SMELLS GOOD!" Harry blew in the back door the next evening, the black Lab at his heels.

"Corkeeee!" DaShawn hollered, and a moment later the boy and dog were rolling around on the kitchen floor. "Oh, hi, Gramps."

"Hmph. Guess I know where I fit on this totem pole," Harry growled, tossing his duffle bag into the corner. But he grinned as he knuckled DaShawn's head and then reached for Estelle. "Hey, babe, gimme some sugar."

Estelle was all too glad to be folded into his strong arms, in spite of being clad in her big white apron and still holding a long-handled wooden spoon. His lips pressed against hers in a long, warm kiss, and then he nuzzled her neck, murmuring, "Sure is good to be home." She relaxed in his arms, head on his shoulder. Whatever the stresses of the week, all was well now. Harry was home.

"Do I have time to hop in the shower?" he asked as they pulled apart.

"You better." She shooed him out with the wooden spoon. "I can still smell train all over those clothes." Boy and dog had disappeared while they were smooching, so Estelle had the kitchen to herself for the next ten minutes as she served up a pot of savory pinto beans to serve over hot cornbread and whisked the coleslaw from the refrigerator onto the kitchen table.

Harry came back into the kitchen—"smellin' like a rose," Estelle teased—and soon they were all talking at once as they piled food on their plates. DaShawn wanted to hear every detail of Corky's role taking down the drug mule in the Denver train station, which Harry relished telling—*after* reminding DaShawn he was "under oath" not to ever mention that his grandfather and K9 partner worked undercover as part of their Amtrak security job.

119

Story over, Harry cut himself another large square of cornbread. "So . . . how are the party plans comin' along? How many kids we got comin'?"

"Six—counting DaShawn," Estelle piped up. "Right, DaShawn?"

The boy fixed his eyes on his plate as he shoveled more beans into his mouth. "Mm-hm."

"I made a few invitations for him to take to school," she explained to Harry. "Haven't got any callbacks from the parents, though." Hadn't got a callback from Karl Molander or Isaac Horowitz either, she realized.

DaShawn swallowed his mouthful. "It didn't say RSVP. You just said call if they had any questions."

Estelle frowned. "So how are we supposed to know if they're coming? I'm not cooking all that food for nothin'."

"Don't worry, Grams. They *said* they're comin' . . . Can I have more cornbread?"

Only when DaShawn had been excused from the table did Estelle fill in her husband about her idea for a different kind of petition.

Harry settled back with a cup of fresh coffee. "Sounds good . . . at the right time. But right now a petition—any kind of petition— seems premature, like you said. Folks need more information. Besides, sounds like Bridges hasn't even made an offer on the Alvarez's two-flat. Could be a moot point."

Estelle frowned. "But what if Horowitz and Molander go ahead with it?"

Harry shook his head. "We can't micromanage this situation, Estelle. Some things are out of our hands. This really isn't about us, you know. It's about the Alvarezes being able to sell their place, and Bridges finding a suitable building for their group home. But . . ." He leaned forward and laid a hand over Estelle's. "If the time comes when a petition would be appropriate, I think the idea you came up with is a good one."

Small comfort. Estelle felt frustrated. Was she supposed to just wait around to see what happened? That was the whole point of proposing a more neutral kind of petition, one that would be fair.

But it was basically worthless if the opposition went around the neighborhood first.

The reality was, she didn't have time in the next few days to even think about canvassing the neighborhood. Friday was another busy morning at the shelter—getting there in time for Edesa's weekly Bible study, making menus for the coming week, preparing lunch and supervising cleanup . . . not to mention rescuing a load of laundry after Ramona accidentally threw in a new red towel with a load of dirty sheets. It took two run-throughs with bleach to get the pink out.

Back home, she made up her shopping list for the party, ordered the chocolate sheet cake, vacillated on whether to buy Popeyes chicken or make her own, and at the last minute ordered fourteen helium balloons from the Party Store for Harry to pick up tomorrow afternoon. After all, what was a party without balloons?

She sent Harry to the grocery store after supper with her shopping list—the Jaspers had conveniently invited DaShawn over to watch a movie with the twins—leaving Estelle to agonize about the scavenger hunt. What would the neighbors think of a group of teenagers knocking on doors to collect such crazy items as an old toothbrush, a takeout menu from a Chinese restaurant, a business card, a two-for-one coupon, a cookie, dryer lint—*dryer lint?*—just to name a few of the items Gabby Fairbanks had suggested. "Things they don't have to return," the red-haired activity director had explained.

Estelle finally had a list of twenty items and printed out several copies. The idea was to divide up in teams—either two teams or maybe go out in pairs. She couldn't help chuckling. Who would DaShawn choose as his partner? Tabby Jasper?

"Oh, stop it, Estelle Bentley," she scolded herself. "Don't you start matchmaking. They're only fourteen."

On Saturday morning she was up early so the pot of greens and ham hocks could simmer a long time. Harry wandered into the kitchen after a while in his pajama bottoms, scratching his jaw, which needed a shave. Pouring a cup of coffee, he leaned back against the counter. "So what are we getting DaShawn for a birthday present?"

Estelle stared at her husband. As far as she was concerned, the party *was* his birthday present. "I have no clue," she finally said. "He could use a new pair of jeans, I guess, and a couple T-shirts . . ."

Harry rolled his eyes in mock horror. "From you, maybe. Think I'll go shopping this morning after I take Corky out, see what I can pick up."

"This morning? Harry Bentley! You said you'd—" She stopped. She didn't really need Harry for the last-minute errands till this afternoon. "Never mind. Fine. Go shopping. But I want you at my beck and call all afternoon. You need to pick up the cake, chicken at Popeyes, and, um, fourteen balloons at the Party Store."

Somehow Estelle managed to get DaShawn to clean his room, get his homework done, and take out the trash before he disappeared to hang out with the twins across the street. She was just as glad to get him out from underfoot as the bewitching hour drew closer. By five thirty, the greens were done, a big pan of mac 'n' cheese was bubbling in the oven, and Harry was tying a few of the balloons to the railing on the front steps so the guests would know which house to come to. He still had to pick up the chicken, but they'd decided to do that after the kids got here so it'd be hot.

She called the Jaspers. "Can you send DaShawn home? The twins can come now, too, if they'd like. The party's supposed to start at six, so the other guests could arrive at any time."

Harry put Corky in their bedroom away from the party, but it was six thirty before the first guest from school arrived. The twins and DaShawn ran down to the door. "It's Jaivon!" DaShawn yelled.

Estelle beamed a welcome when they brought him up. Nice-looking kid, in spite of his saggy pants. "Hello, Jaivon. Did your parents bring you? Are they still here?"

Jaivon shook his head. "Nah. My big brother just dropped me off. Told me to call him if I can't get a ride home."

Estelle shook her head. What kind of parents just let a big brother take a kid Jaivon's age to a party and drop him off? And what was that about getting a ride home?

"C'mon," DaShawn said, grabbing his basketball. "We can play ball out in the alley till the others get here. Whoever comes next, send them out back, okay, Grams?" The four young teens thundered down the outside back stairs.

Simon showed up next, skin as dark as long-roasted coffee beans, and he had an accent as though Swahili or Kirundi might be his first language, though he spoke English well. No parent in sight. "Thank you for inviting me, Mrs. Bentley, Mr. Bentley," he said politely when he got up to the apartment. He handed a small box to her. "A gift for DaShawn. He is a good lab partner."

The doorbell rang again.

"The other kids are out back playing basketball—Harry, will you show Simon the way? I need to get the front door."

Good thing this was the last guest. She hadn't counted on all this going up and down the stairs. Huffing slightly, she opened the door. A pretty teen wearing jeans and gym shoes, her hair in long extensions, stood on the stoop next to a light-skinned black man wearing a business suit and glasses. "Mrs. Bentley? Sorry we are late," he said. "I just got home from work. Kristy was invited to your son's birthday party? He said to dress casual."

"Grandson." Estelle stuck out her hand. A proper parent at last. "Yes, they're out back playing basketball. You might as well go around to the back by the sidewalk, Kristy, rather than come upstairs and have to go back down again."

"Bye, Dad." The girl darted off and disappeared around the side of the house.

Estelle waved good-bye as the man walked back to his car. Good. Everyone was here. Now Harry could run out to Popeyes and pick up the chicken. Should they eat first or do the scavenger hunt first? She wasn't sure.

Harry had been gone twenty minutes or so when she became aware of the noise level in the alley. What on earth? The *bump, bump* of the basketball and kids calling back and forth seemed to have risen to a new level. And then a man's voice yelling,

"What's going on out there? You kids better scram or I'm gonna call the police!"

Karl Molander.

Estelle shook her head. Good grief, it was just kids playing basketball. But maybe she better go down and tell the kids to quiet down or come in . . . Wait, what was that smell? Oh no! The mac 'n' cheese. She'd forgotten to take it out!

Grabbing a couple of potholders, she whisked the large pan out of the oven and onto the counter. Hmm, a bit brown around the edges, but probably still all right.

Now the noise out in the alley seemed even louder. Where was Harry? He should be the one to go down and tell the kids to cool it. Going out onto the back landing, she squinted into the fading light beyond the garage out into the alley . . . Wait a minute. What on earth? There were a lot more than six kids out there. Where did *they* come from?

Just then she saw three or four more kids appear down below coming around the side of the house and heading through their yard for the alley. "Hey, hey!" she yelled. "You can't—"

But that wasn't all. A whole group of teenagers was meandering up the alley toward their house, laughing and calling out to the group already there. No, no, no, this wasn't supposed to be happening. She had to get down there quick.

Before Estelle could even get to the bottom of the back stairs, she heard sirens and flashing blue lights—and suddenly she saw police cars coming from both ends of the alley and screeching to a stop, boxing in the kids directly behind their house.

Chapter 18

Cops were getting out of the cars, hands hovering near their nightsticks. "What are you kids doin' out here?"

"What's it look like? Just playin' some ball." "Yeah, yeah. We ain't doin' nuthin'."

Estelle didn't recognize those voices. Not DaShawn anyway. But she had to do something! She started for the back gate—and suddenly realized her husband had come around the house from the front and was right beside her. "I'll take care of it, Estelle," he said tersely.

"Everybody, listen up!" one of the cops was yelling out in the alley. "All of you kids go on home, quiet-like. You're disturbing the peace. Go on, now."

Harry strode to the back gate and stepped out into the alley. Estelle followed, but stayed on their side of the gate. "What seems to be the trouble, officers?" Harry flashed his Amtrak Security badge.

One of the policemen, a fifty-something white man with bushy eyebrows, eyed the badge, and then eyed Harry. "You the home-owner here?" Harry nodded. "Any of these kids yours?"

Harry pointed at DaShawn. "My grandson. He's having a birth-day party with five *invited* guests. DaShawn!" he ordered. "Get over here. Tavis . . . Tabby, you too. And the three kids we invited from school."

The six kids meekly moved close to Harry. Kristy looked close to tears.

"The rest of these kids, don't know where they came from. When I left thirty minutes ago, just these six were playing ball." He pointed up at the hoop attached above the garage door. "My wife was here. I just got back with the party food."

The cop smirked a little. "Okay, got it. Word gets around . . ." He raised his voice. "You heard the man. You weren't invited. So scram. Down that way . . . Go on, now. No messin' around."

Estelle watched from behind the garage gate as the crowd of teenagers noisily moved down the alley, some laughing, others muttering and banging the tops of the garbage cans. Some of those kids looked like high schoolers—not eighth graders. How did they find out about DaShawn's party?

"Get in here. C'mon. Upstairs." She motioned to DaShawn and his guests.

"Thank you, officers," she heard Harry say. "Sorry about that. We were just having a small party—had no idea these other kids would show up."

"It happens." One of the officers shook Harry's hand. "I'd keep your party inside for the rest of the evening if I were you."

Estelle followed DaShawn and the others as they made for the back steps up to the second floor, but a movement next door caught her eye. Farid Jalili to the north of them had come out onto his back stoop and was squinting his eyes her way. She waved and called, "It's okay, don't worry." But he just stood there watching curiously.

Glancing into the opposite backyard, she saw Karl Molander standing on *his* back stoop, the scowl on his face perfectly illumined by the back door light, watching the crowd of kids moving off. "And don't come back!" he yelled, shaking his fist. Then he turned and went back into the house, slamming the door.

As Estelle reached their back landing on second floor, she glanced down the alley over the garage rooftops. One of the police cars was slowly following the group of teenagers, its lights still flashing. But where was Harry?

She looked down over the railing. Harry was standing in their backyard talking to Jared Jasper, the twins' father. Oh Lord! Jared too? He must've seen the flashing lights over here clear across the street! Was he going to make the twins go home?

A few minutes later Harry came upstairs and saw her anxious look. "Don't worry. Everything's fine. Jared understands. Said the same thing happened with Destin one time—Oh." He made a sheepish face. "I left the chicken out in the car—just came running when I saw the flashing lights in the alley. Be back in a sec."

Harry threaded his way through DaShawn's friends, who were standing around the living room looking at each other. "Eats comin' up!" he said cheerfully before disappearing down the stairs. "Let's get this party back on!"

Estelle breathed a sigh of relief a while later as she watched DaShawn and his crew piling their party plates with Popeyes chicken, mac 'n' cheese, and savory greens. Food was the ticket. Except . . . what next? It didn't seem like a good idea to do the scavenger hunt now. The police had said to keep the kids inside. And frankly, she didn't want them bothering the neighbors, not after having the police rattling the whole neighborhood.

Darn those kids who practically ruined DaShawn's party!

As she gathered up the dirty paper plates, Estelle pulled DaShawn aside just as he came out of his bedroom with a handful of CDs. "I feel real bad about it, DaShawn, but I don't think we should do the scavenger hunt. It wouldn't be a good idea after—"

"Don't worry about it, Grams. We don't wanna go out anymore. We're gonna listen to some music and, you know, just hang out. Until dessert." He gave her a big grin and wiggled his eyebrows— just like Harry did sometimes.

She watched him scoot back to his friends. That was one good kid.

Harry had taken Corky out for her nighttime walk, and by the time he got back the music in the living room had gotten louder. And the kids were gyrating around and laughing.

Harry frowned. "What's going on?"

"They're dancing."

"Huh. You call that dancing? Looks more like flailing around in a patch of poison ivy."

Estelle's chuckle was interrupted by a *thump, thump, thump* on the floor beneath their feet. "What's that?"

Again, *thump, thump, thump.*

Estelle and Harry looked at each other.

"Uh-oh," Harry said.

"Miss Mattie."

Thump, thump, thump, thump, thump!

"She's using her broom handle." Harry was trying to keep a straight face—and failing.

"Oh, dear. I hate to rain on their parade *again*. But . . . I'll call time-out for birthday cake, and Harry, you go downstairs and placate Miz Mattie. Go on, hurry." She shooed him out of the kitchen, even as the thumping beneath her feet continued. She leaned against the counter, fanning her face, trying to compose herself before bringing out the cake and ice cream. What now? A movie . . . After dessert they could watch a Netflix movie. She'd make popcorn. That would be quiet enough—as long as it wasn't some loud, shoot-'em-up movie.

If she ever let Harry talk her into throwing a birthday party for DaShawn at home again, they ought to have their heads examined.

✧ ✧ ✧ ✧

The movie wasn't over till ten thirty, and most of the parents picked up their kids by eleven—except for Jaivon, who couldn't get in touch with his brother, so Harry drove him home. When pressed, DaShawn said he didn't know how word got around about his party, though somebody may have snatched one of the invitations and passed it around.

Estelle shook her head. Hmph. So much for putting their home address on a flyer that flew around the whole school.

But by morning, her mind was full of other things. Even during the worship service at SouledOut, her mind wandered. Should she or Harry go next door and try to make peace with Karl Molander about last night? His wife had said he hadn't been feeling well. And Miss Mattie? Estelle had been so busy serving up cake and ice cream last night, she hadn't even asked Harry if he'd been able to mollify their downstairs neighbor.

Nick Taylor, the young pastoral intern who assisted Pastor Cobbs, preached that Sunday. Well, not exactly preached, she mused as they drove home from church. The recently graduated seminary student was more of a "teacher" than a "preacher." More like their former Pastor Clark, who'd had an uncanny resemblance—at least in manner and tone—to Mr. Rogers of the famed

TV program for kids, *Mr. Rogers' Neighborhood*. Remembering, Estelle couldn't help a few chuckles. Pastor Cobbs and Pastor Clark had made an endearing team—sort of like "Mutt and Jeff" in the comic papers. Pastor Cobbs was short, sturdy, and African American, while Pastor Clark had been tall, skinny, and lanky, as well as white. What a pair they'd made! But it was because of their mutual vision to bring together believers across the color and cultural divide that SouledOut Community Church had been born.

Lord, Lord, what a crisis it'd been when Pastor Clark died of a heart attack—right in the middle of a Sunday morning service! And that hadn't been the only crisis. The most mature and experienced leaders to come alongside and assist Pastor Cobbs would've been Avis and Peter Douglass—but they were also African American. Some members worried that SouledOut would become "just another black church" if all the primary leaders were black.

Estelle was still lost in her thoughts as Harry turned onto Beecham Street and dropped off Ramona. The Douglasses had graciously stepped back and recommended Nick, since the white seminary student needed an internship and would keep the leadership diverse. In spite of his inexperience, so far it'd been a wise decision—though Nick's wife, Kat, hardly fit the bill as a typical pastor's wife. Estelle grinned. Lord have mercy, what a pistol that girl was!

"So, Gramps," DaShawn said as Harry parked in front of their graystone, "when you an' me goin' to Lou Malnati's for pizza today? You didn't forget, right?"

Harry chuckled. "Didn't forget. But I'm feelin' a nap comin' on right now after all that excitement last night. How 'bout four o'clock?"

A shrug. "Okay. Can I go over to the Jaspers' till then?"

Lunch was easy—leftovers from the party last night. But within minutes after eating, DaShawn was off across the street and Harry had shut himself in the bedroom. Estelle sat staring at the leftover mac 'n' cheese. Leroy used to love her mac 'n' cheese. Should she hop in the car and take him some? Could she be back with the car by four o'clock? Probably not. It was already after two. But if she was late, maybe Harry could take his work car—

No, better not risk it. Harry didn't use the work car for personal stuff unless absolutely necessary. She'd go see Leroy next weekend. She'd been trying for every other week anyway, and she and DaShawn had gone just last Saturday.

Estelle sighed. She knew what she *should* do this afternoon. Might as well get it over with.

✧ ✧ ✧ ✧

Eva Molander opened the door when she rang the doorbell. "Oh . . . Mrs. Bentley."

"Please, call me Estelle. May I call you Eva, Mrs. Molander?"

Mrs. Molander seemed a bit flustered. "Well, *ja.*" She still hadn't invited Estelle to come inside.

"Is Karl at home?"

"Well, *ja.* Karl?" she called over her shoulder. "Mrs. Bentley to see you."

When there was no reply, Eva Molander motioned Estelle to step inside. "He's vatching football on TV . . . Karl!"

Estelle followed her neighbor into the living room of the one-story frame bungalow. Karl Molander was sitting in a recliner, footrest up, remote in his hand. A football game was playing loudly on a TV that had to be at least twenty years old.

"Oh, it's you." The elderly man pushed the footrest down and started to get up.

"No, please, don't get up. I'm only here for a minute." To Estelle's relief, Eva Molander had confiscated the remote and put the sound on Mute. Estelle sat on the edge of an overstuffed couch with lacy doilies on the back and arms and took a deep breath. "I wanted to apologize for what happened last night."

Karl Molander scowled. "Yeah. Those kids sure were making a racket. Used to be a peaceful neighborhood around here."

"I know. It was very upsetting—to us too. We didn't invite those teenagers. We were having a very small birthday party for our grandson, but somehow word got around the school and a lot more kids showed up."

"Used to be a quiet neighborhood around here," the man muttered again. "Everything changes. All kinds of people movin' in—like them Muslims other side of you, and those two queers with their kid."

Estelle hardly knew what to say. The "two dads" on the other side of the Jalilis kept very much to themselves. They were hardly disruptive. And the Jalilis . . . she really should say something. "Farid and his wife are Middle Eastern, Mr. Molander, but I'm pretty sure they aren't Muslim."

"Well, whatever."

"Karl," his wife spoke up, "remember, it was the Jalilis' little boy who discovered Mattie Krakowski had fallen down the stairs. They seem nice enough."

"Didn't say they weren't nice," he growled. "Just . . . whatever happened to the ethnic neighborhoods Chicago used to have? People with their own kind, happier that way. Now you folks want to add some mental nut cases to this neighborhood."

Oh, Lord, help me here. Estelle counted to ten before she spoke. There was no point in arguing. "Well, I just wanted to apologize about the noise in the alley last night and promise that it won't happen again." She stood up. "Oh. I stopped by the other day to ask if you'd consider holding off on your petition against the group home until we get more information about what that would mean. And if a petition is necessary, would you consider this petition instead, which I think would be more balanced and fair?" She drew a copy of the petition she'd created out of her big purse and handed it to Eva Molander.

Karl Molander just grunted as his wife passed the paper to him.

Eva accompanied her to the door. "Don't mind Karl, Mrs. . . . uh, Estelle. He hasn't been feeling too vell lately—he has heart problems, you know."

Estelle nodded, then made her way down their front steps. Hmph. Heart problems. Exactly. And not just the physical kind.

Chapter 19

DaShawn and Harry came home from their "guy time" at Lou Malnati's with corrugated boxes of leftover pizza and fist bumps about what a great time they had.

"So what did your grandpa give you for your birthday?" With all the hullaballoo going on Saturday, Estelle had never asked Harry what he'd gotten the boy for a present.

DaShawn grinned and dug into the pocket of his jeans. "He gave me Great-Grandpa Mac's pocketknife." He held it up. The knife was probably four inches long, the handle slightly curved and nubby brown. "It's so cool! Look, two blades"—he pulled out each one—"and a bottle opener, and a flat thing that, I dunno, can't figure out what it's for."

Harry grinned and gave a shrug. "Me neither. Used to use it to clean my fingernails. Which wouldn't be a bad idea for you either." He gave DaShawn a playful punch on the shoulder.

Estelle waited until DaShawn had gone to his room to finish some homework before she spoke her mind. "Harry Bentley! What were you thinking! A pocketknife? That's considered a weapon around here."

Harry looked offended. "Every boy should have a pocketknife."

"Hmph. In the last century. Or out in the country. Maybe down South. But where can he carry it around the city? Not to school. Not through any metal detectors."

"Well . . ." Harry frowned. "I wanted to pass something on to him, something meaningful from his ancestors. We don't go back that far, records wise, you know." His tone got testy. "Not many heirlooms from slavery days."

Estelle winced. She hadn't meant to bring up a painful topic.

"Fact is, that knife is all I've got from my dad. I do like passing it on, though."

His dad. She'd never known Mac Bentley. The man had passed before she ever met Harry, and Harry hadn't talked about him much. "You didn't give it to Rodney?"

Harry glanced away, then slowly shook his head. "I missed doin' a lot of stuff I should've done with Rodney. Tryin' to make it up to my grandson, I guess."

Estelle's heart melted. "Oh, honey. I'm sorry. I can see why you wanted to give it to DaShawn. I just . . . worry, you know. Wouldn't want him to take it to school."

Harry sighed. "You're right. They'd take it away . . . if it didn't get stolen first. Maybe one of these days I can take him fishing, show him how to use it to gut a fish, stuff like that."

She leaned close and kissed him on the cheek. "That's a great idea."

For some reason, Harry wanting to pass something on to his grandson stayed with her that week as she went back and forth to Manna House with Ramona. She'd tried to leave her house to Leroy—had moved out and let him stay when it became apparent they couldn't live together—but that was gone along with everything in it, lost to a fire. She didn't have much of anything to leave to Leroy now . . . except her love and attention. And who'd give that to him once she was gone?

Which made it all the more important to give that to him now.

She didn't call Nicole Singer again about the Tuesday night prayer time at Grace's, but to her surprise the young mom was there already, still dressed in business casual, when Estelle arrived at seven. Michelle arrived fifteen minutes late, out of breath and looking decidedly pregnant. "So sorry," she huffed. "Had to work late today. Charlotte's out of the office looking at possible listings for the new group home, which means I'm covering for her."

Estelle felt a twinge. Was the Alvarezes' two-flat still a consideration? At the same time, it seemed as if Nicole's whole expression perked up. "Well," the young woman burbled, "I sure hope they're paying you time and a half for all the extra work."

Michelle's mouth tipped in an ironic smile. "Fortunately or unfortunately, I'm salaried, not an hourly worker, so I'm afraid it comes with the territory."

Estelle decided not to ask anything about the group home tonight. She'd talk to Michelle later when she'd feel freer to ask specific questions. If she could lay it aside emotionally, that is . . . which was where trusting God came in, she supposed.

"So." She took a deep breath and smiled at Grace. "What's this I hear about your young man coming to town soon?" She winked at Ramona, who was perched precariously on the arm of Grace's couch next to where Estelle was sitting, holding Oreo the cat. "I get all the low-down, you know, now that Ramona rides to work with me every day."

Grace flushed but couldn't hide the smile. "Oh you do, do you? And after I told Ramona that what happens in this house stays at this house." She shook a teasing finger at the Hispanic girl. "Watch out, young lady, or your bed might get short-sheeted."

Ramona's eyes went wide. "Short sheets? What is that? Did they shrink in the wash? I didn't ruin the laundry here, too, did I?"

The others laughed. After assuring the girl it was a joke, Grace got back to Estelle's question. "Yes, Jeff has a business trip to the East Coast in a few weeks and is planning a stopover in Chicago a couple weekends from now. Oh, wait, is that Halloween?" She pulled out her smartphone calendar. "Oh, good. There are five weekends in October, so it'll be the fourth, not the last."

Michelle and Estelle glanced at each other, the same thought obviously on both their minds. An engagement party! But Estelle gave a slight shake of her head. Making it a surprise would be fun.

Ramona giggled. "So! Are we going to have—" Before she could say more, Estelle elbowed her just hard enough so that Ramona shrieked, "Oh!" as she landed on the floor and the cat made a beeline out of the room.

Estelle was out of her seat faster than she thought possible, given her age and size, helping Ramona to her feet, at the same time mouthing softly, *"Shh. Surprise party."*

The girl was quick to catch on. "Oh, so clumsy of me. I was just, uh, gonna say, are we, um, gonna have tea tonight? I'll make it, Miss Grace. You *amigas* go ahead."

"Thanks, Ramona. Actually, I already made a tea tray—there's hot water in the carafe. You can bring it out, if you would." Grace looked pleasantly surprised as Ramona practically bounced toward the kitchen. "Will wonders never cease," she murmured after the girl had disappeared. "She's actually developing some social graces."

"Very sweet," Estelle said. "So while she's getting the tea, why don't we share our prayer requests so we have plenty of time to pray?"

✧　✧　✧　✧

To be honest, Estelle was glad they hadn't talked any more about the group home at prayer Tuesday night, because Nicole had seemed very relaxed and open the rest of the evening. She asked for prayer for her and Greg—and the kids too—as they all adjusted to the new family schedule. "Everything's different," she said. "Greg's got a new job, I'm working now instead of being at home, and Becky and Nate are in school instead of being homeschooled. It's a lot of adjustment." Then she looked sheepish. "But I have to admit I'm glad Greg got a job working for Potawatomi Watercraft instead of doing a home business. Our house just isn't big enough for the four of us 24/7!" She rolled her eyes and everyone laughed.

Grace asked prayer for some local area concerts coming up that fall, plus some decisions she needed to make regarding a Sweetheart Tour in February . . . Michelle said she was planning to work till mid-December, which would give her six weeks or so before her due date. She'd like to quit sooner, but they need the money . . . Estelle had them all laughing about the cops showing up at DaShawn's birthday party—except for Ramona, who got bug-eyed and said, "I would've been so scared!" Then they got serious when she told them Harry was struggling with DaShawn spending the upcoming weekend with his dad, especially since "that woman" would be there. Though, truth be told, Donita *was* the boy's mom.

Later, Estelle realized it probably wasn't the wisest thing to share stuff about DaShawn with Ramona there, since the two had become friends the week she'd stayed with them. So when they drove to Manna House the next day, she took the opportunity to tell Ramona that what they shared at prayer meeting should be considered confidential—"not to be talked about with others."

"Sí. I understand." The girl picked at some cat hairs on her jeans. "So if I tell something in this prayer meeting, that is confidential too?"

"Yes, of course." Estelle cast a quick glance at Ramona. Come to think of it, even though the girl came to the prayer group from time to time, she'd never shared anything or asked for prayer. How much did they know about this mysterious teenager from LA, anyway? Just that she'd been duped into helping that fiend, Max, transport drugs across the country and had been given probation in exchange for her testimony against him. Which was bad enough. But were there other hurts and concerns she carried?

✦ ✦ ✦ ✦

The rest of the week fell into a normal routine—including the return of Angela Kwon to her normal post at the reception desk at Manna House. Estelle had had enough of the gum-chewing Lacee. Several times that week she'd told the girl to "spit it out" and had barely resisted the urge to stick the gummy glop on her nose.

Her third grade teacher had done that to her once. Very effective.

Almost before she knew it, the weekend was upon them. Rodney had called, said he had to work part of Saturday driving for Lincoln Limo, but he'd asked his boss if he could pick up DaShawn in one of the limos and let the boy ride around with him as he had several customers he needed to take to the airport at different times. Give the boy a glimpse into what his dad did for a living.

"Oh great." Harry had looked disgusted. "He's trying to wow DaShawn by riding him around in one of Lincoln Paddock's limos, when his own car is that old beater of a Ford he picked up." Harry was even unhappier when Estelle reminded him that Monday was a school holiday—Columbus Day—and Rodney had said they'd bring DaShawn back by suppertime.

When Rodney showed up Saturday morning and honked— at least the limo was a sedan, not a stretch limo—Harry gave DaShawn a fist bump and growled, "Just remember what I said."

"Yeah. Thanks, Gramps. Bye, Grams! Bye, Corky!" And DaShawn thundered down the stairs and out the door with his school backpack and duffle bag.

Harry moved to the front windows to watch them drive off. Estelle came up beside him, feeling suspicious. "What'd you tell him?"

"Nothin' much." He shrugged. "Told him to have a good time—and not do anything I wouldn't do."

She swatted his shoulder. "Oh you. I bet you told him to check in with you every two hours and call 9-1-1 if Donita looks sideways."

Harry just grinned at her and waggled his eyebrows. "C'mon. You wanted to go see Leroy today, didn't you? Just don't take *all* the leftover mac 'n' cheese."

So far October had ushered in perfect fall weather—next to no rain, mostly sunny days with temps in the eighties and down in the pleasant fifties at night. Saturday was no exception. It'd be a nice day to walk along the lakefront with Leroy and eat a picnic lunch. She'd keep a container of mac 'n' cheese warm for him.

Leroy was waiting for them in the reception room of the Lighthouse, though he kept looking behind them as if expecting someone else. "Where's DaShawn? I thought he was gonna come too. I, uh, made him somethin' for his birthday."

"Oh, baby, that's so sweet of you." Estelle got a lump in her throat. "He's with his dad this weekend. Do you want us to take it to him?"

"Nah. I'll give it to him next time I see him." Leroy looked a little embarrassed. "It's back in my room. We can go now."

Estelle had just finished signing him out for a few hours when one of the Lighthouse staff came into the reception room. Estelle remembered her as one of the social workers they'd talked to when they placed Leroy here . . . a Mrs. Finch.

"Hello!" The dark-haired woman, maybe in her forties, shook their hands, smiling generously. "Leroy said you were coming today. Did he tell you that he's looking for a job?"

"A job?" Estelle stared at Leroy. "What's this about, son?"

"Aw, nothin'. I mean, it's just an idea . . ." Leroy looked imploringly at the social worker. "Maybe it won't happen."

"Well. Didn't mean to spill the beans. I'll let Leroy tell you about it. You all have a good visit." Mrs. Finch gave Leroy a reassuring touch on the arm and disappeared down a hallway.

Chapter 20

A COUPLE OF HOURS LATER, Estelle stared out the passenger side window as they drove home on Lake Shore Drive. Such a beautiful day. Oaks, elms, and maples along the lakefront were starting to turn color, standing out like ruby and opal gemstones among the evergreen trees, while waves on the lake in the distance danced and sparkled in the sunlight. The boaters were still out on the water enjoying the mild weather—but soon the marinas along the lake would empty out as winter's chill crept into the city.

"You want to talk about it?" Harry broke the silence.

"What?"

"Leroy. Wanting to get a job."

Estelle sighed. "I don't know. Why are they encouraging him? I mean, a job in a hospital burn unit? He doesn't have any kind of training for something like that."

"Depends."

She looked at her husband. "What do you mean, depends?"

"Depends on what kind of job. Hospitals have orderlies who take patients from place to place, housekeeping staff—jobs like that."

"But he says he wants to work in a burn unit, of all things. I mean, that's a highly specialized unit."

"Are you surprised? How many months did he spend in that burn unit at Stroger Hospital? That's what he knows."

"I know, but—"

"It's actually very commendable. I think he wants to give back. He knows what those patients are going through."

"Harry! Not you too."

Harry was quiet for several moments as they drove past the high-rises on their left and the busy parks on their right. Then . . .

"What's going on, Estelle? When Leroy told us what he'd like to do, I thought you'd be excited for him. He's thinking about a future. A job would give structure to his days, give him a purpose."

Tears clouded her eyes, which she dabbed away with a tissue. "I am. I mean, I'm proud of him for thinking about getting a job, doing something positive with his life—that shows how far he's come lately. But . . ." She dabbed at her eyes again. "I . . . I just don't want to see him set himself up for disappointment." Disappointment led to frustration, and frustration was a trigger that sometimes sparked one of his episodes.

She didn't want to say it aloud, but . . . no hospital was going to hire Leroy if they dug into his background. People with certain mental health challenges, maybe yes. But Leroy's schizophrenia had actually gotten dangerous for her at one point—

Estelle brushed the thought away. What was she doing? That kind of thinking might raise questions about his suitability for a group home too. No, Harry was right. She needed to be supportive. After all, Mrs. Finch at the Lighthouse had sounded supportive of his desire to get a job. Maybe she should talk to the social workers there. What chance did Leroy have really? If they could find a way to be both supportive and realistic at the same time, maybe . . .

✦　✦　✦　✦

Harry wanted to pick up the phone and call DaShawn Sunday morning to wish him happy birthday "on his real day," but Estelle cautioned him. "Let it be, hon. We celebrated his birthday big time last weekend, remember? They'll know you're just checking up on them."

"So? What's wrong with that?" he growled. But he didn't call.

Still, Estelle could tell Harry was frustrated that Rodney didn't bring DaShawn to church. On the way home he let it blow. "They want him for a weekend? Fine. Next time we tell 'em they gotta bring him to church 'cause that's how we've been bringin' him up."

"Maybe they took him to church someplace else. Maybe they've got their own church."

Harry gave her a look.

"Okay. Didn't think so. But who knows?"

The rest of the weekend seemed to drag. Columbus Day might've been a holiday for schools and public institutions, but Monday was a workday like any other for both Harry and Estelle. When Estelle got home, she made a big pan of lasagna with extra mozzarella cheese, the way DaShawn liked it. She imagined him enthusiastically downing two or three large gooey servings, along with the hot garlic bread and tossed salad she made—a welcome home treat.

Harry and Corky got home by six, but six thirty, then seven passed and no sign of DaShawn. Harry called Rodney's cell but it went straight to voicemail. The lasagna was done—past done—so Estelle finally served up two plates, but they both poked at it with their forks. Didn't taste as good without DaShawn to enthuse over it.

At 7:35 they heard the door at the foot of the stairs open and DaShawn shouting, "Bye, Dad!" Then his heavy footsteps pounded up the stairs. "I'm home!"

"We're in the kitchen!" Estelle called, giving Harry a warning look.

They heard thumps as DaShawn dumped his bags, then he breezed into the kitchen and flopped into the chair by the empty plate. "Whatcha eatin'? Oh, man, lasagna. Looks good. But we just ate. Dad and I stopped at Olive Garden on our way here."

"Your dad"—Estelle could tell Harry was trying to control himself—"said he'd have you home by *suppertime*." Harry glanced pointedly at the clock. "We assumed that meant six or six thirty— the time we usually eat. Your grandma went to a lot of trouble to make a welcome home meal for you."

"Oh, man, sorry 'bout that. Dad had to take someone to the airport by six thirty, so he said we'd stop at Olive Garden on our way home, just him and me. Didn't know you were cookin' somethin' special, Grams—I mean, I was just gone for a couple'a days."

"Well." Estelle exchanged looks with Harry. "Just a misunderstanding, I expect. Tell us about your weekend. What'd you do?"

"It was great! On Saturday we just hung out at the apartment, you know, watched movies an' stuff. But for my birthday yesterday, they took me to this trampoline park out in the 'burbs." For the next ten minutes, DaShawn rattled on about a whole room full of trampolines built right into the floor, playing dodge ball on the tramps with some other kids there while a DJ spun pop music. "Man! I've never had so much fun. We gotta go sometime, Gramps!"

Harry grunted. "Maybe." He got up from the table. "Glad you had a good time." Then he headed for the living room and turned on the TV.

Estelle started to clear the table. "So. I assume sometime this weekend you did your homework since you had an extra day."

DaShawn snitched a piece of garlic bread. "Uhhh, not really. Didn't exactly have time. Like today. I rode around with Dad while he did some of his limo pickups, then we stopped at Lincoln Park and watched the college rowers practice on the lagoon for some big race. Then he had to pick up another passenger—you know, the one to the airport—and then the Olive Garden, an' . . ." DaShawn shrugged.

Estelle wagged a finger at him. "Then you better disappear into your bedroom, young man, and get down to business before your grandpa finds out." She watched him go. *Hmph.* Neither Rodney nor Donita asked him the whole weekend if he had any homework he needed to do? Shaking her head, she stuffed dishes and flatware into the dishwasher. Those two had a long way to go before they were ready to parent a teenager.

✧ ✧ ✧ ✧

Grace called to say she had evening practices with her band all this week in preparation for two concerts at a big church in South Bend on the weekend, so could the Tuesday prayer time meet someplace else? Estelle told her not to worry, she'd contact the others. But when she called the Singers, Nicole said Becky was home with a bad chest cold, so she couldn't come anyway. That left Michelle— and when Estelle called Michelle at work, Michelle told her she'd appreciate a night off because she'd been having to work late almost every day while Charlotte Bergman pursued options for the proposed group home.

Estelle licked her lips. "So, is the Alvarez place still an option?"

"I think so. At least Charlotte hasn't put any money down or signed any papers on any other property yet. But . . . I know she's arranged an info meeting for this coming Sunday afternoon with the neighbors of one property she looked at. Just between you and me, it might be a good thing to do the same thing in our neighborhood. Think you could arrange a meeting like that with our neighbors? Maybe for the following Sunday? I could check Charlotte's calendar—I think she'd be open to that."

Estelle thought fast. "Uh . . . sure, sure. I'll make up a flyer and take it around to the neighbors."

"Yeah, taking it around in person is a good idea. Tell people it's their chance to ask questions, share their concerns. Keep it neutral if you can."

Yes. Estelle knew she needed to do that. "Just one more thing, Michelle. Could you . . . you know about my son, Leroy. Could you find out how I—we—can get him registered as a client of Bridges Family Services and put him on the list as a possible candidate for the new group home? I mean, especially if Bridges buys the Alvarezes' two-flat and he could live near us."

Michelle's voice was sympathetic. "I understand, Estelle. I'll see what I can do. But don't get your hopes up too high. There are already several candidates on the list for this group home. Still, God wants the best for your son, even more than you do. If it's meant to be, I know it can happen. We'll keep praying, okay?"

Yes, *she* needed to keep praying—which was one reason she regretted that they had to cancel the prayer time this Tuesday. She needed these weekly prayer times as much as Grace said she did to help keep her focus where it needed to be. Especially since her Yada Yada Prayer Group was only meeting once a month now.

Only after she and Michelle hung up did she realize she had one more thing they needed to talk about—pulling off a surprise engagement party for Grace Meredith and Jeff Newman a week from Saturday!

✧   ✧   ✧   ✧

Turned out Ramona had the same idea as she bounced into the RAV4 Wednesday morning. "So, Miss Estelle, what are we gonna do for a surprise party for Mr. Jeff and Miss Grace when he comes next week?"

Estelle chuckled. "You're right, we better get busy. Hmm. Grace is gone this weekend . . . How about if you and I and Michelle Jasper—and Nicole Singer, too, if she'd like to—get together on Saturday to plan the party?"

"But I can't this Saturday! Grace invited me to go with her and Sam to South Bend this weekend, since they're driving. She says Oreo will be all right since it's just Saturday and Sunday. I've never been to one of Grace's concerts, so I'm excited. Sam said maybe I could help with the CD table." She grinned. "I like Sam. Can we invite her to the engagement party too?"

"Oh." At least Ramona wouldn't be left alone while Grace was gone. "Sure, we can invite Sam." Samantha Curtis was Grace's personal assistant who traveled with her on tour. "So you'll be gone this weekend . . . Hmm. I know, you and I can talk to Gabby Fairbanks at Manna House for some ideas, and while you're gone I'll get some more ideas from Michelle and Nicole. Then . . . next week we'll put it all together." She grinned at Ramona. "Somehow.

Chapter 21

MICHELLE JASPER CALLED ON FRIDAY to say her boss was open to an informational meeting in the Beecham Street neighborhood a week from Sunday—just give her the time and place. Which meant Estelle needed to get busy.

The first hurdle was Harry—would he be okay with them hosting the meeting at their house? On a Sunday afternoon?

"Sunday's our day of rest," Harry protested when she brought it up after work that night. "Why not Saturday?"

"Well, I would . . . except that's the weekend Jeff Newman is in town and we're planning an engagement party for Grace and Jeff."

"At her house, right?"

Estelle hadn't thought that far ahead. "Uhh, probably not. Because we want it to be a surprise. We need to invite them over for supper or something."

"At *our* house."

He sounded annoyed. Estelle went over to the kitchen wall calendar. Uh-oh. That weekend was also the Sunday when Yada Yada met this month. October had five Sundays this year, but the fifth one was Halloween, and none of the Yadas thought that was a good evening to be away from home with trick-or-treaters ringing doorbells.

"Why can't somebody else host one of these things? Or put off the group home meeting till another weekend."

Still looking at the calendar, Estelle shook her head. "The weekend after that is the last weekend in October—and Manna House is having a Harvest Party that Saturday and Halloween falls on Sunday. We can't wait till November—Bridges will be making a decision soon." She turned. "Guess I could ask the Jaspers to host the engagement party—just kinda hate to do that since Michelle works full time and is in her second trimester."

Harry threw up his hands. "Whatever! You're gonna do what you're gonna do. Trouble is, you drag me into it too." He grabbed the dog leash. "C'mon, Corky. Let's go for a walk."

Estelle rolled her eyes as the back door slammed and his footsteps faded down the back stairs. Huh. Had he forgotten it was *his* idea to host DaShawn's birthday party at their house instead of taking the kids out for pizza? But when something was *her* idea . . .

By the time she heard his footsteps coming back up the stairs thirty minutes later, she was feeling a bit more meek. Harry had good reason to feel overwhelmed by so much happening on one weekend. Even she felt overwhelmed by it.

She reached out a hand to him as he came in the door. "Honey, I'm sorry. I realize it *is* a lot for one weekend. I'm not sure what to do, because Jeff's only here that weekend, and Michelle thinks an informational meeting ASAP would be a wise thing to do if Bridges wants to put a group home in the Alvarezes' two-flat . . . But would you pray with me about it? Maybe there's something we can do besides host everything here. I know I sometimes go rushing ahead—"

"Sometimes?" But there was a teasing tone in his voice. Harry sat down at the kitchen table and took her hand. "Sorry I flew off the handle, babe. But it does feel like too much. Yeah, let's pray about it . . . ."

And it was right in the middle of Harry's prayer that Estelle got the idea.

✧   ✧   ✧   ✧

Michelle Jasper volunteered most Saturday mornings at Lifeline Care Center—a crisis pregnancy center that also offered post-abortion counseling—but she thought she'd be home by two. "We can meet on our front porch to plan the party for Grace and Jeff," she offered. Nicole Singer seemed pleased to be included in the party plans. And two o'clock was just fine with Estelle—that gave her time to follow up on her idea.

She rang the Alvarezes' doorbell at eleven, bringing a loaf of homemade banana bread fresh out of the oven. Mrs. Alvarez answered the door, but Estelle was able to ask in her limited Spanish if her husband was available, since he spoke a little more English. *"Sí, sí."* Mrs. Alvarez motioned her to come in and sit on the sofa in the living room while she went for her husband.

By fits and starts, Estelle was able to ask and get the answer that, no, they did not have a buyer for the house yet, but the Alvarezes were still very eager to sell. Curious, Estelle thought, that the Horowitzes' rabbi hadn't sent some Jewish families to make an offer on the house—if, as Rebecca Horowitz had let slip, that was their intention. At least it meant the door was still open for Bridges to make an offer.

"The woman from Bridges Family Services is still interested in your two-flat. But they would like to have a meeting with the neighbors to explain how they want to use the two-flat for a group home and see how people feel about having a group home in this neighborhood. It might help sell your house." It took a few more minutes of "Spanglish" to communicate what she meant, but the Alvarezes seemed to understand. "They need a place to meet. Would you be willing for the neighbors to meet *here* next Sunday— uh, *el próximo Domingo*—to talk about it?"

Husband and wife looked at each other. Mr. Alvarez said something to her in rapid Spanish, and they went back and forth for a few moments, then he said, "Here? Like another open house?"

Estelle shrugged and nodded. "Something like that. But to talk. And only for an hour or so. Not all afternoon."

The couple talked between themselves again, then Mr. Alvarez nodded. *"A la tres el próximo Domingo."* He held up three fingers. "Three o'clock. Next Sunday."

Estelle left after exchanging many smiles, handshakes, and repeated, *"Gracias, gracias."* She felt a strange peace. Was this in answer to their prayers last night? She hadn't been at all sure the Alvarezes would consent to having a neighborhood meeting at their house. But having the meeting at the two-flat in question had more benefits than just keeping life sane for Harry's sake—though that was her initial motivation. Whatever happened with the group home or even with Leroy, this might help the Alvarezes sell their two-flat sooner rather than later, which was obviously a high priority for them. And maybe the discussion would be more polite with the Alvarezes present. At least she hoped so.

She glanced at her watch. Still time to make a flyer about the info meeting to pass out to the neighbors. And after meeting with Michelle and Nicole at two, maybe she'd have time to . . . no. Actually going door to door with the flyer could wait till tomorrow after church. Because she just got another idea: Ask Harry out on a date. Tonight. She'd take him out for dinner. With candlelight. A good wine. Maybe a movie afterward. Or a walk along the lake.

No DaShawn. No Leroy. No group home. No engagement party.

Just the two of them.

✧ ✧ ✧ ✧

Estelle woke up early in spite of getting in rather late with Harry. She listened. He was still asleep, his breathing slow and steady. Mmm . . . Going out on a date was just what they'd needed. After all, even when there weren't extra activities going on, she and Harry were raising a grandchild. A *teenage* grandchild. Which meant they were "on duty" 24/7, just like when their kids were kids—except they weren't in their thirties anymore. And they'd only been married a few years. They needed time for themselves too.

She lay staring into the darkness. Planning for the engagement party had been fun. They'd decided to keep it simple. She would invite the couple for supper with her and Harry, but instead surprise them with a party. The guest list was fairly short. A few neighbors—the Bentleys, Jaspers, Singers, and Ramona—plus Grace's brother and his family, who lived in the western suburbs. And Samantha, Grace's assistant. Even that short list counted eight kids. Food could be potluck—maybe a Mexican theme with Ramona's help. She and Ramona would get a few fun game ideas from Gabby Fairbanks at Manna House . . . and that was it.

As for the info meeting, all that was left to do this weekend was take that flyer around to the neighbors. What would be the response to the possibility of a group home on Beecham? So far it was about even-Steven for and against. But what about the rest?

Estelle rolled out of bed and slipped on a cozy caftan, trying not to wake Harry. Wouldn't hurt to pray about it. She'd also promised to pray for Grace's concert, which was last night, but Grace had also been invited to sing at some big megachurch this morning. She'd cover that girl in prayer for today too. Besides, it'd been a few days since Estelle had had some real quiet time, just her and God.

She crept out of the bedroom, slippers in hand. Corky, curled up in her dog bed by the back door, barely cracked an eyelid when she came into the kitchen to start the coffee. Good. She'd let them all sleep so she could have the house to herself for at least an hour.

A fresh cup of hot coffee in hand, Estelle settled in Harry's big ol' recliner by the front bay windows. The sky had barely begun to lighten and the streetlights were still on even though it was past six already. If she was lucky, she just might see the sunrise through the trees and over the tops of the houses.

Where had she been reading in her Bible last? It was tempting to turn to that tried-and-true verse, Jeremiah 29:11—"'For I know the plans I have for you,' declares the LORD, 'plans to prosper you and not to harm you, plans to give you hope and a future.'" A verse she and some of her Yada Yada sisters quoted a lot, confirming the good plans God had in store for them. She'd claimed it for Leroy a bunch of times.

But the last time she'd turned to that chapter, she'd read it in context—a letter to the exiles who'd been carried away from Jerusalem to Babylon, telling them to make the best of it, and after seventy years—a whole lifetime basically—God promised He'd bring the nation of Israel home again. A promise that didn't see the light of day for God's people until the next generation.

Estelle didn't want to wait that long.

She decided to skip Jeremiah and go back to the Gospels. She'd started Matthew a few weeks ago. But as she opened her Bible, a bookmark fell out and landed on the floor. She picked it up—a handmade laminated bookmark Jodi Baxter had made for her birthday a couple of years ago when she first came to Yada Yada. It had *"ESTELLE"* on one side with the meaning of her name beneath it: *"STAR."* And Jodi had written, *"Even when God feels far away, look up—He will guide you with a steady light, even on the darkest night."*

For some reason, a lump caught in her throat. She turned the bookmark over. On the other side Jodi had printed a verse:

> *Trust in the LORD with all your heart, and lean not on your own understanding; in all your ways acknowledge Him, and He will make your paths straight. ~ Proverbs 3:5–6.*
> *Trust.*
> *Don't lean on your own understanding.*

Estelle reached for a tissue and blew her nose. She hadn't been doing too well in that department lately. In fact, Harry might say she'd been pushing her own plans. Trying to make things happen the way she thought they ought to go.

"Oh, God," she groaned. "Sometimes I don't really know how to balance 'doing what seems best to do' with 'trusting You to work things out.' Am I supposed to just sit around and accept whatever happens as 'God's will'? What does trusting You really mean, anyway?" She dabbed at her eyes with the wadded-up tissue. Huh. As many years as she'd been a Christian, you'd think she'd have this figured out by now.

The sky had turned a pale golden color, streaking the cirrus clouds above the treetops in the neighborhood. The sun would be coming up soon. She sighed. She better do some praying or it'd be time to wake up Harry and DaShawn and the Sunday scramble would begin. But as she stuck the bookmark back in her Bible, she read the verse on it again: *". . . in all your ways acknowledge Him, and He shall direct your paths."*

That was it. At least the place to start. Acknowledge she really needed God to direct her path, no matter what her plans were or how well she thought she understood what should happen.

A good place to start her prayer time.

Chapter 22

WORSHIP AT SOULEDOUT WAS GOOD FOR THE SOUL that morning. Estelle let the gospel music roll over her. "The Lord Is My Rock" . . . "The Name of the Lord Is a Strong Tower" . . . even a good ol' hymn, "On Christ the Solid Rock I Stand." Avis Douglass was the worship leader that morning and interspersed several good scriptures between the songs. Estelle especially liked the one from Psalm 114:8—"He turned the rock into a pool of water; yes, a spring of water flowed from the solid rock."

"That's who Jesus is, saints," Avis said, "a solid foundation to stand on, and at the same time He is the Source of life-giving love and forgiveness, like a spring of water flowing out of the Rock to revive a thirsty soul or rescue a dying spirit. Oh, glory!"

After the service, Estelle found Avis and gave her a hug. "Thank you, Sister Avis. I needed that reminder today. Too easy to get swept away by all the concerns and challenges in my life and forget I've got a solid rock under my feet."

Avis looked at her with concern. "Is everything all right, Estelle? Anything I can pray for?" She looked around. "Where's Ramona? Hasn't she been coming with you to church lately?"

"Oh, she's fine. She went with Grace Meredith to Indiana this weekend—Grace had a couple of concerts." Estelle hesitated. Should she ask Avis to pray about talking to the neighbors this afternoon about the group home? Knowing Avis, she'd stop and pray right now. Well, why not?

She gave a fifty-words-or-less version of the upcoming group home info meeting, and sure enough, Avis started praying right then and there ". . . that Your purpose, O God, would become evident for all concerned—the residents of the proposed group home as well as the neighbors. Come, Lord Jesus!"

Harry had rounded up DaShawn and waved at her, ready to go home. "See you next week at Yada Yada," Avis said, giving Estelle one last hug. "I'll be eager to hear what God does in your neighborhood."

Estelle had noticed Avis didn't pray that the neighbors would welcome the group home into the neighborhood, just that "God's purpose" would become evident. Which felt like tacking "but Your will be done" onto a prayer to give God an out if the prayer wasn't answered the way you wanted. Didn't Jesus tell us to pray "in faith"? That if you believed, to "ask what you will" and it would be done?

But as she set out sandwich makings for Harry and DaShawn a while later, it suddenly hit her: even Jesus prayed, *"yet not my will, but yours be done"* after asking the Father to release Him from the severe trial He was about to go through.

Whew. That was one heavy-duty "but" . . .

Lunch over, Estelle gathered up the flyers she'd made about the group home info meeting next Sunday and headed downstairs. But her thoughts still dogged her. Was she really willing to pray for God's purpose and God's will if it didn't line up with her own request?

"Okay, Lord," she breathed, heading next door to the Jalilis. "I get it. I really do want Your will to be done about the group home, but it does seem like a win-win-win situation if Bridges could buy the Alvarez place and if Leroy could live there too."

Lily Jalili answered the door. "Hello," she said shyly. "Is everything all right?" The woman had a pleasant face, which was all one could see since the rest of her head was covered by a dark brown scarf fastened under her chin.

"Yes, everything is fine." Estelle smiled cheerfully. She explained briefly about the house that was for sale, the agency that wanted to buy it for a group home for mentally challenged adults, and if she or her husband had any questions they could come to a meeting at the Alvarezes' house next Sunday afternoon. Farid's wife took the flyer, nodded politely, and closed the door.

The boy Danny opened the door at the brick bungalow next to the Jalilis. Cute kid—straight blond hair, blue eyes, about eight years old. She wasn't sure about his last name, though, because his two dads each had different last names. "Dad!" he yelled. "Lady here to see you!"

Tim Mercer appeared at the door. A smile broke out on his face. "Mrs. Bentley! How are you? Heard you had a little excitement at your house a couple weeks ago."

Estelle's face went hot. "Oh no. You heard about that?" She shook her head. "We had a small birthday party for DaShawn, but I guess word got around school and a horde of party-crashers showed up. So sorry about all the drama."

Tim laughed. "Don't forget, I teach high school. I hear about party-crashers all the time." He eyed the flyers in her hand. "What's that? Doesn't look like cinnamon rolls."

She had to laugh too. "Not this time." She handed him a flyer, explained what it was about, and he nodded. "Good idea. Not sure we can make the meeting, but Scott and I wouldn't have any problem with a group home on this block. They're usually well supervised and regulated. But people have funny notions . . . a neighborhood meeting would be a good thing."

Friendly guy—friendlier than some in the neighborhood. She and Harry didn't really know either of them very well, though both Tim and Scott had come to the "Welcome Home Party" for Mattie Krakowski last summer. Next time they had a backyard cookout, they should invite them over—maybe with the Jalilis. She'd seen their boy Karim playing with Danny now and then, though Karim was a couple of years older.

Estelle headed for the McMansion that sat across the north end of Beecham Street, creating the dead end. No cars sitting in the cul-de-sac—Lincoln Paddock might not be home. The man was a lawyer and had a successful limo business on the side. He could certainly afford this big house, but why a single man like Paddock needed such a big house was beyond her. Rodney Bentley had been working for him as a limo driver for several months now— the man had been willing to give an ex-con a break. Far as she knew, Rodney was hanging on to the job and doing well.

As she guessed, no one answered the doorbell, so she put a flyer through the mail slot in the door.

The Jaspers started the row of houses on the east side of the street. No need to explain the meeting to them, but she left a flyer in their mailbox. Grace Meredith wasn't home from Indiana yet . . . another flyer in the mailbox. Same with the couple on the other side of Grace. Yellow-brick home with beveled bay windows that covered the whole front, lovely lace curtains inside. But she hardly ever saw them—a mixed couple, he was white, she was black. Grace once said they were both professionals, no kids, gone a lot, but Estelle couldn't remember their names. Another flyer in the mail slot.

Estelle stopped briefly at the Alvarezes' home and gave them a flyer, then paused on the sidewalk in front of the next house. The Singers. Nicole had already let her know how she felt about a group home next door. Estelle breathed a quick prayer and rang the doorbell.

Greg Singer opened the door. "Mrs. Bentley! Come in. How's Harry?"

She shook her head. "Hi Greg—and please call me Estelle. Harry's fine. I can't stay, just passing out these flyers to all the neighbors."

He took one and scanned it, then frowned. "A group home is going into the two-flat next door?"

She shook her head. "No one's bought the building yet. But they're interested. They realize people will have questions about what that would mean, so they've scheduled a meeting to explain what a group home is and to let people ask questions. Can you and Nicole come?"

"Maybe. I don't know . . . The whole idea seems kind of risky to me. And right next door? We have kids . . ."

Estelle kept her voice even. "I know. It's normal to have concerns. It's a good opportunity to get information and ask questions. Nothing's set in stone, but since this is one of the properties Bridges Family Services is looking at, it seemed like a good idea."

"Okay. I'll talk to Nicole about it. She's real protective of the kids, you know."

Understatement. Estelle was still surprised that Nicole had gone back to work and let Becky and Nathan go to public school after homeschooling for several years. But from what Nicole had shared at Tuesday prayer, they were digging their way out financially from Greg losing his job earlier that year.

Still, Estelle felt good as she left a flyer at the corner house, then walked across the street to the Horowitz home. Greg had concerns, but he didn't seem totally closed. Hopefully she'd get at least that much openness from Isaac Horowitz. Sunday . . . hopefully they were home since their Sabbath services had been yesterday.

Isaac answered the door. He just raised his heavy eyebrows when he saw who it was. Estelle greeted him pleasantly, handed him the flyer, and invited him to the meeting.

He had the same reaction as Greg Singer. "They've already bought the two-flat?" Isaac looked past her and across the street. "Sign still says For Sale."

Rebecca Horowitz came to the door with little Benjy on her hip, listening in as Estelle explained once again that the group home was just a prospective buyer. "I, uh, saw the petition you and Karl Molander started to pass around, so I know you have questions or concerns. This meeting would be a good time to get more information."

Isaac just scowled. "Yeah, well, just wish those *goyim* weren't so trigger-happy, trying to sell so quick. They should give more notice, give more people time to check it out. Might get a better deal if two families bought it—isn't that what a two-flat is for?" The tall bearded man handed the flyer to his wife and disappeared back into the house.

Estelle and Rebecca looked at each other. The toddler grabbed hold of the colorful scarf covering his mother's hair and pulled. "No, no, Benjy. Leave mama's *tichel* alone." Rebecca loosened his fingers and bounced him on her hip, turning her attention back to Estelle. "You need to understand"—she lowered her voice almost to a whisper—"it's not really about the group home. Our rabbi would like more time to see if there are Jewish families who might be interested in buying on this block. So far"—she shrugged—"no one."

Estelle felt a pang. She could see why it would be nice for the Horowitzes if there were other Jewish families on the block. Most of the homes on Beecham were single family, but a two-flat . . .

As she said good-bye and headed up the street, Avis's prayer replayed in her head. *". . . that Your purpose, O God, would become evident for all concerned—the residents of the proposed group home as well as the neighbors."* She sighed. Not sure how the sale of the Alvarezes' two-flat could end up being good for *everybody*. Somebody was going to lose out—maybe her. Was she really willing to say "not my will but Yours be done"?

She had just finished leaving flyers at the next two houses when Estelle saw Grace Meredith's sporty red car sail past and pull up in front of Grace's bungalow. Samantha Curtis, Grace's assistant, jumped out of the driver's seat and pulled it forward so Ramona, who'd been sitting in the back of the two-door Ford Focus, could squeeze out and run toward the house.

Potty emergency, Estelle guessed with a grin. She crossed the street. Might as well take advantage of the moment and extend her fake invitation for next Saturday. "Welcome home, Grace!" she called. "Hi Sam! Glad you're all home safe. How was the weekend?"

Samantha waved. "Great! Grace brought down the house." The perky young black woman looked fresh as a daisy in spite of spending the last three or four hours in the car. "But I've got one tired soprano on my hands who's catching a cold. Gotta get her inside and into bed."

Grace had climbed out of the passenger side and was stretching. "Don't listen to her, Estelle. I'm fine. Just tired is all, and I've got a sniffle. Going to bed early tonight."

"You should go to bed now," Sam muttered, unloading bags from the trunk. "You don't want to be sick when that man of yours shows up next weekend."

Grace just wagged her head and headed toward the house, pulling a wheeled suitcase behind her. Estelle watched her go. Probably not the best moment to invite Grace and Jeff to their "surprise party." She'd catch her tomorrow.

Chapter 23

RAMONA, WEARING SKINNY JEANS and her thick dark hair braided in one long braid, was waiting by the RAV4 when Estelle came out the next morning. Estelle gave the girl a hug as she unlocked the car. "So did you have a good time on tour with Grace this weekend?"

"Oh, *sí, sí!* It was awesome!" Ramona giggled. "The guys in the band are nice. Especially Zach. He plays bass guitar."

Estelle wanted to roll her eyes. Of course. Take a teenager to a music concert, and she's going to zero in on the guys in the band. But as Ramona chatted on their way to Manna House, Estelle realized that the themes of Grace's concerts were not lost on the girl.

"I liked Grace's songs . . . and the way she talked about God's grace, you know, that God loves us and forgives us, no matter what we've done in the past . . ." Ramona's voice trailed off.

Estelle let the silence fill the car. Was Ramona thinking of her foolish cross-country trip with Max, helping him transport drugs from LA to Chicago? More than foolish—dangerous! Maybe she wanted to talk about it.

But Ramona abruptly changed the subject. "So what's happening with the surprise party? Mr. Jeff called last night and it sounded like he and Miss Grace were making plans for the weekend. Did you ask her to come to your house for supper or anything?"

Uh-oh. Estelle grimaced. Was she too late? She'd have to think fast if Grace and Jeff had already made plans for Saturday night. Couldn't move the party to Sunday—she had Yada Yada after the group home meeting at the Alvarezes'. Estelle accelerated her speed a notch. She'd better call Grace as soon as she got to Manna House . . . which she did, ducking into Gabby Fairbanks's tiny office to use the phone even though staff meeting was about to start. The phone rang at least five times before Grace answered.

"Oh, Grace, did I wake you? You probably wanted to sleep in this morning after your busy weekend."

"Uhhh, no, I was awake. Still in bed . . . just being lazy—uh, just a minute." Estelle heard Grace blowing her nose, followed by some coughing, and then she picked up the phone again. "Sorry. I think I caught a cold down in Indy. So . . . what's up?"

"You said Jeff is coming this weekend, so Harry and I are wondering if the two of you could come to supper Saturday night. We'd really like to get to know him a bit better."

"Oh! That's sweet of you. I don't know. We have a bunch of business to do in a short time. He has a new tour possibility for me, plus some concert invitations and schedules to coordinate. On top of that, we're trying to decide on a wedding date! Uh . . . wait." Grace went offline again and Estelle heard her coughing. Then she was back again. "Uhh, sorry." *Sniff, sniff.* "Let me talk to Jeff. Can I let you know tomorrow?"

Estelle wanted to say, No! I gotta know now because we're planning this big party for you! But instead she said lightly, "Oh, sure. But I really hope you can. You take care of that cold now . . . Tell you what, I'll bring you some homemade chicken soup tonight. My surefire cure for the common cold!"

Estelle hung up Gabby's phone and hustled up the stairs to the staff meeting. She and Ramona would grab Gabby after lunch and pick her brain for some fun ideas for the engagement party anyway. Surely Grace's cold would be better by the weekend. It was only Monday.

But when Estelle delivered the pot of chicken soup that evening, Ramona opened the door, holding Grace's black-and-white cat to keep him from escaping. "She's pretty sick. It got worse during the day. I bet that soup will help. Smells really good." She tipped her head toward Grace's bedroom. "She's talking to Mr. Jeff on the phone now. I'll let you know in the morning what he says about Saturday night." Then she grinned and lowered her voice. "I hope it works out. I think Miss Gabby's idea of doing a piñata is *fantástico!*"

✧ ✧ ✧ ✧

Grace sent word via Ramona the next morning that she and Jeff would love to accept the Bentleys' invitation for Saturday night. But she needed to beg off hosting the Tuesday night prayer again, because of her cold.

"Which works in our favor," Estelle said, winking at Ramona. "We can meet at my house with Michelle and Nicole and finish planning the surprise party."

Ramona was able to get numbers from Grace's phone book for Samantha Curtis and Grace's brother. "It's really last minute," Nicole worried as they gathered that evening. "Do you think they can come?"

"Won't hurt to try." Estelle called Mark Meredith first and got his wife, who introduced herself as Denise. But she said they'd try to make it—especially after Estelle assured them kids were invited too. They had two boys, six and nine—close to Nicole's Nathan and Becky.

Samantha Curtis screeched with excitement when she got the call. "Is that a yes?" Estelle asked, laughing.

By the end of the evening, they'd planned the menu—a taco salad buffet—and decided who'd bring what. Estelle and Ramona would go shopping for the piñata, Nicole would pick up the family-size package of toilet paper for the silly game, and Michelle said she'd order a sheet cake from Jewel's bakery.

Harry poked his nose into the living room. "Better tell the guests to go through the alley and come in the back way. Won't be a surprise if they see everybody traipsing up our front walk."

They ended with a short time of prayer for Grace's cold. Estelle noticed that Nicole had been a little subdued during the evening, though she'd been willing to do her share for the party. She seemed to hang back as Michelle and Ramona said their good-byes and left. Nothing had been said all evening about the info meeting on Sunday, but Estelle wasn't too surprised when Nicole said, "Greg showed me the flyer about that meeting on Sunday. Said you'd brought it by. Why are you pushing this group home thing in our neighborhood, Estelle?"

Estelle wanted to say, *Why are you so against it?* But she tried to answer carefully. "I don't mean to be pushin' it, Nicole. But I have a grown son who's mentally challenged, and I know he would benefit from a home-like environment instead of an institution. So I guess I support the idea of group homes."

"Well, I didn't know about your son. But—excuse me for saying so—I still don't think people who are . . . are *mental* should live in the same neighborhoods with children. And we live right next to the Alvarezes!"

Estelle searched for the right words. "You have a right to your opinion, of course. But since a group home has shown some interest in purchasing the Alvarezes' two-flat, it seems like a good thing to have a neighborhood meeting so we can all get accurate information about what that would actually mean. Don't you agree?"

"No. They'll just try to make it sound all hunky-dory. They won't tell you all the problems and dangers."

Estelle sucked in a breath. *O Lord, You gotta help me here.* "Well, if you have concerns you should come and—"

"Oh, I will. Those people need to know how the neighbors really feel about this. The Alvarezes too."

Estelle's thoughts and feelings felt like a mess of tangled wire. Did the woman have any idea how her comments made her feel? People who are "mental"? But she didn't want their conversation to end with bad feelings. "Do you . . . should we take a few minutes to pray about this, Nicole?"

Nicole picked up her purse, her chest heaving slightly. "Thanks, but . . . I think I should go." She headed for the door, and then turned at the top of the stairs. "Guess we'll see you Saturday night for the party."

✧   ✧   ✧   ✧

The October weather continued mild and dry, with temps in the sixties during the days and not too cold at night. Estelle couldn't remember going so long in the fall without any rain, but she didn't hear anybody complaining.

According to Ramona, who gave her a blow-by-blow progress report of Grace's cold as she and Estelle drove to Manna House that week, each day the singer was feeling a bit better, though she'd developed laryngitis. "Good thing she doesn't have any concerts *this* weekend, 'cause no way could she sing."

That wasn't Estelle's only concern. Normally this would be the weekend she'd visit Leroy, but there was too much going on. Hopefully they could have a good, long talk by phone at least.

And after weeks of dry weather, it drizzled Saturday morning, causing momentary consternation about where they were going to hang the colorful six-point Fiesta Star Piñata she and Ramona had picked out and filled with chocolate candies. But the weather cleared by late morning, so Harry nailed a long pole to the back porch railing and attached the piñata to the end so it dangled about seven feet above the ground. A quick call to the Singers netted a plastic bat and Harry reluctantly donated one of his treasured bandanas for a blindfold. The kids would love it.

By the time guests began to arrive at six o'clock, Estelle had the dining room table ready for the buffet and Corky had been banished to the bedroom. Samantha Curtis was the first to arrive by the back stairs, and immediately offered to organize the food as it arrived for the do-it-yourself taco salads. Estelle chuckled to herself. That young woman was a keeper. No wonder Grace sang the praises of her assistant.

Soon the kitchen and dining room were crowded with adults as the Jaspers and Singers arrived bearing the sheet cake and toilet paper, though all the kids gravitated to DaShawn's bedroom like iron filings to a magnet, where he showed off some magic tricks he'd been practicing.

Estelle glanced at the clock: 6:40 already. Grace and Jeff were supposed to arrive at seven. "Oh, dear. I hope Grace's brother gets here on time," she worried. Ramona hadn't arrived yet either.

Just then Harry announced, "They're here!" as he opened the back door.

Ramona slipped in first, breathing hard as if she'd run all the way around. "I had to sneak out the back. They think I'm in the bathroom."

Behind her, the young man in the doorway, probably mid-thirties, had to be Grace's brother. The family resemblance was strong—dark brown hair, warm amber eyes, pleasant features. Mark introduced his wife, Denise, and the two boys, Luke and Marcus. Only then did Estelle realize there was someone else with them. Two someones. Who—?

"And I hope you folks don't mind," Mark said as they all crowded into the kitchen, "but my parents have never met Jeff. When I told them about the surprise engagement party you folks were throwing, they drove up from Indianapolis this afternoon and showed up at our house, wanting to surprise them too." He turned to the beaming silver-haired couple behind him. "These are my parents, Margaret and Paul Meredith."

The whole kitchen erupted in claps and cheers. "Aw-riight!" "Super!" "What a great surprise!" "Thank you so much for coming!"

The senior Merediths were beaming. "We got to attend Gracie's concert in Indy last weekend, but Jeff wasn't there and she didn't say anything about this party. Guess she didn't know about it. We're eager to meet Jeff." Mr. Meredith winked. "Gotta put my stamp of approval on any young man who wants to marry my daughter, you know."

"Now you're talkin'," Jared Jasper grunted to general laughter.

Estelle was so flustered and excited, she almost didn't hear Samantha calling from the living room. "Hey, everybody! Quiet! Quiet! They're coming!"

Somehow everyone managed to stifle the whispers and giggles and comments as they shut off the lights in the kitchen and dining room and crowded together. The doorbell rang. "DaShawn!" Estelle hissed. "You go down and answer the door." She and Harry went out into the living room to receive their guests as they came up the stairs.

Jeff was as good-looking as Estelle remembered him—dark curly hair, the hint of a five o'clock shadow on his jaw, a boyish grin, wearing jeans, tan sport coat, and an open-necked white shirt. She liked that he held Grace's hand as they came into the room. Grace looked lovely as usual. Couldn't tell she'd been struggling

162

with a terrible cold—until she tried to speak. "Better not hug me," she croaked. "Don't want you folks to catch the bug I had."

"Well, come on in," Estelle said, starting for the kitchen. "Supper's almost ready and—"

"*SURPRISE!!!*"

Grace's mouth fell open as her neighbors burst out of the kitchen, kids jumping up and down and yelling. But the look on her face when she saw her brother and her parents was priceless.

✦   ✦   ✦   ✦

The party quickly moved into full swing. The taco salad buffet was a big hit, and like the biblical five loaves and two fish, somehow everybody got fed. Then Harry ushered everyone down the back stairs and into the yard, where the piñata hung, swaying in the breeze. They blindfolded Grace first and gave her the bat, but she did little more than send it spinning. Next all the kids had a try. Destin Jasper gave it a good whack and broke off one of the star points, but finally it was Jeff's turn. Blindfolded and teasing Harry about promoting "games of violence," he whacked it good on his first swing and the piñata burst open, spilling chocolate candy in every direction.

The mad scramble that ensued brought Karl Molander out onto his back stoop next door, frowning under his porch light. "Don't worry, Mr. Molander!" Estelle called hastily. "We're done here. We're going back inside now."

Once again upstairs, Ramona gleefully introduced the "Dress the Bride and Groom" game à la Gabby Fairbanks. Dividing the TP rolls—six to the guys, six to the women—she sent the women into the living room to "dress the bride," and the men to the dining room to "dress the groom." Ten minutes later the bride and groom posed for pictures—Grace swathed in swirls and loops of toilet paper, including a long trailing "veil," and Jeff's whole body wrapped in a "suit"—including a top hat that kept sliding down over his face creating a perfect mummy.

Jeff grinned as he took Grace's hand amid cameras and smartphones flashing. "Hey, sweetheart, we could save a lot of money on the wedding if we wore these."

"How'd you guys do that top hat?" Samantha wanted to know.

"Professional secret!" Mark Meredith hooted.

As the future bride and groom finally shed their "finery," Michelle Jasper, looking more pregnant every day it seemed, brought out the cake to the dining room table. It was decorated with green and yellow script that said, CONGRATULATIONS JEFF AND GRACE! and GOD BLESS YOU!

Michelle handed the couple a cake knife and server. "You two get to cut the first piece."

People started to clap, but Jeff held up his hand for silence. "Uh, before we cut the cake, Grace and I have an announcement to make. And since this special woman can't talk right now above a whisper"—he grinned at Grace and squeezed her hand—"I get to do the honors." The room hushed as Jeff looked around until he saw Grace's parents. "Mr. and Mrs. Meredith, we are so honored that you came to this wonderful surprise party for us. And we hope you don't have anything on your calendar the first week in February, either, because"—again he grinned at Grace—"we've set our wedding date for February second. And you're *all* invited!"

Someone must've checked their smartphone calendar because a voice said, "Hey Jeff, that's a Wednesday! Why'd you pick a date in the middle of the week?"

"Seriously?" Jeff pulled a poker face. "February second is my birthday, and I figured I'd never forget our anniversary if we got married on my birthday." That got a big laugh.

"Smart man," Harry snickered, poking Estelle. "Wish I'd thought of that."

Estelle poked him back. "Don't worry, I won't let you forget our anniversary. Besides, it's always right around Thanksgiving."

"Okay, it's actually more complicated than that," Jeff was saying. "Most of you know I'm also Grace's agent, and this weekend we've been trying to juggle her concert schedule for next year with wanting to get married as soon as possible. Grace has been invited to do another January tour, a reprise of the "New Year—New You" tour she did last January, except in different cities. Then in February, she's been invited to Hawaii—yeah, you heard me right, *Hawaii*—to do a weeklong Sweetheart tour in the

Islands. We figured a few extras days in the Islands before the tour might be a good time to squeeze in a honeymoon, right, hon?"

He pulled Grace close and kissed the top of her head as the clapping and congratulations swirled around them. Then Jeff picked up the cake knife. "So . . . who wants some cake?"

Chapter 24

T HAT WAS A GREAT PARTY, ESTELLE." Harry came into the kitchen the next morning knotting his tie and kissed her on the back of the neck. "Sorry I dragged my feet about having another party at our house. You did a great job."

"Huh. Wasn't me. Everybody pitched in. And it was Ramona's idea to do a piñata." She turned from the stove and grinned at him. "But it *was* a great party, wasn't it? With a couple extra surprises— you know, Grace's folks turning up and Jeff announcing their wedding date."

Harry whistled for the dog. "Say, any chance I've got time to take Corky out for a short walk before breakfast? Hated to leave her shut up all last evening. She's eager to get out."

Estelle shooed the pair out the door. They'd be back soon— it was drizzling again. So what if they were late to church? God would understand. Frankly, what she'd really like to do is have a day off. But no . . . she was looking at another busy day. Church . . . then the info meeting about the group home . . . then Yada Yada. At least today her primary responsibility at all three things was just to show up. She even had a birthday card already for Yo-Yo—the only Yada Yada sister with an October birthday.

By the time they got home from SouledOut a few hours later, she only had about an hour before the neighborhood meeting at the Alvarezes. She wished she had a reading on who was "for" and who was "against" a group home in the neighborhood . . . but like Harry had said, taking the petition around earlier would've been useless. People would've voted on gut reactions, not based on any real facts. A petition would make a lot more sense once people had more information.

166

To be honest, it could go either way. Nicole Singer certainly had strong feelings about it. And Avis's prayer still niggled in Estelle's mind, that God's purpose would become evident for *all* concerned. She didn't see how . . . but then she wasn't God either.

Harry waffled on whether to go—he didn't feel strongly one way or the other. But at the last minute he said, "Wait up, I'll go with you. Won't be more than an hour, ya think?"

When Estelle and Harry arrived at three o'clock, Charlotte Bergman was already at the two-flat talking to the Alvarezes. A large pot of coffee sat on a small table in the living room alongside stacks of Styrofoam cups and containers with milk and sugar. Other neighbors soon arrived—Farid Jalili, Tim Mercer, Greg and Nicole Singer, Isaac Horowitz *and* Rabbi Mendel, and even Karl Molander, looking slightly florid. Jared Jasper hurried in, but no Michelle. He whispered to Estelle that his wife really needed to get off her feet that afternoon. Grace Meredith wasn't there—guess that was understandable. But that still left four households on the block missing . . .

Charlotte thanked everyone for coming and introduced herself and Bridges Family Services, a private social service agency. "I appreciate having a chance to share about the possibility of establishing a group home in this neighborhood. We work with a substantial number of adults who have mental health challenges that impair their ability to live independently on their own. They need support. Some also have physical disabilities that may affect their vision, communication, or ambulation. These individuals require assistance in their day-to-day living—but most do not need to be institutionalized and they often thrive in home-like settings . . . Oh, welcome. Come on in. We just started."

Lincoln Paddock had just slipped in. "Sorry." He got himself a cup of coffee and leaned against the mantel of the gas fireplace.

Ms. Bergman went on to share that one of the primary goals of a group home was to increase the independence of the residents. "Live-in staff members teach daily living skills such as meal preparation, laundry, housecleaning, home maintenance, and money management, as well as self-care skills, including bathing, toileting, dressing, nutrition, and taking their medications—"

"Good grief," Karl Molander snorted. "They need *help* knowing how to go to the bathroom? Sounds like a bunch of two-year-olds."

"Let her finish," Lincoln Paddock said sharply, much to Estelle's delight.

"Thank you." Ms. Bergman didn't smile, but simply outlined the other social services that would be available to the group home residents such as medical care, occupational therapy, vocational training, education, and mental health services. Estelle got the feeling she was a no-nonsense type.

"A two-flat such as this one offers some obvious advantages—primarily that the in-home staff couple could live on one floor, giving them some personal privacy while at the same time being on-site, and the residents could live on the other floor, providing a sense of independence. Bridges is very interested in this property. The price is right and the owners—Mr. and Mrs. Alvarez here—are eager to sell quickly." The woman looked around. "But of course, the success of a group home partially depends on the receptivity of the potential neighborhood. I'm sure some of you have questions and concerns—"

"Ms. Bergman." The rabbi spoke slowly and deliberately. "All that sounds well and good. But this is a residential neighborhood. You're talking about a social service agency. Don't you need a zoning variance? Seems like the neighbors would have a say in something like that."

"Of course we want neighbors to have a say—that's why we're having this meeting. One of the goals of a group home is integrating the residents into the neighborhood in a positive way. But a zoning variance? No. The Fair Housing Act of 1968, amended in 1988, prohibits discrimination in housing toward people with disabilities."

Estelle saw Isaac Horowitz and the rabbi exchange glances. Isaac frowned.

Farid Jalili raised a hand. "Ms. Bergman, do you have any statistics or facts about how a group home affects property values in a neighborhood?" Greg Singer nodded. He was obviously concerned about that too.

As far as she knew, Ms. Bergman answered, she was not aware that the presence of a group home affected property values to any significant degree.

"Come on, now," Karl Molander growled. "You can't tell me that having mental cases wandering around the neighborhood acting all weird isn't going to affect our property values. Huh. Property values been goin' down already ever since anybody an' everybody started movin' in here. Not like the old days."

An uncomfortable rustle and murmur spread around the room. Estelle wanted to toss Molander out the door on his ear—the nerve of the man! "Anybody and everybody" indeed. Two-thirds of the neighborhood were people of color or different ethnicities.

To her surprise Harry was the first one to speak up. "Excuse me, name's Harry Bentley. We're pretty new here on the block ourselves, and I'll be first to admit change isn't easy. Most of us like hangin' with folks like ourselves. I'm talkin' 'bout myself. But one thing we like about this neighborhood is gettin' to know a whole lot of different kinds of people. You all aren't as scary as we first thought."

That got a laugh and the tension in the air seemed to ease.

"So I'm thinkin' that'd be the same with folks with some disabilities. Once we get to know 'em, probably a whole lot o' ways they're just regular folks."

"Excuse me." Nicole Singer's hand shot up. "I know you mean well, Mr. Bentley, but people with mental issues aren't 'just regular folks.' Nobody's mentioned the biggest issue—and that's *safety*. Haven't you seen the news stories about people who suffer from schizophrenia or severe depression or . . . or any number of mental illnesses who go off half-cocked and kill people? Or steal stuff, or . . . or . . . at the very least, they can be scary. Especially to children." She stood up and wagged a finger at Charlotte Bergman. "We live right next door to this two-flat. I have two young children. If a group home moves in here, I'm telling you . . . we'll be putting our home up for sale." She sat down.

Estelle gasped. She felt like she'd been slapped. The group in the living room murmured and shifted. All Estelle could think of was Leroy. Without ever meeting her son, Nicole was saying

Leroy—people like Leroy—were so scary the Singers would *move*?

Charlotte Bergman held up her hand for attention. She spoke directly to Nicole. "I'm sorry to hear you say that, but if that's how you feel, Ms. . . . Mrs. . . . ."

"Nicole Singer. This is my husband, Greg."

"You said it, lady," Karl Molander grunted.

Ms. Bergman ignored him. "If that's how you feel, Mrs. Singer, of course we need to consider how welcoming a neighborhood will be. Many of our clients with disabilities have been rejected and made fun of all their lives. We are trying to give them the best possible chance at living a normal and productive life. Many of the people you read about in news reports did not have a supportive environment or proper treatment. For some, their illness was not even known, much less treated. But I do want to assure you— and everyone else here—that we screen our clients carefully. The residents we assign to group homes have no history of violence, and they are supervised carefully—both by live-in staff and social services who meet with each one on a regular basis."

She started to gather her bag and papers. "I have some printed information here about Bridges Family Services as well as some FAQs about group homes if anyone would like to pick them up on your way out." She turned to the Alvarezes. "Thank you, Mr. and Mrs. Alvarez, for hosting this meeting. I, uh, think we're done here."

The meeting broke up. Estelle hardly knew what to do. Should she try to talk to Nicole? She didn't trust herself. Harry and Greg had a pretty good relationship—maybe he could talk to him, find out if his wife was really serious.

Estelle made her way over to the Alvarezes', both of whom looked rather distressed. She thanked them, said she hoped they'd get a buyer for the two-flat soon, and then picked up some of the printed information Charlotte Bergman had brought, hoping to get a chance to speak to her. However, Lincoln Paddock and Tim Mercer were talking to her, so Estelle just said, "Thank you for coming, Ms. Bergman, very helpful," before finding Harry and heading for the front door.

To her relief, the Singers seemed to have left already. But as she and Harry came down the front walk, she heard someone call out, "Jalili! Just a minute." Estelle looked up. Isaac Horowitz had crossed the street and was flagging Farid Jalili to stop. The sturdy Iranian walked back and met Isaac in front of the bushes lining the edge of the Horowitzes' yard.

Harry was inclined to walk up the middle of the street to their house, but Estelle headed for the sidewalk. Now they could hear Isaac saying, ". . .They're dead now, see?" He pointed to two of the bushes. "Two hundred dollars it will cost me to replace mature bushes. I hold you responsible!"

"Me? What are you talking about?"

Harry was trying to tug Estelle's elbow to walk a little faster away from the confrontation going on, but she slowed her steps.

"Your plow! Driving down the sidewalk last winter. Ruined these bushes, you and your truck. I want compensation."

"You're crazy," Farid Jalili said. "That was six months ago. Anything could have killed those bushes. Besides, it was an emergency. You know that as well as anyone."

"Two hundred dollars." Isaac Horowitz folded his arms across his chest.

Farid Jalili made a gesture as if swatting down those last words and walked away in disgust.

"On purpose you did it!" Isaac called after him. "We know you people don't like Jews!"

"You're crazy, man," Farid shouted back and kept walking.

Estelle felt a strong tug on her arm. "Estelle Bentley, you stay out of it," Harry hissed in her ear. "It's not your business. Come on. Let's go home."

Chapter 25

THE WHOLE DAY HAD BEEN CLOUDY with an occasional drizzle, but the wind had picked up and the sky had rolled itself into a dark angry boil as Estelle drove to Jodi Baxter's house for Yada Yada a few hours later. Trees that had been holding onto their glory whipped this way and that, sending mad showers of twigs and dried leaves into the gloom.

They were in for a thunderstorm, no doubt about it.

Might as well. Matched the storm in her spirit since the group home meeting that afternoon. What in the world was happening in their neighborhood? Ever since they'd moved in last winter, she and Harry had been going out of their way to be friendly to all their neighbors and had at least gotten to know everyone's names. And they'd already made good friends with Grace Meredith and the Jaspers—and, she'd thought, with the Singers too. She'd even bragged to some of the staff at Manna House that their little block on Beecham Street was becoming a *real* neighborhood.

Now Karl Molander's sarcastic comments showed how *he* really felt about his neighbors, and it was obvious that Isaac Horowitz held a grudge against Farid Jalili. How much of that was a stupid misunderstanding between two neighbors, and how much was it a reflection of years—decades, centuries—of animosity between the Jewish people and the Muslim neighbor-states that surrounded them? Some of both no doubt.

And was Nicole Singer *really* threatening to move if Bridges Family Services bought that two-flat for a group home? O God! What was happening here?

Estelle backed into a parking space half a block from the Baxters' two-flat and hustled back toward their house. The temperature must've dropped a good ten degrees just in the last fifteen minutes. But as she mounted the steps to the porch, she paused, memories flooding back. The door on the right, next to the bay windows, led into the Baxters' first floor apartment. The door on the left led upstairs to the second floor apartment where Leslie Stuart, another Yada Yada sister, lived—and who'd offered Estelle a place to stay when the old Manna House shelter burned down a few years ago. Faulty wiring. They'd all gotten out safely . . . Hallelujah, thank You, Jesus! She'd been a resident at the shelter back then, after Leroy got hard to live with and she'd let him stay in the family home rather than kick him out.

That was before . . . everything. Before she went back to volunteer when the new Manna House had been built, then came on staff. Before Harry came to one of Gabby's Fun Nights at the shelter and—almost literally—swept her off her feet doing the Macarena. Before a bunch of druggies took advantage of Leroy and turned her house into a drug den. Before an arsonist burned it down, almost taking Leroy if the firemen hadn't pulled him out. Before the long months of treatment for his burns . . .

Lord, Lord, she'd lived enough lifetimes for two or three people!

Shaking off the memories, she pushed open the door on the right and walked in.

"Estelle! So glad you got here before the storm." Jodi Baxter took her jacket. "Hope the rest get here soon—don't think it'll hold off much longer." She raised her voice and called back into the kitchen. "Stu! Estelle's here. Is that tea ready?"

Stu—Leslie Stuart—brought in the tea tray and set it down before giving her a quick hug. "Hey, roomie. How's your man? By the way, I found an earring in the guest room—gotta be yours." She held up a baggie with a dangly gold loop in it.

Estelle took the baggie, eyeing the earring. "Yep. Was. I threw out the other one after a couple years, never thought its mate would show up."

Becky Wallace arrived next, apologizing that she'd been out of town last month and just forgot to let the sisters know. The others arrived in waves over the next ten minutes, still beating the rain. But the first loud crack of thunder rattled the windows just seconds before Delores and Yo-Yo darted in . . . and then the rain came down in sheets.

The hot tea with lemon and honey felt good going down, and Estelle started to relax in the company of these familiar sister-friends. Avis Douglass opened with a familiar worship chorus and prayer, then Jodi disappeared into the kitchen with a couple of others and reappeared with a flaming cake in a 9"x13" pan singing lustily, "Happy birthday, dear Yo-Yo . . ." as others joined in.

Yo-Yo's real name was Yolanda, a name that meant "violet flower"—which was a misnomer if there ever was one. Yo-Yo was anything but a delicate flower. Estelle had never seen her in a dress or wearing pastel colors. Now thirty-two, the young woman still wore overalls or cargo pants of some sort, and she usually kept her hair cut short and spiky, streaked in changing hues—blue, blonde, purple, green, even black. Her concept of jewelry consisted of body piercings here and there along with a few tattoos. Yo-Yo had come to the group unsure about "all this Jesus stuff," raising her two teenage half brothers by herself in lieu of a drugged-out mother. Her baptism in Lake Michigan was like the starting gun in an unfamiliar cross-country race, and she still had no patience with churchy language and clichés. She kept the Yadas on their toes by her constant refrain: "What in the heck does that mean?"

In spite of Yo-Yo's tough demeanor, Estelle noticed she quickly brushed away some telltale moisture as the various sisters gave her cards and read their blessings for her new year. "All right already," she finally blurted. "Can we cut this doggone cake?"

Avis deftly moved them into the sharing time as they finished up the crumbs from Jodi's homemade red velvet cake. Seemed to be a lot of prayer requests for "kids" who were no longer kids but finishing college or in the military—one of Yo-Yo's brothers—or pounding the pavement looking for jobs. Estelle put Leroy into that prayer pile too . . . then asked if she could share something that'd happened that day that had her tied up in knots.

"Of course," Avis said. The room quieted.

Estelle shared as best she could about the neighborhood meeting that day, stopping now and then to go back and fill in the blanks with things that had happened since their last meeting in September. "Feels like our neighborhood is falling apart—people for, people against. Makes me wish I'd never brought up the whole idea of the Alvarezes selling their two-flat to Bridges Family Services—even though it *still* seems like a really good thing for both parties! But . . ." Estelle rubbed her forehead, which had started to ache. "Guess what I'd really like prayer for is how to relate to Nicole Singer. I mean, she's in this little prayer group we started in the neighborhood—four of us women—but this afternoon she said if a group home moves into the neighborhood, they're moving out!"

The Yada Yadas reacted. "You're kidding!" "Really? She said that?" "Why?"

Estelle shrugged. "Safety issues, I guess. She said people who are 'mental' are dangerous. She's worried about her kids. I mean, she practically freaked out!"

"Well, a few of them can be." Stu said. "As a social worker, I've run into a few I wouldn't want in my neighborhood."

Others protested, coming to the defense of group homes they'd known about or relatives who had mental health challenges but were harmless.

"The thing is," Estelle said, still rubbing her forehead, "I don't want this group home thing to drive the Singers out of the neighborhood. Yet the Alvarezes really need to sell their house right away, and I think Bridges is the only real buyer on the horizon right now. Although . . ." Her frown deepened. "The Horowitz family wants more Jewish families to move into our block, so they're against the group home too. But it's mostly smoke and mirrors. I don't think they actually have a potential buyer." She sighed. "Well, there it is. Not sure how to ask you to pray."

The room was quiet for a long moment. Then Adele Skuggs spoke up. "Sounds like that gal has a story. Needs someone to listen to it."

"What?"

Adele shrugged. "People all the time tellin' me stories when I got 'em in the chair at the shop. First they got opinions—huh. Loud opinions, off-the-chart opinions." A few snickers greeted this. Adele's Hair and Nails was a favorite shop for a loyal clientele, and

NETA JACKSON // DAVE JACKSON

free gossip was included in the price. "But if I listen long enough, those opinions usually have a story in back of 'em. Sometimes a hurt that goes way back, maybe a loss or sorrow, oftentimes a fear."

Florida was nodding big time. "Now you're talkin', girl."

"I agree," Avis said. "Let's pray that God would give Estelle an opportunity to talk to Nicole—"

"Not talk, listen," Adele interrupted.

"Yes, that's what I mean. Give Nicole an opportunity to share why she feels the way she does. Not to change her mind but just to care about whatever it is."

"*Sí!*" Edesa Baxter's eyes had grown wide. "Maybe she has experienced a big hurt that has never been healed. You could pray for her."

Estelle felt the breath wheeze out of her. Talk to Nicole? Listen to her story? If there was one. When could she do that? Would she come to the prayer time on Tuesday? Would she feel comfortable sharing there? Or—

Avis had started to pray, praising God for His loving care for Nicole Singer and asking God to give Estelle an opportunity to come alongside this woman who might be hurting underneath all the anger about a group home moving in next door. But as Avis prayed, Estelle was wrestling with whether she felt up to this.

It was hard enough carrying her own burden about Leroy—a story that didn't have an ending yet—without carrying someone else's burden, whose story might be too close for comfort.

✦   ✦   ✦   ✦

She'd forgotten to add DaShawn to the prayers back at Jodi's house, but should've. When she got home around nine, she found Harry brooding over a cup of lukewarm coffee. "Rodney called. Wants DaShawn to come for another weekend—the one comin' up."

"So soon? That's Halloween."

Harry rolled his eyes. "That's the point. He's got some big idea for goin' to a Halloween bash at a friend's house. Says his friend's got a couple teenagers who'll be there too."

"I don't like it."

"Neither do I."

"Besides, isn't the SouledOut youth group having a Harvest Party Saturday night?"

"That's what I told him! But he said, 'No problem! Our costume party is Sunday night.' Said he'd make sure DaShawn gets to his party and church, too, if we want."

Estelle frowned. "Still don't like it."

"Me either."

Estelle looked at her husband. "But you said okay, didn't you."

Harry nodded glumly. "DaShawn heard me talkin' to Rodney, said oh yeah, his dad told him about it when he was there and he'd kinda like to go. Told me he and his dad talked about dressing up in costumes like some kinda famous duo." He shrugged. "Didn't say who."

"Hmph, right. Probably Jekyll and Hyde . . . or Dr. Frankenstein and his monster."

"Said I don't know," Harry snapped. He pushed his chair back, got up, and headed for the bedroom. "I'm goin' to bed."

Chapter 26

Ramona seemed in a funk when she got into the RAV4 the next morning.

"You okay, sweetie?" Estelle asked, starting the car.

"Yeah. Sure." But she just stared out the window.

Estelle sighed and just drove. Whatever. She had her own dilemma. Should she try to go see Nicole Singer like her Yada Yada sisters had suggested *and* prayed could happen? Or just wait till tomorrow and see if she came to their prayer time at Grace Meredith's house—maybe feel her out then.

Chicken.

Well, yeah. She had to admit it. She—

Don't be afraid. I am with you.

Estelle almost wanted to pull a "Samuel" and cry out, *"Lord? Is that You?"* But she had a passenger in the car who'd think she was really weird.

Nicole needs you. She needs a friend.

What? She'd been trying to be Nicole's friend since day one, but it wasn't easy. They were too different—and not just because Nicole was white either. Grace was white, and a contemporary concert artist as well, a world Estelle knew nothing about. But . . . Grace had let herself be vulnerable. Had owned her past mistakes. Had experienced what *grace* was all about. But Nicole—

"The engagement party was nice."

"What?" Ramona's voice jarred Estelle out of her thoughts.

"I thought the engagement party was nice. The piñata was a lot of fun. All the *niños* seemed to like it."

"Thanks to you. You did a lot to pull it off—the piñata, the toilet-paper-dress-the-bride-and-groom thing, the Mexican theme."

Estelle smiled at her passenger. "I think Grace and Jeff really loved the surprise and the party."

"Yeah." Ramona fidgeted with the small shoulder purse that lay in her lap, then looked up at Estelle. "When's the trial gonna be? What if it doesn't happen before Miss Grace and Mr. Jeff get married? What am I gonna do then?" Her voice rose. "I can't go home. I gotta stay here to testify or . . . or they'll put me in jail for helping Max. But it's . . . it's taking too long! What if Max finds me before then? Maybe it's better to go to jail than . . . than . . ."

"Oh, honey." Estelle suddenly felt helpless. She didn't have answers to these questions. "Baby, I don't know when the trial's gonna be. I'll ask Harry to see if he can learn anything. As the arresting officer, he may be able to find out." She reached over and laid a hand over one of Ramona's. "But one thing I know— Harry and me, and Grace, and the Jaspers, and your friends at Manna House . . . we're gonna stick with you, no matter what. Okay?"

Ramona sniffed and nodded, then fished for a tissue in her pocket and blew her nose.

They rode again in silence. And again Estelle heard the voice in her spirit: *Don't be afraid. I am with you. Nicole needs you. She needs a friend who'll stick by her too.*

✧　✧　✧　✧

Mattie Krakowski was sitting in her plastic lawn chair on the square concrete stoop that passed for a front porch when Estelle arrived home from work that afternoon. "Well, look at you, Miss Mattie! Enjoying the nice weather after the storm, I see." The temperature was a pleasant seventy-two and a light breeze chased lazy clouds across the sky.

"Eh? Storm? What storm?" Mattie squinted up at Estelle.

"Last night. All that thunder." Surely even someone as deaf as Mattie would've heard the bone-shaking cracks of thunder and seen the flashes of lightning.

"Thunder? Huh. Thought it was fireworks—Fourth of July or somethin'."

"No, the Fourth was a couple months ago. It's the end of October now." Estelle hid a smile and was just about to head upstairs when she felt a tug on her sleeve.

"You got any lemonade or sumthin'?" Mattie asked. "Kinda warm out here."

"I'll bring you something." Upstairs, Estelle had no sooner dumped her bag and headed for the kitchen when her cell phone rang. She looked at the ID . . . Leroy. "Hi, baby! What's up?"

"Ma? It's me, Leroy."

"I know, son. Everything okay?"

"You didn't come visit me on this weekend."

"I know, baby. We called you, remember? We couldn't make it. But we'll come next weekend, okay?" Oh dear. Next Saturday would be crazy. Gabby wanted her to come early to help set up for the masquerade party at Manna House that night. "Maybe Sunday."

"Can I come stay with you for the weekend, Ma? Miz Finch said I could have a weekend pass. That mac 'n' cheese you brought me last time was good. Can you make some more?"

"Uh . . . baby, I don't know. I'll have to talk to Harry, see what all's happenin' here next weekend." Estelle grimaced to herself. She was pretty sure Harry wouldn't be too keen on the idea. Why did every weekend get so crazy full? "Look, I'll call you back, hon. If it doesn't work out to come here for the weekend, I'll for sure come to see you."

Estelle stood in the middle of the kitchen, her mind a muddle. She'd come in here for some reason . . . oh, right. Lemonade for Miss Mattie. Might fill a picnic jug and have a glass herself. It was only four thirty—Harry wouldn't be home yet for a couple of hours.

Ten minutes later she was back down on the stoop with Mattie, sipping lemonade. For once she was glad Mattie wasn't much of a conversationalist. It felt good to just sit . . . though the concrete stoop was hard. For half a minute she was tempted to cross the street and sit on Michelle Jasper's porch swing. But just then movement down the street caught her eye . . . Becky and Nathan Singer had just come out the front door of their house and were starting to draw on their front sidewalk with sidewalk chalk.

Which meant Nicole must be home.

Without giving herself time to think, Estelle grabbed the picnic jug, heaved herself up off the steps, and started across the street. "Hi, Becky. Hi, Nathan," she said as she reached the second house from the end of the block. "Your mama home?"

"Hi, Mrs. Bentley," Becky, the eight-year-old said. "Mommy's inside."

Estelle rang the doorbell. The door was open, and through the screen door she saw Nicole coming down the hallway, blonde hair pulled back into a ponytail, but still wearing her go-to-work pantsuit. "Hi, Nicole! Hope this isn't a bad time."

Nicole didn't hide her surprise. "Oh . . . hi, Estelle."

Estelle hefted the picnic jug. "I've got some lemonade here. Do you have a few minutes just to sit a spell?"

"Well . . . okay." Nicole opened the screen door. "I have a few minutes. Greg has to work late, so the kids and I were just going to have some hot dogs and baked beans."

Estelle settled in at the built-in breakfast booth in the compact kitchen while Nicole got out two tall glasses. Estelle poured and Nicole slid into the opposite bench. "Um, nice of you to stop by."

They chatted a little while, sipping lemonade. Nicole's job as a legal assistant was part time, letting her get home in time to pick up the kids from school. So far she really liked her job, wasn't sure she had much future there, but it was good for now. Estelle debriefed about typical Mondays at the homeless shelter—staff meeting, making lunch, a sewing class, Ramona coming with her each day. But after a few minutes Nicole said warily, "Are you mad at me—for what I said yesterday at the Alvarezes'?"

There it was. Her opportunity. Estelle shook her head. "No. I'm not mad. Concerned though. I got the feeling you have a good reason for feeling the way you do about having a group home next door."

"Well, sure. Like I said, safety issues, especially around kids. You hear all the time about mentally ill people going crazy and doing all kinds of violent stuff."

It was so tempting to jump on that sweeping generalization, but Estelle reminded herself to not argue. She was there to listen. "What I mean is, it sounded personal. Did something happen to you? A person with a mental illness who frightened you or . . ." She stopped. Nicole had looked away and was blinking back tears. Estelle reached across the booth and laid a hand on Nicole's. "I'm sorry. I don't mean to bring up bad memories. But we are sisters in the Lord, Nicole, and I care about you."

"'Scuse me." Nicole slid out of the booth and disappeared out of the kitchen. Estelle gaped after her. What now? Should she leave? But a few moments later Nicole was back with a box of tissues. "Just wanted to check on the kids," she said huskily, but dabbed at her eyes and blew her nose.

Taking in a deep quivering breath, she let it out slowly. "You . . . you might think this is silly, but . . . but when I was growing up, there was a . . . a retarded man on our block. I say 'retarded' because I . . . I don't really know what was wrong with him. But he was grown and still living with his parents. And he was so . . . so weird. He would stare at us kids when we were outside playing. Just look. Not say anything. Though"—she grimaced—"some of the kids would yell at him to go home and throw things at him— you know, sticks and pebbles. Then he'd scream, 'Stop it! Stop it!' and he'd run inside, babbling. And one of his parents would come out and yell at us to leave him alone. I never threw anything at him, but . . . he scared me. If he was outside, I didn't want to go outside and play." She dabbed at her eyes again.

Estelle nodded slowly. "I'm so sorry, Nicole." She wanted to ask, did your family ever go over to his house and try to get to know him? Understand why he looked at you? Maybe he wanted to play! Sometimes adults with limited mental capacity were very childlike at heart. But she just let the silence sit between them.

Nicole sniffed and sat up straight. "So, you can see why I don't want my children to be scared to play out in their own neighborhood. I'm serious about moving if that group home buys the house next door. I don't want Nathan and Becky to go through what I went through."

Again words sprang to the tip of Estelle's tongue. *That doesn't have to be the only choice—to live scared or move!* But with great effort, she bit them back and heard herself saying, "Can I pray with you, Nicole?"

Her neighbor nodded and they held hands across the table as Estelle prayed for the comfort of the Holy Spirit for her precious sister and her family, even adding the gist of Avis's prayer: ". . . and Lord, we pray that Your purpose would become evident for all concerned—for the Singers and their children, the Alvarezes, our neighborhood. Show us Your way, Jesus, and we'll give You the glory. Amen."

Nicole walked her to the door. "Thanks for coming over, Estelle. I appreciate it."

Estelle gave her a hug. "And just to let you know, I don't want you and Greg to move. We need to trust God to work this all out." On the porch she turned back. "See you tomorrow night at Grace's?"

Nicole shrugged. "If Greg doesn't have to work late."

As Estelle navigated the chalk-covered sidewalk, Nathan Singer jumped up. "Hey, Mrs. Bentley! See the dragon I drawed? That's his head an' his tail goes all the way over to the next house!"

Estelle admired the chalky dragon and then hustled on home. Harry would be home soon—DaShawn too—and she hadn't even started supper. But her mind kept replaying the prayer she'd prayed and she felt conflicted. Was she being honest asking God to work out His purpose—no matter what? Listening to Nicole's story had touched her. Kids should be able to play outside like Nathan and Becky were doing now without being afraid. And she really didn't want the Singers to move. But . . .

Maybe the group home wasn't supposed to happen on Beecham Street. Maybe she needed to let go of her hopes about Leroy moving close by. But even if she did, what would the Alvarezes do if Bridges didn't buy their two-flat? They had hoped for a quick sale—and for good reason! It must be hard to be so far away from family in Guatemala at a time like this when they were needed. But as far as she knew, there weren't any other buyers on the horizon, in spite of Isaac Horowitz's bluster.

"O God," she groaned aloud, "I hope You can figure all this out, because it feels like somebody's gonna lose out big time, whatever way it goes."

Chapter 27

Tuesday was Estelle's easy day at the shelter. Just had to put lunch together and stay through cleanup. Ramona still seemed in kind of a funk, but she helped set out the soup and sandwich makings and did her share of cleanup, so Estelle let her be. As Estelle was doing a last-minute check of the kitchen—all stove burners off, dirty dish towels in the laundry, a shopping list for tomorrow, lights off—Gabby Fairbanks poked her head out of her tiny office.

"Oh, good, you're still here, Estelle." The curly redhead popped over to the counter and looked around as if making sure no one else was listening. "Just wanted to ask if Harry is coming to the masquerade on Saturday. With people in costumes and some extra guests, we could use some extra security that night."

Estelle chuckled. "Well, that's one way to get him to come. Tell you what—he's more likely to come if *you* ask him. You have his cell number, don't you?" She had her own agenda to ask Harry. Let Gabby do the begging for the party.

"Yep. Will do." Gabby turned to Ramona, who had just come out of the laundry room. "What about you, Ramona? Are you coming to the party Saturday night? It's a masquerade, you know. Come dressed in a costume—just nothing evil or scary. It'll be a lot of fun."

Ramona pulled a puppy dog pout. "Wish I could, Miss Gabby. But I'm helping with the youth group at SouledOut and they're having a Harvest Party on Saturday too."

"Oh. Too bad. But you'll have fun with the teens."

"So what costume are you going to wear, Miss Gabby?"

Gabby wiggled her eyebrows. "That's a secret. It's a masquerade, you know."

"Uh-huh," Estelle chimed in. "Good luck hiding that mop of red hair. My costume is a secret too—even I don't know what it is."

Which tickled the program director's funny bone and she left laughing.

Apparently Gabby got on the phone right away and called Harry, because he brought it up at supper. "Ah, the Firecracker wants me to come to this masquerade thing she cooked up at Manna House on Saturday—said she could use some extra security. Told her I'd do it"—he eyed Estelle as a warning—"as long as I don't have to dress up in some silly costume."

"Fine." Estelle sniffed. "Just don't blame me if I end up dressing like Lady Godiva or somebody."

"Who?" DaShawn said, his mouth full of enchilada casserole. "Hey, 'bout this weekend. Dad said he wanted to pick me up Friday after school since I have that party at church Saturday night, you know. Guess he wants to go bowling or somethin' Friday night. But it's cool—he said he'd help me come up with a costume."

"Like what?" Harry growled. "They don't want any ghosts or ghouls or monsters or gangsters."

DaShawn shrugged and shoveled in his last bite. "I dunno. I'll think of somethin' . . . Can I be excused?"

"Clear your dishes first." Estelle watched the boy go. Now was the time to ask Harry about Leroy . . . but a little sugar wouldn't hurt.

"Hon, want some peach ice cream?" She knew it was a favorite. As she handed him a dish with two large scoops she said casually, "As long as we're talkin' about this weekend, uh, Leroy called, said he'd like to come spend the weekend. You know," she added hastily, "since we didn't go see him last weekend. It's been a few weeks now."

The ice cream failed to sugarcoat the request. "Leroy here? All weekend?" Harry rolled his eyes. "Babe, how many things are we gonna pile on every weekend? DaShawn's goin' to his dad's, the Firecracker's got us goin' to this crazy party at the shelter. We never have any time when nothin's happening!" He glared at his bowl of ice cream. "Besides, that would mean *two* trips to the South Side to pick him up and take him back."

Estelle toyed with her own ice cream. "I know, hon. But in one way it's a good weekend, 'cause DaShawn will be gone, so Leroy can sleep in his room. And I thought Ramona and I could run down to the Lighthouse after we finish lunch at the shelter Friday and pick him up. That'd be one trip taken care of. I could even take him back Sunday afternoon by myself since it'll just be to drop him off."

"I'm not just thinkin' 'bout me, Estelle. You run around like a chicken with its head cut off. *You* need to slow down, take some time for yourself too."

"I know. It's just . . . I'd like to say yes this time. He could go to the party with us—that would be fun for him."

Harry sighed. "Yeah. Whatever." He glanced at the clock. "I gotta go. Men's Bible study is startin' up again, meeting over at Peter Douglass's place. You goin' over to Grace's?"

Five minutes later Estelle was heading across the street to Grace Meredith's house, hoping to get there early and ask Michelle Jasper what her boss was thinking after the neighborhood meeting on Sunday. Before Nicole got there—if she came.

❖ ❖ ❖ ❖

For the rest of the week, Estelle's thoughts and emotions felt like pulled taffy—stretched first this way, then that, up, down, around . . . and sticky too. Nicole did come to the prayer time at Grace's house, which was good, right? Estelle had been afraid she'd drop out over this disagreement about the group home. But she told Grace and Michelle about Estelle's visit, recounting the same story about her childhood scary neighbor and why she felt so strongly about not having a group home next door. The sisters had been kind and sympathetic, and Michelle had even prayed that God would heal the childhood memories that still haunted her.

But did it change anything? Not that Estelle was aware. In fact, when she got a chance to speak to Michelle alone, her friend acknowledged that Charlotte Bergman felt hesitant to pursue the two-flat on Beecham for the group home. Bridges certainly didn't want to disrupt a neighborhood by people moving out.

Estelle found herself mumbling the same prayer all week: "Work Your purpose out, Jesus . . . work Your purpose out . . ." Because she certainly had no idea what that purpose was.

187

Thankfully, Ramona was willing to ride with her to pick up Leroy after lunch at the shelter on Friday. As they passed the receptionist's cubby in the foyer on their way out, Angela Kwon called after them, "Make sure you push those doors shut! They haven't been totally closing on their own lately, and then the safety buzzer's useless."

Estelle acknowledged her with a wave and once outside pushed the double oak doors shut until she heard them click. Good for Angela. Her diligence in being the gatekeeper for Manna House was an important factor in Ramona's safety—as well for a few other residents who took refuge there when domestic abuse was a factor in their homelessness—even though there hadn't been any incidents since that one time when Max showed up.

Leroy was waiting for them in the reception room at the Lighthouse, a duffle bag slung over his shoulder, talking to Mrs. Finch, the social worker. "Hey, Ma!" he grinned. "I'm ready." His smile faded when he saw Ramona and he ducked his head, as if suddenly shy.

"Hi, sweetie." Estelle gave her son a kiss on the cheek. "Mrs. Finch, good to see you. Thanks for giving Leroy a weekend pass—we're looking forward to it. Oh!" She indicated Ramona, who was standing uncertainly off to the side. "This is Ramona, one of my neighbors. She volunteers at the shelter where I work, so I give her a ride to and from each day. But we came here to pick you up first, Leroy."

Ramona held out her hand. *"Buenos tardes, Señor* Leroy. I am happy to meet you."

The smile slowly returned on Leroy's face and he shook her hand slowly. "Me too, *Señorita* Ramona."

"Looks like you'll have a chance to practice your Spanish, Leroy." Mrs. Finch beamed. "Leroy signed up for our beginning Spanish class just last week. Well, you all have a good time." She turned to go. "Leroy should be back here by six o'clock Sunday evening. We have one of our required group times at seven."

Ramona hopped into the back seat of the RAV4 leaving the front seat for Leroy, and Estelle gave her a grateful look. Leroy climbed in and buckled his seatbelt. "Will DaShawn be home when we get there? I brought the birthday present I made for him." He tapped the duffle bag he still held on his lap.

"Oh, Leroy." Estelle felt stricken. She'd forgotten Leroy had made a gift for DaShawn. "He's going to go to stay with his dad again this weekend. But . . . he might still be there if we get on home right away." She pretended to gun the engine. "Buckle up, ladies and gents. We're off!"

She needn't have worried. DaShawn hadn't even gotten home from school yet by the time they arrived at the Bentleys' graystone. When he did come bounding up the stairs, he gave a big high five to Leroy. "Hey, Uncle Leroy! Glad I got to see ya before my dad gets here. How ya doin', man?"

Estelle lifted an eyebrow. Uncle Leroy? Where did that come from? But it made sense. Harry's son was DaShawn's dad, so it would be natural to think of her son as his uncle. And Leroy practically split his face with a wide grin, obviously liking the handle.

"Sorry I missed your birthday, DaShawn." Leroy rummaged in his duffle bag and pulled out something wrapped in tissue paper. "I made this for you. Hope you like it."

Estelle was just as curious as DaShawn as he ripped off the tissue paper. He pulled out a leather belt that had all kinds of tooled designs in it. "Hey, cool. A belt." He looked at it closely. "It even has my name designed on it! How'd you make this, Uncle Leroy?"

Leroy shrugged, trying to act like it was no big deal, but he was obviously pleased. "Lighthouse has a craft room, and this guy came in and showed us how to make stuff out of leather—wallets and belts, stuff like that. You like it?"

"Yeah. Thanks a lot." DaShawn even threaded the belt through the loops on his jeans. "Well, I better pack my stuff. Sorry I gotta leave, Uncle Leroy, but you can sleep in my bed."

Estelle could've hugged him.

After DaShawn left, the rest of the evening was low-key. She fried catfish and made mac 'n' cheese for supper, two of Leroy's favorites, then Harry and Leroy watched a football game on the sports channel as Estelle stewed over the next big question: What kind of costume could she and Leroy wear to the masquerade party tomorrow night? And would Leroy even want to dress up?

When she told Leroy about the party and broached the question the next morning, Harry—who was off the hook—told her she ought to go as Della Reese, the actress. "All ya gotta do, Estelle, is wear your hair down, maybe powder a few white streaks in it. Told ya before you look a lot like her."

"Huh. I wish." But the idea had a certain appeal. All she'd have to do was wear a mask over her eyes to make it a "masquerade," and maybe a *Hello! My Name Is . . .* nametag with the word *Della* printed on it. Easy.

"What about you, Leroy? Who would you like to be for the masquerade party?"

To her surprise Leroy had a ready answer. "Batman!"

"Batman?"

"Yeah. He drives that cool Batmobile."

Harry gave Estelle a *you-figure-it-out* look and hustled out the back door with Corky to give the dog her morning walk. Huh. So much for Helpful Harry.

"Well, let me think about it, Leroy. See what I can do." She knew one thing—she needed help.

Leroy turned on the TV to a cooking show while Estelle called Michelle Jasper. Not home. Jared said she volunteered at the Lifeline Care Center Saturday mornings. Right. Estelle had forgotten. Should she call Grace? Somehow Grace didn't seem like the dress-up-in-costume type. Nicole? . . . Maybe. She was a homeschooling mom—or had been—and homeschoolers always seemed to be doing creative things.

"Batman?" Nicole said when Estelle called and explained her dilemma. "Oh, that shouldn't be too hard. Does Harry have a pair of black pants? And a black turtleneck?" Estelle thought so, and Leroy was about the same height, though a bit thinner. "Believe it or not," Nicole said, "I've got some black silk that would make a good cape, and I think I could make a helmet and mask with some black felt. We've got tons of that stuff. Give me half an hour and I'll be over. Can I bring the kids? Greg's at work today."

Estelle didn't ask, just informed Harry when he got back with Corky that he was donating a pair of black pants and his black turtleneck to the cause. "Put these on," she told Leroy. When Nicole arrived, Leroy's eyes lit up at the black silk "cape" she'd brought, tied in front with a pair of black shoelaces.

"Now . . ." Nicole studied Leroy's head. If she noticed the scarring on the left side of his neck and head, she didn't say anything. "Okay, let me fool around with this black felt for a while, see what I can do. I don't need you for a while."

Nathan had been watching the proceedings with wide eyes. When his mom sat down at the dining room table where Estelle had set up her sewing machine, the six-year-old tugged on Leroy's sleeve. "Mr. Leroy, you wanna play a game?" He held up a pack of colorful playing cards. "I brought Uno."

Leroy grinned. "Sure. I like Uno. We play it at the Lighthouse."

Becky joined in, and soon the three of them were hunkered around the living room coffee table, calling out colors and numbers and "Reverse!" and "Skip you!" until they were all giggling.

Praise Jesus! Estelle was torn between watching the game and watching Nicole fashion a Batman "helmet," complete with pointy ears. When Nicole heard Estelle was going to go as Della Reese, she offered to make a soft eye mask out of the squares of black felt she had. "Softer than those awful plastic masks you get at the Dollar Store."

The moment had come for the final fit. Nicole had even made a wide "gold" belt out of yellow felt. "All you need now, Batman, is a pair of black gloves."

"Got 'em," Harry volunteered. He was obviously impressed.

Leroy stared at himself in the full-length mirror on the back of Estelle and Harry's bedroom door. When he came out, he gave a surprised Nicole a hug. "Thank you, Miz Nicole. I like it. Wow, you can really sew!"

Nicole gathered up her material and sewing supplies, and Estelle walked her and the two kids down the stairs to the front door. "Don't know how to thank you, Nicole. Leroy will never forget it. You've really made his day."

Nicole had a funny look on her face as they stood on the stoop outside. "Did you . . . did you say your son is mentally ill? I mean, Leroy seems pretty normal to me."

Estelle sucked in a breath. "He does have mental challenges. He's been diagnosed borderline schizophrenic. Not multiple personalities," she said hastily, "just . . . inconsistent and sometimes contradictory emotions, thoughts, and behavior. But as long as he takes his meds, you're right, he's pretty normal."

"Not many adults have the patience to play Uno with my two." She tipped her head toward Nathan and Becky who were already skipping down the sidewalk. "They loved it."

Estelle smiled sadly. "Mmm. Mentally, he's often rather childlike. Yet he sometimes surprises me with his adult decisions. He's actually trying to get a job in a hospital burn unit, because he spent a long time as a burn patient after . . . after getting third-degree burns in a house fire a few years ago. Knows what patients go through."

"Oh. I'm so sorry." Nicole stared after her kids, who'd arrived at their front porch and were waiting for her. "But . . . it's wonderful he wants to give back."

Estelle shrugged. "Well, we'll see. I just hope he's not in for a big disappointment."

Nicole seemed lost in thought. Estelle finally broke the silence. "Anyway, thanks so much for pulling that costume together, Nicole. And for the eye mask you made for me too." She gave her neighbor a hug. "I'll let you know how the party goes tonight."

"Great." Nicole headed down the walk, then tossed back, "Take pictures!"

Chapter 28

MANNA HOUSE WOMEN'S SHELTER WAS BRIGHTLY LIT when Harry let Estelle and Leroy off at the front door, then left to park the car. Josh and Edesa Baxter arrived seconds later with their two little ones, all dressed as Wizard of Oz characters. "Aw, you guys are too cute!" Estelle chuckled. Josh must've used a whole roll of aluminum foil to create his Tin Man. Edesa had a tousled mane of tan yarn, tan sweats, and a long rope "tail" as the Cowardly Lion. Gracie made a cute miniature Dorothy in a blue dress and Mary Jane shoes, her dark wavy hair parted and tied in two hair ribbons. Little Julian was a mini-Scarecrow in a flannel shirt, patches sewn on his baby sweatpants, and a straw hat.

Estelle introduced Leroy. "Great costume, man," Josh said, shaking Leroy's hand. "Say, where's Harry?"

"He's—wait a minute." Estelle frowned. "Aren't you Baxters supposed to be at the party for the teens at SouledOut? DaShawn is going . . . and Ramona said you asked her to help. That's tonight, isn't it?" Or had she gotten the date wrong. After all, Halloween wasn't till tomorrow, but tomorrow was Sunday. Surely they wouldn't—

"Yep, we're on our way," Josh said. "But we promised Gabby we'd stop in for fifteen minutes. She wanted to see the Wizard of Oz costumes. So . . . we better get movin'." He hustled his little family up the steps and pulled open one of the big oak doors.

"You're supposed to ring the buzzer," Edesa reminded him.

Josh shrugged. "It opened, didn't it? After you, ladies."

"Welcome!" a booming voice said as they entered the foyer. "Sarge"—a former Marine and the no-nonsense night manager at Manna House—waved them in, her only costume a nametag that said *Security*. "Party's right through those double doors on the main floor. Only staff allowed on the lower level tonight." The short, stocky woman turned to the next visitors coming in behind them. "Welcome!"

Estelle grinned. Between Sarge and Harry, security should be well covered.

But she felt Leroy tense up and pull back a little as they moved through the double doors into the main room. Forty or fifty people, all in some sort of costume, milled around, some sipping from Styrofoam cups. The large multipurpose room was decorated with long streamers of brown, yellow, and orange crepe paper, pumpkins with black marker faces here and there, and pop music playing on a boom box.

She took Leroy's arm. "It's all right, son. Just stick with me. Want something to drink?" They moved in the direction of the refreshment table where a couple of the shelter residents—a clown with a red rubber nose and a black cat with a cat-eye mask and whiskers drawn on her cheeks with eyebrow pencil—served up hot cider and paper cones of popcorn.

"Estelle!" Gabby Fairbanks bustled over, decked out in a red Orphan Annie dress, white lacy socks, and patent leather shoes.

Estelle chuckled. "Definitely goes with the hair."

Gabby ignored the comment and gaped at Batman. "This isn't . . . Harry, is it?"

"Now that's funny! No, this is my son, Leroy. Leroy, this is Gabby Fairbanks, our program director . . . or, ah, should I say Orphan Annie. She and her red hair get all the credit and the blame for whatever happens tonight."

Leroy held out a black-gloved hand. "Pleased ta meet you, Miz Gabby. Thanks for letting me come to your party."

"I am so glad you came, Leroy!" Gabby looked genuinely pleased. "My sons are around here somewhere—look for Luke Skywalker and a Jedi." But she glanced around nervously. "Harry is coming, isn't he? Sarge could use a little help. Don't know what I was thinking, encouraging a masquerade party when you don't know for sure who's who!"

"He's here—just parking the car." Estelle rolled her eyes. "Can't miss him. He's dressed up as Harry." But she smiled reassuringly. "Don't worry, Gabby. I'm sure Sarge and Harry will take care of any problems. But everyone seems to be enjoying themselves—oh! Did you see Edesa and her family? Over there—the Wizard of Oz gang. But they're only here for half a minute—they've got a teen group party going tonight up at SouledOut. Otherwise Ramona would've come, too."

"Yeah, I know. Thanks. Nice to meet you, Leroy." And Orphan Annie scooted away, threading herself through the crowd toward the Baxters.

Estelle saw Harry come through the double doors, and a few moments later saw him and Gabby talking briefly. He came their way, gave Estelle an approving once-over and murmured in her ear, "You look beautiful tonight, 'Miss Della Reese.'" He always did like it when she wore her hair down. Then he grabbed a cup of hot cider and said, "The Firecracker just wants me to mingle and keep my eyes and ears open. Should've brought Corky—ha. Anyway, you two have fun." He moved off.

Both shelter residents and staff had gone all out dressing up. Some people—mostly board members or outside guests—came in rented or store-bought costumes. Mabel Turner, the shelter director, came dressed in a colorful African dress and head wrap, similar to ones Estelle had at home. Why didn't she think of that?

But the shelter residents had obviously gotten creative with what little they had. Funny hats, mismatched clothes, and outlandish makeup were the most common, but there was also a princess with a glitter-decorated paper crown wearing an old-fashioned prom dress, and a western "dudette" with cowboy boots, jeans, and leather vest, wearing a clothesline "lariat" looped over one shoulder. But Estelle thought the person who dressed in rags and pulled a wire cart around stuffed with who-knows-what, shaking a Big Gulp paper cup and begging for change from other partygoers, was a bit gauche—like a bad reality show.

Chairs and couches had been moved out of the way, and soon the dancing began. Estelle was surprised that Leroy really got into it, his black silk cape swirling this way and that. Several of the shelter residents flirted and even danced with him—sort of, since it was all pretty much individual, do-your-own-thing. Estelle watched from the sidelines this time, remembering the party four or five years ago when she'd first met Harry and they'd danced the Macarena.

She waded into the dancers at one point to tell two of the residents who were grinding and bumping in a vulgar way to cool it *now* or get off the dance floor. One of them—a hefty white girl with a bit too much skin and cleavage showing—got in Estelle's face, hands on hips, a snarl on her painted lips. "Who you think you are, lady? I ain't no kid. You ain't gonna be tellin' me what I can't do."

Estelle glared right back. "We've got rules here, sister—and yes, I can tell you what you can and can't do. And if you don't listen, you can move right on out of this shelter tonight!" Which, Estelle hoped, was true. Sarge had kicked out mouthy residents for less. Mabel Turner too.

The woman—must be a recent addition to the shelter's roster because Estelle didn't know her name—flounced out of the room and up the stairs to the bunkrooms.

As she returned to the sidelines, Estelle heard Harry's voice in her ear. "You tell 'er, babe. With you around, why did the Firecracker think she needed me?" He moved away, chuckling to himself.

The music stopped and Gabby got up on a chair to announce a costume parade—with prizes! Everybody clapped and hooted as the first category—the staff and volunteers—paraded in front of the wall mural that designated the "front" of the big room. Estelle made herself invisible behind Leroy's black silk cape—no way was she going to parade herself as Della Reese. What had she been thinking! Too bad the "Baby Baxters," as Precious liked to call them, had had to go to the other party. Their Wizard of Oz quartet would have won hands down. As it was, Gabby tried to disqualify herself, but her Orphan Annie costume won anyway by the loudest clapping and cheering. Everybody laughed when her face turned almost as red as her hair when Mabel handed her a Starbucks card.

As the next category was being announced, someone said, "Hey, Miss Estelle. Where's Ramona?" Estelle turned. Behind the eye mask of the black cat she recognized Piper, who'd been taking her Thursday cooking class. "Somebody was asking if she was here. I thought maybe I'd see her in the staff and volunteer parade, but I didn't see her."

"Oh, she had to help with a teen group party at our church, Piper. But I'll tell Ramona she was missed."

"Oh. Okay, thanks—oh, I gotta get in the residents parade!" And the cat ran off.

The western "dudette" won the next Starbucks card when the shelter residents paraded, which puzzled Estelle at first . . . until she saw the forty-something woman shake out the "lariat" and twirl it in a perfect circle, up, down, and around. Now that woman must have a story—had she once been a rodeo trick rider or something back in the day? A lot of these homeless women had surprising stories—

Wait. What did Piper mean, Somebody was asking if Ramona was here? Estelle tried to quiet the alarm bells suddenly ringing in her head. Probably just another one of the residents—she'd become fairly popular with the women in the cooking class especially. But it wouldn't hurt to ask Piper who'd been asking.

"Now for our guest parade!" Gabby announced from her perch on the chair.

"Ma!" Leroy tugged on her sleeve. "Should I—?"

"Yes, yes, go on, son," Estelle said, half distracted. Now where was Piper? Her head swiveled from side to side . . . there, back at the refreshment table, which was being replenished with plates of cookies, chips and dips, veggie and fruit trays. "Piper!" she called and hustled to the black cat's side. "Uh, who did you say was asking if Ramona was here?"

Piper shrugged. "Some guy. Didn't recognize him 'cause he had one of those clown wigs on, you know, all different neon colors, and a plastic eye mask. But otherwise, just regular clothes I think. Do you know him?"

Some guy . . . clown wig . . . The alarm bells were sounding louder now. Why would a *guy* be asking about Ramona? Estelle thought she'd seen someone with such a wig across the room at one point, but hadn't paid much attention.

"Piper! What did you say to this guy?"

"I just said I hadn't seen her, wasn't sure if she was here or not—"

Estelle didn't hear the rest. Harry! Where was Harry? She had to tell him to look for a guy with a clown wig. *O Lord, if it's Max,*

197

now he knows Ramona is known to people here at the shelter, which means he might keep looking for her here. It wasn't Piper's fault. Only the staff had been told they were taking precautions when Ramona was here—keeping her work on the lower level, alerting Angela Kwon, the receptionist, to be extra diligent about who she buzzed in on the days when Ramona came to volunteer. One problem: the automatic door lock wasn't working at the moment. But even if it were, people had been coming in and out all evening for the party. It'd be so easy for Max to slip in—

She heard clapping and cheering and saw Batman raising his hands like a boxer who'd just won a fight. "Ma! Ma!" Leroy yelled across the room. "I won the costume parade!" Both residents and staff were shaking his gloved hand or giving him high fives—including Harry.

She made a beeline for her husband. "Harry!" she hissed. "Some guy in a clown wig was asking if Ramona is here. What if it's Max? Who else—?"

Harry's swore under his breath. "Saw the clown wig just a few minutes ago. Wondered why whoever it was didn't join the costume parade. But . . ." He scanned the room quickly. "I don't see him now. Go tell Sarge to be on the alert. I'm going to check the lower level. Call my cell if you see him."

Estelle made her way to the foyer where Sarge was still on door-duty, though the flow of people had stopped and she'd snagged a chair. Estelle started to tell her to alert Harry ASAP if she saw a guy in a clown wig leaving, when Sarge popped out of her chair, all five-feet-four of her. "Clown wig you say? Plastic eye mask?"

Estelle nodded.

Sarge jerked a thumb at the door. "Guy wearing a clown wig just left, not two minutes ago." The ex-Marine sergeant quickly pushed open the door and stood out on the steps, Estelle right behind her. The narrow street in the Wrigley North neighborhood was quiet, the streetlights dim. No cars, no pedestrians. Lights from the Laundromat next door spilled out onto the sidewalk and Sarge hustled down the steps and cased the inside of the coin-operated laundry, but came back shaking her head. "Don't see him now. What's the problem?"

Estelle briefly brought her up to date as they went back inside. Frankly, she didn't know if she was upset or relieved that the "clown" got away.

"Man! Wish I'd known," Sarge growled. "Guy just nodded at me and said, 'Nice party. Hate to leave.' So I said, 'Good-night.' Shoulda asked who he was here with."

Estelle pulled out her cell phone. "Not your fault, Sarge. But I gotta tell Harry."

Harry, Estelle, Gabby, and Mabel Turner huddled in Mabel's office. Sarge was still out in the foyer, shepherding the last of the guests out into the night as the staff and residents cleaned up the multipurpose room.

"But you don't know for sure it was Max," Mabel said, half statement, half question.

"Pretty darn sure it was," Harry shot back. He could hardly stand still he was so mad.

Estelle nodded. "What other male would be asking around if Ramona came tonight? The only people Ramona comes in contact with here are the female residents and some of the staff."

"Well, thank God Ramona wasn't here," Gabby said. "At least he didn't find her."

Harry stopped pacing. "Sure. Tonight. Problem is, if the clown wig *was* Max, now he knows Ramona comes here often enough so that people like Piper know her. Which means if he's trying to get to her, to threaten or silence her so she can't testify against him at trial, he'll be on the lookout. This is the closest clue he has where to find her."

Silence settled on the little group as they all looked from one to the other. Finally Mabel cleared her throat. "Which means . . . maybe Ramona shouldn't come to volunteer here anymore." The shelter director eyed Estelle and Harry. "You two want to be the ones to tell her?"

Chapter 29

Ramona rode with the Bentleys and Leroy to church the next morning, but neither Harry nor Estelle said anything about what had happened at Manna House last night as the girl burbled excitedly about how much fun they'd had at the teen group party. Grace had helped her dress as a Mexican folk dancer, and some of the teens had begged her to do the Mexican hat dance. "But I didn't have a partner," Ramona giggled. "Can't do a courting dance with only one person."

DaShawn, they learned from Edesa after church, had come as Michael Jackson. "He even did a moonwalk," she said, laughing, "while lip-syncing to, uh, 'Beat It,' I think it was. But your grandson was the hit of the party."

"Oh brother," Harry muttered. Estelle knew what he was thinking. Where did DaShawn get the *bling* to dress up as Michael Jackson?

Estelle drove Leroy back to the Lighthouse after lunch, even though he didn't actually have to be back until six. But as she accompanied him inside and signed him in, he said, "Thanks for takin' me to the party, Ma. It was fun. You tell DaShawn hi for me, okay? Uh, will he be there when I come see you again?"

"When I come see you again . . ." Estelle chose her words carefully. "I'll see you in a couple weeks, okay? And then, maybe you can come for Thanksgiving. I'm sure DaShawn will be there then."

"Yeah. I'd like that." Leroy gave her a hug and disappeared through a door.

It had been a good weekend with Leroy, Estelle mused as she drove home. He seemed to be doing very well. Maybe now was a good time to ask Bridges Family Services if he could apply for the group home they wanted to establish. She'd call them this week.

But as she drove up Beecham Street and passed Grace Meredith's brick bungalow in order to turn around in the cul-de-sac, her heart sank a little. They couldn't avoid it—she and Harry had to go talk to Grace and Ramona today and tell them it wasn't safe for Ramona to continue volunteering at Manna House.

❖   ❖   ❖   ❖

The drive to Manna House that week felt oddly cheerless without Ramona's bouncy chatter—sort of like the weather, which had suddenly turned chilly and cloudy. Typical November weather. At the shelter, Estelle was bombarded left and right by residents and staff alike: "Where's Ramona?" And when she made a lame excuse about a conflict that made it impossible for the girl to volunteer anymore, people whined, "But we didn't even get to say good-bye!"

And Tuesday night at prayer—just Estelle, Michelle, and Grace that week—Grace lowered her voice and indicated that Ramona was holed up in her room, sulking. "I really need to find something else for her to do! It's not going to work having her moping around the house 24/7." On top of which, Grace said, she had a four-day concert trip to Denver coming up at the end of next week. "I can't take her with me this time—Sam and I are taking the train. She'll need someplace to stay."

Which probably meant their house, Estelle thought. But she didn't promise anything. That would be their next weekend to visit Leroy, and she'd promised Harry she'd try not to schedule so many things all at once on the weekends.

But coming home from work late Thursday afternoon, something seemed . . . different as she turned into Beecham Street. And then she did a double-take. The For Sale sign in front of the Alvarezes' house had a bright red sign with white letters sitting on top: SOLD.

Sold? Oh, no! Who bought it? She was tempted to pop right over to the Alvarezes' and ask. But after parking the RAV4 in front of her house, she pulled out her cell phone while still in the car and called Michelle Jasper's work number. Michelle might know something . . . or not. But if Bridges was still on the fence about pursuing this two-flat, they needed to know it was off the market now.

"Michelle? Estelle here. I just got home from work and guess what. There's a Sold sign now in front of the Alvarezes' two-flat."

"I know. I was going to call you—"

"What do you mean you know? It wasn't there this morning when I left for work, and you leave before I do."

"I mean I just got out of a staff meeting where Charlotte announced that Bridges signed a deal with the Alvarezes yesterday for the group home."

Estelle stared out her windshield at the two-flat down the street, phone clamped against her ear. "They . . . what?"

"Bridges signed a deal with the Alvarezes yesterday." Michelle's voice had laughter in it. "I just found out myself."

"But . . . last I heard your boss was having second thoughts about pursuing it because of the strong objections at that neighborhood meeting two weekends ago."

"Go figure. Charlotte just said there'd been more interaction with the neighbors, and the purchase seemed feasible now."

Estelle felt her heart beat a little faster. "What neighbors? I mean . . . the Singers? Or the Horowitzes?" Or even Karl Molander—though it was hard to take the old guy seriously.

Now Michelle did chuckle. "She didn't say. Just said the major objections had been withdrawn."

Estelle blew out a long breath. "Lord have mercy. It had to be Nicole. She didn't come to prayer Tuesday night, so I haven't seen her since she helped Leroy with his Batman costume last weekend . . . oh."

Leroy. Had spending time with Leroy last Saturday had something to do with Nicole's change of heart? If it was Nicole . . .

Estelle hardly knew what to do after she hung up. She just sat in the car for several minutes, her mind racing. What did this mean? It meant the Alvarezes could move now. It meant a group home was going to move into their two-flat—but how soon? It meant—

O good Lord. Hallelujah! She quickly redialed Michelle's work number.

When her friend answered, Estelle blurted, "Michelle! What do I need to do to get Leroy signed up as a client with Bridges and on the list for that group home?"

✧ ✧ ✧ ✧

A large truck drove onto Beecham Street early Saturday morning and unloaded a pod along the curb in front of the Alvarezes' two-flat and then left. Soon after, Mr. Alvarez and a couple of other Hispanic men started carrying furniture and boxes out to the pod.

Estelle watched curiously from the bay windows at the front of their apartment. The Alvarezes weren't wasting any time moving now that they had a buyer. Though they'd probably been packing for weeks, since they'd said they wanted to move as quickly as possible. She was happy for them—but hadn't ever considered how people moved their stuff all the way to Guatemala. What were they going to do with that pod?

Harry wandered to the window in sweats, holding his first cup of coffee. "Looks like they plan to ship their stuff," he said. "That's usually what they do with those pods. I wondered if they'd sell it or store it. Guess they figure it's worth it to ship it there rather than having to replace everything."

Estelle heaved a sigh. "Doesn't feel right that they're moving and none of us neighbors are helping. Maybe we should wake up DaShawn and all go over there and help out."

Harry raised an eyebrow. "Hon, not everyone wants to have a bunch of strangers come over uninvited and start handling their stuff. It's not like we actually got to know them"—he raised his hands in self-defense as she opened her mouth—"I know, I know. It would've been great if we'd gotten to know them better. But, Estelle, we've only been in this neighborhood six months ourselves." He leaned in and kissed her on the cheek. "You don't have to be the mother of the world, my sweet."

Estelle pressed her lips together as her husband wandered back toward the kitchen. A moment later she heard him whistle for Corky and then the back door slammed.

Hmph. Mother of the world, indeed.

Still. It didn't feel right for the Alvarezes to just move out without doing *anything*. Food. That's what she'd do. She'd make a big pot of chili or something and take it over. The high today was only going to hit the mid-forties—something hot would be nice.

✧ ✧ ✧ ✧

The Alvarezes and their helpers seemed to appreciate the pot of chili she brought over, along with paper bowls and plastic spoons and a jug of lemonade. When Estelle returned to pick up the chili pot, Mrs. Alvarez gave her a woven table runner in bright blues and yellows. At first she protested, but the beaming woman said, "*Sí, sí,* you take!" The woman said more in Spanish that Estelle didn't comprehend, but realized it would be ungrateful to refuse. On impulse she gave the Guatemalan woman a hug and got a hug back. "*Adiós, mi amiga,*" Mrs. Alvarez said.

For some reason, Estelle felt like crying.

Sunday there was no sign of anyone coming or going all day— just the pod still sitting in the street. And when Estelle got home from work on Monday, the pod was gone. The truck must've returned and picked it up. The Alvarezes were gone.

When Estelle left for work on Tuesday, a construction crew was already at work inside the house. Obviously Bridges wasn't wasting any time preparing the two-flat for its new group home. She wondered what Greg and Nicole thought of all the work going on next door, but she still hadn't talked to Nicole. Everything seemed to be happening so fast.

Unlike the previous week, which had sent a few nighttime temperatures below freezing, the sun came out and temperatures hiked back up into the high sixties. Pleasant Indian summer. Estelle still felt badly about Ramona not being able to come with her to Manna House each day, but at prayer Tuesday night Grace said that Edesa Baxter had called on Sunday afternoon and offered to host Ramona for the four-day weekend she'd be away. "Ramona must've told her about my upcoming concerts in Denver. Edesa said she'd love to have a mother's helper and Ramona was so good with Gracie and Julian—said she'd pick her up tomorrow night. I leave early Thursday, so that's perfect. Ramona's happy about going to the Baxters, for which

I'm grateful. But she's still spending a lot of time holed up in her bedroom." Grace tipped her head toward the guest room down the hall, from where the little group in the living room could hear music from a Spanish station seeping through the door. "I think hearing that Max showed up at the masquerade party at the shelter really spooked her."

It had spooked Estelle too. "We still haven't heard a date for Max's trial, even though Harry asked. We need to pray that it happens soon."

Nicole came late to the prayer time—but she came. "Sorry, ladies. Greg had to work late again, so I couldn't leave till he got home. But he's giving the kids baths and putting them to bed. That's pretty new for my macho husband—but he seems to like it." She grinned a little. "Me too."

No use beating around the bush about the SOLD sign on the building next to the Singers. "Uh, Nicole, are you okay? You probably know that Bridges Family Services bought the Alvarezes' two-flat," Estelle ventured. "You felt so strongly about it . . ."

Nicole nodded soberly. "I know. Still feel nervous about the whole thing. But, well, spending time with your son that day, helping make a costume for him . . ." Her eyes teared a little. "I don't know. The way he played Uno with my kids . . . I thought about what you said to me that time you came to my house, how a group home would be a great place for him rather than a large institution."

Estelle felt a little teary herself.

"That didn't really sink in until I met him in person. I prayed about it all weekend, fighting with my fears . . ." Nicole grimaced. "But a couple days later I called Bridges and told Ms. Bergman I'd overreacted that day at the neighborhood meeting. She was really decent, told me they would do everything possible to vet the, um, residents for the group home and not assign anyone who might be a danger to themselves or others. And she told me if I had any questions or concerns at all to call her personally." The young mom gave a nervous laugh. "Which I might do more often than she thinks. I still get cold feet—but I think it's the right thing. God gave me some peace about it. Mostly."

Shaking their heads and sharing some tears, the prayer time that evening seemed especially sweet.

Estelle smiled big the next morning as she passed the rehabbing going on in the two-flat across the street. God was working things out, even bringing some healing to her neighbors and restoring the peace. "Thank You, *Jesus!*" she sang out loud. "I feel good!"

Chapter 30

A FEELING THAT DIDN'T LAST LONG . . .
The rehabbing of the two-flat across the street continued all week, starting at seven in the morning, walls being torn out, hammers pounding, machines grinding. Which made Estelle wonder how long *that* was going to go on, though she guessed she could live through it, since at least she and most of the neighbors went to work during the day and the construction crew usually knocked off by five.

Grace left for Denver on Thursday—which happened to be Veterans' Day—and Ramona was picked up by Josh Baxter for the long weekend. DaShawn had no school that Thursday because of the holiday, or Friday either, which was parent-teacher conferences and report card pickup at Stone Academy, giving the kids a four-day weekend. Estelle wasn't too excited about having their grandson underfoot for four days in a row, but the weather stayed mild and mostly sunny, so DaShawn and the Jasper twins spent a lot of time out in the alley behind the Bentleys' graystone playing basketball or bouncing back and forth between the two houses—though Michelle mentioned that Nicole had hired Tabby to babysit for Nathan and Becky for several hours on Thursday and Friday so she could do some work from home for her law firm.

Nice. Estelle wished DaShawn could get some odd jobs like that. What did young boys do these days to earn spending money—mow lawns? Walk dogs? A lot of working people hired a lawn service like Farid Jalili's. And she knew Harry, for one, wasn't about to hire someone else to walk *his* dog.

On Friday afternoon, Michelle picked up Estelle and they drove together to Stone Academy for their parent-teacher conferences—but Estelle had no sooner sat down across the desk from DaShawn's homeroom teacher than she heard the schoolroom door open and someone flopped down into the chair beside her. Estelle stared, speechless. DaShawn's mother sat next to her big as life, dressed in a short red skirt, a low-cut white top, and black high-heeled boots, her big hair dyed blonde, and smacking gum.

"I'm Donita Stevens, DaShawn's *mother*," she informed the teacher. "I'm here for th' parent-teacher meetin'. She"—Donita refused to look at Estelle—"can leave."

The teacher seemed momentarily flummoxed, looking back and forth between Estelle and Donita. Then she quickly gathered her wits. "You're welcome to sit in on our conference, Ms. Stevens. But since our records indicate that Mr. and Mrs. Bentley are DaShawn's custodial guardians, my meeting is with Mrs. Bentley."

Donita rolled her eyes. "Huh. She ain't even DaShawn's *real* grandma." But she half-turned her back to Estelle and let the teacher get on with it. At the end, when the homeroom teacher deliberately handed DaShawn's report card to Estelle, Donita got up and flounced out of the room.

Michelle was slack-jawed when Estelle told her what happened. "I think that earns you a caramel macchiato," she said, pulling into a Starbucks parking lot on the way home. They spent half an hour comparing notes about the three kids, all of whom seemed to be doing pretty well, considering. "Can you believe Jared and I have to go through all this *again* for twelve years once this little rug rat comes along?" Michelle moaned, pointing at her expanding stomach and slurping her macchiato noisily.

So it was almost suppertime when Michelle dropped her off. Estelle was trying to decide what to make for supper to celebrate DaShawn's report card, which was all solid Bs except for an A- in Science and a C+ in Language Arts, so she almost didn't notice her next-door neighbor standing next to his lawn service truck, scowling angrily at a piece of paper in his hand.

"Farid?" She approached tentatively. "Are you all right? Is something wrong?" Her Iranian neighbor didn't say anything, just handed the piece of paper to her and then banged a fist on the hood of his truck. Estelle read the note, which was written in a bold script with a thin-tipped black marker.

Mr. Jalili.

I am waiting for the $200 you owe me for the bushes you ruined with your truck last winter. If I don't receive payment by the end of the month, I will be forced to take you to small claims court.

Isaac Horowitz

❖ ❖ ❖ ❖

Estelle stewed about the note on Farid's truck all weekend. What was wrong with the man, anyway! Harry didn't say much when she told him about it, but he, too, seemed disgusted. If anyone owed Isaac Horowitz for his damaged bushes, it was Mattie Krakowski. The whole incident with Farid's snowplow had been an emergency on the old woman's behalf—but Estelle couldn't see even Isaac Horowitz hitting up Mattie for the money.

And good grief, it was November! Not exactly the right time to be planting new bushes. The whole thing didn't make sense.

But soon the problem between Farid and Isaac got overshadowed by complications closer to home . . . Thanksgiving weekend. Their anniversary was the day after the holiday this year, but as Estelle studied the kitchen calendar, she thought maybe she and Harry could go out to dinner or something another time since she'd pretty much promised Leroy he could come again that weekend. Harry shrugged and said, "Whatever," so on their visit to Leroy at the Lighthouse on Saturday, Estelle invited him to come spend Thanksgiving with them. In fact, Estelle realized she was looking forward to it—just the four of them, she and Harry, Leroy and DaShawn. Her three favorite men . . . now that'd be worth cooking up a storm.

But that was before the message from Rodney on the house phone when they got home, asking if DaShawn could come spend Thanksgiving weekend with him and Donita. "It'd mean a lot to us, Dad," Rodney's voice crackled on the answering machine. "Haven't had Thanksgiving dinner together in . . . well, a long time."

"Absolutely not!" Harry exploded to Estelle. "DaShawn lives with us and Thanksgiving is . . . is family time. He stays here."

Estelle was relieved. She'd promised Leroy that DaShawn would be here.

But when DaShawn heard about it, he said, "Why don't we all have Thanksgiving together? My parents could come here, and then I could go spend the rest of the weekend with them. I'd kinda like my whole family to be together, instead of having *two* Thanksgiving dinners."

Harry was shaking his head. "I don't think—"

"What your grandpa's trying to say is—"

DaShawn held up his hands. "Okay, *okay*. I get it. You don't like my mom. But she and Dad are trying. She's been pretty decent when I've been there the last couple times. I really think she's gonna stay clean this time." The boy's face hardened a little. "Seems like you could try a little, too, Gramps." With that, DaShawn disappeared into his room and shut the door, harder than necessary.

Harry ran a hand over his shaved head and looked helplessly at Estelle. "I dunno, babe. I swore that woman would never come under my roof. Ever! Don't know which is worse—letting DaShawn go have Thanksgiving with them, or having them here for Thanksgiving dinner. I mean, if it was just Rodney . . ."

Estelle sighed. Her sentiments exactly. After her run-in with Donita at the parent-teacher conference, she couldn't think of anything more disagreeable than trying to have Thanksgiving dinner together with the woman.

But then there was DaShawn.

O Lord, what do You want us to do?

✧　✧　✧　✧

Estelle could tell Harry was struggling all through the worship service at SouledOut the next morning, but she wasn't totally surprised when he told her he thought they ought to call Rodney back that afternoon and suggest that he and Donita join them here for Thanksgiving, and then DaShawn could go home with them for a few days. She knew he'd do anything for DaShawn, and if that meant "trying harder," then he was going to man up and gut out Thanksgiving dinner with Donita. Just like she'd been willing to give up celebrating their anniversary in order to invite Leroy for—

Wait a minute. She looked at the calendar again. Why not?

Estelle made a fresh pot of coffee and brought Harry a steaming cup to where he was slumped on the living room couch flipping channels with the remote. She gently traded the coffee mug for the remote and turned off the TV, then sat on the padded arm of the couch. "Harry, hon, maybe there's an upside to this. I'd pretty much given up doing anything on our anniversary if Leroy and DaShawn were going to be here all weekend. But if DaShawn is going to his dad's for the rest of the weekend, we could take Leroy home Thursday evening and get away somewhere for a few days—just you and me." She stroked the trim beard that circled his mouth and chin. "Mmm, what do you think?"

Harry looked up at her. "Go away somewhere? Just you and me?" A slow grin widened his cheeks. "How about Mexico . . . or Jamaica . . . or—"

"Oh, you." She backhanded his shoulder. "We need more than three days to go that far. But yes, go away." She got up from the arm of the couch. "I'll find a romantic place to go, and *you* make sure you can get the time off."

Settling down at the dining room table, she booted up the computer, and by bedtime that evening, she'd locked in a bed-and-breakfast suite at a charming country inn for three days and two nights just a couple hours south of the city. Wait till she told Harry about the Jacuzzi for two and the in-room fireplace.

✧   ✧   ✧   ✧

"It cost how much?!" Harry was incredulous when he saw the printout receipt.

Estelle snatched the paper back. "It's our fifth anniversary," she sniffed. "Happens to fall on a holiday weekend with holiday prices. Besides, we never did have a real honeymoon. It's high time." Now that they'd decided to go, she wasn't going to let a little thing like the cost derail their plans.

She got nervous though when he came home Monday evening saying Captain Gilson had just assigned him to another undercover assignment that week on the Texas Eagle, and he and Corky would be gone for a few days. "Okay. But you tell that Captain Gilson of yours that *next* week you want the whole Thanksgiving weekend off. Tell him it's our anniversary—no, tell him it's our belated honeymoon, and he'll answer to *me* if he tries to ruin it."

On the upside, she had good news. "Charlotte Bergman called and said to bring Leroy in for an interview if we'd like him to be evaluated as a client at Bridges."

Harry was packing his train bag for the next day. "You sure about this, Estelle? What if he's not a candidate for the group home? If he switches from the Lighthouse to Bridges Family Services, but doesn't get assigned to a group home . . . what then?"

She pursed her lips. Good question. But in order to get assigned to the group home, he had to be one of their clients. It felt like a catch-22. "Well, it won't hurt to have the interview."

But to her surprise, when she called Leroy to ask when he could do the interview, he got all huffy. "Ma! What'd you go do that for? I . . . I got my social worker here, and she's tryin' to get me a job."

"Well, I know that, baby. But I thought you wanted to, uh, live in a smaller setting—not a place as big as the Lighthouse. Bridges might be able to place you in a group home that's closer to us." She regretted mentioning that possibility as soon as she said it.

Leroy was quiet for a long moment. "So you sayin' I might be able to live in a group home close to you an' Harry?"

"It's . . . it's just a possibility, Leroy. A maybe. But we'd have to do the interview first."

Another long silence. "I don't know, Ma. I gotta think about it." Another pause. "Brenda came back. Forgot to tell you. We're really good friends."

Estelle racked her brain. Brenda? Brenda who? And then she vaguely remembered. A girl at the Lighthouse Leroy had been kind of sweet on, but she'd had to leave over something or other. So Brenda was back. "Look, honey, you think about it. It won't hurt to have the interview. I'll call you in a day or two and we can plan a time."

She told herself he just needed time to think about it. Change wasn't easy for him, but after all, this whole idea came about because Leroy said he didn't like living in an institution and he missed her cooking.

In spite of Harry being gone, the week seemed to pick up speed. The weather seesawed from a high in the low fifties down into the thirties and back up again. A light rain one day broke the dry spell, and one night there was even frost on the ground. Typical mid-November weather. The rehab work on the new group home continued—painters, electricians, and tuck-pointers swarmed the place. Grace got back from her trip to Denver and gave a good report at their prayer time on Tuesday night. Even Ramona seemed in better spirits after her weekend being a "mother's helper" at the Baxters', and sat in on the prayer meeting. "I like kids," she said. "I helped Gracie with her numbers and she can even read a few words. She's really bright. Thinking I might wanna be a schoolteacher someday."

Nicole lit up. "Would you be interested in spending some time with Becky and Nathan after school or on weekends a few times a week? I've got some homeschool projects I'd like them to do, even though they're going to public school now, but I just haven't had the time."

Ramona and Grace exchanged delighted glances. Estelle had to smile. Guess you could take a homeschooler out of the home, but you couldn't take home school out of a homeschooler. She breathed a little thank-you prayer. God was working things out.

Harry got home Friday night, bushed from his nights on the train. He seemed dispirited. "Didn't get our man. Bad intel. Not only that . . ." He pulled out of his bag a *Chicago Tribune*, which was folded open to page three. "Did you see this?" He thumped one of the articles on the open page. "Read it."

The headline read, WAS SNITCH SKUNKED? She skimmed the article. A documented member of the Vice Lords in Chicago who had turned state's evidence against one of the known leaders of the gang heavily involved in the drug trade had died the day before the trial in a one-car accident. According to a police source, the "accident" looked suspicious and was being investigated. She looked up at Harry.

"We better hope and pray," he said tersely, "that Ramona doesn't hear about this."

Chapter 31

According to a phone call from Grace, Nicole Singer had talked to Ramona about maybe helping her kids do extra-credit projects after school a couple of times a week. ". . . but she said it'd have to wait until after Thanksgiving since Tuesday is also her birthday," Grace said, "so I'm guessing she won't be at prayer. But I'm already wondering, since it *is* Thanksgiving this week . . . do you think we ought to cancel?"

As far as Estelle was concerned, she'd as soon go ahead with their weekly prayer time, but both Grace and Michelle seemed to think it was a good idea to cancel given extra holiday preparations and family visits. Grace said she and Ramona had been invited to her brother Mark's for Thanksgiving Day, and her folks were coming up from Indianapolis "to talk wedding plans." The Jaspers were joining Jared's family on the South Side, much to Michelle's relief. "I know I've still got a couple more months to go," she told Estelle, "but I feel like I could drop this baby anytime now. No way am I gonna cook for all the Jaspers this year." And Estelle's birthday call to Nicole on Tuesday revealed the Singers' plan to spend Thanksgiving Day with Nicole's mom.

Good. Looked like everyone in the prayer group had plans for the holiday.

Harry seemed concerned that the *Sun Times* and *Chicago Tribune* both had stories every day that week about the ongoing investigation into the suspicious death of the key witness in the trial of the Vice Lord gang leader. He asked Estelle if Grace got a newspaper delivered, but she couldn't remember one way or the other.

Besides, she had other things on her mind. To her relief, she was able to set up an interview for Leroy on Wednesday afternoon, so after lunch cleanup at Manna House she drove to the South Side, picked up Leroy and his overnight bag, and drove him to Bridges Family Services.

Charlotte Bergman was professional and courteous as she conducted the interview with Leroy. Estelle decided she needed to be honest about why they were considering a change from the Lighthouse, and told Charlotte they were hoping Leroy could be considered a possible candidate for Bridges' new group home.

The director looked at Leroy. "Is that what you want, Leroy?"

Leroy hesitated. "Yeah, I guess. I mean, yeah, I think so. But I'm going to get a job, you know. And Brenda lives at the Lighthouse. Brenda's my friend."

"I see." Ms. Bergman tapped her pencil. "I appreciate your candor, both of you. But I have to be honest with you as well. We already have vetted our four initial residents for the group home on Beecham Street—"

Estelle stiffened. The air in the room suddenly felt as if it had been sucked out.

"—but we are hoping to establish a second group home sometime in the coming year. If you're interested in completing the application process, we can do a second interview in the next few weeks and put Leroy's name on the list for the other group home."

Estelle could hardly speak as they left the offices at Bridges Family Services. She'd been so sure God had brought everything together for Bridges to buy the two-flat in their neighborhood as an answer to her prayers for Leroy! Why was God jerking them around? "Well," she said finally as she and Leroy drove toward home, "we might as well finish the process. Who knows, one of the residents might drop out and there would be an opening."

✧　✧　✧　✧

The neighborhood was strangely quiet when Estelle awoke Thursday morning. At first something seemed wrong . . . but when she tiptoed past Leroy, still asleep on the couch, and peeked out the front windows, she realized that construction work at the two-flat had stopped for the holiday.

Well. *That* was something to be thankful for on Thanksgiving Day.

Harry and DaShawn were sleeping in, too, so Estelle let Corky out into the backyard—going down the outside steps to make sure the side and back gates were closed and locked—and then put the turkey in for its slow roast. Rodney and Donita were supposed to arrive about one o'clock, so she had the morning to prepare the rest of the dinner: a ham, mac 'n' cheese, cornbread and sausage stuffing, and collard greens. She'd made the sweet potato pie and an apple crumb pie last night. What else did they need? Hot rolls, cranberry sauce, pickles and olives . . .

As Estelle cooked, she prayed. *Lord, I don't know what You're doin', but I gotta admit I'm mighty disappointed that Leroy didn't get on the list for the new group home. I want to trust You, Lord, but I'll just be honest and say I don't understand.* She added smoked ham hocks to the pot of simmering collard greens, then poured the dry macaroni into the other pot of boiling water and set a timer. *And today, we need some of Your special grace. Harry and I don't care for Donita, and she doesn't especially like us either. But for DaShawn's sake—and Leroy's too—fill this house today with a peace beyond our own understanding.*

Her men folks got out of bed one by one and went through two pots of coffee, then settled down in front of the TV to watch the McDonald's Thanksgiving Day parade downtown, flipping back and forth to the pregame show for the Saints/Cowboys football game. Well, she'd put them to work closer to mealtime with last-minute stuff. Would Donita bring anything? Probably not. Rodney hadn't mentioned anything. Oh well. Thanksgiving was family day, and like it or not, this was their family.

At noon Estelle heard the doorbell ring. What? Had Rodney and Donita come early? She wasn't ready! She wasn't dressed, hadn't done her hair, put on her face, anything. Then she heard Mattie and a male voice down in the foyer and realized it was Mattie Krakowski's son picking her up. Well, praise Jesus. She'd been so distracted by their own plans, she hadn't given a single thought to whether the old woman had any place to go for Thanksgiving. But as Mattie drove off with her son, Estelle wondered whether

Karl and Eva Molander next door had family in the area to spend Thanksgiving with or if they'd eat alone. Should she—?

No, no. She knew what Harry would say. *"You're not the mother of the world, Estelle! You don't need to take care of everybody."* And frankly, a dinner mix with Karl Molander *and* Donita *and* Leroy had so many disastrous possibilities, she was sure it wasn't a good idea.

By the time Rodney and Donita did show up—only half an hour late—Estelle had donned her blue and silver caftan with its matching head wrap, done her lips and cheeks with Bronze Glow Glaze, and had shanghaied all three couch potatoes to take out the trash, set the table, and wash up the pots and pans. Rodney looked as handsome as she'd ever seen him in black slacks, purple shirt, and gray sport coat. "Hey, Miss Estelle," he said and gave her a kiss on the cheek. Donita was dressed up in a gray-and-white striped two-piece suit that showed a lot of leg between the hem of the mid-thigh short skirt and her four-inch white sling-back heels. But she handed Estelle a bouquet of fall-colored mums. "'Preciate y'all invitin' us to Thanksgiving dinner. God, I hate ta cook!"

Estelle pasted a smile on her face and decided flowers covered the sins of a too-short skirt and taking the Lord's name in vain. "Glad you could come. You can put your coats in our bedroom, and then make yourselves at home in the living room—got some chips and dip and veggies on the coffee table."

But she felt like slapping the woman's face a few moments later when she overheard Donita mutter to Rodney, "Who's the retard hangin' out with DaShawn out there?"

Estelle banged a few pots. *Argh! Lord, You gotta help me here!*

When the pair came out of the bedroom, she said brightly, "Did you meet my son, Leroy, when you came in?" emphasizing the word *son.* "He and DaShawn are great friends. Made DaShawn a hand-tooled leather belt for his birthday. You should ask DaShawn to show it to you."

She saw Rodney shoot Donita an irritated look, then he hung back till he was alone with Estelle in the kitchen. "Sorry about that, Miz Estelle. I didn't know Leroy was comin', should've prepped Donita a little."

Estelle nodded, not trusting herself to do more than that.

But once she'd called everyone to the table, she could tell Donita was trying to be on her best behavior. Or maybe Rodney had told her to just shut up and eat, because the woman said next to nothing during the whole meal except, "Pass them greens please," or "Got anymore gravy for the stuffin'?" Harry was pretty tight-lipped too . . . but after a while, he loosened up and got into an animated argument with DaShawn and Rodney about whether the Chicago Bears would make it to the playoffs this year.

"They're seven to three so far, Pops," Rodney said. "They even beat Green Bay."

"Yeah, Gramps. The Miami Dolphins didn't get even one touchdown last week—and they were playin' in Miami!" DaShawn crowed.

"Uh-huh, but they lost three games last month . . . Pass that turkey, will ya?" Harry reloaded his plate. "I'm not holdin' my breath."

Estelle let the sports talk ride. Pretty safe topics. Leroy basically paid attention to his plate.

Meal over, Estelle asked everyone to please take their plates to the kitchen, creating a momentary gridlock around the sink area. But when they all wandered back to the living room to watch the New Orleans Saints play the Dallas Cowboys, she stayed in the kitchen to put leftovers away, grateful for the momentary solitude. She'd even let Harry off the hook since he'd already washed the pots and pans.

Two hours down, two to go . . .

Estelle served pie and coffee in the living room, trying to ignore the amount of skin Donita was showing sitting down in that short skirt . . . And when the tight game was over—Saints 30, Cowboys 27—Rodney stretched. "Guess we better get goin'. Thanks, Pops. Thanks, Miz Estelle. Great dinner." He stood up. "You got your bag packed, DaShawn? An' don't forget your homework if ya got any."

Estelle and Harry exchanged glances. Score one for Rodney. Maybe he was learning how to be a dad after all.

Harry said he'd drive Leroy back to the Lighthouse while Estelle finished cleaning up the kitchen and doing a bit of laundry so they could pack for their weekend away. Then he was going to drop Corky off at the Amtrak station to be cared for by one of the dog handlers she was used to till Monday when he came to work.

Estelle grinned to herself once everyone was out the door. Hallelujah, thank You Jesus! They'd survived Thanksgiving dinner with the whole family. Now . . . "Let the weekend begin!" She laughed out loud.

✧   ✧   ✧   ✧

Harry checked the weather before they left the next morning. "Whoa!" he said. "It's below freezing out there. What happened to that nice Indian summer weather we've been having?"

The drop in temperature didn't seem to stop the construction going on at the two-flat across the street, though. The workers were hard at it again by 7:00 A.M.

Estelle was disappointed. She'd been imagining nice walks in the countryside, enjoying the last of the beautiful fall colors. But she put a good face on it. They'd just have to make good use of the in-room fireplace and that Jacuzzi for two.

Just as they were getting ready to leave, the home phone rang. The phone ID said *Grace Meredith.* "Oh dear, I forgot you guys were going to get away for the weekend," she apologized. "I just . . . please pray for Ramona. I think she overheard my brother and my dad yesterday talking about that Vice Lords' case here in Chicago, where the key witness was found dead the day before the trial. Supposedly an accident—but the authorities think it was murder."

Estelle's heart sank. She put the phone on Speaker so Harry could hear.

"Anyway, she seemed pretty upset and got real moody. I'm not sure what to do. Guess we could both use prayer. I'm not sure how to encourage her."

"Of course. Let's pray right now." Estelle prayed right there on the phone, that God would protect Ramona both physically and emotionally. "Lord, protect her from fear, because we know fear is not from You but from the evil one. And show us all how to come alongside Ramona to support and encourage her during this time of waiting and uncertainty."

"Thanks, Estelle," Grace said. "Okay, you kids go have fun this weekend. Sorry I bothered you. Just keep praying, okay?"

Chapter 32

Traffic was light as Harry and Estelle drove through the city, and even though a few clouds drifted across the sky, no rain or snow was predicted for the weekend and the sun danced off the windows of the tall buildings along Lake Shore Drive. Estelle put some of her favorite gospel CDs into the player and hummed along as they headed down I-57, the main route to Champaign-Urbana, home to the University of Illinois, and eventually to Memphis, Tennessee, if they stayed on it long enough. But they turned off 57 at Paxton, a quaint town just two hours south of Chicago, and followed the directions to their destination. A long lane surrounded by lush meadows, maples, oaks, and various evergreens led them up to the two-story inn with its wraparound porch, dormer windows, and white shutters.

They were early. Check-in time wasn't supposed to be until three o'clock. But the hostess just smiled. "No one stayed in the Maple Sugar Suite last night, being Thanksgiving and all, so you might as well settle in. And there are some nice restaurants in town if you want lunch. Here . . ." The pink-cheeked woman, her silver hair piled in a loose bun on top of her head, handed them several brochures of local attractions. She gave them two room key cards and led the way up the polished wood stairs to the second floor. "Oh, just to let you know, we're hosting a small wedding reception on the grounds tomorrow. In the summer and early fall we have our weddings outside, but as chilly as it is, looks like they'll be using our two lounges and meeting rooms here on the first floor most of the afternoon. But you'll probably want to be doing some sightseeing off grounds anyway—I hope they won't bother you."

Estelle and Harry exchanged a glance. A wedding party? They'd both been hoping for a long, quiet weekend.

The Maple Sugar Suite was even more amazing than the online photos, with its king-size bed, Jacuzzi set back into the wall, and marble front fireplace—but hunger sent them into town, where they had lunch at the Country Thyme Tea Room. Estelle ordered the fruit and spinach salad with homemade bread, and Harry had the baked tilapia with steamed vegetables. They liked the food well enough that they considered coming back for supper—until they found out that "tea room" meant luncheon only.

While they ate they looked at the brochures of local attractions. "Look! There's an old-fashioned drive-in theater nearby!" Estelle said.

Harry gave her a look. "Even if it's open at this time of year—which I doubt—we'd have to keep the car runnin' all night just to keep warm." Scratch the drive-in.

Estelle thought it'd be fun to visit one of the Amish villages for shopping and supper, but the closest was over an hour away. They finally settled on the Chanute Air Museum in Rantoul just fifteen minutes away—definitely right up Harry's alley—and Estelle decided there'd be plenty of weekend left to do some of the things she'd enjoy. Maybe even the Amish village on Saturday when they had all day.

Harry seemed tireless meandering through the air museum, checking out everything from the huge B-25 Stratofortress to Lockheed's F-104A Starfighter jet and everything in between, large and small. But Estelle pooped out and found a seat near a replica of the Wright Brothers 1903 Flyer.

When they finally headed back to Paxton, they decided on Mexican food at the Pueblo Lindo. "Almost as good as the Mexican food back in Chicago," Harry said, stuffing the sizzling steak fajitas into his mouth. While they waited for their after-dinner coffee, Estelle sighed happily. It felt so good to finally kick back, to get away from everything and everybody. Even Harry seemed relaxed. He reached across the small table and took her hand. "Thanks, babe. Really glad you pushed us to get away. Can't believe we still have another two days before we have to head back."

Estelle gave him The Eye. "Uh-huh. But I'm about ready to forget that coffee and head back to the inn. I can hardly wait to sink down into that hot, bubbly Jacuzzi"—her voice lowered to a husky whisper—"with my *man*."

A sly grin put a twinkle in Harry's eyes. "Me either, babe. Let's go."

✧ ✧ ✧ ✧

A familiar stanza of music—all *Da da dum* and mysterious—invaded Estelle's slumber, the same ominous tones repeating over and over until finally she recognized it: Harry's *Law and Order* ringtone. "Uhhhh, Harry," she groaned, shaking his shoulder. "Harry! It's your phone."

Her husband groped for his cell on the nightstand. "Bentley," he grunted, still half-buried in the big, soft pillows. Estelle turned over. Better not be his boss bothering them on their weekend *off*.

"She what? When?" The bed jostled as Harry sat up.

Rising up on one elbow, Estelle glanced bleary-eyed at the bedside clock—8:56. The big country breakfast they'd been promised by their hosts was good eight till ten. She hadn't meant to sleep this late, but at least they hadn't missed—

"... don't know!" The voice on the phone jumped into the room as Harry put the call on Speaker. The voice was Grace Meredith. "I didn't realize she was gone until just ten minutes ago when I went into the kitchen to make coffee. I found a note on the counter in Ramona's handwriting—just said, 'So sorry. Please forgive. *Gracias* for everything.' I immediately checked her bedroom and the bed is made, and her duffle bag is gone. Her jacket too! Oh, Harry, I'm scared! I don't know where she's gone!"

Ramona? Gone? Wide-awake now, Estelle started to say something, but Harry waved her off. "All right now, Grace," he said, in his best let's-not-panic voice. "Think. Did she have any money? Does she have her own cell phone?"

"Money ... if any, can't be much. I gave her some spending money each week, otherwise she had no income. Yes, we got her a different cell and new number so Max couldn't call her, remember?"

"Okay. Try calling her cell. Maybe she will answer. And do a more thorough search of the house—check the wastebaskets. Also check your computer. Did she look up the train or bus schedule? Even flight info. Anything!"

"Oh . . . okay. I'll look around and call you back. Can I call you back?" The voice was suddenly penitent. "I—I know you're on holiday. I'm so sorry to bother you, but—"

Now Estelle did interrupt. "Of course you can call us, Grace! Don't worry. You get off the phone and start looking for any clues. Harry and I are going to pray."

The phone went dead. Harry and Estelle looked at each other. Neither said anything for a moment, but she knew they were both thinking the same thing: *There goes our anniversary.* Estelle reached for Harry's hand and lifted her voice. "We need help, Lord! Ramona's taken off, and we don't know what to do. Protect her, Jesus! Surround her with Your guardian angels, wherever she is. And give us some insight, some clue where she is."

Harry headed for the bathroom. "Might as well shower and get dressed. Get something to eat. Just in case . . ."

He didn't finish but Estelle knew what *just in case* meant. Just in case they needed to head back to Chicago.

But a moment later Harry stuck his head out of the bathroom. "On the other hand, the girl is . . . what? Eighteen now? Legally an adult. We can't make her do anything. If she wants to go, we can't stop her." His head disappeared and Estelle heard the shower turn on. But a few minutes later, the shower stopped and Harry stuck his head out of the door again. "Except . . . if she leaves the state and the authorities find out, she could be arrested. Charges against her were held pending her agreement to testify against Max at his trial."

Estelle stared at him. "Oh, Harry."

❖   ❖   ❖   ❖

The call came while they were eating breakfast in the charming dining room of the inn half an hour later. Mouth-watering waffles with strawberries and sour cream, poached eggs, sausage links, freshly squeezed OJ, hot fragrant coffee—

Harry didn't put the call on Speaker, so all Estelle heard was, "A confirmation email? Ha, good, good . . . Uh-huh . . . uh-huh

. . . What time does it leave Chicago? . . . okay. Look at the first few stops and read them to me . . ." He hissed, "Pen!" to Estelle. She handed him one from her purse and he jotted something on a paper napkin. Then, "She what? . . . Oh, brother, wish she hadn't done that. But Grace, don't worry. Just pray. This is good. Let me talk to Estelle, I'll call you back."

Estelle had stopped eating, fork halfway to her mouth. "What? What?"

Harry glanced toward the kitchen. If there were other guests at the inn, they must've already eaten, and for the moment their cheerful hostess wasn't hovering with her pot of coffee. "Grace checked her email—there was a confirmation from Greyhound for a bus ticket to LA. Leaving Chicago at ten thirty this morning."

"LA! How'd she do that?"

Harry nodded. "Grace's credit card, apparently. *And* Grace thinks there's some cash missing from her purse too. Not good."

Estelle put down her fork. She suddenly wasn't hungry. She looked at her watch. Ten after ten. "Oh dear. No way we can get to the bus station in time to stop her. Not even Grace could get there in time. But do you think the Chicago police—?"

"Not if we don't want this to go public. But here's the thing." Harry pushed the napkin he'd written on toward her. "First stop . . . Champaign, Illinois. At one fifteen."

Estelle's eyes widened. "Champaign is just fifteen minutes from here!"

Harry nodded soberly. "It's just a quick stop to pick up passengers or let them off. We're going to be there to meet it."

Estelle let this sink in. "But . . . what if there are no passengers to get on or get off? What if it doesn't stop?"

Harry shook his head grimly. "Oh, it'll stop . . . potty break or whatever. If she doesn't get off, I'll just show my badge to the driver and explain there's a passenger onboard I need to speak to. The next stop is St. Louis, and I'm not chasing that bus all the way down there. Besides, by then she'd have crossed the state line."

✦ ✦ ✦ ✦

Estelle stared out the windshield of the RAV4 in the parking lot of the big brick Amtrak station in downtown Champaign that also served as the bus stop for Greyhound. They'd been there for twenty minutes already, parked near the main door, not wanting to take a chance on missing the bus when it pulled in. Harry had kept the car running to keep the heater on, since the outside temperature had barely risen a few degrees above freezing. The minutes and seconds seemed to tick by slower and slower . . . 1:05 . . . 1:07 . . .

But when the big blue and grey bus with the familiar greyhound pulled into the parking lot, it almost took her by surprise. "Wait," Harry cautioned. The door wheezed open and they watched as passengers disembarked. A mom and two kids, a bearded guy in a down jacket and ripped jeans, two elderly ladies obviously traveling together . . .

"Oh, Harry," Estelle breathed anxiously. "What if she didn't get on this bus? Maybe that was a ruse to throw us off. What if—"

"There she is."

Ramona stepped down from the bus wearing the same tan suede jacket she'd had when she arrived in Chicago months ago, her long, dark hair blowing loose. The girl hugged her purse and hunched her shoulders against the biting wind as she followed the other passengers headed for the building.

Estelle's heart clenched. Poor thing wasn't dressed for this weather.

"Come on." Harry opened his door. Estelle followed. She knew he wanted to get to her before she went inside, with as few people around as possible. Several passengers had already gone inside, and Ramona was practically coming straight toward them, eyes down, unseeing.

"Ramona," Harry said when she was within a few feet. "It's us. Harry and Estelle."

The young woman threw her head up, stared at them with wide, terrified eyes, then turned and started to run back toward the bus.

"Ramona! Wait!" Estelle called. "We need to talk to you, honey."

The girl stopped, then slowly turned around. Harry and Estelle quickly caught up to her. For a moment no one said anything, then

Ramona stammered, "How . . . how d-did you know? I mean, how did you get *here*?" She hugged herself, shivering.

Estelle wrapped her in a hug. "God planted us in a town not far from here, baby. He knew you'd be comin', knew you'd be needin' a friend."

Ramona pulled away. "I—I gotta use the restroom. We only have a fifteen-minute break. Then I need to get back on the bus."

"Ramona, you can't do that," Harry said. "We know you're scared and you don't want to testify against Max. But if I don't bring you back and you leave the state, a warrant for your arrest will be issued, and then you'll be in big trouble. Please believe me . . . We're your friends, your family. We aren't gonna let anything happen to you."

Tears started in Ramona's eyes. "But . . . but he's looking for me! Max came to the shelter—you said so yourself. And that . . . that witness in the news who had an accident the day before *he* was going to testify against that big gang chief—you know that was no accident! That could happen to me too!"

"Oh, baby." Estelle pulled the girl into her arms again and let her cry. Then, "C'mon, sit in the car. You're freezing, and it's warm in there."

With a reluctant look back at the bus, Ramona let Harry usher her into the front passenger seat of the RAV4. Estelle climbed into the backseat. He turned the heater on full blast. Five minutes later, Harry and Ramona got out and walked back to the bus. Estelle held her breath as they disappeared inside . . . then blew it out as they reappeared a few minutes later with Ramona's duffle bag. Harry spoke to the driver, who had returned to the bus, and Estelle saw the driver question Ramona, who nodded.

A few minutes later, the bus pulled out of the parking lot. Harry headed out the opposite way. No one spoke. Estelle spent a few silent moments, making peace with the fact that they were going back to the inn to pick up their luggage, and then they'd be heading home to Chicago. She sighed. Maybe the inn would give them a rain check for their unused night tonight.

But as they drove up the lane, something didn't seem right . . . wasn't there a big wedding reception at the inn that afternoon? Where were all the cars?

The three of them walked inside. All was serene. The silver-haired hostess was at the front desk, reading glasses perched on the end of her nose, frowning at some papers. But as they came in, she looked up and beamed. "Welcome back! I thought you were gone for the day." She noticed their puzzled look at the empty lounge and dining area. "Oh . . . the wedding reception. Cancelled." She made a face. "In fact, the wedding this morning got cancelled—well, postponed. The bride came down with the flu last night, poor thing. They've rescheduled for two weeks from now." She peered over her reading glasses at Ramona. "So! Who's this lovely young lady?"

Harry chuckled, then leaned over and whispered in Estelle's ear.

Her mouth dropped open but she nodded. "Uh, this is a special friend of ours. And if you've got an extra room, we'd like to include her in our reservation for tonight."

The inn hostess rolled her eyes. "Extra room? Hmph. Got lots. Some of the wedding party were going to stay over—but they cancelled too." She studied her registration book. "Hmm. I think our Honey Bear Room would be perfect for this young lady." She winked and handed over a room key.

Estelle made a mental note to let Grace know they weren't coming straight home. Ramona was wide-eyed, but ran out to the car to get her duffle bag.

While they waited for her, Estelle murmured, "Harry, you told her you weren't gonna let anything happen to her, but Max is still out there, and I'm afraid she might have reason to be scared."

"Yeah, maybe. But as far as we know, Max doesn't know where she is, so she's safe if she stays put."

"That's not enough if he's still lookin' for her."

Harry frowned thoughtfully. "Okay. I'll speak to the state's attorney, see if she can get the judge to pull Max's bail for intimidating a witness."

"Could you? Oh, that'd be a big relief—shh, here she comes."

As Ramona came scurrying back in with her bag in her hand, Harry said. "Don't know about the two of you, but I'm famished. How 'bout we grab a bite here in Paxton for lunch and then head on down to the Amish village? I hear Amish women are mighty fine cooks."

Chapter 33

CHECKOUT TIME WAS ELEVEN O'CLOCK, though the hostess said noon was fine. On the way home, Harry's cell dinged and Estelle read the text to him: *Dad, will bring DaShawn back by six. Do you have a few minutes to talk? Rodney.*

Before she got a chance to ask Harry if he wanted to respond, she got a text on her cell from Jodi Baxter: *Sisters! Just a reminder about Yada Yada, last Sunday of the month. Meeting at Edesa's apt tonight at the House of Hope 5 P.M. P.S. Adele's birthday was Nov. 4.*

Good grief. Life just picked up and took off running the moment they got back. Still, she didn't want to miss Yada Yada, not when they only met once a month now.

Ramona slept in the backseat most of the way back to Chicago, and when they dropped her off at Grace Meredith's house, Estelle and Harry decided not to go in. They could debrief with Grace later. It had been good to let everyone chill out for another twenty-four hours before bringing Ramona home. Once Grace knew Ramona was safe, she needed some time to process the breach of trust and whirlwind of emotions caused by Ramona running away. Estelle figured Ramona had needed the extra time, too, to own the decision to go back and think about the impact on Grace of just disappearing. Hopefully she and Grace would be able to talk it through—an initial reunion and conversation anyway.

Estelle had time to unpack and start some laundry before she headed over to Yada Yada. She wouldn't be home to welcome DaShawn back, but maybe that was for the best. Give space for Harry and Rodney to talk about . . . whatever it was. Though she had a pretty good guess what it was about.

231

The House of Hope six-flat where Edesa and Josh Baxter lived was an extension of Manna House, but for the express purpose of providing housing for homeless moms with kids. Four units were dedicated to this purpose, with two set aside for staff. Gabby Fairbanks and her family lived on the first floor as house parents, and Josh Baxter, who was the property manager, lived in one of the third floor apartments with his wife and kids.

But no elevator. Estelle puffed her way to the third floor. How Edesa managed to climb these stairs every day with two little ones, laundry, or groceries, she couldn't imagine.

"Hola!" Edesa greeted her with a big smile and warm hug. Several of the Yadas were there already in the brightly painted living room and others arrived shortly. Birthday cards and blessings for Adele Skuggs took first priority once everyone showed up—which reminded Estelle she really needed to get her hair done and a mani-pedi at Adele's Hair and Nails soon. After they'd demolished the birthday cake, Avis Douglass led in some *a capella* worship before opening the meeting for sharing.

All the sharings took longer than they used to when they met every week and kept up with each other a little more, so by the time it was Estelle's turn she was about to burst. She had so many things for both prayer and praise! The group home, she said, was actually becoming a reality in their neighborhood—but Leroy didn't get on the list of residents. She still didn't know what God was doing about that. Harry's son, Rodney, was stepping up, wanting to spend more time with DaShawn . . . but he wanted "a talk" with Harry tonight—which was probably happening right now, so could they pray for that? Then the shock of discovering that Ramona had spooked and run away that weekend—but how God had put her and Harry in her path . . .

Yo-Yo rolled her eyes. "Estelle, listening to you makes me dizzy as ridin' a roller coaster. How d'ya hold on to all those ups an' downs? God answers some prayers, acts like He's ignorin' bunch of others. Sheesh."

"Yeah, but this sistah got her prayer seatbelt strapped on," Florida put in. "Only way to survive *that* kind of roller coaster."

Estelle liked that. *Her prayer seatbelt.* If only it were always true. Too many times she felt like she was riding that roller coaster of prayers answered, not answered, different answer, waiting for an answer . . . as if she was barely holding on for dear life—no seatbelt, no safety bar, no nothing.

She'd have to remember to keep her prayer seatbelt buckled.

✧　✧　✧　✧

Harry met Estelle at the door. "You wanna go for a walk?"

"You're kidding. I just got home. What I wanna do is go to bed."

He jammed his hands in his pants pockets, shoulders hunched. "Okay. It's just . . . I don't pick up Corky till tomorrow morning and I'm used to taking her for a walk about this time of night."

Estelle had the grace to laugh. "So, you want to walk your wife since your dog's not here?"

Harry grinned sheepishly. "That came out wrong. What I meant was, I wanna tell you about Rodney's phone call, but don't want to do it with, you know . . ." He tipped his head toward DaShawn's closed bedroom door with the strip of light showing beneath.

That was different. They bundled up and meandered slowly up one side of their block and down the other as stars came out in the crisp night sky. "Rodney says he and Donita want DaShawn to come live with them next semester. Come for the Christmas holidays and if all goes well, stay through the rest of the school year."

Estelle sighed. "I thought as much. Did they talk to DaShawn?"

"Don't think so. Rodney said he wanted to talk to me first. That much I appreciate. But I gotta tell you, Estelle, it kinda kills me inside."

"I know." She hugged his arm tightly, and they walked in silence for several minutes.

"But the boy's fourteen. Guess I need to ask him what he thinks. What he'd like to do."

"He loves living with you, Harry. Maybe he'll choose to keep things the way they are—visiting with his folks for a weekend now an' then, but living with us."

Harry sighed. "Hope so. But guess we won't know unless we ask him."

✧   ✧   ✧   ✧

Estelle couldn't believe it. After temps dipping below freezing all during the Thanksgiving holidays and their anniversary getaway, the last two days of November practically felt like a heat wave, topping off at fifty degrees.

"Go figure," Harry snorted as he set off with a happy, tail-wagging Corky for work on Tuesday. "*Now* we get some Indian summer."

Estelle knew it wouldn't last. This was Chicago. So she was going to enjoy it while she could. Tuesday was her short day at Manna House and she left as soon as lunch cleanup was over. At home, she dragged a lawn chair out of the garage and set it up in the backyard. She was going to catch a few rays if it killed her.

The sun felt good on her face—the only skin actually exposed, since she wasn't brave enough to sit out without her coat. She actually dozed off . . . but came to with a start at the banging of metal on metal—*clank, clank, clank*—from behind the garage next door. Curious, she struggled up out of the lawn chair and went out into the alley.

Faird Jalili was attaching the snowplow to the front of his utility pickup.

"Farid! You're going to jinx this beautiful weather with that thing," she said in mock horror.

"To wait for the snow to fall is too late," the muscular Iranian grunted. *Bang, bang, clank, clank.*

Farid's snowplow . . . Estelle suddenly remembered Isaac Horowitz's threatening note. Would the man really take his neighbor to small claims court over his damaged bushes?

Almost as if reading her mind, Farid straightened and wiped sweat from his face with a big handkerchief. "Me, I try to help people with my plow. Miss Mattie, she would have died last winter if not for my plow. But—" He spit on the ground. "No thanks do I get from that Jew on the corner. He will not get one cent from me. And this winter? Do not ask me to do anyone any favors."

Estelle hardly knew what to say. "Oh, Farid. I am sorry. You did a good thing plowing a way for the ambulance to get to Miss Mattie last winter." But the man had returned to work and her words were lost amid the metallic banging.

✧ ✧ ✧ ✧

Estelle didn't get a chance to say anything to Harry about her conversation with Farid Jalili when he got home from work, because he was in a hurry to get to his men's Bible study at Peter Douglass's house. But first he wanted to deliver some good news.

"State's attorney didn't even have to mention Ramona to the judge. Turns out they did a surprise drug check on Max and he dropped dirty. Claimed he was clean, had to be secondhand pot smoke from a party he'd attended the night before. But that was enough for the judge to revoke his bail. So he's off the street . . . at least for now."

That *was* great news. Estelle would have to reassure Ramona when she got to Grace's house for their Tuesday prayer time.

When Grace answered the door that evening, Nicole was already there, talking to Ramona about hiring her to tutor Becky and Nathan three days a week after school, giving them help with homework . . . "Also, how do you feel about helping them learn to speak Spanish? No better way to learn than everyday conversation with someone who speaks it well."

Ramona's face was alight, and Grace, standing behind Ramona, winked at Estelle. Sounded like Grace might have been conspiring with Nicole to give Ramona something meaningful to do that would keep her busy, and a chance to earn a little money as well.

Sounded like a good time to give Ramona some more good news. When she announced that Max was back in jail for violating his parole with a drug drop, she burst into tears and threw her arms around Estelle. "Tell Mr. Harry *gracias*," she blubbered.

Later, during their sharing time, Nicole admitted she'd been asked to increase her hours as a paralegal, so hiring Ramona to help with the kids was actually selfish on her part.

"I don't think that's selfish," Grace said. "Just God taking care of both of you with the same answer to prayer."

The talk moved on . . . Grace had gone shopping for a wedding dress with her mom over Thanksgiving but didn't find what she wanted. Michelle had given her notice to stop work in mid-December—"if I make it that long." And general curiosity about what was happening at the two-flat next to the Singers. Painters had replaced the noisy construction, and Michelle said she thought the group home residents and staff might move in as soon as this coming weekend. Nicole was nervous about it but asked for prayer to give it a chance.

Estelle let the talk swirl around her. God had answered her prayer about the group home, but not about Leroy moving in. So what was the point? Wasn't that what this was all about—having Leroy nearby, being able to see him more often, but not under the same roof? At least as far as she was concerned. What was it Grace had said a few minutes ago about Nicole and Ramona? *"Just God taking care of both of you with the same answer to prayer."* Huh. Didn't seem that way for her and Leroy.

Just keep your prayer seatbelt buckled, a Voice in her spirit seemed to say.

✧   ✧   ✧   ✧

The weather report called for snow flurries all day on Saturday. "Harry, come look!" Estelle called as she peeked out the front windows after breakfast.

"I know. White stuff," he grunted. "I've already been out with Corky."

"No, come look. Somebody's moving into the group home this morning."

Sure enough, a rental truck had pulled up to the two-flat across the street, along with a pickup, an ancient station wagon, and a big black SUV. A crew of people was moving back and forth from the vehicles to the front door, unloading furniture and boxes and bulging plastic bags and disappearing inside.

"Hmm. Don't blame 'em wanting to move in before we get some *real* weather around here. These flurries shouldn't bother 'em though." Harry chugged the last of his cup of coffee. "Well, guess I better get my coat on and get out there myself."

"What? Are you going to help with the move?"

"No, babe," he said patiently. "Remember what we talked about when you told me what Farid   said a few days ago? I want to do it this morning when people are home before Horowitz makes good on his threat. Or even if he was just bluffing . . . it's still the right thing to do."

Right. She watched him shrug into his coat with the Amtrak Security patches and head down the front stairs. Corky whined, wanting to go too, but stretched out at the top of the stairs, nose on paws, to wait. Estelle breathed a quick prayer as she headed for the kitchen and the breakfast dishes. *Lord, open our neighbors' hearts. And wallets.*

It had been Harry's idea. "This problem shouldn't be between Isaac Horowitz and Farid Jalili," he'd said. "It's a neighborhood problem. There was an emergency, Farid and his snowplow came to the rescue, but, okay, we accept that the Horowitz bushes were damaged in the process. So . . . what's two hundred bucks? Not much if it's shared among us." He'd nixed the idea of just coming up with the money themselves. "That would feel like charity to Farid. But if the neighborhood owns this problem, that's different."

From time to time Estelle peeked out the front window. DaShawn had finally woken up and was supposedly cleaning his room. The snow flurries stopped, then started. The pickup, station wagon, and SUV were gone, but the rental truck was still being unloaded. An hour passed . . . and then she heard Corky give a happy *woof*, followed by Harry thumping up the front stairs.

He was grinning. "Didn't have to go to all the neighbors. I started with Danny's dads and they added a twenty to ours. Paddock insisted on giving a hundred-dollar bill, even though I told him we were all chipping in—so by the time I stopped by the Jaspers and

Grace and the Singers, who each gave a twenty, we had our two hundred!"

Estelle felt giddy. "That's wonderful! But . . . you didn't include Farid?"

Harry smiled slyly. "Just now—after I collected all the money. Thought I should let him know what we're doing and assure him it is our responsibility as a neighborhood, not his. His wife insisted they contribute twenty dollars too." He waved the envelope. "So we actually have more than enough. Want to go with me to deliver this to the Horowitzes?"

"Yes—oh, wait. They might not be home. It's their Sabbath, remember? Maybe we should wait till tomorrow afternoon."

The snow flurries hadn't left anything to speak of by the next day, but a biting wind made it clear that winter had arrived. Estelle had baked a double batch of cinnamon rolls to take over to the group home after they stopped by the Horowitzes, but she planned on keeping both visits short. It was cold.

Rebecca Horowitz answered the door. "Oh. Mr. and Mrs. Bentley." She looked momentarily uncertain, and then opened the door wider. "Please come in. It's cold today. I was going out in a few minutes, but I have a moment."

Harry cleared his throat as they stepped into the small foyer. "We won't stay long. Is your husband here? It is him we came to see."

Rebecca looked wary, but said, "One moment, please," and disappeared. A few moments later, Isaac Horowitz appeared in his shirtsleeves carrying a newspaper, white fringes trailing from beneath his shirt and showing up against his black pants, Rebecca close behind him. The tall bearded man peered over his glasses. "Yes?"

Harry handed him the envelope. "We heard that your bushes were damaged during last winter's snowstorm when the ambulance had to come up the sidewalk to get to Mattie Krakowski, so several of the neighbors took up a collection to replace them."

Isaac Horowitz glared at the envelope. "Did that coward Jalili put you up to this?"

"No, no, not at all. Our idea actually. But the Jalilis contributed, along with many others. After all, you're our neighbor."

The man continued to stare at the envelope until Rebecca said, "That is very kind, Mr. Bentley. We are grateful, aren't we, Isaac."

Isaac cleared his throat. "Thank you." He took the envelope and nodded. *Das iz gut.* Good, good." He shook Harry's hand and they turned to go.

Standing on the front porch a moment later, Estelle said, "Do you want to go with me across the street to deliver these?" She held up the plastic container with the cinnamon rolls.

But before he could say anything the door opened again and Rebecca Horowitz came out, bundled in a long gray wool coat and carrying a large soup pot. "Oh. You are still here!" She smiled at them from beneath the warm scarf she had wrapped around her normal head covering. "I was just going to take this soup to our new neighbors to say welcome. I hope they don't mind kosher." She laughed a little.

Estelle chuckled. "I was just going to take these cinnamon rolls."

"Well, you two go on then. You don't need me." Harry gave a little wave and headed back up the street to the graystone.

"That was a very nice thing you did," Rebecca said, as the two women headed for the two-flat across the street. "Isaac is a good man, if you knew him like I do."

"I'm sure he is." Estelle grinned at her companion. "I'm glad we are welcoming our new neighbors together."

She rang the doorbell. A moment later, a forty-something woman came to the door wearing clogs, tights under a longish black skirt, white turtleneck, and sweater. "Come in, come in!" the woman beamed. "Please excuse the mess—we just moved in, you know." She shut the door behind them.

"I'm Estelle Bentley. My husband and I live in the other two-flat on this block." She held out the cinnamon rolls. "We brought some food. Hope there is enough for all of you." Rebecca seemed to be staring at the woman, so Estelle said, "And this is another neighbor, Rebecca Horowitz."

"So pleased to meet both of you. I'm Sarah Cohen. I'm afraid my husband Samuel is upstairs helping our residents put their beds together. Do you want to—"

"Sarah Cohen?" Rebecca found her voice. A smile spread across her face. "You are Jewish!"

Chapter 34

I AM?" THE WOMAN FEIGNED ASTONISHMENT. "Well, that explains it. My auntie keeps trying to marry me off to a nice Jewish boy." Sarah Cohen winked. "Auntie is still miffed that I chose my own husband instead of the future rabbi she had picked for me."

Rebecca giggled. "Is she a *shadchan*?"

"Matchmaker? Thinks she is. But in reality just an old *yenta*." Now both Sarah and Rebecca laughed as the three headed for the kitchen, passing a large dining room table with a brass menorah as a centerpiece. Five of the nine candles had been lit. Hanukkah must have started already.

It was Estelle's turn to feel speechless. Really? A Jewish couple had moved into the Alvarezes' two-flat as staff for the group home?

"The soup is kosher," Rebecca was saying. "I was hoping you wouldn't mind—and then you turned out to be Jewish! I can't wait to tell Isaac."

Sarah made a face. "Well, yes and no. I mean, Samuel and I are Jewish, and we come from conservative congregations. But, we . . . well, I'd have to say we have lapsed a bit. We only attend services on *Shabbat* now and then, and"—she shrugged—"it's hard to keep kosher with four adults with mental health issues who *aren't* Jewish going in and out of the kitchen. And this is our second group home."

"*Oy vey.*" Rebecca nodded sympathetically.

"Still, helping our fellow man *is* one of our Jewish core values, yes?"

Feeling a bit left out of the conversation, Estelle held out the cinnamon rolls again. "I'm afraid these *aren't* kosher."

Another peal of laughter. "No worries! Our hungry residents will polish them off in an hour—if Samuel doesn't get to them first."

✧   ✧   ✧   ✧

Estelle watched Rebecca scurry across the street once they left the group home, probably in a hurry to tell Isaac the "good news" about their new neighbors. Estelle felt a pang as the young woman disappeared into their brick bungalow. The Horowitzes had two unexpected good fortunes today—the neighborhood collection to help Isaac replace his damaged bushes, and now, the very thing they'd hoped for when the Alvarezes' For Sale sign went up: another Jewish family on the block.

Well, a Jewish couple anyway.

The wind had died and Estelle walked home slowly. Avis's prayer at Yada Yada a month or so ago tickled the back of her mind—something about God's purpose becoming evident "for all concerned," the residents as well as the neighbors. Well. Looked like the Horowitzes were getting their prayers answered. The Cohens weren't as religious as Isaac and Rebecca, and they didn't seem to have kids at home—but still.

"But what about Leroy, Jesus?" Her breathy prayer came out in puffs of frosty air. "Did You forget about him?"

Harry and DaShawn seemed to be having a talk in the boy's bedroom when she got home, so she pulled a couple of cans of tomato soup from the cupboard and some bread and cheese to make toasted cheese sandwiches for a light Sunday evening supper. The soup was almost hot when Harry came into the kitchen, face sober, the black Lab close on his heels. Estelle looked at him questioningly.

Harry sighed. "Says he'll try it at his dad's during Christmas break, and if all goes well, move to their place. He doesn't want to change schools in the middle of the year, though. And he said he'd like to be here for Christmas Eve and Christmas morning."

Estelle hesitated. How to be encouraging? "Well, that's a good thing. Sounds like he's thinking straight—oh!" She snatched the soup pot off the burner just before it boiled over.

"Yeah. Uh, think I'll take Corky for a walk. How soon till supper?"

She gave him fifteen minutes, but it was more like thirty when he got back with the dog and the toasted cheese sandwiches were cold. But she called DaShawn to join them and served it up.

"So, did you meet the new guys at the group home?" Harry seemed to have made his peace with the transition they were facing—for the moment anyway.

"Just the wife of the staff couple, Sarah Cohen. They're Jewish."

Harry stopped in midbite, strings of cold melted cheese hanging from his mouth. "You're kidding. . . " He actually grinned. "You're not kidding. Ha. God certainly works in mysterious ways."

Estelle pushed past her own questions about God's mysterious ways. "Sarah said they plan to have a Christmas open house in a couple weeks once they get settled so we can meet the residents."

"Christmas?" DaShawn said, his mouth full. "I thought you said they're Jewish."

"But the residents aren't. At least I don't think so. Sounded like they celebrate all the holidays. They don't keep kosher either." Estelle couldn't help a smile. "I like Sarah. She's got a sense of humor."

Harry chuckled. "Guess you'd need one to be house parents for a group of—"

Estelle gave him a look.

"Uh, mentally challenged adults," he finished. "You know what I mean."

Without Ramona riding with her to and from Manna House, Estelle had lots of time to think and pray in the car each day—mostly about Leroy. Seemed like God was answering a lot of prayers surrounding the group home moving into the neighborhood, all except the one she cared about most: having Leroy nearby. Was God testing her? Seeing if she'd give up? Maybe God still wanted her to fight for Leroy, do what she could do rather than expect God to deliver her answer to prayer all tied up neatly with a ribbon.

The temperature hung around the low twenties most of the week, but there was no snow, even a few days of bright sunshine. "Nippy but nice" was the weather guy's assessment. Harry ended up with an undercover assignment that took him and Corky out of state over the following weekend, so Estelle drove herself to see her son at the Lighthouse that Saturday. She smiled to herself as she parked the car and walked into the residential institution. Hopefully Leroy could get a pass for next Wednesday too.

Leroy was waiting in the reception area as usual, but he was talking quite intensely with a white girl who was sitting beside him and didn't see her at first.

"Leroy? I'm here. Come give me some sugar, baby. I've got some news for you."

Leroy's head swiveled and he jumped up with a grin. "Hey, Ma. This is Brenda. Remember I told you about her? Brenda, this is my mom." He kept grinning in a nervous way.

The young woman stood up too and held out her hand. "How do you do? I'm Brenda." Estelle nodded and shook her hand. Yes, this was the girl she'd met once before, Leroy's friend. Pretty face, bright red lipstick, light brown hair worn long and loose, a bit plump but not fat.

"Can Brenda come with us, Ma? Miz Finch said she could come if it's okay with you."

"No, what I said was, you need to ask your mother about that," said a familiar voice. They all turned. Mrs. Finch, the social worker, had just come into the room.

Estelle felt irritated at being put on the spot in front of the girl. "I—I don't know, son. There's something I want to talk to you about." She should just come out and say no. She did not want Brenda coming along.

Leroy's grin got wider. "I got something to tell you too—right, Miz Finch?"

The woman smiled. "That's right. Why don't we all sit down here?" The social worker pulled a chair over for Estelle and another for herself.

"I got a job, Ma! That's my good news!" Leroy was almost beside himself with excitement.

Startled, Estelle looked at Mrs. Finch. "A job? What job?"

"At Stroger—the county hospital. It's a part-time job in the burn unit, fifteen hours a week to start, transporting patients by wheelchair to and from their various therapy sessions." Mrs. Finch smiled. "They were very impressed with Leroy. Willing to try him out on a trial basis."

"That's . . . that's wonderful, son! I'm so glad for you." Estelle hadn't thought it possible. Had her expectations for her son been too low? Then she frowned. "But, uh . . . when do you start?"

Leroy looked questioningly at Mrs. Finch. "Right after the New Year," the woman said.

"Oh, good." Estelle felt relieved. "Because I have news, too, Leroy. I set up a second interview for you at Bridges Family Services next week, Wednesday. You know, to get on their list for the next group home."

The little group suddenly got quiet. Leroy looked at Mrs. Finch, then at Brenda, then back at his mom. "But, Ma! I don't want to get on any list. You should have asked me. I want to stay here!"

"Here? But Leroy, I thought—"

"I just told you, Ma. I got a job!"

"I know, but—"

"And I'm real close to the job if I stay here at the Lighthouse. I can even walk, takes only fifteen minutes. Ain't that so, Miz Finch?" The social worker nodded.

Estelle took a deep breath and tried to gather her thoughts. Brenda's pale face with the bright red lipstick had gone all worried and she was tugging on Leroy's sleeve. This wasn't going exactly like Estelle had thought. She should have taken Leroy out to lunch and just talked to him there. Alone.

"It's . . . it's just an interview, Leroy. It's just to get you on a list. You can stay here and start your job, then when a group home opens up in the New Year, maybe next spring, I'm sure we can work out the transporta—"

"No!" Leroy set his jaw. "I don't want to go to any group home. I'm not going to no interview. You shoulda asked me first. Besides . . ." He reached out and took Brenda's hand and his leathery face softened. "My friend Brenda's here. I wanna stay here too."

❖   ❖   ❖   ❖

Estelle drove home from the Lighthouse, her emotions banging around in her chest like gym shoes in a clothes dryer. She knew Leroy could be stubborn, but this took the cake! Not even go to the interview? Shut the door on the group home option? That didn't make any sense!

But Harry had a different take on it when he got home Sunday night. "Hold on, babe. Just think about it. Your son is doing *great*. I mean, he set his mind on getting a job, on being a productive citizen—and he did it! And sounds like he's making friends there at the Lighthouse—"

"Hmph. *Girlfriend* is more like it. Which is another whole thing."

Harry threw up his hands. "Girlfriend then. So what? He's happy. He's excited. He's hopeful. He's looking to the future. Isn't that what you want for him?"

Estelle set her own jaw. "He wanted more of my home cookin', that's what he said."

Now Harry burst out in a loud guffaw. "Just listen to yourself, Estelle Bentley." He pushed back his chair from the kitchen table and headed for the living room, shaking his head. "More of her home cookin', the woman says," he muttered.

Estelle felt teary the next day or two. Why did she fight so hard for the group home to move into their neighborhood if Leroy was going to insist on staying at the Lighthouse? Not that she was against the group home being there, but the whole thing had seemed like a divine plan, with all the puzzle pieces fitting together. For the Alvarezes. For the group home. For Leroy. For her.

She walked slowly across the street to Grace's house Tuesday evening, stars glittering in the clear night sky in spite of the "light pollution" from city lights. The weather had still been "nippy but nice." Should she share her feelings with her neighbor prayer sisters? Or would they be like Harry, only see it as "Leroy's good news"?

She was met with a red-eyed Ramona who looked like she'd been crying, and an equally sober Grace. Estelle looked from one to the other. "What?"

Grace handed her an official-looking letter. The letterhead said *Circuit Court of Cook County* and in large letters at the top it said, *Subpoena*. Estelle hardly breathed as she skimmed the letter. Ramona was being subpoenaed to appear before the court to give testimony in the trial of Michael "Max" Wagner on January 19, a Wednesday.

Estelle blew out a long breath. "So. Now we know the trial date." She put an arm around Ramona and drew her into a hug. "That's only a month away, honey. It'll soon be over."

The girl nodded, but her lip trembled. "Except . . . except Miss Grace . . ." She started to cry.

Grace looked distressed too. "What she means is, I'll still be gone on my "New Year—New You" reprise tour. I had really wanted to be here for her."

Chapter 35

THE ELEPHANT IN THE ROOM, Estelle realized as they prayed together that night, was where would Ramona stay for two whole
weeks while Grace was gone? It'd be great if she could stay in the
neighborhood, so she could continue her job tutoring Nicole's kids
and where the people who knew her best could keep an eye on
her. Was there someone who could stay with Ramona at Grace's
house? Estelle couldn't think of anyone.

On the other hand, she admitted to herself, DaShawn might be
living at his dad's by then, which would free up a bedroom at their
house. But Estelle was pretty sure Harry wouldn't want to give
away DaShawn's bedroom for two whole weeks in January, just in
case his grandson wanted to come back early.

Estelle had to remind herself not to close her eyes as she prayed
on the way to Manna House the next morning. *Lord Jesus, we need
You to make a way out of no way, just like You did when Ramona tried to
run away a couple weeks back. I know You're takin' care of that girl, Jesus.
So I'm gonna trust You for a place for her to stay too.*

A flyer announcing "A Holiday Open House at Casa Shalom"
showed up in their mailbox when she got home from work on
Wednesday. *Casa Shalom* . . . House of Peace. What a nice name
for the group home. But she felt the familiar pang of loss. If only
Leroy . . . no, no, she wasn't going there. She reread the flyer:
Sunday at 3:00 P.M. Probably in deference to the Jewish Sabbath.
The Horowitzes should be happy about that.

When she wrote "Open House" on her kitchen calendar, she
had a shock. Christmas was a week from Saturday! And she'd
hardly done a thing to get ready. School was out for the holidays
that Friday, and Harry took DaShawn shopping for a Christmas
tree. They put it up in front of the bay windows and discovered it

was a bit lopsided—"But only twenty bucks!" Harry protested—
and it wasn't too bad once they decorated it on Saturday with the
hodgepodge of ornaments and lights she and Harry had pooled
when they got married.

Then Estelle braved the crowds and went shopping for Harry,
DaShawn, and Leroy. They'd better be happy with some clothes.
Lord knows Harry and DaShawn needed new underwear—which
she'd tuck under a couple of new shirts. Should she get anything
for Rodney and Donita? Probably. Something not too personal. She
picked up a nice basket with a variety of nuts, cheeses, smoked
sausage, and fancy crackers.

Sunday was the fourth Sunday of Advent, Avis Douglass
announced during worship the next day. Estelle couldn't remember
who'd introduced celebrating Advent at SouledOut—the weeks
leading up to the "advent" of the Christ Child. It hadn't been part
of her church tradition growing up. But watching the junior high
girls do a candle dance as they lit each of the Advent candles in a
wreath on the Communion table was lovely. As the candles were
lit, the praise team led the congregations in singing, "O Come O
Come Emmanuel . . ." Estelle noticed, as if for the first time, that
all the verses expressed the longing of Israel for the coming of the
Messiah. *"Rejoice! Rejoice! Emmanuel shall come to thee, O Israel."*

Hmm. Maybe this song was something she could share with
Rebecca Horowitz, or even Sarah Cohen. A song that spoke to both
their religious holidays at this time of year.

Estelle was eager to get home so they could attend the Christmas
Open House at Casa Shalom. The weather was still holding at
"nippy but nice" with several sunny days in a row and only a slight
dusting of snow on the ground. Which might encourage a large
turnout from the neighborhood, she hoped, if not sheer curiosity
about the new neighbors.

Coming up the walk with Harry and DaShawn, Estelle noticed
an electric candle in each of the windows of the two-flat, though
they weren't turned on this early in the afternoon. A young man
with obvious Down syndrome greeted them at the door with a big
smile. "Hello. My name is Jack. Welcome to Casa Shalom. Please
make a nametag." He gave Estelle a vigorous handshake and

pointed to a basket with nametags and red and green markers. Then he turned to the Jasper family coming in: "Hello. My name is Jack. Welcome to Casa Shalom . . ."

DaShawn balked at making a nametag, but gave in after a warning glare from Harry. Jared Jasper made his kids make nametags, too, though later Estelle noticed DaShawn and the twins had slapped their nametags on the legs of their jeans. Oh, brother.

Inside, an artificial Christmas tree sat in a corner of the first floor living room next to an upright piano, and ropes of tiny LED lights outlined the wide doorway between living room and dining room. Votive candles flickered in little glass holders on the fireplace mantel, the top of the piano, and on various side tables. All very festive.

Harry stopped to talk to Samuel Cohen, who was mingling with the guests, so Estelle and Michelle Jasper wandered together into the dining room, where Sarah Cohen was ladling hot spiced cider into paper hot cups. A young man wearing a nametag that said *Stephan* was handing them out. Estelle guessed he might be around thirty and had some kind of disability, as his eyes roamed in awkward, sideways glances, not really looking at them.

"Hello!" Sarah smiled warmly. "Estelle, right? So glad you came. And this is—?"

Estelle introduced Michelle. "And Baby Bump," she added with a chuckle, "who is supposed to make his or her arrival in early February."

"Congratulations," Sarah beamed. "Every neighborhood needs a baby or two. Ours have grown up and moved away, and unfortunately haven't produced any grandchildren yet."

"This is my name." Sarah's helper tapped his nametag vigorously. "It's pronounced *Stefan* with an 'f,' not Steven with a 'v.' Do you want some hot cider?"

More neighbors arrived—even the interracial couple between Grace Meredith and Casa Shalom who never seemed to be home. Their nametags read *Jason Smith-Owens* and *Jamila Smith-Owens*. Estelle heard them ask Samuel Cohen, who'd been mingling with the guests, if they could see the upstairs. He hesitated for a brief moment, then spoke quietly to a young Latino who'd been sitting on the stairs just watching. The young man hesitated a moment, then disappeared up the stairs.

"Rodrigo will show you around upstairs," Samuel said, "but please do not go into the residents' bedrooms. Their bedrooms are private space, so please respect that."

Michelle begged off climbing the stairs, but Estelle joined the small group for a tour of the second floor. Rodrigo was waiting for them at the top of the stairs. "Th-this is our l-lounge," he said, indicating the living room, which had a mismatched assortment of comfy chairs and a couch. "We have a T-TV and stereo and DVDs. And b-books. P-personally, I like to read b-books better than watch TV."

Besides the stutter, the young man seemed intelligent. Estelle wondered why he qualified as a resident for a group home.

The second-floor dining room had been remodeled into a fourth bedroom, and the kitchen had been expanded to include an eat-in area. "For b-breakfast and s-snack times," Rodrigo explained. "We eat s-supper d-downstairs with the C-Cohens."

The doors to the bedrooms were open but Rodrigo said, "You c-can look in, but please d-do not go in." But as the little tour group passed one of the bedrooms, someone inside firmly closed the door.

"It's okay, B-Bernie," Rodrigo said through the door. "We'll be g-gone in a few minutes." He smiled apologetically at the group. "You will m-meet Bernie later."

Estelle saw Jamila Smith-Owens roll her eyes and whisper something to her husband. Hmph, Estelle thought. How would they like it if half the neighborhood wanted to peek into *their* bedroom? Though she had to admit she was curious about the fourth resident behind the closed door.

As they went back downstairs, Estelle realized that the stairs had been remodeled to come directly into the first floor apartment instead of out a second front door into the foyer. More neighbors had arrived. Both Karl and Eva Molander were parked on a couch in the living room, and Lincoln Paddock had arrived with a woman he introduced as "an old friend." Grace and Ramona were talking to Sarah Cohen and getting refills of hot cider. The last to arrive were the Horowitzes, and Estelle saw Isaac and Farid Jalili nod cordially to each other, but that was about it.

Well, it was a start, she thought.

Jack, the self-appointed doorkeeper, rang a bell. "Ladies and gentlemen, we now have a special treat for you. Please find a seat in the living room or dining room." As the neighbors found places to sit or stand, Samuel Cohen disappeared up the stairs and a few moments later came back down, followed by a twenty-something young man dressed neatly in jeans, a plain dark T-shirt, and tan corduroy sport coat. He had longish hair that hung over one eye and brushed his coat collar. This must be Bernie, Estelle thought.

Bernie didn't look at anyone as he came into the living room, but headed straight for the piano. Samuel said, "This is Bernie Wilson, and he'd like to play some familiar songs for the holiday season for our new neighbors."

"I didn't say I'd like to," Bernie said from the piano bench, eyes focused on the piano keys. "You *asked* me to and I said yes."

"That's right," Samuel corrected. "We asked Bernie if he would play some songs for the holiday season and he said yes."

People looked at one another but quieted. Bernie hunched over the keys and then started to play. The familiar strains of "I'm Dreaming of a White Christmas" flowed from the piano. Estelle saw people's eyes widen. The young man was good.

When he finished, a few people started to clap, but Samuel Cohen held up his hand and shook his head. "Go on, Bernie," he said.

"White Christmas" was followed by a rousing rendition of "Deck the Halls" and then the gentle melody of "Silent Night."

As the last notes of the familiar carol faded, Karl Molander spoke up from the couch. "Can you play 'Joy to the World'? That's my favorite Christmas carol."

Bernie tensed. "That is not what I planned to play! I told Sam I would play four songs, but 'Joy to the World' is not one of them. I want to play the songs I planned!"

His voice had risen and Samuel Cohen laid a gentle hand on Bernie's shoulder. "That's fine, Bernie. Play the last song just as you planned."

"Well, excuse me!" Karl Molander muttered sarcastically, but Eva laid a restraining hand on his knee.

There was a long pause at the piano bench. But finally Bernie began to play, "O Come All Ye Faithful." Then he stood up abruptly and nodded his head in a slight bow as people clapped, then he quickly crossed the room and disappeared up the stairs.

As people began to move and murmur, Samuel held up his hands. "Just a moment, please. Thank you for your attention. Bernie is a very accomplished pianist, but he also has Asperger's syndrome. A person like Bernie needs a great deal of structure, and it's hard to deviate from a plan once it's made. So thank you for your patience. I hope you enjoyed our little concert. Now . . . please help yourself to more hot cider and cookies and thank you all for welcoming us into the neighborhood with your presence."

People began to put on their coats and drift out the door. Jack took up his post and nodded and smiled at the departing guests. "Thank you for coming . . . Please come again . . . Thank you for coming . . ."

Michelle wagged her head wearily at Estelle. "Gotta get home and get my feet up. Baby Bump is bumping around like she wants to pop out. Not sure she's gonna wait another six weeks. Uhh . . . don't think I'll make prayer on Tuesday. Too much Christmas stuff left to do."

"'She,' huh. Thought you didn't want to know the baby's sex ahead of time."

Michelle grinned wearily. "Tabby is convinced she's getting a sister. We might have to send this one back if it's a boy."

Estelle was still chuckling as she and Harry rounded up DaShawn and left the new group home. It was only four thirty, but twilight was settling over the neighborhood. Looking back at the two-flat from the sidewalk, Estelle saw the electric candles in all the windows had been turned on, sending a friendly beam onto Beecham Street.

The Cohens and the group home residents had certainly gone out of their way to reach out to their new neighbors with their Christmas open house. Yes, there might be some challenges knowing how to relate to people like Bernie or Stephan, but—

Only then did Estelle realize that she hadn't seen Nicole Singer or anyone else in the Singer family at the open house.

Chapter 36

Estelle puzzled about the Singers' absence from the group home Open House. It would have been the perfect time to meet the Cohens and the residents in a casual setting. But maybe Nicole's mother was ill or something. She'd check in with her when they got together at Grace's house Tuesday night—oh wait. Michelle said she wouldn't be there, and maybe not Nicole either since the kids were out of school for the winter break.

Well, she'd just call.

Which she did as soon as she got home from Manna House on Monday. But it was Ramona who answered the phone. "Oh, *hola*, Miss Estelle. Nicole had to work today. I'm babysitting *los niños*. I will tell her you called."

So it was Tuesday afternoon before Estelle had a chance to speak to Nicole.

"I . . . I know we promised to come," Nicole said on the phone. "But . . . didn't you hear the scream Saturday night?"

"Scream? What scream?"

"Next door! From the group home. It was so loud it woke me up."

"Are you sure it was from the group home? Maybe it was just a cat. Sometimes they can sound like—"

"I'm telling you, Estelle, it was a human scream! And it came from next door! And . . . I felt too shook up to take my kids over there. So we went over to my mom's for the afternoon."

Estelle hardly knew what to say. "Well, I can understand something like that would upset you. But there has to be an explanation. The young men there seemed quite friendly and personable in spite of their limitations. One of them even played the piano for us. He has Asperger's but is very high functioning."

255

Nicole didn't say anything for several long moments. Then . . . "I don't know, Estelle. I wish they'd never moved in."

"Nicole, I know you probably need time with your kids tonight, but . . . why don't you come over to Grace's house, even for ten minutes, and we'll pray about this."

Another long pause. "Okay, I guess." Nicole's voice sounded teary.

As soon as they hung up, Estelle called Grace, who said she was still willing to have prayer at her house that evening, " . . . if we can keep it kind of short. Christmas week, you know."

So it was just Grace and Ramona and Estelle when Nicole showed up around seven thirty. Estelle had already told Grace and Ramona about the scream in the night, so the four women held hands and asked God to protect Nicole from fear, to reveal the source of the scream she'd heard, and to give her wisdom about how to relate to the residents of the group home.

When they said amen, Estelle looked around the little circle. "I think we should just go to Casa Shalom and ask about the scream Nicole heard."

"I was thinking the same thing," Grace said.

Nicole was shaking her head. "What if they deny it? What will I do then?"

"Just promise you'll think about it, Nicole," Estelle said gently. "I'll go with you. We can go together. Sarah Cohen, the house-mother, is really a lovely person. You'll like her."

Nicole was still shaking her head when she left.

Estelle got up to leave soon after, since she'd promised to keep the prayer time short. "So what are your Christmas plans, Grace? Is Jeff coming?"

Grace rolled her eyes. "I wish. But he can't come until New Year's. Ramona and I are invited to spend Christmas Eve with Mark and his family, but we don't really have any plans for Christmas Day. What about you?"

"Leroy is coming for Christmas, but then Rodney is picking up DaShawn around noon Christmas Day for the rest of the holiday— and maybe longer. I told you, didn't I, that Rodney and Donita want DaShawn to come live with them?" She snorted. "Huh.

That's another whole prayer request! Anyway, Harry and I might go to Manna House to help serve Christmas dinner later that day. They need more volunteers. I think Leroy might like to go too. He had a great time at the masquerade party."

"Oh! I'd love to go to Manna House to serve Christmas dinner!" Ramona said, her eyes alight. "I miss all my friends there. I mean, it is safe now, *sí*? Max is in jail, so I don't have to stay away."

Grace smiled. "Sounds like a great idea to me. Can I come too, Estelle?"

✧   ✧   ✧   ✧

Gabby Fairbanks was delighted to have extra volunteers to set up and serve Christmas dinner, which was being catered by a church group from the suburbs. "And some of the ladies like to play board games or play Ping-Pong in the rec room, so we can always use more volunteers to just hang out—before and after Christmas dinner!"

Estelle couldn't help grinning as she drove home from the shelter, in spite of having to turn on the wipers because of the spitting snow. Serving Christmas dinner at Manna House would be just what the doctor ordered to keep Harry from moping around the house after Rodney picked up DaShawn.

The light was blinking on the kitchen phone when she got home. A voicemail from Nicole: *"Greg thinks going over to the group home and asking about the scream is a good idea. He says he'll go with me. But will you come too, Estelle? Ramona said she could come stay with the kids this evening."*

Estelle called back and said of course she'd go too. "But we should ask the Cohens for a good time to come. We should probably talk to them alone—not in front of the residents."

Which turned out to be at eight o'clock that evening. "The guys are usually upstairs watching TV," Sarah said when Estelle phoned. "Or doing their laundry or whatever by then."

The snow had stopped, leaving only an inch or so on the ground when the Singers and Estelle rang the doorbell of Casa Shalom. The electric candles in the windows and the bright porch light made the two-flat seem welcoming. "Please, come into the den," Samuel said, leading the way into a second bedroom on the first floor that had been made into a private den with a TV and bookcases and comfortable chairs. Sarah brought in a tray with herbal tea.

Nicole was fidgeting with a tissue in her lap, so Greg Singer explained why they were there. "The scream was very upsetting to my wife," he said. "Fortunately, our children did not wake up. But we want to know what went on here that night."

"This is what we were afraid of!" Nicole's eyes flashed. "We don't want frightening things happening in our neighborhood, scaring our children."

Samuel nodded. "I can understand that it upset you—especially if you didn't know what was happening."

"You see," Sarah said gently, "Rodrigo is an army vet—he served two tours in Iraq. But he's now suffering from PTSD—Post-traumatic Stress Disorder. And he occasionally has nightmares. That's what happened the other night. Fortunately, the other residents understand what's happening, and Jack, especially, has a very tender heart and knows to wake him up, make him some tea, and even read to him for a little while."

Nicole's eyes were wide. "Oh my goodness. I had no idea. He was in Iraq? The poor man."

"Yes. Rodrigo's really a great guy. He started stammering because of the stress, and of course he's getting professional treatment. But he's single, and that's why living in the group home is a good thing, so he's not alone."

Greg nodded. "Thank you. That's very helpful. Still . . . we live right next door, and we're afraid his screams in the night will frighten our children."

"It might help for them to meet Rodrigo," Samuel said, "get to know him as a person, and explain to them about the nightmares caused by war. You might be surprised how empathetic children can be when they know the facts. And the scream was unusual. More often he just wakes up in a panic."

Nicole looked at Greg. "We could help Nathan and Becky pray for Rodrigo about the nightmares."

"A wonderful idea," Sarah said, smiling. "Why don't you bring the children over sometime soon."

Nicole nodded. "Maybe Friday during the day? That's Christmas Eve and both Greg and I have the day off."

They said goodnight and left Casa Shalom. Nicole gave Estelle a hug out on the sidewalk. "Thank you, Estelle. You and Grace were right—we just needed to come here and ask."

Estelle was thoughtful as she walked back across the street to their graystone, grateful for what just happened. Hopefully it was another step in healing the fears Nicole had carried since she was a kid herself. Who knew what else God had in mind by bringing Casa Shalom to Beecham Street? She'd prayed for the group home to come into their neighborhood—mostly for her own selfish reasons, she had to admit. But she hadn't thought about praying for the residents once they moved in. Jack . . . Stephan . . . Bernie . . . Rodrigo . . . the Cohens . . .

Okay, Lord, I think You're telling me I need to be praying for them too.

✦ ✦ ✦ ✦

It snowed on and off all day Christmas Eve, leaving five inches of the white stuff. "We're having a white Christmas!" Leroy said, coming into the house after Harry picked him up using his work SUV. But he wasn't so excited about the snow Christmas morning when Harry told Leroy and DaShawn first thing to bundle up and handed them both shovels. "Leroy, you do the side and the back. DaShawn, you shovel the front. By the time you're done breakfast will be ready."

Estelle wagged her head. What a way to start Christmas morning! But it did give her time to warm up the cinnamon rolls she'd made the day before and bake the egg-and-sausage casserole. When she checked on the boys from the front window, she saw them working together on the front walks instead of splitting up front and back as per Harry's instructions.

Thank You, Jesus. It meant a lot to her that Leroy and DaShawn got along so well.

She didn't see anyone else out shoveling snow. Maybe because it was Christmas morning and nobody had to go to work. But she was grateful Harry had insisted on clearing their walks when she heard the doorbell ring and Daniel Krakowski's voice in the foyer below, come to pick up his mother for Christmas Day.

The boys had worked up a good appetite by the time they came back in and Estelle suggested they fill up a plate and take it into the living room while Harry read the Christmas story from Luke 2. Estelle relaxed with her coffee and cinnamon roll, feeling content as Harry's deep voice read the familiar words of Scripture. A perfect Christmas morning . . . just her and Harry and DaShawn and Leroy.

It didn't take long to open presents. Leroy apologized, said he didn't have money to go Christmas shopping until he started work at Stroger Hospital after the holidays. But he did make a key ring for Harry, a bookmark with Estelle's name on it, and a leather wallet for DaShawn in the craft room at the Lighthouse. Her men all seemed to like their shirts—though Harry gave her a funny look when he got to the underwear. Estelle was glad to see that the black turtleneck she got Leroy covered up most of the scarring on his neck from his burns. "Thanks, Ma," he said, giving her a hug.

Estelle's biggest surprise was her gift from Harry—several yards of a beautiful African print to make one of the caftans she liked to wear. "There's enough for a head wrap too," he said, looking slightly embarrassed. "A lady at the fabric store helped me."

Rodney arrived promptly at noon to pick up DaShawn. "Donita's back at the apartment, trying to cook Christmas dinner." He punched DaShawn playfully on the shoulder. "Don't set your expectations too high, son. Your mom's tryin' though."

Estelle gave him the basket of Christmas treats, wrapped in green cellophane and red ribbon. Rodney looked embarrassed. "Sorry. We don't have anything for you. Our, uh, first Christmas together in a long while, ya know. Just tryin' to get it together."

Harry went to the front windows to watch them drive away. Estelle knew what he was thinking. Was this just a long holiday visit? Or would DaShawn be back to move more of his stuff over to his dad's house next weekend?

✧ ✧ ✧ ✧

All five of them piled into the RAV4 for the drive to Manna House an hour later, but Harry insisted on taking Corky too. "No way I'm leaving the dog alone on Christmas," he growled. "She can stay in Mabel's office if she gets in the way."

Ramona got an enthusiastic welcome from the staff who were on holiday duty, as well as some of the shelter guests who remembered her from Estelle's cooking class. "Ramona! Would you and Grace like to help decorate the tables for Christmas dinner?" Gabby Fairbanks, the program director, gave Ramona a hug, then turned to introduce her to two strapping teenagers. "These are my sons. Paul is a junior in high school, and this is P.J. He's home for the holidays from his first year at Goucher College."

Estelle kept giving Gabby's boys furtive glances as she headed for the kitchen. P.J. Fairbanks had started college already? Seemed like just yesterday he was a freshman in high school. But he was looking more and more the spitting image of his father.

Speaking of P.J.'s father, where was Philip Fairbanks? He and Gabby had been back together for at least two years after a near divorce.

The food, which had been ordered and paid for by a church group, arrived by delivery and Estelle set to work with a few of the shelter residents keeping the turkeys and ham warm till time to slice them, and dishing up the various salads and side dishes into proper serving bowls. By the time Gabby rang the bell for dinner, the tables had been decorated with red and green plastic tablecloths, fake pine boughs, red and silver balls, and candles in safety glass jars, and Estelle had platters of sliced turkey and ham on the counter along with all the side dishes, plus cranberry relish, black olives, and sweet pickles.

As shelter guests, staff, and volunteers all stood in a circle holding hands for the blessing, Gabby asked Grace Meredith to start them on "Joy to the World." Estelle was touched by how beautifully the thirty-some shelter residents sang the familiar carol. Then it was food and laughter and bedlam for the next forty-five minutes—especially when Estelle set out the ten pies that had been delivered: sweet potato, mock mince, apple crumb, blueberry, banana cream . . . Glory! What a feast.

After dinner, Harry and Estelle pitched in as a cleanup crew, while Grace and the younger set played Clue and Scrabble and a rowdy game of Blitz with some of the residents. Three of the shelter guests needed a fourth for doubles Ping-Pong and shanghaied Harry, who actually could slam a mean ball. Estelle noticed that P.J. seemed to end up doing whatever Ramona was doing, and she was laughing and flirting right back. Gabby must have noticed it, too, because one time her eye caught Estelle's and she looked at the two young people and then made a face that had "Yikes!" all over it.

They stayed till nearly seven o'clock. Ramona sighed happily as they drove home. "That was the best Christmas ever! Can we do it again next year?"

Next year? Estelle half-turned and gave Grace a look in the backseat. Wouldn't Ramona be back in LA by next year?

Chapter 37

ESTELLE WAS GLAD both she and Harry had to go back to work Monday. The house was too quiet without DaShawn. Ramona had asked about going back to Manna House with Estelle regularly now that Max was off the streets—but as it turned out, Nicole Singer wasn't able to cut her hours at the law firm during the school holiday break as she'd hoped, so she asked Ramona if she could be "nanny" for Becky and Nathan until the kids went back to school. "She's paying me too!" Ramona told Estelle when she called to say she wouldn't be going to Manna House after all.

Grace would be leaving on her "New Year—New You" tour a week after New Year's Day, so was in a tizzy working on wedding plans. At Tuesday night prayer a few days after Christmas, she modeled the wedding dress she and Samantha had found at an After Christmas Sale that day for half price. "My mom's disappointed we didn't find one at Thanksgiving when she went shopping with me, but . . . do you like it?"

The dress was lovely. Simple lines—a square neckline, small cap sleeves, an empire waist, with sheer Schiffli lace covering the silky underlining that fell to the floor and ended in a small train. But Estelle was puzzled. "Didn't you already have a wedding dress when you were, uh, you know—?" As soon as she said it, she knew she'd stuck her foot in her mouth. Grace had been engaged before to a man who'd dumped her. "Oh. Grace, I'm so sorry. That was so thoughtless of me."

Grace made a face. "That was then. This is now. This one is for Jeff and me." She twirled around, her long dark hair a beautiful contrast to the white gown. Then she stopped. "I don't have any regrets. God had a better plan for me—a better husband." She suddenly got teary, even though her smile was big. "I'm so happy. I wish we could get married this weekend and skip all the fuss. But . . ." She shrugged. "Oh. I have a question for you sisters. Jeff and I are making our guest list this weekend. Do you think I should invite the rest of the neighbors on this block? I mean, besides you three and your families? I don't know if anyone else would come, but we aren't having a sit-down dinner reception—just a buffet, which could accommodate more people."

Estelle and Michelle and Nicole looked at each other. "I think that's a great idea," Estelle said.

Michelle shrugged. "Well, sure, if you want." Then she laughed. "More presents!"

Grace looked horrified. "Oh no. I hope people wouldn't think that's why they're getting an invitation."

Michelle laughed. "Just kidding. Sure, invite the neighbors."

But Nicole frowned. "Everyone? I mean, even the guys at the group home?"

A thunder-crack seemed to shake the whole house on New Year's Eve. "What odd winter weather," Estelle murmured, bringing a mug of hazelnut decaf coffee to Harry, who was watching the Times Square celebration on TV. "First we have a white Christmas—just enough snow, not too much. And now the temp is back up in the fifties, the snow has all melted, and we're getting a thunderstorm."

They'd decided to forgo the New Year's Eve service at Souled-Out. Harry had offered to cover New Year's Day on Saturday for a fellow security officer who wanted the day off—which, Estelle suspected, was Harry's way of keeping busy to avoid thinking about what DaShawn would decide about staying with his dad and mom for the next school semester.

They didn't have to wait long for the answer. "Hey, Happy New Year!" DaShawn said when she answered the phone the next day. "Is, uh, Gramps there?"

"Sorry, DaShawn. He's working today."

"Oh." A pause. "Well, I just wanted to tell you guys that it's been goin' pretty well over here, so I guess I'll come get some of my stuff Sunday afternoon. Dad said he'd bring me over. Uh, will Gramps be there tomorrow?"

Estelle tried to keep her voice even. "Yes, yes. We'll make sure we're both here. What time do you think you'll come?" She should warn Harry, so he didn't offer to cover for someone else on Sunday too.

"Two o'clock okay? I wanna go see the twins too. I—" DaShawn's voice cracked a bit. "I really miss hanging out with my friends over there on Beecham. But at least I'll get to see 'em at school." Another pause. "Really miss you and Gramps too, Gram."

Estelle got a lump in her throat. "We miss you too, DaShawn. Please, come back and visit on the weekends—or whenever you can. It would mean the world to your grandpa and me."

She called Harry as soon as she got off the phone with DaShawn. He didn't say much, just, "Well, that's it then. Yeah, two o'clock is okay."

Church seemed to drag the next morning—or go too fast. Estelle couldn't tell which. She had a hard time focusing on the worship, and Harry definitely seemed out to lunch. People greeted them after the service with, "Happy New Year!" but this New Year promised to be not so happy at the Bentley household. Not with DaShawn moving out and Leroy not moving nearby. *What's all this about, Lord?* Estelle fussed in her mind, but didn't really expect an answer.

Just before they got out the door of SouledOut, Jodi Baxter caught Estelle. "We didn't have Yada Yada last week because it was Christmas weekend. But January has five Sundays, so Avis and I thought we could meet tonight *and* the last Sunday of the month this time. Okay with you? My house, five o'clock."

Estelle nodded but she wondered if she should leave Harry alone that evening after DaShawn moved out. Well, she'd see.

Rodney and DaShawn showed up at two as promised. Harry followed his grandson into his bedroom as the boy packed some of his stuff, leaving Estelle to keep Rodney company. "Is Pops mad at me?" Rodney asked her in a low voice.

"No, no. Just give him some time, Rodney. DaShawn's been living with his grandpa for five years, you know, and it's hard to let him go. But he understands. He's proud of how far you've come this past year. He respects that, wants to respect DaShawn's wishes too." She gave Rodney a questioning look. "Are you sure Donita is up for this?"

"Yeah, yeah. We've talked about it a lot. She's his mother, you know."

After DaShawn had gathered a bunch of his stuff, he ran across the street to say good-bye to the Jaspers. Estelle went into the kitchen, leaving Harry with Rodney. Couldn't hear what they were saying, but she guessed Harry was giving his son an earful about what was good for DaShawn. She heard voices raise a time or two, but when DaShawn returned, Harry gave both of them a hug.

And then they were gone.

Harry left with Corky a few minutes later, saying he needed to walk the dog. Right. He was probably going to give Corky an earful too. At least the dog was a good listener.

When he got back an hour later, Harry told Estelle to go on to her Yada Yada Prayer Group. "You don't have to babysit me. I'm fine," he growled. "Corky and me, we're gonna watch a real shoot-'em-up thriller, ain't we girl." He gently knuckled the dog's noggin. "You don't wanna be around for that, Estelle."

✧   ✧   ✧   ✧

Estelle sank into a corner of Jodi's couch. It felt good to be surrounded by her Yada Yada sisters. Since they weren't celebrating anyone's birthday—Chanda George had had a December birthday, but she'd gone home to Jamaica for the holidays and wasn't back yet—they took extra time to share what was going on in everyone's life and pray for each other as they headed into the new year. Most of the requests were the usual: kids going back to school or college, job stresses, too full schedules. Estelle found herself asking prayer for a lot of other people: Michelle Jasper's baby due in early February . . . Grace Meredith's upcoming two-week concert tour . . . needing a place for Ramona to stay while Grace was gone . . . Ramona getting the subpoena to testify at Max's trial in a few

weeks . . . Leroy starting his job at Stroger Hospital tomorrow . . .
DaShawn moving in with his dad and mom and the loss Harry
was feeling . . .

"But what about you, Estelle?" Avis asked gently when she'd
spun out her list. "How can we pray for you?"

Estelle just shook her head. Why was she feeling so . . . so down?
Many of the prayer requests she'd just mentioned were also cause
for praise! Max had been taken off the street. Leroy had gotten an
actual *job*. Grace was getting married to the love of her life, a really
great guy. Ramona really liked taking care of the Singer kids and
getting a chance to teach them Spanish.

Still, it felt as if God was moving on all fronts except for the
one prayer that had been on her heart for months. Years, really.
That she could be a real mother to her son. A chance at redemption
after the years of loss and guilt. It didn't help that Harry had just
had to give up DaShawn too. Raising DaShawn had given Harry
a chance to be the father he'd failed to be for Rodney. But now . . .
she didn't know how to encourage her husband and didn't want
to burden him with her feelings about Leroy, which he'd already
heard a dozen times anyway.

Estelle shook her head again. She couldn't explain it. She would
just sound petty or peevish. But Avis prayed anyway. "Lord God,
You know what's on our sister Estelle's heart. Give her renewed as-
surance of how much You love her and how much You care. Thank
You for her big heart and all the concerns she carries for others, but
Lord, help her know that she can lay *her* burden down and let You
carry it . . ."

✧　✧　✧　✧

Temperatures had dipped again, back to "nippy but nice." Estelle
had to be careful walking out of the house to the car, as the melted
snow over the New Year's weekend had turned to a thin veneer
of ice on walks and roads. Now that Mattie Krakowski was back
home from her holiday visit with her son, Estelle made sure to tell
her *not* to go outside unless she had someone with her. The old
woman didn't need another broken hip!

Harry didn't talk much about DaShawn, just buried himself in his work. Estelle let it go. This was their new reality and they better just suck it up.

Grace was eager for "the sisters" to meet Tuesday night and pray for her concert tour, which started that Saturday in Memphis. "Sorry none of you got to see Jeff over the weekend," she said. "We were really busy with tour business on top of wedding plans. But . . . Nicole came with some good news. Tell them, Nicole."

Nicole flushed. "Well . . ." She reached out and shyly took Ramona's hand. "Ramona, my kids love having you for their nanny—*and* their tutor. I've watched you with them—you're really patient and fun and . . . I don't know, just good with them. Like a big sister. So Greg and I talked about it and we'd, um, like to invite you to stay with us while Grace is gone on her concert tour. You could have Becky's room, and she and Nathan could bunk together for the two weeks. If you'd like to, I mean. I—"

Ramona squealed. "Oh, Miss Nicole! I'd love to stay with you! Thank you so much!" She threw her arms around Nicole in a big hug.

When Nicole was able to pry Ramona's arms off her neck, she said, "I realize that leaves you alone three-fourths of the day, since the kids are back in school, but—"

"Not a problem," Estelle cut in. "Ramona could come to Manna House with me on school mornings and volunteer like she used to. We always get back before kids are home from school."

"Wait, wait." Now Michelle jumped in. "Tell you the truth, I was going to ask Ramona if she might like to help *me* out until the baby gets here." She rubbed a hand over her extended stomach. "This little rug rat is sapping all my energy and I can't seem to get anything done, even though I quit work two weeks ago! We're trying to make room for the baby, and I could really use help for three or four hours every day—you know, before Nicole's kids get home from school. And I'd pay you, too."

Ramona's mouth dropped open, but the smile on her face grew. "*Sí!* I'd love to help you get ready for the *bebé*, Michelle! And if you don't need me some days, I could go with Miss Estelle to the shelter that day. Oh, Miss Grace, God is working it all out, just like you told me He would!"

A few weeks ago Grace had said, *"It's God taking care of both of you with the same answer to prayer."* Except in this case, Estelle thought, God's answer to prayer was taking care of three at once.

Let it go, Estelle, that inner Voice said. *Just keep your prayer seatbelt buckled.*

"—be sure to come back to the house to take care of Oreo at least once a day," Grace was telling Ramona. "But don't come alone. Maybe Greg or Nicole could come with you."

"Don't worry about Oreo," Ramona assured her as the others all gathered around Grace. They laid hands on her and prayed for the upcoming tour—safety for the days on the road, strength and health for her voice so it wouldn't give out as it did last year during her first "New Year—New You" tour. But mostly for the young people who would come to the concerts, that God would use Grace's songs and testimony to touch kids with the reality of God's grace, especially for the ones who felt they'd messed up already. That God's love and mercy and grace were there for them too.

✦ ✦ ✦ ✦

Grace and Samantha flew out on Friday to meet Grace's band in Chattanooga. Then they'd tour several of the southern states for the next two weeks in the rented tour bus until she and Sam flew home on the next to the last Sunday—a total of sixteen days.

Max's trial was in less than two weeks. Good thing Ramona had responsibilities to keep her busy. Who knew what would happen that day? If the trial dragged on for a few days, they'd need to come up with a different plan for Nicole's kids if Ramona wasn't back in time to meet them after school.

January . . . after all the holidays in the fall, the days seemed to fall into the usual winter doldrums. Dark when they got up, dark even before suppertime. Even though the temperature was mild for a Chicago winter, hovering in the twenties, the cold seemed to seep into Estelle's bones. It snowed an inch or two every few days, but the accumulation wasn't much. Five or six inches at most. Maybe they'd get away with a mild winter and spring would come early.

Estelle was looking forward to her Saturday visit with Leroy to break up the long workweek. She was eager to hear how his job was going. But when she called the Lighthouse, he said, "Sorry, Ma. I can't come this Saturday. Or Sunday either. I have to work at the hospital this weekend."

What? She hadn't expected this. "Well, when do you get a day off?"

"I dunno. Next Thursday I think. It changes every week."

Thursday! That was her long day at Manna House, teaching the cooking class in the afternoon.

"I'm disappointed, baby. I was looking forward to seeing you."

"I know, Ma. Me too. But I like my job. It's a good job. I'm helping people."

"I know, baby. That's good. It's just—"

"And me an' Brenda—we're gettin' to be real good friends." There was laughter in Leroy's voice. "I like Brenda, Ma. Maybe we'll get married."

Estelle was speechless. This was too much! She finally found her voice. "Baby, don't rush into anything. One thing at a time. Just get used to your job. I'll come see you when you get a day off, okay? You let me know, promise?"

"Sure, Ma."

Estelle was close to tears when she hung up the phone. She was losing Leroy! She looked at the calendar. Leroy said Thursday . . . But today was Thursday. So he must mean next week Thursday. Well, she'd call again and make sure.

It was time to fix supper for Harry. She needed to pull herself together. *Buckle your prayer seatbelt, girl.* DaShawn had been gone almost two weeks and she was still cooking as if they had to feed a teenager with a hollow leg. The refrigerator was full of leftovers. Maybe they'd just eat leftovers tonight.

She was setting the kitchen table when the phone rang. "Bentleys."

"Gram? It—it's me." DaShawn sounded as if he was crying.

"DaShawn! What is it, baby? What's wrong?"

"Is . . . is Gramps there? I gotta talk to Gramps. Right away!"

"No he isn't. But I expect him real soon. Wait . . . hold on. I think I hear the garage door."

Still holding the cordless, Estelle pulled open the back door and went out onto the small deck. A light had gone on in the garage. "Yes, he's home. Hold on . . ."

Shivering, she waited for Harry and Corky to come out the side door and then she yelled, "Harry! Hurry. It's DaShawn on the phone. Says he needs to talk to you!"

Harry made it up the back stairs two at a time and grabbed the phone. "DaShawn! I'm here. What's goin' on? . . . What? . . . Where are you?" Harry looked wild-eyed. "DaShawn, you stay right there. I'll be there in twenty minutes."

Estelle looked at her husband, her heart pounding. "What?"

Harry was already at the back door, his eyes flashing fire. "Don't know for sure. Says he's at that drugstore on the corner down the street from my mom's old place. Wants me to come get him. Right now."

Chapter 38

Estelle jerked off her apron. "Wait. I'm comin' too." No way was she going to just sit here at home if DaShawn was in some kind of trouble.

Her husband paused for half a second. "Then we gotta take your car. Don't have room for three in the Durango."

Harry drove crazy fast in spite of the spitting snow that had been coming down on and off all day. Estelle was afraid a cop would pull them over before they even got to her mother-in-law's old neighborhood. She knew the drugstore well enough, because she'd helped take care of the old lady in her job as an elder caretaker before she and Harry got married. She'd often gone down to the drugstore to pick up a prescription for Mother Wanda before she passed. Harry had been happy enough about Rodney moving into his mom's apartment after the funeral, giving him a place of his own to get his life back together. Until Donita moved in, too, that is.

Tires squealing, Harry pulled into a No Parking space in front of the drugstore, punched the emergency flashers, and left the car running. As he disappeared inside, Estelle swiveled her head anxiously, hoping a police car wouldn't come by.

Even before Harry reappeared with DaShawn, Estelle got out and climbed into the backseat of the RAV4. Best to let DaShawn sit up front with Harry. It'd be easier to talk if he was next to his grandpa. At least it didn't sound as if DaShawn had gotten into any trouble. According to Harry, all he said on the phone was, *"My mom—she went kinda nuts. I can't stay there! Please come get me."*

The front car doors opened and Harry and DaShawn climbed in, his school backpack slung over one shoulder. She wasn't sure if the boy knew she was there, so she said, "Hi, DaShawn. I'm here too," so as not to startle him. He cast a glance over his shoulder and gave her a nod. "Thanks for comin', Gram," he mumbled as he buckled his seatbelt.

Harry was grim-faced as he drove around the block and headed back home. But once they were on Western Avenue headed north, he glanced at DaShawn. "Okay, son. What happened? What about your mom?"

DaShawn just stared out the side window. From where Estelle was sitting behind the driver's seat, she could see his jaw clenching.

"DaShawn," his grandfather said, a little more firmly. "I gotta know what happened. It's okay. Just tell me."

Soon it all came tumbling out between big gulps of air. "Got home from school today kinda late—takes a little longer 'cause I gotta take the 'L' then the bus. Dad was out, still drivin' some bigwigs to the airport for Lincoln Limo. But when I let myself in the apartment, I could hear my mom laughin' and talkin' with somebody, an'"—DaShawn's voice rose angrily—"I could tell she was wasted. That shrill laugh of hers when she gets high." He spit out the words and hit the dashboard with his fist. "An' I couldn't believe it! That . . . that rotten guy she used to hang out with when my dad was in prison, that pimp was sittin' there on Great-Grammy's couch, grinnin' like a fool. I could tell he was wasted too. 'Hey there, boy,' he said all friendly-like. 'How ya doin'?'" DaShawn imitated the guy's voice sarcastically. "'Ain't seen ya for a long time, boy. Look at you, all grown.'"

DaShawn paused, breathing heavily. Estelle could see Harry's face in the rearview mirror, eyes narrowed, a storm cloud ready to shoot lightning bolts.

"I yelled at the guy—can't remember his name—told him to get outta there or I was gonna call the police. Then he got mad, jumped off the couch, an' made like he was gonna hit me. I ducked an' he yelled, 'You better shut your face, you little—'" DaShawn spit out the nasty words like a pro. Harry shot him a glance but said nothing, just tromped on the gas and swerved around a slow vehicle. Estelle bit her tongue. Now was not the time to clean up DaShawn's language.

"I yelled at my mom, told her I was leavin' an' not comin' back."
DaShawn's shoulders heaved suddenly as he broke down in sobs.

"You don't have to go back, son," Harry said tersely. "It's all
right. Gonna be all right."

They rode in silence until Harry pulled into the garage. DaShawn
climbed out of the car and hustled up the outside back stairs. By
the time Harry and Estelle got up to the apartment, DaShawn was
down on the floor tussling with Corky, whose tail was wagging a
furious welcome. With a final hug for the dog, DaShawn stood up
and headed for his bedroom. "Guess I better call my dad, let him
know where I am," he muttered as he disappeared into the room.

"I'll call him!" Harry called after him and took out his cell
phone.

Estelle stopped him. "No, let DaShawn call his dad." She pulled
her husband aside and lowered her voice. "Let DaShawn tell his
dad what happened. If you call, then it becomes between you and
Rodney."

"It *is* between me and Rodney," Harry hissed. "He never
should have let that . . . that hellcat back into DaShawn's life. An'
I'm gonna—"

"Not now!" Estelle insisted. "Right now Rodney needs to hear
from DaShawn about what happened when his son got home,
and that DaShawn was the one who called you to come get him.
Now—before he gets a different story from Donita."

Harry hesitated, his jaw working, then he picked up the house
phone and carried it into DaShawn's bedroom. "On second
thought," she heard him say, "maybe you should call your dad."

✧   ✧   ✧   ✧

Somehow Estelle was able to put together supper for Harry and
DaShawn out of the leftovers crowding the fridge. But it wasn't
long before the house phone rang. Estelle picked it up, looked at
the caller ID, and handed it to DaShawn. "It's your dad."

DaShawn took the phone. "Hi Dad . . . yeah, I left a voicemail
for you . . . I'm at Grandpa and Grandma's house . . ." He listened
for a long while. Then, "I *told* you in my message what happened.

I—I don't want to come back tonight . . ." The boy listened some more, then handed the phone to Harry. "He wants to talk to you, Gramps."

Harry took the phone, shoved his chair back, and walked into the next room. Estelle followed him. "No, don't come up here tonight, Rodney," Harry was saying. "You gotta give the boy some room . . . Go home and deal with the mess in your own house . . . Yeah, DaShawn's gonna stay here for a few days. He's pretty upset . . . Yeah, yeah, we'll talk later."

DaShawn had run out of the apartment with only his school bag, but Estelle found something for him to sleep in and washed the clothes he took off so he'd have something clean to wear the next day. She and Harry sat up talking, long after DaShawn was asleep.

Harry was still livid. "No way I'm gonna let that woman stay in my mom's apartment. Mom made me executor in her will, so my name is on that lease now, even if Rodney is payin'."

"Harry—"

"And no way is DaShawn goin' back there. If Rodney doesn't have the good sense to kick that woman out of his life, he doesn't have the good sense to raise my grandson."

"Harry—"

"What?"

Estelle just lifted an eyebrow.

Harry sighed. "Yeah, yeah, I know. Rodney's gotta be the one to deal with Donita, or she'll make it about me interfering. But I just can't stand by and let DaShawn—"

"I agree with you, Harry. She can't be usin' drugs and inviting that pimp into a house where our grandson is living. We have a right to say what happened was totally unacceptable and DaShawn can't go back as long as she's there. Period. After all, you're still his legal guardian."

Harry argued. He didn't trust Rodney to have the guts to kick her out. And he didn't want DaShawn to go back there even if he did. But finally they decided to just sleep on it. And ask God to show them what to do.

✦ ✦ ✦ ✦

DaShawn grabbed a piece of toast and ran out of the house the next morning to meet up with the Jasper twins on the way to school. Estelle watched from the front window as the threesome playfully pushed and laughed and threw a few snowballs at each other as they walked to the bus. Looked to her like DaShawn was glad to be home.

Pulling on a bulky sweater, Estelle went downstairs to get the newspaper and noticed a Meals on Wheels van driving up the street as if looking for an address. The van turned around in the cul-de-sac in front of Lincoln Paddock's house, then parked in front of their house. "This Mattie Krakowski's place?" the driver called as he got out.

"You got it." Well, good for Mattie. Or maybe it was her son, Daniel, who lined up meals for his mom. Especially in the winter when it was hard for her to get out to the grocery store, even by taxi.

As she went back up the stairs, she heard Mattie answer her door. "What? Deals on wheels? Sorry, don't want no solicitors . . ."

Chuckling, Estelle headed back to her kitchen. Hopefully the Meals on Wheels driver would succeed in leaving the food. Mattie could be pretty stubborn. But it made her wonder . . . how were Eva and Karl next door doing? Maybe they could use something like Meals on Wheels. She ought to go next door and check on them. Hadn't seen them for a while—not since the Open House at the group home. Good grief, had that been almost four weeks already?

✧   ✧   ✧   ✧

Rodney showed up on Saturday between pickups for Lincoln Limo to talk to DaShawn. It took almost all of Estelle's physical strength and powers of persuasion to get Harry out the door to walk Corky, long enough to give father and son some time alone to talk. "Just ten minutes," she told him. "Then come back and we can talk to them both."

"But what if he talks DaShawn into coming back, some sob story about how sorry his mom is? No way—"

"Harry, just go. Give them ten minutes."

Was she doing the right thing? Estelle stayed in the kitchen while Rodney talked to DaShawn, though she was tempted to eavesdrop. Instead she prayed. *O God, not our will but Yours be done.* Wait. Was that what she wanted to pray? Not really. She wanted to tell God what to do! But she just kept praying, *God, do what's best for DaShawn.*

Harry was back in ten minutes on the dot. Rodney looked embarrassed as they came into the living room. "Don't say it," he said to his dad. "Shouldn't have happened. I—yeah, I know. Donita an' me got some stuff to work out."

Harry snorted. "Got that right."

"Uh, DaShawn says he wants to stay here right now. Okay with you?"

"Of course," Estelle hastened to say. "But he needs his clothes and other things."

"Yeah. I'll, uh, get his stuff together and bring it tomorrow."

"Rodney, he's been wearing the same clothes for three days."

Rodney's shoulders slumped. "Okay. Tonight then." His phone reminder went off. "Uh, gotta go. Got a client to pick up."

As they stood up, Rodney grabbed DaShawn and pulled him into a tight hug. "So sorry, son. So sorry." Then he hustled down the stairs and out the door. To Estelle it looked like the man was crying.

Chapter 39

IN A WAY, ESTELLE WAS GLAD she didn't have to be away from the house for several hours that weekend to see Leroy, as it seemed important to be around for DaShawn as he got resettled in his room. She made some of his favorite food—BBQ chicken and oven-baked home fries—and did a whole lot of laundry. Hmph. Didn't look as if Donita had done any laundry since DaShawn had moved his stuff to their apartment New Year's weekend.

That woman!

Harry got a phone call Sunday night that he took in their bedroom with the door closed, but he didn't say anything when he came out. "Rodney?" she asked. He shook his head, got Corky's leash, and went out into the night for the dog's walk.

Now what was *that* about?

On Monday night, Estelle called Michelle and Nicole and suggested they meet for prayer at her house Tuesday night. She didn't feel comfortable meeting at Grace Meredith's house while she was away on tour, even though Ramona insisted it'd be okay. "The trial is this Wednesday," Estelle told the others. "We should pray with Ramona. I'm sure she's really nervous about having to testify with Max right there in the courtroom."

Michelle sighed on the phone. "Well, for Ramona I'll scale the mountain to your second floor apartment. I'd invite you all to our house, but three teenagers plus a husband who just spent a nerve-racking day in the control tower at O'Hare wouldn't be exactly conducive to a prayer meeting. You haven't installed an elevator recently, have you?"

Nicole said her house wouldn't work either—not with a spouse trying to give baths and get kids into bed. So it was DaShawn who got banished to his bedroom to do homework, though Estelle took pity on Harry and let him have the living room TV while the girls gathered around the kitchen table for prayer.

"So tomorrow's the trial," Estelle said after putting out the tea things. "You doing okay, Ramona?"

The girl shrugged. "I'm kinda scared. Max will be there."

"I know, child. But Harry's pretty sure he'll be going away for a long time. And God's bigger than Max and that drug cartel. We're going to cover you in prayer right now." Which they did, holding hands in a knot in the center of the table and pounding heaven with their prayers.

"Wish Miss Grace were here," Ramona sniffed, wiping her eyes with a tissue after the prayers.

"I'm sure she wishes she could be too. But she'll be with you in spirit, I know."

"I've got some good news," Nicole Singer said, a bit shyly. "Greg and I took our kids over to Casa Shalom last week, and we met Rodrigo and the other guys. The kids were a little scared to meet the man who screamed—but once they actually met him, they warmed right up. He was so kind and gentle as he answered their questions."

"Yeah," Ramona chimed in. "They've been busy ever since making cards for him and writing notes."

Nicole grinned sheepishly. "Not sure who was helped more by meeting those guys personally—the kids or me. That Jack is really sweet. Stephan . . . he's a little strange, but seems harmless. Bernie is really intense though. I've never met anyone with Asperger's before. We've decided to do some homeschool-type projects learning more about Down syndrome and Asperger's and . . . whatever Stephan's problem is."

Harry walked Michelle home, not wanting her to fall when she was almost nine months pregnant. Estelle sat at the kitchen table for a while after the women left, thinking about Nicole and the group home. Seemed like God was already using Casa Shalom to do some healing in the neighborhood.

Greg Singer arranged to work from home on Wednesday on the chance Ramona wouldn't be home in time to receive the kids from school. The trial at the Cook County Court House in Skokie was set for ten o'clock, but it was ten twenty before the jury filed in. Harry and Estelle and Ramona sat on the right side of the small courtroom behind the state's attorney's table. Harry wore his Amtrak Security uniform as the arresting officer, ready to testify. Nicole had braided the sides of Ramona's hair and tied them at the back of her head that morning, letting the rest of her rich brown hair fall in waves below her shoulders. She was wearing new jeans, leather snow boots, and a thick pullover sweater, looking like the eighteen-year-old she was. But she'd only been seventeen last spring when Max had coerced her into traveling with him across state lines, helping him deliver drugs from LA to Chicago, meriting the kidnapping charge and contributing to the delinquency of a minor, as well as dealing drugs.

Max was brought in from a side door by a police officer. He was dressed in street clothes, and as he walked to the defense table on the left of the courtroom, he saw Ramona and winked at her. Estelle felt a surge of hot anger and put her arm protectively around Ramona, who'd ducked her head.

The judge came in—a woman. *Praise God,* Estelle thought. "All rise," the clerk intoned. Instructions were given and everyone sat down again. The jury was fairly diverse this time—mostly whites, but also three blacks and two Hispanics. After the clerk read charges, the state's attorney began to state his case. Estelle had an inkling how Ramona must be feeling. Her own heart seemed to be beating triple-time.

Harry kept turning around and glancing at the back of the small courtroom. Estelle was about to ask who he was looking for when he was called to the witness stand by the prosecution. In response to the lawyer's questions, he told his story about traveling undercover for Amtrak Security after getting intel that a "mule" would be bringing drugs into Chicago from LA by train. His dog, Harry said, was trained to sniff out drugs, which the dog discovered in one of the suitcases onboard. Later the owner of the suitcase changed her travel plans and departed early in New Mexico, after which he witnessed the defendant threatening his companion, a young girl, about letting the passenger out of her sight.

The lawyer asked Harry if that young girl was in the courtroom, and Harry indicated Ramona before continuing.

Since the evidence was only circumstantial at that point, he had to wait until the suitcase and its owner arrived a day or two later in Chicago, at which time he witnessed the defendant stealing the suitcase in question while the owner was distracted, at which time Harry made the arrest.

The defense lawyer then questioned Harry harshly, why he didn't arrest the owner of the suitcase as the one carrying the drugs. But before he could answer, there was a slight commotion at the back of the room. A broad smile spread across Harry's face. "I think it'll become clear when you hear the next witness."

All eyes turned to the back. Ramona gasped and Estelle could hardly believe her eyes. *Grace Meredith.*

The state's attorney said, "The prosecution would like to call Grace Meredith to the stand."

Grace gave Ramona a smile as she made her way to the witness stand and whispered, "I'm here, sweetie." Prompted by the state's attorney, Grace told her story—about meeting the young girl in the LA train station, trying to get to know her, having a sense something wasn't right. The girl seemed to be terrified of her so-called boyfriend—

"Objection!" called the defense.

"Of the man she was with," Grace corrected.

"Objection, your honor. My objection was also to the witness's *speculation* that the girl was *terrified*."

"Sustained."

Grace hardly knew what to do until the judge turned and told her to continue. She explained that the defendant seemed much older by at least ten years, and Ramona was still a teenager. She told how she'd accidentally spilled coffee on the girl's jacket, offered to get it cleaned and return it to her in Chicago, even though the girl seemed afraid the guy she was with would find out. Things got complicated when Grace had a sudden change in her own travel plans, causing her to get off in New Mexico and return to Chicago a day later. She'd planned to contact Ramona and return the jacket once she got it cleaned, but the girl had met her as she got off the train, demanding her jacket right then, then suddenly seemed to faint right there in the station. As Grace attended to the girl, her suitcase disappeared. Only later did she learn from Amtrak Security that they'd caught the thief who'd stolen her suitcase in order to retrieve drugs that had been stashed inside the area housing the suitcase handle.

During cross-examination, the defense tried to make it sound like Grace was the one transporting drugs. It was her suitcase! When it came out that charges against Ramona for her complicity had been dropped if she would testify against the defendant, the defense jumped on the fact that Grace had shown a great deal of concern toward the girl from the time they first met, took her under her wing so to speak. "How do we know the girl isn't testifying against my client because she feels some obligation to protect you?"

Estelle realized she was holding her breath. What if it came out that Grace had actually taken Ramona into her home for "witness protection"? That might give the defense more ammunition for his bogus charge—and even worse, would let Max know where Ramona was staying!

But to her relief it didn't come up. Must be something about witness protection that disallowed information about a witness's whereabouts to come out during a trial.

The judge allowed Grace to step down. She squeezed past Estelle and sat down on the other side of Ramona. "Told you I'd be here for you, honey," she whispered. Ramona leaned against her and started to cry.

Would Ramona be called now? Estelle tensed as she saw the state's attorney whisper to his two cohorts at the prosecution table, frown, whisper some more, glance back at Ramona . . . and then he said, "Your Honor, I'd like five minutes to confer with our witnesses."

"Five minutes, counselor."

The state's attorney came over and huddled with Harry, Estelle, Grace, and Ramona. "Miss Meredith, I know you were hoping your testimony would be enough to support Officer Bentley's testimony and convict the defendant without having to call the young lady to testify, but we're pretty sure the defense is going to claim that their client is guilty only of stealing your suitcase and didn't know there were drugs inside. I'm afraid we need Ramona to testify. She's the only one who can verify he was transporting the drugs and coerced her to help him find a mark."

Harry swore under his breath. "I caught the guy red-handed with the drugs!"

"It's not enough. We need Ramona's testimony. I'm sorry."

Ramona took a deep breath. "That's all right. I'm ready."

"Good girl." The state's attorney returned to the table. "Your Honor, I would like to call Ramona Sanchez to the witness stand."

✧   ✧   ✧   ✧

Grace had to leave directly from the courthouse to go to the airport to rejoin her tour. "You did great, honey," she told Ramona out in the hallway. "I'll be home Sunday. Then you can help me get ready for the wedding!" A hug and then she was gone.

Ramona was subdued as she rode home with Harry and Estelle. "Did you know Grace planned to show up at the trial?" Estelle asked Harry.

He nodded. "That's who called me the other night. Asked me if she testified, if that might be enough to help convict Max without Ramona having to testify. I talked to the state's attorney and he was willing to consider it, but—well, you heard what he said."

"What happens now?" Ramona asked from the backseat.

"The defense will present their case tomorrow. Then the case will go to the jury and . . . we'll see what happens. Since the judge didn't tell you to, you don't have to go back—unless you want to."

"No." A long pause. "Guess it's in God's hands now."

Estelle looked at Harry, then turned her head to glance at Ramona. "That's right, honey. It's in God's hands now."

✧　✧　✧　✧

Estelle went to see Leroy after her sewing class the next day—his day off—and took him out to supper. He was so excited about his job he almost forgot to eat. "Ma! This kid got burned real bad, don't know how, but I talked to him about all sorts of stuff, you know, the Cubs an girls an' school, an' he said it helped him forget how much it hurt. Made me feel real good. An' . . ." Estelle had to smile as the stories went on. Leroy was really upbeat. But when he talked about Brenda, she realized her smile felt a little more forced. *O God, don't let him get hurt by this woman.* How could it ever work for two people with substantial mental health issues to get married?

When she got home Harry had just gotten a call from the state's attorney. He quickly put the phone on Speaker so Estelle could hear. "The jury was out only four hours. Guilty of transporting a controlled substance across state lines, but not guilty of the kidnapping charge."

"What?" Estelle cried. "He took a minor across state lines without the permission of her parents!"

"Yes," the attorney said patiently, "but as the young lady admitted on the stand, she agreed to go with him because he'd befriended her when she ran away from home. Only later did she become afraid of him when their mark left the train with the suitcase. But it's good news, folks! Sentencing will be in a few weeks. I'll be in touch."

"Well, praise God," Estelle breathed after they hung up. "We need to go tell Ramona right away."

✧　✧　✧　✧

As scheduled, Grace Meredith got home Sunday evening. From her second floor view, Estelle saw the taxi drive up and Grace and her assistant trudge through several inches of snow on her unshoveled walks, taking bags inside. A few minutes later Ramona came out of the Singers' house with her duffle bag, ran up the block, and disappeared into Grace's house.

Estelle smiled to herself. Happy reunion going on there.

She was eager to hear about Grace's concert tour when they got together for prayer on Tuesday night. But Grace laughed nervously. "It was wonderful. God was so present . . . but the tour seems like ages ago already! I only have one week now to get ready for the wedding, and my head's spinning with stuff to do." She picked up a box of invitations. "My mom sent out the ones that needed to be mailed, but I didn't get these in time to pass out to the neighbors. Would, uh, one of you volunteer?"

Estelle ended up with the invitations for the neighbors. "Okay now, slow down, Grace, and tell us your plans for the wedding. Maybe there are other ways we can help."

Grace grabbed her list. Jeff was arriving on Saturday. His parents got back from a ten-day cruise on Sunday and would be flying in on Tuesday but probably wouldn't get there in time for the rehearsal Tuesday morning. "That's the only time we could reserve the church—they have a lot of programs going on over there." Grace's parents would drive up from Indy on Monday, stay with her brother Mark, and be there for the rehearsal. The wedding party and family—which included Samantha as maid of honor, her brother Mark as Jeff's best man, Mark's wife and sons, and both sets of parents—would meet somewhere at a restaurant for the traditional rehearsal dinner.

"Jeff's parents are supposed to take care of that, but I want you sisters and your husbands to come too. Please?"

"But we're not doing anything!" Michelle protested.

"Uh, I was just getting to that," Grace teased. "My parents are making all the arrangements for the buffet reception at the church, but I still need help at the wedding."

When all was said and done, Ramona was excited to be asked to be the candle lighter. "Sam will take you shopping for a dress," Grace promised. Michelle needed a job where she could sit down, so offered to do the guestbook at a small table, and Nicole became official greeter, directing people where to hang coats, deliver gifts, and sign the guestbook.

Grace looked imploringly at Estelle. "I need someone to be my wedding coordinator—you know, who will tell the wedding party when to come in at the right time. Estelle, would you—"

"The wedding boss!" Ramona crowed. "Perfect job for Miss Estelle!" Everyone laughed—except Michelle, whose face suddenly contorted and her eyes went wide.

"Michelle! What is it?" Estelle was immediately at her side.

Michelle had her hand on her stomach. "A contraction. I think. Pretty strong."

"What? You're not due for two weeks, right?"

Michelle nodded, but struggled to her feet. "Been feeling something goin' on for a couple hours. I—I think I better get home."

"You stay right there," Estelle commanded. "I'm going to call Jared."

"I live right next door," Michelle protested.

"You're not twenty-five, Michelle Jasper. You're forty-two and this is a late-in- life baby. I think Jared should take you to the hospital."

Chapter 40

ESTELLE COULD HARDLY SLEEP THAT NIGHT, wondering what was happening with Michelle's baby. But by the time she got Harry and DaShawn out the door to work and school the next morning, she still hadn't heard anything. So she called Jared Jasper's cell.

"Oh, hi Estelle." Jared sounded tired. "Yeah, we're still at the hospital but no, no baby yet. In fact, the contractions stopped altogether about two hours ago and they're getting ready to send Michelle home."

"Ohh, I'm so sorry. False alarm I guess."

"Yeah, doctor said they were just Braxton-Hicks contractions. Michelle says she feels stupid coming in to the hospital. The kids got all excited, thought they were going to have a new baby brother or sister today."

"Well, she shouldn't feel stupid. I was the one who encouraged her to go."

"And I agreed with you. Better to be safe than sorry at our age. Anyway, I gotta go. But don't call Michelle till tomorrow. She didn't get any sleep last night, and I think she wants to lay low. I didn't either, but I gotta go to work now."

Estelle hung up. At least Michelle's husband was a supervisor now at the O'Hare control tower rather than an air traffic controller himself. Wouldn't be a good idea to do *that* nerve-racking job on no sleep.

She waited till the next day to check on Michelle, who wearily said she hadn't had any more contractions since early Wednesday morning. "Wouldn't mind this baby coming early though. I feel like a blimp that's been grounded. But my obstetrician said I'm barely dilated. So those contractions the other night didn't help much."

Things got extra busy at Manna House the next few days because the hot water heater went out, so Estelle had to heat water on the big stove for all kinds of necessities besides cooking—so it was Saturday before Estelle had a chance to go over to the Jaspers' to check on Michelle again. Still no new contractions. On her way back home, she was surprised to see Daniel Krakowski parked in front of the graystone, stowing suitcases in the back of his SUV.

"What's going on, Daniel?" Estelle asked, shivering inside her bulky jacket. She hadn't dressed to be out long.

"Oh, heard we might get a real dump of snow next week, so I decided to bring Mom over to our house. Don't want something like what happened last winter to happen again." He slammed the back of the SUV and hurried back into the house to get his mom.

Estelle waited outside to say good-bye to Mattie—and suddenly realized she had an invitation with Mattie's name on it that she'd never delivered. She hustled inside and up the stairs as fast as she could, but was huffing when she came back outside with Grace's wedding invitation.

"But I'm gonna miss my favorite TV shows, Danny." Mattie was whining as her son put her in the car. "Can I come home tomorrow?"

"No, Mom. You can watch your shows at our house. We have TV too."

"Wait," Estelle called, reaching the car before he closed the door. "I have something for you, Miss Mattie." She handed the envelope to the old woman. "Grace Meredith across the street is getting married. It's an invitation."

"Who?"

By then Daniel was in the car and impatient to be off. Well, the invitation was self-explanatory.

Estelle went back into the house shaking her head. Mattie's son had a good heart, bless him. But what did he mean about a "real dump of snow" next week? She hadn't been paying much attention to the weather lately. After all, it was almost the end of January, and even though they'd had snow showers every other day or so, the accumulation wasn't much. Pretty mild winter so far—and no one was complaining.

But she'd totally forgotten about those wedding invitations for the neighbors! And the wedding was next Wednesday! She better bundle up and deliver them right now.

✧　✧　✧　✧

She apologized at each house for delivering the invitations so late—totally her fault. But she assured each person that Grace would be delighted if they could come.

Responses were interesting, she told Harry later. "It's a morning wedding, eleven o'clock, so some people will be at work of course. But Farid has his own business, so he said he'd see. Tim Mercer said Scott had to work, but he'd try to make it since he works at home. Lincoln Paddock said he'd absolutely come, seemed real tickled to be invited. The Smith-Owenses weren't home—no surprise there. The Cohens at Casa Shalom seemed surprised to be invited. Sarah wasn't sure if all four boys could come, might depend on the day. But she said some of them would definitely try to make it."

The Horowitzes were the most interesting, Estelle said. Rebecca confided she'd never been to a Christian wedding. "She said Isaac probably wouldn't come—he has to work anyway. But she said she'd like to, if she can get a babysitter for little Benjy."

"And the Molanders?" Harry asked, one eyebrow raised.

"Probably not. Eva said Karl wasn't doing too good lately. Not getting out much these days because of his heart and the weather." Estelle frowned. "We really should look in on them more. Eva sounded pretty worried."

Rodney showed up late Sunday afternoon wanting to talk to DaShawn just as Estelle was getting ready to leave for the last-Sunday-of-January Yada Yada Prayer Group meeting. *Should I stay?* she mouthed at Harry, but he waved her out, probably wanting "the talk" to be just father, son, and grandson.

If she'd known how hard the wind was blowing, she might've stayed home anyway. Even though it hadn't actually snowed for a few days, the wind tossed it around like one of those snow globes kids shake. But Estelle was glad she went because Nony Sisulu-

Smith, who had moved home to South Africa a few years ago, was their only January birthday, and they Skyped her on Avis Douglass's computer, even though it was one o'clock in the morning in KwaZulu-Natal! It was crazy and wonderful at the same time—everyone talked at once, cried, crowded together for a glimpse of their precious sister, laughed at how they looked on Skype, sang "Happy Birthday" to her a bit off-key. Nony wanted everyone's news, so the Skype call lasted a while.

When Estelle finally got home, DaShawn said his grandpa was out walking Corky. "Which means they'll be back soon," she said dryly. "It's a biting wind out there. Uh . . . would you like some hot chocolate?" Shameless bribery, she knew. But she wanted to hear about Rodney's visit.

"So," she said as she heated a mug of milk in the microwave, "what did your dad want?" Two heaping tablespoons of mint-flavored hot chocolate mix into the hot milk equaled one captured grandson.

"Got any of those mini-marshmallows?" DaShawn held out the mug.

Estelle dug out the mini-marshallows and waited while he took a few sips. "So, your dad?"

DaShawn shrugged. "Dad said my mom's not gonna live at Great-Grammy's apartment anymore, and he wanted to know if I'd come back to stay with him—just him and me."

Estelle took a deep breath and told herself not to say anything. But he was quiet so long, just sucking mini-marshmallows off the top of his hot chocolate, that she finally blurted, "DaShawn!"

He looked up and grinned. "Just messin' with ya, Grams. I told my dad I didn't want to go back right now. I want to finish the school year here with you and Gramps. But I could visit weekends sometimes, ya know, like we were doin'."

"You scalawag!" Estelle reached over and pulled DaShawn into a big hug. Then she laughed. "You better be careful who you mess with, young man. Or you just might get a refill on that hot chocolate!"

✧ ✧ ✧ ✧

While driving to work Monday morning, Estelle realized she couldn't come in to cook lunch at Manna House the next day, because she had to go to Grace's wedding rehearsal out at that big suburban church. After all, she needed to practice when to tell the wedding party to start down the aisle. She stayed longer at the shelter on Monday, cooking up a big batch of chili and a couple of pans of cornbread for the staff to serve the next day. Luckily the water heater had been repaired, so she didn't have to deal with *that* again.

Early Tuesday, Grace called to ask if Ramona could ride to the church with her, since Jeff was picking her up in his rental car. And could she also take some boxes of stuff she'd rented for the reception?

It was snowing again—not much, a light snow—but Estelle figured she better add some extra time to the forty-five minute trip out to the church. So she asked Ramona to be ready to leave at nine thirty. Ramona was excited. Now that the trial was over and Max was going away for a long time, hopefully, the girl seemed more relaxed, upbeat. Estelle hadn't heard anything about when she'd be going back to LA and her parents, but that decision was probably waiting until after Grace's wedding.

The rehearsal was scheduled for eleven. Grace and Jeff Newman were already at the church when Estelle and Ramona arrived, but Jeff was on his cell phone walking back and forth, running his hands through his dark, curly hair. "Something wrong?" Estelle asked Grace.

She shrugged. "Not sure. I think he's talking to his parents."

Samantha Curtis and the rest of the wedding party were arriving, stamping snow off their feet as they came into the beautifully carpeted foyer. The foyer rang with squeals as Grace greeted and hugged her parents, who'd stayed overnight at Mark's house. The church's event coordinator met them and showed them the side rooms where the bride and other women could dress, the groom's room, and a lounge where the family and others could wait.

Jeff joined them, shaking his head. "Bad news. My parents said their flight into Chicago was cancelled. Not just delayed. Big storm warnings in the Midwest."

"Too bad, but not surprised," Grace's dad murmured. "Weather report said Chicago might get a lot of snow tonight."

"Oh, honey, I'm so sorry." Grace tucked her hand into the crook of Jeff's arm. "Maybe they can fly in late tonight or early tomorrow and still get here in time for the wedding."

Jeff shook his head. "They didn't sound too hopeful. But . . . who knows." He rubbed his hands together as if trying to shake off his mood. "Let's get this show on the road! I want to marry this here girl, and we may have to elope if you all don't shake a leg."

Laughter broke the tension and they moved toward the sanctuary. The pastor met them at the front, assured Grace's parents it was his privilege to marry this fine young couple and he was glad to make his church available to Mark Meredith's sister—"Fine family, the Merediths"—and he had a meeting in thirty minutes so could they go through his part first?

That threw Estelle off a bit, but they went through the part with Grace and Jeff and the pastor at the altar, then practiced the coming in of the parents and wedding party with the organist, as well as the recessional. Grace had wanted her keyboardist from the band to play the processional, but the band had a gig. Grace had no flower girl—Mark only had two boys—so they'd dispensed with both flower girl and ring bearer, so Ramona was the first to walk in to light the candles. *Bless her*, Estelle thought as she had the young woman practice again, coming in slower, in time to Pachelbel's lovely "Canon in D" processional. *Hopefully she'll also find a wonderful Christian young man someday and walk down the aisle in her own wedding.*

Since the wedding party wasn't large, they were done before twelve thirty. Jeff said, "Snow has stopped. But it might be a good idea to head back before it starts up again. My parents said to go ahead with the rehearsal dinner tonight at Pete Miller's in Evanston, even if they don't make it. Anybody need the address?"

Estelle was glad that Harry was invited to the restaurant tonight, as well as Michelle and Jared and Greg and Nicole. That would be fun.

Grace's parents went home with Grace and Jeff instead of going to Mark's, since Mark had to go back to work at UPS after the rehearsal. He and Denise would join them later tonight at the restaurant with their boys. Samantha decided to hang out at Grace's until the rehearsal dinner too. Quite a houseful over there, Estelle chuckled. But personally, she was glad she was coming home to a quiet house for a few hours, since Harry was still at work and DaShawn at school. She needed a nap!

✧   ✧   ✧   ✧

Estelle woke to the incessant ringing of her cell phone. Groping for the phone on the bedside table, she said "Hello?" groggily without even looking at the ID.

"Hey, babe." Harry's voice. "Look, weather conditions have gotten really bad down here in the city. They're cancelling most of the trains. I got a few things to finish up here, but then Corky and I are going to start home. Uh, what time does DaShawn usually get home? I'm kind of worried about the buses up there."

By now Estelle had swung her feet off the bed, wide awake. "What? The snow had stopped when I got home a while ago." What time was it, anyway? She looked at her watch. Almost three? She'd slept longer than she intended. She started to say more, but Harry had already hung up.

She walked into the living room and stared at the front windows. She could hardly see across the street. Heavy snow was blowing sideways across the windows and the wind whined like a cat stuck in the walls. Flipping on the TV, an emergency weather band ran across the bottom of the screen: "Heavy snowfall . . . Blizzard conditions expected by early evening . . . Wind gusts currently up to 40 mph . . . Lake Shore Drive already bumper to bumper . . . Stay home if at all possible . . ."

Now she did feel anxious. How was Harry going to drive home in this? And DaShawn? *O Lord, I don't know what to do! Please keep my boys safe!*

The front door downstairs opened, then blew shut with a *bang,* and she heard DaShawn stomping up the stairs. "Thank goodness you're home! How—?"

DaShawn shook off a thick layer of snow from his coat and boots. "Mr. Jasper came and picked us up from school 'bout an hour ago. Guess they closed down O'Hare and he came for the twins. Man! It's murder out there!"

The house phone rang. It was Jeff Newman. "Just calling to cancel the rehearsal dinner." His laugh was hollow. "Guess that's obvious. But . . . pray for Grace, will you? She's afraid the whole wedding will have to be called off. And we're supposed to fly out of here on Thursday for Hawaii. As husband and wife."

"Oh, Jeff. Maybe it'll stop later tonight and they'll have the main roads cleared by morning. Don't give up hope yet."

But when she went back to the TV, they were predicting heavy snow until at least noon tomorrow.

And what about Harry? The minutes ticked by. Four thirty . . . five. Had he left the train station yet? Maybe he should just stay there instead of trying to come home. She hesitated to call. The TV was saying "white-out conditions" and "wind gusts up to sixty miles per hour." He might not pick up if he was trying to drive in these conditions.

But at 5:20 her cell phone rang. "Harry! Where are you? Are you all right?"

"Hey, babe, I'm all right. But . . . uh, it's gonna be a while before I get home. Lake Shore Drive is one big parking lot. Nothing's moving. And I mean nothing. Can't see a thing either. Visibility is maybe twenty feet."

Estelle was aware of DaShawn hovering nearby. "Oh, Harry, I'm scared. You could freeze to death out there!"

"Don't worry, babe. I've got Corky. We'll snuggle up. I've got some emergency equipment—flashlight, stuff like that. Some people have already abandoned their cars and are trying to walk to safety. Hate to do that—abandoned cars aren't gonna help this log jam, though I can't blame 'em. But if necessary, I'll leave the car and try to make it over to one of those high-rises along the Drive."

"Just call me, Harry! Every half hour. I gotta know you're okay."

"I will, babe. Love you."

But hours went by and her phone didn't ring again.

Chapter 41

Estelle insisted that DaShawn go to bed, but she sat up in the living room, glued to the Weather Channel. She tried to call Harry's cell several times but only got his voicemail. *O God, why doesn't he call?* News reports came in, estimating several hundred cars and trucks marooned on Lake Shore Drive. More and more drivers and passengers were abandoning their cars and walking to safety, though some insisted on staying with their cars because they didn't want to be ticketed.

A loud crack of thunder nearly sent Estelle off her seat on the couch. What? Thunder? In a snowstorm? The thunder cracked and rumbled for nearly forty-five minutes. DaShawn came out of his bedroom, unable to sleep. As soon as the rumbles of thunder faded about eleven, however, she sent him back to bed.

She kept the TV on low and dozed on and off—but came awake with a start when her phone rang. Harry! But the ID number was unfamiliar. She answered anyway.

"Estelle? It's Harry. I—"

"Oh, Harry, thank God you're safe! Why didn't you call? I'm a wreck!" She checked the time. After midnight.

"I'm really sorry, babe. My phone died. Can't believe I forgot to charge it last night. Corky and I finally abandoned the Durango and we're in the lobby of a high-rise along the Drive. Emergency crews are checking all the cars, helping everyone to get to safety. A nice lady here let me borrow her phone, but I can't stay on long. Just wanted to let you know we're okay, and we'll make it home somehow. Don't worry. Go to bed now, okay? Get some sleep." He hung up.

Get some sleep . . . Hmph. Not likely.

But she must've fallen asleep on the couch anyway because she again woke with a start when her cell phone rang. Harry again, praise God! "Still here at the high-rise. Borrowed another phone. I was hoping I could get to the Red Line and take the 'L' home, but we just got word that the rail switches are all frozen. The wind is really bad—gusts up to fifty, sometimes sixty miles per hour. But . . . some of the residents here in the building are bringing us coffee and stuff to eat. Had to take Corky out once—hope I don't get a ticket for not picking up her poop." His laugh was hollow. "Gotta go, babe. Don't go outside. Love you."

Bleary-eyed, Estelle checked her watch: 5:52. Good grief, she'd slept almost five hours! A banner running across the bottom of the TV screen said Chicago public schools were closed that day—first time in over a decade. Well, she'd let DaShawn sleep, but she got up, made a pot of fresh coffee, and took a cup doctored with milk and sugar back to the TV. Snowplows were out, but heavy snow was still predicted for several more hours with blowing winds. Tons of cancellations and closings.

As Estelle stared at the TV, a multitude of thoughts tumbled through her head. Good thing Daniel Krakowski had come for his mom a few days ago . . . Grace must be a wreck, there'd be no way they could get out to the church this morning, poor thing . . . Michelle better not have her baby today . . . and Harry? How was he going to get home? Reports now saying more than nine hundred cars and trucks were stranded on Lake Shore Drive.

The morning dragged. No more calls from Harry. A tearful call from Grace. According to the local weather station, snow was starting to let up mid-morning, but blizzard conditions still existed because of strong winds blowing the snow.

DaShawn got up, crazy happy that he didn't have to go to school, but worried about his grandpa. He called his dad. Safe at home. Lincoln Limo had cancelled all drivers and clients. A call to the Lighthouse confirmed Leroy was safe too. Estelle told DaShawn to fix whatever he wanted to eat while she stayed glued to the TV.

But at eleven thirty she heard a new sound outside. Not the wind, the roar of machines. Couldn't be snowplows. The city wouldn't touch side streets like theirs until the major arteries had been cleared, which might take days. Estelle got up and went to

the front window. Was that Farid Jalili out there with a snow blower? The snow was deep—had to be at least two feet out there, and
the snow had blown drifts over the parked cars, burying them in
drifts four or five feet high. But it wasn't just one snow blower . . .
someone else had a snow blower across the street, and she made
out several bundled figures out there with snow shovels. Someone came out of Casa Shalom and pointed toward the Molanders'
house. Two figures waded through the heavy snow in the street
and started to tackle Karl and Eva's sidewalk.

Those were the group home guys!—and the Cohens, too, if she
counted right.

"DaShawn, get your coat and boots on, and go help those folks
shovel snow," she ordered.

"What? Gram! It's like—"

"Now, young man!"

Estelle stood at the window and watched. The snow had
stopped falling, even though the wind was still tossing it around.
What time was it? Almost noon. As she watched, she saw more
people coming out of their doors with shovels. Jared Jasper and his
three kids . . . Danny's dads . . . Jeff Newman and another man—
must be Grace's father . . . and then another snow blower joined
the fray, the noise coming from the big house on the cul-de-sac.
Ha! Even Lincoln Paddock was out there.

A smile grew on Estelle's face. She felt like laughing. What she
was watching was . . . a neighborhood.

Estelle refreshed her coffee and resumed her post at the front
windows. Lincoln Paddock had stopped and was talking to Jeff
Newman. Lincoln pointed back toward his house. After what
seemed like several long minutes, Jeff motioned his father-in-law-
to-be over and the three men talked some more. Then Jeff and Lincoln shook hands and Jeff hustled back into Grace's house. What
in the world was going on?

She didn't have to wait long to find out.

Her phone rang. It was Grace. "Estelle! You're never going to
believe this but . . . Lincoln Paddock just told Jeff we could use his
house for the wedding. I mean, we *have* to get married today, because we're supposed to fly out tomorrow for Hawaii. Our tickets,

our reservations for our honeymoon, the Sweetheart concert tour next week . . . I was just about to give up and say we should just forget the wedding and go to a justice of the peace or something once we got to Hawaii. But my folks are here, and Sam, and Ramona, and all of you friends here on the block, and . . ."

Estelle couldn't get a word in edgewise as Grace talked breathlessly a mile a minute, but she was so astonished, she didn't know what to say anyway. Grace said she had her wedding dress there at the house, and Jeff and Samantha and her folks all had to stay over because of the storm last night so all the essential people were already here, so why not?

"Grace, it's crazy . . ." Estelle found her voice. "But crazy wonderful. I say go for it. Except . . ." She had a sudden thought. "Who would do the marrying? Don't think Mark's pastor could get here."

A silence fell on the other end of the phone.

But Estelle suddenly had another crazy idea. "Grace, what about Rabbi What's-his-name—you know, the Horowitzes' rabbi. He has to live nearby. They walk to their synagogue. Maybe he would do it."

"A rabbi?" Grace started to giggle. "Do you think . . . I guess it wouldn't hurt to ask the Horowitzes if they would ask him. Under the circumstances, you know. I think Jeff and I could get over to their house by now. Everybody's out shoveling. Don't go anywhere. I'll let you know what happens."

Don't go anywhere. Yeah, right.

For a few brief minutes, Estelle had almost forgotten her chief worry. Harry. Harry still wasn't home.

✧　✧　✧　✧

According to Grace, the Horowitzes were certain Rabbi Mendel couldn't perform a wedding ceremony for non-Jews—Orthodox Jews just didn't do that. But Rebecca had been excited about the idea of Grace and Jeff still being able to get married in spite of the blizzard. "She said her cousin is a conservative Jewish rabbi and only lives half a mile from here. She said she'd call and ask him. 'My cousin has always been a little *un*orthodox anyway,' she said." Grace laughed into the phone. "We're still waiting for her call back. But . . . Estelle, we're going to do it anyway. Whether we have a preacher or rabbi or not. Five o'clock at Lincoln Paddock's house. Maybe Harry would do the vows for us. Or you. You've both been spiritual mentors to me. I don't care if you're licensed to do weddings. It's in God's eyes anyway. Then we could go to a justice of the peace to make it legal when we get to Hawaii."

Estelle hesitated. She didn't want to worry Grace about Harry. "Well, we'll see. Wait till you get word from Rebecca Horowitz about her cousin. But what about your brother? He was going to be Jeff's best man."

"I know. I called Mark and told him what we're thinking. He said we should absolutely go ahead. After all, he said he got to go through the ceremony yesterday at the rehearsal. Said that ought to count for something."

Estelle chuckled. "Now that's a good big brother for you."

"Yeah, he's the best—oh, Estelle, can I ask you for a favor? Would you call the neighbors on this block and tell them they're still invited to the wedding? Tell them since none of us can go to the wedding, the wedding has come to us!" Grace laughed again and hung up. She sounded a bit giddy to Estelle.

Estelle reached for her phone book. If she was going to call all the neighbors on Beecham Street, she'd better get started now. Better use the kitchen phone in case Harry called her cell again. But she was sure going to give Harry the dickens about not making sure his cell phone was charged—at a time like this! Oh! That man!

Four thirty. Still no Harry. Estelle left him a prominent note and bundled up for the trek to Lincoln Paddock's house to do whatever she could to help out. The sidewalks had been pretty much cleared, though there were mountains of snow everywhere and most everyone's cars were still buried. She was glad for DaShawn's arm to hold onto. This was only the second time she'd been inside the "McMansion," as some of the kids called it. On the right, a wide modern stairway curved gracefully from the second floor down to a spacious living room. A baby grand piano stood off to one side of the large room, and a mixed array of couches, chairs, and stools had been arranged to face a small decorative wooden table with a beautiful cloth draped over it holding an elaborate silver candelabra of three candles. A couple of large green plants and some fancy silk flowers stood on either side of the little table, creating a semblance of an altar. Candles in different size glass jars flickered and danced from every conceivable flat surface.

Mm-hm. That Lincoln Paddock was something else.

Their host, dressed impeccably in a tailored black suit and narrow blue tie, was beaming, welcoming each guest who came in, acting as an usher, showing people to their seats. Isaac and Rebecca Horowitz and their children arrived, stomping snow off their feet and giving up their coats, accompanied by a young man dressed in a suit and tie and wearing a yarmulke on his head. Must be Rebecca's cousin, the Conservative rabbi.

Jared Jasper arrived with Michelle leaning on his arm, as if he was half-carrying her. "Oh, don't give me that look, Estelle Bentley," Michelle murmured. "Wouldn't miss this for anything."

Estelle didn't see Grace or Jeff or even Grace's parents or Sam or Ramona for that matter. But other neighbors arrived—Tim and Scott and their son Danny, the Jalili family, the Singers . . . and the entire contingent from Casa Shalom, dressed to the nines, though Stephan's suit was a bit baggy and his shirt and tie didn't match.

A grandfather clock along one wall bonged five times, and Lincoln Paddock raised his voice over the murmurings going on. "If you can all be seated, we have a wedding to witness."

The young rabbi had draped a white prayer shawl with black embroidery and long white fringes around his shoulders, and now stood behind the candelabra table. Estelle found a seat, though she kept glancing out the window. If only Harry would come! A note on the piano surprised her and she turned to the baby grand. To her shock, the young man named Bernie, the one with Asperger's, had taken up residence on the piano bench and started to play Bach's "Jesu, Joy of Man's Desiring." Tears sprang to Estelle's eyes. Unbelievable. A resident from the group home playing for Grace's wedding. God really did have a wonderful sense of humor. What a blessing.

As Bernie played, footsteps were heard on the stairs. Heads turned and watched as Ramona came down the stairs looking lovely in a knee-length baby blue chiffon party dress, carrying a lit taper candle. Smiling shyly, she moved through the "aisle" created by the couches and chairs and lit the two side candles on the candelabra. Then blowing out her candle, she stood over by the baby grand.

Jeff appeared from somewhere on the first floor and stood to one side of the small table wearing the tux he'd rented a few days earlier, not even trying to hide his grin. Bernie kept playing the sweet notes, and Samantha Curtis came down the stairs, wearing a dress the same color blue as Ramona's but a different style, carrying some silk lilies. Did Lincoln Paddock have silk flowers all over his house? If so, they sure came in handy for an emergency wedding.

The music stopped . . . and then started again. Oh my goodness. It was the traditional wedding march. All heads looked up. Grace Meredith appeared in her lovely wedding dress at the top of the stairs, accompanied by both her mother and father. Estelle heard Stephan say in a loud whisper, "Stand up, everybody! We're supposed to stand up!"

They all stood as Grace and her parents walked through the little throng and stopped before the table. The parents kissed Grace and sat down. Jeff reached out for his bride . . .

Estelle couldn't help grinning at the wonderful mishmash in front of her. Ramona Sanchez, a typical Hispanic teenager . . . Samantha Curtis with her lovely caramel skin and perky twists . . . Grace and Jeff, both dark-haired but very Caucasian . . . the Jewish rabbi . . . a young man with Asperger's at the piano . . . oh my. God must be enjoying this one! She certainly was.

The improvised ceremony included a bit of this and a bit of that, though Estelle was somewhat distracted, still glancing out the window at the deepening gloom outside, hoping Harry would show up. Grace and Jeff each took one of the lit candles and lit the candle in the middle as a sign of "becoming one." The young rabbi, whose name was David Ackerman, asked them to exchange rings, then wrapped his prayer shawl around their hands, saying some kind of blessing in Hebrew or Yiddish—Estelle didn't know the difference. At some point Jeff, and then Grace, said their vows to each other. Then they each took a sip from a goblet of wine, and Rabbi Ackerman said he was going to say the *sheva b'rachot*, or seven blessings, over this couple, which he did in Yiddish. Estelle noticed that Isaac Horowitz was also saying the blessings under his breath as the singsong words conveyed their intended blessing over the couple.

The rabbi beamed. "And now, if there are no objections, I will—"

"I do object!" boomed a deep voice.

Estelle whirled. Her heart leaped. Harry! How in the world did he—

But her husband, quickly shedding his winter parka and still dressed in his Amtrak Security uniform, strode through the room full of startled people and walked right up to the bride and groom. "I object to these two people getting married without *my* blessing!" And Harry Bentley wrapped his big arms around Jeff and Grace and pulled them into a big embrace. Smiles and chuckles spread around the room.

"Just in time to be my best man!" Jeff grinned as Harry let them go.

At this, David Ackerman beckoned to Harry and whispered in his ear. Harry grinned and nodded—and together the young rabbi and the Christian cop said in unison, "We now pronounce you husband and wife!"

People all over the living room erupted in claps and cheers as Jeff and Grace kissed. But the rabbi said, "One more thing, people!" He took the empty wine glass and wrapped it in a cloth napkin. The room hushed and necks craned. Ackerman set the wrapped goblet on the floor and nodded at Jeff. "Stomp on it."

Grinning, Jeff lifted his foot and stomped on the cloth—hard. The whole room heard the breaking of glass. Samuel Cohen shouted, "Mazel tov! Mazel tov!" Now everyone stood up as more shouts of "Mazel tov!" filled the room.

Suddenly another cry rose above the others. "Oh no! Oh no!" Michelle Jasper had a stricken look on her face as she reached for her husband and stared at the floor. Even Estelle could see the widening puddle at her feet. "Oh no!" Michelle cried again. "My water just broke!"

"What?" Jared looked stunned. "We'll never get to the hospital in this snow!"

Rebecca Horowitz, her hair neatly contained in a pretty snood, practically climbed over the people between her and Michelle. "It's all right. It's going to be all right." Her voice was commanding. "I'm a midwife. I've delivered many babies. Michelle, you remember that time we talked in the grocery store and I told you I was a midwife?"

Michelle nodded, her eyes wide.

"All right then. Mr. Paddock, do you have a bedroom here on the first floor? Yes? Good. I need clean sheets, a plastic tablecloth, boiling water . . . Michelle, you and your husband come with me. Everyone else, go on with your wedding party. We're going to have a baby here!"

Chapter 42

ACCORDING TO THE MORNING NEWS, emergency crews had worked all through the night towing cars off Lake Shore Drive and opened the Drive by the morning rush hour. But the city was not able to keep track of all the license plates of the towed cars, so Harry spent all day on Thursday trudging from lot to lot looking for the Durango.

Estelle got a call from him at four thirty that afternoon.

"Yeah, I finally found the car. But, uh, still can't get it out—they stacked the cars in here bumper to bumper. Not sure *when* I'll get it out."

"Oh, Harry, can you come home now?"

"Not yet. I'm gonna go check in at the station, then come back to see if they've been able to move some cars around so I can get the Durango out. If not, I'll catch the 'L' home. Don't wait supper on me. I'll keep you posted."

Estelle sighed. She felt exhausted . . . but she couldn't help smiling. The past forty-eight hours had been a roller coaster of chills and thrills—not the least of which had been staying with Michelle Jasper and her husband as their "go-fer" and support person as labor progressed through the night under the watchful eye of Rebecca Horowitz. And then, at 3:36 a.m., that beautiful squall as the baby slipped into the world on Lincoln Paddock's guest bed. "It's a girl!" Jared had whooped—and then got all teary as Rebecca cut the umbilical cord with a pair of sterilized scissors and placed the baby in his arms.

And thus Melody Hope Jasper had entered the world during one of the largest snowfalls in Chicago's history.

Farid Jalili, meanwhile, had got out his snowplow and managed to plow a swath down the middle of Beecham Street during the night, even though it added more snow to the already buried cars on both sides. An emergency call to 9-1-1 soon after the baby was born had resulted in a fire station ambulance following a city snowplow to Beecham Street and taking mother and baby to the closest hospital to get checked out.

Michelle and Melody were both fine and going to stay a couple of days.

Chicago public schools remained closed one more day. Youthful laughter filled the street as kids of all ages romped in the deep snow, making snow forts and having snowball fights. Neighbors all up and down Beecham Street helped dig each other's cars out from under the drifts and several folks even made it to work. 'L' trains were running again, though completely off schedule. And O'Hare Airport had reopened, slowly but surely getting stranded passengers back into the air.

Even the newlyweds got word they could fly out that evening, only twelve hours behind schedule.

Well, Harry wouldn't be home anytime soon, so Estelle bundled up and made her way carefully across the street to Grace Meredith's house to say good-bye. *Correction. Grace Newman's house*, she reminded herself, and chuckled again. Grace and Jeff's wedding wouldn't be forgotten by this neighborhood for a long time. She still had to laugh at the look on their faces when Lincoln Paddock asked where they were going to spend their first night. Forget the downtown hotel they'd reserved. But Grace's house was full of guests—her parents, Samantha, Ramona—who certainly weren't going anywhere *that* night anyway. As if it wasn't enough that he'd hosted their wedding and a baby was on its way into the world in a first floor bedroom of the "McMansion," Lincoln had offered the newlyweds his master suite with a king bed. "Cleaning lady was just here two days ago," he'd assured them. "Don't worry about me. I've got a futon in my office downstairs. You can have the whole second floor to yourselves."

Jeff Newman answered the door. "Estelle! Come in. Did Harry get his car back?"

"Not yet." She noticed suitcases lined up in the front room and the smell of something cooking in the kitchen. "Didn't come to stay. Just wanted to say good-bye to you two, send you off with a prayer."

Grace appeared and gave Estelle a big hug. "Oh, so glad you came over. Is Harry with you? How can I ever thank you two for . . . just everything. For being you. For—" Grace got a little choked up, but tried to laugh it off. "It's just been a little crazy, you know."

Ramona poked her head out from the kitchen. "Oh, hi, Miss Estelle. Guess what? The Singers invited me to stay with them again until Miss Grace and Mr. Jeff get back. Then . . ." She shrugged. "But maybe I could still go to work with you some mornings when Becky and Nathan are at school?"

Estelle nodded. "Of course, honey. Just let me know." Ramona bounced back into the kitchen. So. Ramona wasn't heading back to LA right away? Estelle wanted to ask more, but now wasn't the time.

Grace swept a hand at the suitcases. "Can't believe how much stuff I've got to take because of the Sweetheart tour in the islands right after our honeymoon. Samantha will fly over and join me before the tour starts. Not the band though. We're going to have to use digital tracks of their music."

"And can you believe that Lincoln Paddock is dispensing one of his limos to pick us up? He's confident they can get through to O'Hare . . . though it'll take longer than usual." Jeff said. "Grace asked if Rodney Bentley could be our driver—so guess he'll be here soon."

Grace smiled ruefully. "Allowing a lot of extra time. Traffic is still crazy out there, we heard. Don't know how to thank Lincoln though. None of this would have happened without his generosity."

Estelle nodded. "Amen to that." Whoever would've thought the big house at the end of the block—the house they all thought didn't belong in this neighborhood—would become a house of hospitality for a wedding, the newlyweds' honeymoon night, and the birth of a baby during one of Chicago's worst blizzards? The storm all the weathermen and newscasters were now calling "Snowmageddon."

"Well, I'm going to let you go. Just wanted to pray for you two." Estelle grabbed the hands of Grace and Jeff . . . but for a long moment she didn't really know how to pray. Seemed like some of her prayers had just hit the ceiling the last few months. On the other hand God had taken her prayers and done new things, wonderful things, unexpected things. Didn't Leroy have a job that made him happy, a job that gave him purpose, even if he didn't get into Casa Shalom? Hadn't walls of hostility toward the group home broken down, bringing some emotional healing to Nicole Singer and more Jewish neighbors for the Horowitzes? Not to mention helpful new neighbors who shoveled Karl Molander's walk in spite of their mental challenges. Who'd told them the elderly man really shouldn't touch a shovel again, not with his bad heart? And whoever would've guessed that Grace would need an emergency pianist for an ad hoc wedding?

God would. That's who. God in His grace had His own plans for the Beecham Street neighborhood, His own reasons for bringing the group home here. If she could just learn to stay out of the way . . .

Now Estelle knew how to pray. *Better just buckle my prayer seatbelt and hang on for the ride.*

THE END

Book Club Discussion Questions for
Snowmageddon

1. Even though Estelle Bentley has been a dynamic secondary character in several of our novel series (Yada Yada Prayer Group, House of Hope, the Harry Bentley novels, and now Windy City Neighbors), this is the first time a story has been from Estelle's point of view (POV). What would you say is the biggest personal challenge Estelle faces in *Snowmageddon*?

2. Let's take it deeper. What would you say are Estelle Bentley's greatest strengths? What do you see as her weaknesses or areas in need of growth?

3. Estelle thought a group home for mentally challenged adults moving into the neighborhood was a win-win-win situation for everyone. (Turned out that was a little presumptuous.) How would *you* feel if you learned that a group home was moving into your neighborhood—right next door? Why?

4. In what ways does Harry help Estelle be the person God made her to be—and in what ways does Estelle help Harry? If you are married, what are the ways you help your spouse—and vice versa?

5. What do think about the idea Harry came up with to solve the antagonism between Isaac Horowitz and Farid Jalili? Was it wise to get involved? Why or why not? How did it help Isaac? How did it help Farid? How did it help the neighborhood?

6. The story doesn't tell us what happens to Ramona after Grace and Jeff got married. What would *you* like to see happen?

7. Both Estelle and Harry have a hard time "letting go" of their sons, even though both are adults. If you have adult children, in what ways do you have a hard time "letting go"? If your parents are alive, in what ways do you feel they have a hard time letting *you* be fully adult? On the other hand, if there are positive experiences in your family of "letting go," encourage one another in the group with your story.

8. From the final chapter: *Whoever would've thought the big house at the end of the block—the house they all thought didn't belong in the neighborhood—would become a house of hospitality?* In what way might God be calling you and your family to be a "house of hospitality" in your neighborhood?

9. Estelle struggled with what seemed like unanswered prayers—or, as Harry would say, telling God what the answer should be. At the end of the book she said, *"Better buckle my prayer seatbelt and hang on for the ride!"* What did she mean by that? What does that mean to you?

10. You've now completed the Windy City Neighbors series. Has this series challenged you to build deeper relationships with your immediate neighbors? If so, in what ways? What might be a first step? Which neighbor would be the biggest challenge to relate to?

11. Need some help? A great resource for building relationships with your neighbors is *The Art of Neighboring—Building Genuine Relationships Right Outside Your Door* by Jay Pathak & Dave Runyon (Baker Books 2012).

Acknowledgements

Many thanks to **Jennifer Stair,** who has edited many of the novels that make up the "Yada Yada world" and remembers details about our characters that we have forgotten! Thanks, Jen, for jumping onboard to edit *Snowmageddon* in spite of your busy schedule and a trip to Hawaii!

Thanks, too, to **Lelia Austin, Jill King, Jayne Loulos,** and **Michelle Redding** for your willingness to proofread the edited manuscript on a tight deadline, as well as offering many helpful questions and comments. Add another star to your crowns!

To our artistic son **Julian Jackson,** Director of Exhibits at the Milwaukee Public Museum, for his whimsical rendition of a "wedding topper" for the cover of *Snowmageddon,* as well as always being a helpful sounding board for design ideas!
A disclaimer: None of the above are responsible for any mistakes, goofs, or typos that slipped past. Those we take full credit for ourselves!

A big shout out to our **faithful readers!** Thanks for your patience when this book took a little longer to publish than we'd hoped. We so appreciate the reviews you leave on Amazon.com, Barnesandnoble.com, ChristianBook.com, Kobo.com, and other online bookstores—they help more than you know. And thanks *always* for your letters, emails, comments on Facebook, and Twitter posts of encouragement! It's because of you that we keep writing.

Last but not least, this may sound a little weird, but to **Harry and Estelle Bentley,** two of our favorite fictional characters who carried the Windy City Neighbors stories even when they weren't center stage . . . thanks for the journey. Thanks for being "real." Thanks for letting us use you to tell *our* story. You are like old friends—no, more like family—and we will miss you.

Neta and Dave

Sign up at
www.daveneta.com
to receive an announcement of future releases.
Yes, we're both working on
more projects.

CPSIA information can be obtained at www.ICGtesting.com
Printed in the USA
LVOW10s1024020815

448531LV00002B/291/P